DEAD-EYED DRIFTER

DEAD-EYED DRIFTER

A KAREN PANTELLI NOVEL

SCOTT WILLIAM CARTER

Visit our website at *www.flyingravenpress.com* for more information about this book and other titles for sale.

THE KAREN PANTELLI NOVELS

Throwaway Jane
Lethal Beauty
Dead-Eyed Drifter

drifter \drif-tər\ n :
aimless or rootless person

1

————————

The MAID SERVICE sign was hanging on the knob, but inside room 1109 I found a man in a wheelchair.

Heavyset with a woolly, red beard, he was working at a folding table he'd situated near the glass doors that overlooked Cascade Bay. With the overhead lights off and the curtains half closed, he was cast mostly in shadow. Beyond his MacBook Pro, the edge of the computer's silver frame glinting in the late morning sun, I could just make out the fluttering white jib of a sailboat headed onto the sound.

I didn't know his name, not then, but I recognized him as one of the attendees of the math conference taking place at the Orcadia.

"Oh, I'm sorry," I said, figuring he'd just flipped the sign to the wrong side; the other read DO NOT DISTURB. "I'm happy to come back when you're—"

"No, no, it's quite all right," he said in a hoarse voice, barely glancing up. For how expansive his beard was, he had only a little hair on top, like strands of red yarn strewn across a wet volleyball. He coughed. "Sorry, not sick, just allergies. Bathroom's fine, but if you could just change the sheets, I'd appreciate it. I have some business to attend to before I rejoin my colleagues."

He gestured idly toward the bed, which was in the alcove out of my sight, then jotted something on a yellow legal pad. Even without the wheelchair or the mountain-man beard, he would have been memorable. His green plaid shirt and red bow tie would have set him apart even from some of his more eccentric fellow conference-goers, and that was before adding the camel-hair blazer draped over the back of the couch, the jacket I'd seen him wearing when he'd rolled his way up to the Amovar mansion for breakfast.

Although he was hard to make out in the dimly lit room, I pegged him as midfifties, perhaps even early sixties, judging by the silver threads in his beard.

I wheeled my cart inside and let the door swing shut. Should I turn on the overhead? Nah, there was enough light to clean, and I didn't want to disturb him. The room was pleasantly cool—not from an air conditioner, even in late June nobody on Orcas Island needed air conditioning—but from the cracked-open slider. A lot of guests arrived with the mistaken belief that summers on the island would be warmer, then overcompensated by cranking up their gas fireplaces and forgetting to turn them off when they left for the day, which made cleaning their rooms unbearable. More than once, I'd been tempted to work in my underwear, but I did that last year at the Hilton in Miami and paid the price. So did the macho Cuban salesman who walked in on me and took my state of undress as an invitation to join him in the horizontal salsa.

He'd ended up with a broken nose, courtesy of my well-honed front kick, and I'd ended up looking for another job. Which was fine. There were always other jobs.

Partly because of this experience, and a few similar ones over the years, I wasn't keen on cleaning with a guest in the room, but it was just a sheet change, after all, and the guy was in a wheelchair. As I pushed my squeaky cart toward the bed, he didn't say anything, which was fine too. I abhorred small talk. Actually, I abhorred most talk.

Metal crutches leaned against the wall, making it a tight squeeze for my cart. Fishy marina air blew through the screen. The room also smelled of the orange-scented bathroom air freshener, so I figured that was probably the real "business" he'd come back to do. Breakfasts at the Amovar were wonderful, but they could be on the rich side. Not that I was speaking from personal experience. They were on the rich side in another way too, far too rich for my meager wage.

The last I checked, I had 167 dollars in my bank account.

The Bayside rooms were some of the Orcadia's nicest, which made me wonder how much a math professor took home a year. This was what I was thinking when I wheeled the cart to the foot of the bed, a California king with a downy pastel-blue bedspread and a brass frame. Not only was the bed already made, but the pillow still had the mint on it from when I'd placed it there yesterday.

Confused, I turned to the professor. He'd closed his MacBook and was staring at me.

"Sorry for the deception," he said. He coughed and cleared his throat, but when he spoke again, his voice was still rough. "I actually find it easier to sleep in my wheelchair these days. Peculiar, I know, but it works for me." He nodded toward the end of the bed. "Would you take a seat, please?"

That was when I saw that he now had something else on the folding table: a S&W .38 Special, a black, snub-nose revolver. His hand rested on the walnut grip, but he wasn't pointing it at me—yet.

"Don't be alarmed," he said. "It's not for you. It's just for my own protection."

The pounding of my heart, the adrenaline shooting through my veins, the tunneling of my vision so the gun grew ten times in size—these were unavoidable human responses to danger, but I was too well-trained to panic. What I needed was time. Time to assess the situation. Time to weigh my options. Rush him? Swing the mop at his head?

My position relative to both the cart and the bed made neither choice ideal. The .38 Special was popular among the concealed carry crowd for its small size, but it wasn't very accurate beyond a dozen feet. The problem was that I was well within a dozen feet.

"If the gun's not for me," I said, keeping my voice light and easy, "then why did you hide it? Listen, if you're looking for something kinky, I'm not the sort who—"

"It's nothing like that," he said curtly. "Please, Karen, if you'll just sit down, I will explain."

This, more than the gun, made my body go cold: *He'd used my name.* I wasn't wearing a name tag. The Orcadia issued them upon hire, but nobody was required to wear them, so of course I never did. I wasn't a name tag-wearing sort of person. In fact, if there were a national referendum to ban name tags, I'd be the first in line to vote.

I glanced down just to make sure nobody had affixed one to my chest when I wasn't looking, but nope, no name tag.

I swallowed. "Who are you?"

"My name is Colin Welk," he said. "I'm a professor of mathematics at the University of Washington—computational analysis and modeling, actually, but usually I just—"

"How do you know who I am?"

He coughed again, long enough that I actually debated diving for the gun, but he never took his eyes off me. "Sorry again. Must be all the cedar trees. I know a lot about you, Ms. Pantelli. In fact, I've been waiting for you, knowing at some point you'd walk through that very door. Actually, I'm the reason you're working at the Orcadia at all."

The shadow and his beard made it hard to detect, but I thought I could make out a slight grin—not a happy smile, but more of an anxious one. His gaze kept flitting to the door. Maybe this wasn't that complicated. Maybe he'd recognized me from some of the unfortunate press I'd gotten in the past. Concocted a fantasy with the purpose of … what, exactly? What did this woolly-bearded, plaid-wearing, wheelchair-bound man think he was actually going to *do?*

"What's stopping me from shouting for help?" I asked.

"Another maid is cleaning next door right now." This was a lie. Elena was actually working at Hillside, but I doubted he knew that. "No way you get away with this."

"I'm not trying to *get away* with anything. The very idea is insulting. I'm a Rhodes scholar, a chess grandmaster, the holder of seven patents, and I have an IQ of 172. Please, if you'll just—"

"I'm leaving."

I turned toward the door, figuring sweaty-faced Professor Welk wasn't the sort of person capable of shooting anyone. He picked up the revolver and pointed it at me. I stopped. He didn't seem comfortable holding the gun, but he didn't seem like he was playing an elaborate game of pretend either.

"You'd shoot me?" I said. "Really?"

"I'd prefer not to. I've never shot anyone, and I'd rather not start today. I actually find violence of any sort quite distasteful."

"You know there's no way you'll escape. This room is registered in your name—and we're on an island for God's sake!"

"If you walk out that door and shout for help, I'm a dead man anyway."

"What?"

"But I wouldn't shoot you to save my own life. I'd do it for ..." Other than his cough, his manner of delivery was consistently polished, but this actually got him to choke up a little. He shook his head. "Please just sit down. This is all coming out more bungled than I'd hoped. That bit about you being here because of me is true, but I shouldn't have led with that. That was my ego getting in the way. I'm not here to threaten you. In fact, I have some information about your mother. That *is* why you're here, correct? You were following a lead that she worked at the Orcadia as a housekeeper in the early nineties?"

My mother. Now there was something I hadn't expected this wackadoodle to bring up, and it forced me to completely reevaluate the situation. It was possible he'd heard from the staff or others on Orcas Island that I'd been asking about my mother—I hadn't been secret about it since I hadn't thought I needed to be— but the specific way he'd phrased it, *following a lead,* suggested that his interest in me may have been more than an opportunistic coincidence.

"See," he said, "I should have mentioned that first. Got your attention, didn't I?"

"How did you know that? Who are you?"

"As I said—" he began but then stopped abruptly and touched his temple with his left hand, wincing noticeably. "*Oooh.* Sorry. A bit ... a bit of a headache there. Allergies again. Hits ... hits me in all sorts of ways."

His gun, unfortunately, hadn't wavered. It was still pointed directly at me even as he rubbed his forehead.

"Are you sure this isn't more than allergies?" I said. "Your health is nothing to take lightly. Maybe you should take a good nap? You'll definitely be able to shoot me better when you're feeling better."

"Please stop. I'm *not* going to shoot you."

"Oh yeah? Then maybe you should put the gun down and we can hit the reset button on whatever's happening here."

He looked at me steadily, long enough that I heard a seagull cawing out on the bay, then sighed. He placed the .38 on this legal pad, turning it slightly so it wasn't pointed at me. "Fine," he said, "I've put down my weapon as a show of good faith. I just ... panicked a little. Will you please just sit down? I have a very urgent task for you, a matter of life and death ideally suited for a former FBI special agent turned dead-eyed drifter, and I'll tell you what I know about your mother if you just hear me out first."

"Dead-eyed drifter?"

"Sorry. Sounds pejorative, doesn't it? I don't mean it as such. There's something romantic about being so unencumbered. It's just a look you sometimes get. Some of the photos of you have a sort of ... emptiness about them. Not that you have that look now. No, right now you're looking at me as if you're imagining separating my head from my body."

"Picking up on that, are you?"

"Quite clearly, yes. And after researching you, I have no doubt you are capable of such violence."

Now this guy was really getting under my skin. "Listen, pal, I don't know what kind of stupid game you're playing—"

"No, no, no. Sorry, again. I'm really botching this. Will you at least hear me out? I promise, you'll understand why I went to such elaborate lengths once you know what I know. I will make no effort to stop you afterward, whatever you decide. I just need you to hear me. *Please.*"

I crossed my arms. I wasn't about to sit, but I wasn't ready to bolt either. "Tell me about my mother first."

"I will. After I explain—"

"No. *First.* I give you my word I'll hear whatever you have to say, but you tell me what you know about Mom first. And no more of this cockamamie bullshit about you arranging me to come here. I don't see how that could possibly be true. I don't like lying. And I don't like games, Professor Welk. If that really is your name."

"It is, it is. But please, call me Colin. Professor Welk is such a formal—"

"I'm not calling you anything until you start making sense, and quick, or I'm out of here."

He raised his hands. "Fine, fine, we'll do it your way. In the end, it gets us to the same place. And we'll keep our relationship formal. Maybe it's better. Last September, you were in Boise, Idaho, investigating one of your mother's last known addresses— also named Karen Pantelli. Interesting that she named you after herself, isn't it? Men have been doing that sort of thing for generations, but it's far rarer for—"

"How did you know I was in Boise? I didn't tell anyone I was there—or why." Then I thought about it some more. "Hope."

"Yes. Your sister hired a private investigator a year and a half ago to search for your mother. She ran out on your family when you were, what, six? It was actually on Mother's Day, of all days, wasn't it?"

I gritted my teeth. "What does that have to do with anything?"

"Well, it apparently mattered a great deal to your sister because she wrote a lengthy Facebook post about it—a little over fourteen months ago, on Mother's Day. You'd think, being only three years old, her recollection would be foggier, but the way she tells it, every detail is seared in her memory."

"Sorry?"

"You're not active on social media, so you're probably not aware of it, but the post was quite heartfelt. About how her husband hired a private investigator as a Christmas gift, but all he could come up with was a last known address in Boise. About how she was going to stop thinking about her own mother on Mother's Day and focus on being the best mother for her own kids instead. About how she suffered from the same mental illness—she didn't mention it, but I know she's bipolar—and yet she was determined to rise above her disease in a way her mom never could."

My face felt warm. Hope resisted taking her medication. She refused to see Ronnie as the abusive husband I knew him to be. She messed up her life in countless other ways ... but I'd always known she wanted to be better. She'd told me so many times. What I *hadn't* known was that she was at least partly motivated to be better because of Mom's failures. Hope, who'd always said she didn't remember a single thing about Mom, could have told me that herself, and yet she hadn't. Why?

"She told me her social media is locked down just for friends," I said.

Welk waved his hand dismissively. "Please. Any moron with even a rudimentary understanding of how the internet works can get past Facebook's simple security measures. What you should *really* be asking me is how that idiotic private investigator in Atlanta found your mother's last known address in the first place."

"Uh huh. You're not about to tell me you *gave* the address to him, are you?"

Welk started to answer, but his voice was so scratchy that he had to stop and clear his throat before he could continue. "That's *exactly* what I'm telling you. I modified key online databases. He never would have found it otherwise. That wasn't all that difficult either, at least for someone with my abilities. The real trick was leaving a trail of breadcrumbs so that you would end up working here—at the Orcadia on Orcas Island, in housekeeping, during the very weekend that the Northwest Academic Computation Analysis Conference was taking place."

I laughed. He didn't.

"You're actually serious," I said.

"Absolutely."

"Impossible."

"No. Difficult, yes. A challenge, even for a man with my abilities, most definitely. But not impossible."

"You're saying that my mother never worked here?"

"Oh, no, that part is absolutely true. She worked as a waitress at the Amovar mansion in the summer of '93 under the name Karen Westlin. You didn't find any of her timesheets because they were burned up in a kitchen fire in '98, but the IRS has a record of her time here, I assure you. And I have access to anything the IRS has." He offered up another fleeting smile. "Karen Westlin was the same name she was using in Miami when—"

"She worked at the Electric Flamingo," I finished. I was starting to feel light-headed. "A night club. She got a job as a waitress."

"Exactly. It's called Dazzle Dazzle now, with a different owner, but it was called the Electric Flamingo back then. You found that out from Bob Loughlin, the man she rented a house from in Boise, once you tracked him down in that nursing home in Spokane. You probably figured she'd want her mail forwarded, and you were right. Did Mr. Loughlin actually remember the address, or did you find something in his records?"

I chewed on my bottom lip. So Professor Welk didn't know *everything.* I found that at least somewhat reassuring. "He knew it was a nightclub. She told him her friend's brother was working as a manager and could get them jobs. I figured out the rest, based on the time frame and an article in the *Herald* about the club's opening."

"Of course! Once you got to Loughlin, I knew you would eventually figure it out. If he didn't remember anything—he is suffering from early Alzheimer's, after all—you would have tracked down your mother's friend, Lucy Hoffvenk, who would have pointed you in the same direction."

I wasn't rattled by much, but my legs felt wobbly. I half sat, half leaned against the bed. This little island in the Salish Sea was about as far from Miami as I could get and still be in the continental United States—over 3,300 miles, which I knew because I'd driven it in my beat-up Honda Civic, including the ferry that brought me the last leg to Orcas Island itself. It was unfathomable that this strange man in a wheelchair was the reason I was here.

"But you couldn't—couldn't have gotten me to the Orcadia," I insisted. "That tip came from Jenna ... Jenna something. A waitress who used to work with Mom at the Electric Flamingo and then moved to Orlando. She called a few months after I talked to her and said she found a postcard from the Orcadia that Mom sent her, saying she got a job there. She said she'd forgotten about it. She even emailed me a picture of the postcard!"

This time Welk's impish smile, obscured as it was by shadow and beard, wasn't so fleeting. In fact, it looked quite cocky. "Did she now?"

"You're saying I'm lying?"

"Nothing of the sort. I'm saying that while the person you talked to in Orlando was, in fact, Jenna Blochmedt, the person who called you later with information about the postcard wasn't. Nor was the person who sent you the email. I'm saying the postcard wasn't really from your mother. You see, Ms. Pantelli, while I'd already discovered that your mother worked at the Orcadia, I also discovered that other than the IRS, there was no other record of her time here. As resourceful as you are, I doubted you would be very likely to discover she worked here—at least not in the time frame I required."

"I'm sorry, time frame?"

Welk winced again, a very subtle twitch above his eyebrows, and he started to reach for his temple before letting his hand fall away. "Um, yes, that's right. You don't really think this conference is happening at the Orcadia by mere chance, do you?"

"Come on. You're saying—you're saying you actually—"

"Arranged it, yes. I'm chair of NACA this year—again, not by accident, mind you—and I put my finger on the scales quite heavily to ensure that the conference met here. Then it was simply a matter of making sure you got the information that your mother worked here, in the appropriate amount of time that would allow you to drive here and get a job at the Orcadia ... so that I could then rent the room you would clean ... and that we could meet at this very moment, on this warm Saturday morning, with a breeze off Cascade Bay blowing through the window behind me, to discuss the very urgent task I have for you."

"Wait, you're not telling me—"

"A task, as strange as it may seem, that could not be discussed in any other manner. Now, can I tell you about what it is I need you to do? I grant that it will seem equally far-fetched at first, but—"

I put my hand up. "Hold on. You actually arranged for me to get the job with housekeeping?"

"No. But the Orcadia always hires summer help, usually after Memorial Day, so I knew the odds were *extremely* high that if you stopped in at some point in late May and asked if there were openings, you would be hired on the spot, given your ... experience with such menial work. Which you did. And you were. It's your pattern, after all, so I was just playing the odds. Many things in life are about playing the odds, Ms. Pantelli. I may be a man of numbers, but my specialty has always been about probabilities. Predictions, based on—"

"But *why?* Why go to all this trouble?"

He coughed into his hand. His voice had gotten increasingly weaker and softer. "Ah! Finally, we come to the task at hand, the raison d'être of our meeting today, and my singular obsession for over a decade. It is an obsession that has cost me almost everything, an obsession that still carries great risks to those closest to me but one with stakes too high for me to stop now."

"Professor—"

"I need you to catch the worst serial killer this country has ever seen."

Of all the tasks I'd imagined he'd wanted me to do, catching a serial killer hadn't been on the list. I'd had a hard time imagining *any* tasks, bizarre as this whole encounter was, but because I'd already pretty much accepted the great lengths he'd gone to get me here, it wasn't a stretch to believe he was sincere. Crazy, yes, but at least sincere. Even crazy people could be certain that what they were saying was true.

For a long time, neither of us said anything. I heard the hum of the mini fridge in the kitchenette. I heard water in the bay lapping against the dock. I heard myself swallow.

"You want to repeat that?" I said.

"I want you to catch a serial killer. Unfortunately, I don't know his identity, as much as I have tried, but—"

"Why me?"

He sighed. "Well, for many reasons. Your skills, obviously. You've proven yourself to be quite resourceful against ... nearly insurmountable evil. You operate outside traditional law enforcement, which is critical. If Mr. Grim gets even a whiff you're pursuing him, the results could be tragic. He already knows I'm onto him, which is why I've had to be so incredibly careful about how I arranged this meeting. It may seem like an elaborate Rube Goldberg machine to you, going to all this trouble, but I assure you it was necessary."

"Mr. Grim?"

"Yes, that's what I've taken to calling him. I know, I know, it seems a little on the nose naming him after—"

"And why the heck would I take that kind of risk? Assuming he really does exist, you think I'm such a ... such a do-gooder that I can't resist going after him?"

"Oh, trust me, he exists. And yes, I wouldn't use such a prosaic term as do-gooder, but I do believe that you *are* someone who can't stand by if a great injustice is taking place. I'm staking everything on it, Ms. Pantelli. I also believe that you are determined, maybe even desperate for redemption for the tragic reasons you left the FBI."

I shook my head. "I've moved on from that."

"You may have moved on, but you haven't gotten over it."

"What, you have a PhD in psychology too?"

He put up his hand. "I don't mean to offend. Unfortunately, I have a penchant for being … unnecessarily blunt."

"So, what, you're offering to pay my expenses while I travel around the country looking for this guy? Is that what you're saying? If this was a TV show, you'd be the behind-the-scenes techie while I'm the one doing the footwork in the field? No thanks."

He shook his head. "I don't need to pay you. I'd be happy to do so, of course. I'd give you my life savings, but I can't do that. In fact, it's vital that there be no more communication between us after this weekend. However, I am quite certain you will take up this task anyway."

"Is that so?" I was back to crossing my arms, irritated that he thought I was this easy to manipulate—assuming this wasn't all bullshit, a weird game he was playing for kicks. "And what makes you so confident?"

"It's not confidence, Ms. Pantelli. Again, it's just playing the odds. There is simply one more piece of information that I have yet to disclose, information that practically guarantees you will want to go after Mr. Grim yourself."

"Uh huh. And that is?"

Professor Colin Welk looked at me steadily. I still couldn't see his face well because of the shadows, but there was something in his expression, a softening he hadn't shown before now. I may have been a dead-eyed drifter in his book, someone who usually kept her emotions buttoned up and battened down, a characterization I couldn't really dispute, but so far he'd struck me as someone who'd buried his own emotions so deep that it would have taken an excavator to unearth them.

So his sympathetic expression caught me off guard, and it gave extra weight to what he said next.

"I believe your mother was one of his early victims," he said.

2

———

The cell phone attached to my hip buzzed. The phone was set on mute, but in the stillness of the room, in the long, weighty silence as I tried to process what Welk had just said, even the vibration was like a thunderclap. I'd also forgotten I was wearing it. Management may not have required me to wear a name tag, but they'd insisted I wear one of their damn cell phones on the job.

Not much could get me to flinch these days, but that buzz certainly did. Welk didn't flinch, though. The professor didn't even blink. Even if he'd known the cell phone was there, showing so little reaction was impressive. Or disturbing. I didn't know him well enough yet to know which.

The buzzing was rhythmic and steady, which meant a call, not a text.

"You better answer it," Welk said.

"What did you say about my mother?"

"I'll explain in a moment. You better take the call."

"It's probably just Steve. The manager."

"I know. He'll grow suspicious if you ignore him, and we can't afford anything that raises suspicion, no matter how small. Whatever he wants, just tell him there was a bit of a mess in the bathroom and it's taking a lot longer than you thought. Since I'm in a wheelchair, this won't surprise him. Tell him nothing else, Karen. It's *critical* that you tell him nothing else—truly a matter of life and death."

I didn't want to, but I answered it. My head was still spinning from what Welk had said about Mom, so I found it hard to concentrate on anything else. I was no longer worried that Professor Welk was going to shoot me, but I still saw him watching me closely. Did he think I was going to make a plea for help? Even if what he was saying was true, his cloak and dagger routine seemed over the top and hysterical, but I was willing to humor him. For now.

It was indeed Steve. In his high, nasally voice—I always thought he sounded like Alvin the Chipmunk with a head cold—he informed me that a guest in 1302 needed extra towels pronto. Steve was always using the word "pronto," no matter what the request, as if he assumed his housekeepers needed constant horse-whipping to do their jobs. I told him I'd get there as soon as I cleaned up a mess in the bathroom in 1109.

"The guy in the wheelchair, right?" Steve said.

"That's right."

"Okay. Just get to 1302 pronto, all right?"

"Yes, sir."

I clicked off and slipped the phone back onto my hip. "Well, you certainly nailed the wheelchair thing," I said to Welk.

"When someone's handicapped," he replied, "or differently-abled, as my more enlightened students would prefer to say, people make lots of erroneous assumptions. I'm used to it."

"Tell me about my mother."

"She looks a lot like you, you know, from the pictures your sister posted on Facebook. At the same age, you could almost be twins. But the world is full of doppelgängers, more than people might realize. Have you ever had that happen? Run into someone who looks almost exactly like you? It happened to me once. It was quite unnerving."

"Tell me about my mother!"

"Right. Sorry. Rambling a bit. It happens when I get nervous. I can see that I've upset you. Again, that is not my intention. Please understand. I used the word 'believe' quite intentionally. I said I *believed* your mother was one of his first victims. While there is lots of evidence that would point to that conclusion, I cannot say so definitively."

"Why? What evidence are you talking about?"

"Please, Karen. It's vital that you don't raise your voice. Someone might—"

"Damn it, you just told me that my mother was murdered. Tell me why you think that."

Welk didn't flinch, but he did blink. He glanced at the cracked-open glass door. Beyond two Adirondack chairs on his concrete patio, down a grassy slope, I could just make out the sidewalk that ran between the Bayside rooms and the marina. I didn't see anyone down there. I didn't hear anyone either. I didn't hear much of anything except for the steady hum of that mini fridge and, somewhere on the sound, the distant drone of an outboard motor.

The breeze shifted, and I caught the scent of grilling hamburgers wafting over from the Amovar, a sign that the kitchen was already switching to the lunch menu. The sun laid tracks on the bay that looked like gold bars. It was gorgeous, as usual, the kind of day, and the kind of place, for enjoying a burger after a sail, then lounging on those Adirondack chairs and drinking lemonades fitted with tiny umbrellas. Not the kind of day for speculating about a mass murderer. When I spoke again, I tried to lower my voice. It was difficult, but I tried.

"What, you think your serial killer is out there right now?" I said. "Is that it? He followed you to the Orcadia?"

"The possibility is remote, but it is not zero." He tapped his hand on his revolver. "There is a reason I brought this along."

"Oh, it wasn't to scare me?"

"Hardly. I told you, I panicked."

"You don't strike me as the sort of person who panics, Professor Welk."

"Oh, I can panic, I can assure you of that. If I'm displaying a steely sort of resolve, it's because the task at hand demands it. Now, we must be quick since my colleagues will soon miss me. As to your mother, here is what I know for certain: She left employment at the Orcadia on Thursday, September 9, 1993. The previous Saturday, she met a Hollywood actor, John Grolin, who stopped at Cascade Bay when he was on holiday sailing up the coast. I learned that from a busboy who worked with your mother here. Grolin apparently took a liking to your mother, who was his waitress when he came to dinner at the Amovar, and they had what you might call a lover's tryst."

"And you think this guy is your serial killer?"

Welk may have appeared preternaturally calm under pressure, but he wasn't beyond irritability. This question was enough to get him to grimace. "Please. Don't you think a man of my intelligence would have ruled out such an obvious suspect?"

"Sorry."

Welk stared at me another moment, then sighed. "No, it's just my ego getting in the way again, and we don't have time for that. It's a perfectly valid question. There are many reasons Grolin could be eliminated as a suspect, but chief among them is that he died of lung cancer in '04—he smoked like a chimney, you see. And the murders continued."

"Ah."

"The reason I mention Grolin is that he gave your mother the business card of his Hollywood agent, Marv Friedman, and wrote a note on the back to Friedman saying that Karen Westlin was a star in the making. This former busboy, Juan Garcia, said your mother showed him the card and said it was "her ticket to the good life." Garcia, an illegal alien, returned to Mexico not long after and never returned to the US. And no, Friedman is not a suspect either. He died not long after Grolin, mostly of old age, though I'm sure the office liquor cabinet he accessed regularly didn't help."

Mom had always wanted a much more glamorous life than being the wife of an Air Force officer, so I didn't find it hard to believe that she would latch onto the possibility of becoming a Hollywood starlet, no matter how flimsy that possibility was. "Did my mother ever go see him? This agent?"

"I'm getting to that. While I wasn't able to speak to Grolin or Friedman, I was able—well, not me, but through an intermediary —to speak to Friedman's longtime secretary, Anne Lambert. She's quite old herself now and didn't remember your mother, but she had something better: all her appointment books dating back to '89, the year she first started working for Friedman. She said Karen Westlin had a 10:00 a.m. meeting scheduled with Marv on Monday, September 13, but she was a no-show."

"She's sure?"

"Lambert said the appointment had a line through it in her book, which means the person didn't show up. Apparently Friedman always left the first hour on Mondays open for urgent business or last-minute appointments, so Anne said he was probably seeing Ms. Westlin as a favor to a client. She also said that Friedman left for a two-week business trip to London the following morning, so he wouldn't have been in LA during that time period to see her."

"So what happened to my mom?"

"She vanished."

"Excuse me?"

"At some point between when she left the Orcadia on Thursday, September 9, and when she was supposed to show up at Marv Friedman's office on Monday morning, she vanished off the face of the earth. Believe me, I have used all my formidable abilities to try to find her."

"And you think this ... this Mr. Grim killed her?"

"Here's where we get into conjecture, though it is built on a chain of suppositions each grounded in some degree of likelihood. Because of when your mother left the Orcadia, and when the appointment with Friedman was, I *believe* she called Friedman that very Thursday. He probably told her that if she could get to Los

Angeles by Monday at 10:00 a.m., he'd at least see her, and I *believe* that prompted her to quit on the spot and head immediately for LA."

"All right, I'm with you so far."

"The one other thing I learned from Garcia is that your mom said she hitchhiked across the United States to work at the Orcadia. Because of this, because I can find no records at all that your mother ever owned a car or traveled by plane, train, or bus that weekend—I can't rule it out, but I'd say it's unlikely—I *believe* she hitchhiked to LA."

"And it's also why she quit so abruptly," she said. "She needed time to make her way down I-5."

"Exactly."

"And that's important why?"

"Because, Ms. Pantelli, that time frame, the middle of September 1993, and that location, Interstate 5 between Seattle and Los Angeles, would have been when Mr. Grim killed his sixteenth victim."

My shoulders sagged. There was a lot to unpack in what Professor Welk had said, but the number stood out. "Sixteen," I said. "You said my mother was one of his *early* victims."

Welk nodded. "She was. Very early."

"How many—"

"There's a reason I call him Mr. Grim, Ms. Pantelli, aside from the need to call him *something*. I'm not usually prone to flights of fancy, but what other name would suffice other than some variation of the Angel of Death? The evidence indicates he has been killing one person a week, perhaps occasionally more, if circumstances dictated it, but certainly no less, since June 1993."

I stared at him. "That's almost thirty years."

"Twenty-nine years, two weeks, actually."

"That—that would mean—"

"That Mr. Grim has killed over fifteen hundred people."

The number sat in the air, like one of those word bubbles in a cartoon. It didn't seem real.

"Impossible," I said.

"At first, I thought so too. It's such an unfathomable number, but the evidence is unmistakable."

"What evidence? What could possibly lead you to believe that someone has killed that many people? Without getting caught? No way. The worst serial killers in the world have killed, what, a couple hundred people?"

"Thereabouts. Luis Garavito is believed to have killed over three hundred in Colombia, Ecuador, and Venezuela. Javed Iqubal of Pakistan murdered at least a hundred but perhaps more. There are, of course, many others. But Ms. Pantelli, these are the serial killers who were *caught.* Most depraved individuals are, frankly, not very intelligent. I have reason to believe that Mr. Grim is every bit as smart as I am. And there are other reasons why he has flown under the—"

"But fifteen hundred! No matter *who* was being killed or how, people would notice. They'd have to!"

"You think so? There are anywhere from ten to twenty thousand murders a year in the United States alone. Even in a single year, fifty-two murders is a drop in the bucket, especially if they are spread far and wide across the country, as Mr. Grim has done. And fifteen hundred over thirty years? Sad to say, it's barely a blip. I'm sure, as someone who used to work in law enforcement, that you know how many of those go unsolved each year."

I sighed. "About 40 percent."

"Correct. Most people find that number shocking, but I'm sure you know that if the victim exists at the margins of society—transients, prostitutes, or others without family or friends who'd press the police to investigate—the odds are extremely low their murder will be solved unless it's truly a slam dunk case. You remember Sam Little, of course."

"The serial killer who killed all those prostitutes? He died in prison a couple years ago."

"Yes, but six decades after his first murder."

"But he killed, what, a hundred people? Not a thousand. Not even close. There's just no—"

"My point is that it proves that if even a psychopath with

average intelligence, one smart enough to target people on the margins, can potentially get away with killing all those women, then imagine what someone with genius-level intelligence could get away with. Especially one whose thinking is not clouded by the sadistic tendencies that bedevil so many serial killers."

"Clouded?"

"I don't mean that as a compliment. Like Mr. Little, many serial killers are rapists, pedophiles, sadists, and the like. Not all, but probably the majority, and it is usually their undoing. Much of the rest are attention seekers who end up getting caught because they want credit for what they've done. But not Mr. Grim. In fact, many of his victims, like your mother, are never discovered. Quite a few of the deaths were even attributed to natural causes, though I know this is not the case."

"Natural causes? Really?"

"Yes."

"How can you *possibly* know that? What is your proof for any of this? If this guy is so good, how do you even know he exists? You still haven't given me any real evidence that this isn't just some ... some weird fantasy of yours!"

He rubbed his forehead again. "Please. Ms. Pantelli, I will be happy to answer any of your questions in that regard and give you all the proof you need that Mr. Grim is real, but let's hold off on that until tomorrow."

"Tomorrow?"

"Yes. I'd like to propose we meet one more time, when you clean the room again on Sunday at a similar time. I'll be heading back to Seattle on Monday morning. Speaking much longer is a risk we can't afford to take. Anything out of the ordinary, anything at all, risks drawing his attention. We can't do that."

"You make it sound like he's watching your every move."

"I'm quite sure he is. You see, he already killed my wife."

"What?"

Welk put up his hand. "I may not get emotional about much, but I do get emotional about—about my family, so let me only say this for now. Thirteen years ago, my wife—Mona ... Excuse me, this is difficult, even keeping it short. She fell off a cliff while hiking alone in the Olympic National Forest. She frequently hiked alone. It was ... it wasn't something I liked to do. I probably should have, though. Back then, I could walk, you see." He swallowed.

"I'm sorry," I said.

"No, no, I don't want your sympathy. I tell you this because it's necessary for you to understand how I determined that her death was *not* an accident. At first, it was just a feeling. A gut thing. She'd hiked that trail many times. She was careful. She showed no ... no suicidal tendencies. Sorry, again, this is difficult. But you must know."

"And you think this Mr. Grim killed her?"

"I do."

"And why is that?"

Welk cleared his throat. "We'll ... we'll talk more about that tomorrow. I'm serious when I say we can't risk talking much longer. It would put my son in further danger."

"Your *son?* What does your son—"

"No, no, let's not ... not get into that until tomorrow. I didn't mean to—Isaac is one of the few things I just can't ... can't ... " He shook his head. "For now, let me just say that when someone like me has data sets large enough, and computational power significant enough, you can find patterns in just about any amount of noise. The order in the chaos. And I found those patterns, Ms. Pantelli."

"But *what* patterns?"

Rather than answer, Welk tore off the top sheet from his yellow legal pad and handed it to me. I took it. It was a list of names in two columns along with dates and cities next to each name. They were in chronological order, usually one a week, very occasionally two or even three, dating back to January. Welk's handwriting was so neat and tidy that it was almost like type.

"What's this?" I said. "His victims?"

"His *recent* victims. I knew that no matter what I said today, I wouldn't convince you. You'd have to see it for yourself. Simply get the Rand McNally map of the United States that you keep in your Honda and mark off each of these people with a black dot. There's more that will help you narrow your search—this is really the overall pattern that he *wants* us to see—but I will tell you that tomorrow. He essentially repeats this one every year, enough that you'll always recognize it anyway, which is why what I'm giving you here should be enough by itself to put you in a more receptive state of mind."

"How do you know I keep a Rand McNally atlas in my car?"

Welk rolled his eyes at me. "I thought we were beyond such banal questions. Just do it, but please, please, don't show anyone. Don't make any copies of this list. I made this just now, after committing the victims to memory. After Mr. Grim made it abundantly clear how closely he was watching me, everything I record in permanent form is handwritten, locked in a safe in my house, but I knew you would need proof. And don't tell a single soul about this, do you understand?"

"All right, all right." I was highly skeptical that the technology existed that could predict Mr. Grim's victims if he were truly targeting random people, but I was willing to play along if it got me closer to finding out what happened to Mom. Looking at the list again, I noticed something I'd missed at first. "Wait a second. The last three names. The dates—they haven't happened yet. And the last one says 'J. Doe.' As in John or Jane Doe?"

"Correct. While I can't predict exactly *when* or *how* he will kill his victims, I believe I *can* predict both the city and his most likely victim—at least with a 92 percent confidence level for the next two. I list J. Doe until I have a name. Mr. Grim is occasionally opportunistic too, as he was with your mother, though rarely the city. Just the person."

"Opportunistic?"

"Yes, like a spider that has the good fortune to have a second bug get ensnared in his web when he was only hoping for one, he will not pass up an opportunity that presents itself or a secondary opportunity that he creates for … other purposes."

"I see. You're saying my mother wasn't even on his list then. How special for her."

"It has nothing do with being special or not, Ms. Pantelli. You must know that. And my wife wasn't on his list either."

"What?"

He dismissed this with another wave of his hand. "We'll talk about that later. Just know that if he varies at all from what I predict, then new data is fed into the formula and changes who the next predicted victims are. And while sometimes more than one person dies in one of his killing events, he always kills at least one person in a seven-day period. Do you understand? Always at least one every seven days, without fail. So if he kills on a Monday, then he will kill again before the following Monday."

"Killing events?"

"Yes. Again, sorry to make it sound so clinical. The seven-day period seems to match his particular complex, one that fits the pattern you will see when you do what I ask. His most recent victim, Mary Hathfield, was just killed yesterday in Medford, Oregon, and she was on the list, so that means the odds of Mr. Chen dying in the next six days are high indeed. The clock is ticking, as they say."

I looked at the paper again. "Zhao Chen, Butte, Montana. This is insane. You're saying these last three people have a death sentence on them?"

"Not a certainty. But a probability of death, yes."

"A *probability* of death?"

"Remember, we're talking about predictions based on massive data sets. You simply *can't* remove that many people from the population through deliberate means without there being a pattern. Mr. Grim has two main weaknesses. The first is that while I believe he is also some kind of drifter—maybe not a drifter in the literal sense, like you, but at least a drifter through life, without permanent attachments to people—he still prefers to *choose* his victims. It's safer. He's mostly selecting victims who won't be missed, whether because they're from the margins of society or because he can make their deaths look like accidents. Even homeless people, he's mostly selecting them ahead of time. There is other data that can help, but we'll discuss that tomorrow."

"What other data?"

"Tomorrow. We'll discuss it tomorrow. I must—"

"Hold on. How long have you been able to, you know, predict his victims?"

Welk swallowed. "Well, I've had *some* ability for about five years, but it's only in the last six months, with the help of machine learning and AI analytics, that my accuracy has really—"

"Five years!"

"Shh. Ms. Pantelli—"

"And you didn't warn any of them?"

"Oh, yes, I most definitely did—and it cost me dearly. That's why I have to be so very careful this time."

"What? What are you—"

"Please, tomorrow. I must get back to my colleagues, and you must get back to work. For now, put that list in your pocket. Look at this later, when you have total privacy. And if possible, don't use the internet from one of your own computers."

"Seriously?"

"He could already be one step ahead of us—watching you. Monitoring what you do, just as he did with me. It's possible. I won't underestimate him again. Going forward, if you *must* get on the internet for something related to Mr. Grim, don't use your own devices, and do so in some kind of incognito mode. Even better, always assume he could be watching."

I folded the paper into quarters and stuck it in the back pocket of my jeans. "Fine. I'll play it your way. But I have to tell you, I'm still not sure I really believe any of this."

"I know. I predicted that too." He smiled faintly. "But once you think more about what I told you overnight, and do what I told you with the atlas, I think you'll come to see it my way. We simply have no alternative, Ms. Pantelli. We can't let him continue. He's an abomination."

"Okay, say I grant that Mr. Grim is real. What's his other weakness?"

"What's that?"

"You said he had two main weaknesses."

"Oh. While he's definitely not an attention seeker in the literal sense, I believe he does want a worthy opponent."

"He *wants* an opponent? After thirty years of getting away with this?"

"Not just an opponent. A *worthy* one. While I doubt he believes he'll ever be caught, he can't stand the idea that somebody he considers unworthy catches him. I think he likes having somebody on his tail. The thrill, that is. Within reason. He's obviously extremely careful. Plus it validates what he's doing, you see. Like most serial killers, much of his joy comes from the fact that he's getting away with it."

"And you're not worthy? As smart as you are? It sounds like you'd be a perfect match for each other, Moriarty to your Sherlock Holmes."

"Hardly. For one, he's a psychopath."

"Look, I didn't mean—"

"No, no. It's all right. I'm sensitive to this because Mona's frequent complaint about me was my ... my lack of sympathy for anyone except for those closest to me. If I were a little farther over that line, I might be a psychopath myself. I don't know what Mr. Grim considers a worthy adversary—my data doesn't tell me that —but I know that whatever it is, I don't have it. I know that for certain. Otherwise, once he determined I was onto him, he would have killed me instead of ..." He trailed off.

"Instead of what?"

Welk gazed at the bay, as if searching for something. He shook his head, not as if he was answering no but as if he was shaking something off. "There are fates worse than death, Ms. Pantelli. I'm sure you, of all people, know that. Now, if you'll excuse me, I do need to use the restroom again. I'm afraid those breakfasts at the Amovar, while wonderful, are a bit ..." He winced and rubbed his forehead.

"On the rich side?" I finished for him.

Still grimacing, either from the headache or from his upset stomach, he offered the briefest of smiles. "That's right."

"In more way ways than one," I said.

"What's that? Oh, the cost. Right. That reminds me." He reached into his inside jacket pocket, retrieved his wallet, and pulled out a twenty dollar bill, which he handed to me.

"What's this?" I said.

"Your tip," he said. "For cleaning my room. We must keep up appearances, you know. And if you'd like to apply it toward lunch at the mansion, it's on me."

———

I WASN'T TOO proud to take the twenty, but I certainly wasn't going to spend it at the Amovar. That would barely cover the cost of a mimosa.

With the sun gleaming on the cars parked outside Bayside, I left Professor Welk and made my way to the elevator. It was a good thing I was pushing my rattling cart ahead of me because my legs still felt like jelly, and I might have toppled over the railing into the junipers if I wasn't holding on to something.

The breeze swirled across the concrete walkway, making the red cedars at the back of the parking lot, the ones probably giving Welk's sinuses fits, sway like slow-moving dancers. Mom used to dance like that—alone, usually a goblet of red wine in hand, Elton John or Celine Dion on the stereo. It was one of the few times I ever saw her happy. She never danced if she knew I was watching. It was probably no coincidence that she was only happy when she thought her family wasn't around.

Between the last room and the elevator, the path was open to the air, with a partial view of the marina and the backside of the stately white Amovar mansion, where guests lounged in white lawn chairs around the pool. There was a lot of white—beach towels, sunshades, the picket fence around the perimeter ... the people. Generally, it was a pretty lily-white crowd at the Orcadia.

The sidewalk along the bay was lined with blooming pink

orchids. I could still smell hamburger on the breeze, but I was no longer hungry. In fact, I felt downright queasy.

Waiting for the elevator, I leaned against the rail, breathing in the fresh air, steadying myself. I didn't like being manipulated. I didn't like people telling me what to do at all—my old partner at the FBI, Ben Wilde, joked that the best way to get me to follow an order was to tell me to do the opposite—and Welk was doing far more than telling me what to do. He was trying to control me like a kid with a high-tech drone. And he was using my emotions to do it.

I resented him for it. It didn't mean I'd ruled out what he was saying, but I still resented how he was manipulating me. When I got off shift in a couple hours, I'd drive back to my place in Olga, a sleepy little hamlet on Buck Bay, and I'd perform his experiment with the atlas in the privacy of my room, but I'd also use the internet to do my own research despite his warning. I'd dig into Colin Welk too. Maybe I'd even call Ben to see what he could find.

Leaning far over the rail, feeling the weathered wood biting deeper and deeper into my palms, I was struck with a wild thought. What if the killer was Welk? Sure, the guy was in a wheelchair, but maybe that was fake. What great cover, pretending to be handicapped, and what great misdirection, pretending that he was the one looking for the killer instead of being the killer himself.

It was tin-foil hat stuff, and I felt silly for thinking it, especially since it wouldn't be that hard to verify that Welk was really handicapped, and I couldn't think of a reason why the killer would take such a big chance when he'd been getting away with this for thirty years. Still, as I finally punched the elevator's up button, I couldn't shake the feeling that there was something about Welk, or his story, that wasn't quite what it seemed.

When the elevator doors opened, a woman with a stroller got off. As I rode up, my sense of gloom only deepened. Room 1113, a few doors down from Welk's, was the next on my list to clean, but I had towels to deliver for Steve first. The stairs would have been faster, but I'd learned from experience to always bring the cart. A guest may ask only for towels over the phone but then remember that they also needed shampoo, Keurig packets, and quite a few other things once I arrived.

Even so, my whole trip to the third floor of the complex and back, including chatting with the gray-haired Iowan in 1309 who was on the island for her fortieth wedding anniversary and wanted to tell me about each of her seven grandchildren, took no more than ten minutes.

I was wheeling my cart back toward 1113—there was nobody on the path outside the doors but me—when my cell phone rang. It was Steve.

"1109 just called," he said before I'd even gotten out a hello. That was Welk's room, but Steve never referred to the guests by name, just by room. "He said there's a mess in the bathroom that needs to be cleaned up, and that the maid must have missed it." He sighed. "Weren't you just there, Karen? You told me you were cleaning the bathroom!"

"I was! The bathroom was spotless when I left it." This was a lie, or at least not a truth I could verify, because I hadn't seen the state of the bathroom during my visit, but I wondered what Welk was up to now. Did he have something urgent he needed to tell me before tomorrow? "Are you sure this was 1109?"

"You think I'm an idiot? Go take care of it—fucking pronto! I probably don't have to tell you, Karen, but you're on thin ice here. *Thin ice!*"

He clicked off, his shouting still ringing in my ears. I was annoyed. If Welk thought getting me fired was the surest way to get me to help him, he wasn't as smart as he thought he was.

I pushed the cart a little past 1109 and knocked on the door. No answer. The Maid Service sign was gone. Did Welk really just make that call, then head back to the Amovar? What kind of game was he playing? I looked over the parked cars gleaming in the sun, past the low-cut grass and up the path to the Amovar. I saw the lady pushing the stroller, the one I'd passed in the elevator, but nobody else.

I knocked again. Still no answer. Wondering if I had it in me to punch somebody in a wheelchair, I swiped my housekeeping fob over the electronic lock and opened the door.

The bathroom fan—we had some of the loudest fans of any hotel I'd worked at—roared like a jet turbine. Professor Welk no longer sat by the patio doors, but the folding table was still there. The sunlight glared off the bay. I saw his wheelchair next, positioned outside the bathroom door, which was open. The light was on, and that orange-smelling scent still hung in the air. Letting the door to 1109 swing shut behind me, I stepped inside to see what kind of mess was waiting for me and saw blood on the yellow tiles. Just a few drops.

Then, craning my head around the corner, I saw Welk sitting on the can—or what was left of him anyway since most of his face was a bloody mess.

He was dead.

3

A self-inflicted gunshot wound. That was what it looked like—
or at least, what it had been *made* to look like—since the .38
Special was on the tiles next to the wheelchair, underneath his
limp right hand, and it was obvious that the bullet had entered
underneath his hairy chin. It didn't take a forensics expert to know
that was the only way so much blood and brain matter could have
ended up on the ceiling.

There was no need to check for a pulse, that was for sure.
Welk was slumped on the toilet with his head tilted way back,
what was left of his mouth gaping open and blood dripping onto
the tiles. There were still plenty of the left side of his face intact,
including his left eye, which was wide and unblinking, the picture
of someone gripped by terror. His chin was gone, though weirdly
his beard was still holding a lot of that gory mess in place.

Next to all that blood, Welk's hair looked more orange than
red. It was a strange thing to notice, but then I often noticed
strange things in moments like this—a coping mechanism, maybe,
a way to distance myself from the visceral nature of what I was
seeing, to bottle up my emotions behind observation and the cata-
loging of details. Whatever it was, it often served me well in my

past life in the FBI because not only did this reaction keep me calm, the heightened sense of awareness helped me if there was danger close at hand.

The bathroom fan, a steady drone, was loud enough that it might have been hard to make out the discharge of such a small caliber gun even if I'd been standing on the landing right outside, especially with the heavy, fire-resistant door that most hotels used. The shower curtain was pushed all the way open, bunched up on the rod, but there were still red speckles on the vinyl. Plenty on the back of the toilet, the mirror, and the pastel-blue countertop. Metal crutches leaned against the counter next to him, and blood dotted those too. There was blood everywhere.

Not on my black Converses, though, at least not yet. I was making sure not to get any on me.

Welk's jeans were still buttoned and up around his bulky thighs. He was sitting on the closed lid. I absorbed all this in the span of a second or two, then my training kicked into gear. This couldn't have happened more than a few minutes ago. I didn't believe Colin Welk's death was a suicide, not for a second, and that meant his killer was still nearby.

Maybe even in the hotel room.

Leaning just out of the bathroom door, looking past the empty wheelchair, I spied the unoccupied folding table and the patio doors, still cracked open, the sun so bright on the bay that I had to squint. The way the hall ran down the center of the room, I couldn't see the bed or much of the living space, so I swung around flat against the wall next to the wheelchair.

I held my breath and listened. I couldn't hear anything over the roar of that damn bathroom fan, so I flicked it off with my elbow, hoping I didn't mess up any possible fingerprints. The glare from the bay also put me at a disadvantage. I thought about going back for Welk's revolver, but if there was even the smallest amount of evidence that could prove it hadn't been a suicide, I didn't want to contaminate the crime scene. Besides, if Mr. Grim had gone to this much trouble to make it look like a suicide—if that's who we were talking about here—I doubted he really would have stuck around waiting for the body to be found.

My abundance of caution may have been allowing the killer to escape, but it couldn't be helped. I took my time creeping around the wheelchair, staying low, until I could make out both the bed and the living area. The downy white bedspread looked just as it had earlier, as did the green microfiber wingback chairs and the sandalwood coffee table. Nothing looked disturbed. Nothing had changed.

Nobody there.

Nobody on the patio either. The Adirondack chairs were empty. Faster, but still keeping low, I made my way to the sliding glass doors. I spotted no one on the sidewalk path below. I slid open the door and stepped into the cool breeze.

A sinewy old sailor, complete with a Popeye pipe, was tying up his dinghy, but I didn't see any other activity on the dock. The blue wind sock at the end of the boardwalk rippled. Rig lines snapped against masts. Laughter from the Amovar, rising and falling like the wind. Nothing amiss. A normal Saturday. I held my breath and listened. With the building between me and the parking lot, I had to really strain to hear anything coming from the other side, but I thought I could just make out the rumble of a truck starting up.

I raced to the front door and onto the landing, leaning far enough over the rail that I had a sweeping view of the Amovar, the packed parking lot, and the winding road that led to the restaurants and retail shops bordering Cascade Bay.

There it was, the rumble I'd heard: a purple Amazon van, already on its way out of the lot. I recognized the driver, a twenty-something girl with a blonde ponytail, who'd had the job at least as long as I'd been at the Orcadia. Not a likely suspect.

I also spotted three conference-goers on the wide circular steps up at the mansion plus two women loading suitcases into the back of a silver Subaru and a handful of green-jacketed members of the grounds crew, most of whom were laying bark dust from wheelbarrows.

I dashed for the stairs. As I rounded the corner, I nearly crashed into Steve—my short, barrel-chested manager who would have been more physically impressive if he didn't also have a barrel-shaped waist. His black mustache, curled on both sides with enough wax to power a candle for a week, made him look like a villain in a spaghetti western.

"Karen?" he said. "What the hell are you—"

"There was a murder in 1109!" I said, racing past him. "Call 911!—*pronto!*"

———

DETECTIVE MAYA SHAW FROWNED. She'd been frowning a lot since she arrived at the Orcadia, three hours after I found Colin Welk dead in his bathroom and about an hour after I'd already exhaustively answered similar questions posed to me by the sheriff deputy first on the scene and again when the staff sergeant in charge of the Orcas Island substation wanted me to repeat it all again. Just for the record, you know. I always gave the same answers. None of them liked my answers.

My first two interrogators had frowned a bunch too, but their frowns weren't like Detective Shaw's. She had the same kind of frown that my firearms instructor at Quantico had. It made me feel bad disappointing her.

Not *too* bad, of course. I was annoyed that I'd had to twiddle my thumbs while I waited for her to boat over from Friday Island, where apparently the bulk of the San Juan County Sheriff's Office was located, including their only full-time detective. They were supposed to have two—I learned this from Sergeant Henderson while we waited, who was quite the chatty fellow—but the other position was still vacant. Detective Eddie Cobb had apparently taken a position with the Seattle Police Department to be closer to his Microsoft-programmer girlfriend.

This meant Detective Shaw was stretched pretty thin, Henderson explained, when I'd complained about the wait. It might have been why Shaw was frowning at me now. Maybe her frowning had nothing to do with the answers I was giving her. Maybe she was just tired of being stretched so thin. I didn't think so, but maybe.

"So let's run over it one more time," she said, her frown deepening. She had the kind of flawless black skin that reminded me of the polished obsidian bust of Martin Luther King Jr. that Ben had on his desk in DC. "Because I'm confused on a few points. You *did* tell your manager there'd been a murder in 1109, correct?"

So much for her frown being about her heavy workload. Shaw was hung up on this point, as had been the other cops I'd spoken with. It looked like a suicide, but I'd told Steve it was a murder. Why?

We were sitting in 1108, a room identical to the one next door where Welk's body was still dripping blood onto those bathroom tiles, as far as I knew. They might have loaded him into a body bag by now. The walls were thick, but I could still make out a lot of noise over there. Room 1108 had been conveniently unoccupied. It also smelled faintly of bleach since it had just been cleaned. By me, of course. I had the ten dollar tip in my front pocket as proof.

The guests had been a nice couple from Canada, sailing through the San Juan Islands in their catamaran, and I'd predicted they would be nice tippers. They had that good tipper vibe about them. That conversation with the Canadians had been a little after 8:00 a.m. It was now half past two, according to the digital alarm clock next to the bed.

"Yes," I said. "As I told you already—as I told the others—I thought there *might* be a murder. I wasn't sure. It wasn't until I went back in the room later, and saw the body again, that I realized it was probably a suicide."

"But you didn't see anybody in the room when you found Mr. Welk?"

"No."

"Not on the patio either?"

"No."

"And you didn't hear the gunshot?"

"No."

"You just walked in and found him like that?"

"Yes."

Shaw's frown was so deep that it could have been carved with a knife. Her ink-black hair looked like it had been carved by a knife too. She wore it in dreadlocks that ran tight across her scalp and down her neck in a coiled ponytail, the way hair might look on a wooden statue; there was not even a single loose strand. She snapped her tiny spiral notebook closed, placed her pen on top, and leaned back in her wingback chair. Her eyes, with her irises almost as black as her pupils, seemed to grow darker and bigger the longer she stared at me.

I waited her out. She was probably hoping I'd get nervous and start blurting random things I shouldn't, but I was good at waiting. I may have been tired, hungry, and cranky, but I could wait out the best of them. Back when I'd been in the FBI, I'd used that technique myself. Just wait long enough and magically most people would start talking because most people could not stand someone silently staring at them for more than a few seconds.

Shaw's frown was something else, though, either a natural gift or a finely honed technique, but whatever it was, it was an asset that served her well. She was so young, probably late twenties, that she couldn't have had her position long. That she'd become a detective at her age, and as a woman, was impressive enough, but that she was also a tiny thing, probably not even cracking a hundred pounds, made it even more so. I could have stuffed her and two identical twins inside the stocky, double-chinned Henderson and still had room to spare. Not to mention that she was black—*very* black, the kind of black that made the whites of her eyes glow in dimly lit rooms. Rooms like this one.

Orcas may have been an island, with a unique culture that wasn't quite like anywhere else, but it was still small and almost entirely packed with well-off Caucasians. Putting aside her youth and gender, I couldn't imagine that ascending to any kind of position of authority as a person of color had been easy, especially here.

In addition to me and Shaw, there were two other people in 1108: Sergeant Henderson, who'd wandered back after the crime scene tech arrived, and Steve Murray, my ever-vigilant manager, who'd shown up after "triaging a plan for dealing with the situation," as he'd put it, slumping into one of the two maple dining chairs, the collar of his black polo drenched in sweat. His button nose was roughly the color and shape of a radish. The redness in his nose may have been from the stress and exertion, or it may have been because he'd been hitting his special water bottle pretty hard, the one he kept beside the dying fern in his window. His water smelled suspiciously like whiskey.

Shaw glanced at him. "Mr. Murray? Didn't you say you saw Ms. Pantelli rush out of 1109 and into the parking lot?"

Steve was staring into space and stroking his mustache. The sweat dotting his forehead looked like glass beads. I hadn't felt warm until I looked at him, but now I wished someone would open the sliding glass doors.

"Mr. Murray?" Shaw said.

He looked at her. She repeated what she'd said. He blinked and swallowed. In the ten years I spent in the FBI, I'd seen people react in all kinds of ways to seeing a dead body, especially a gruesome one, and nothing surprised me anymore. Some people were all business, like Shaw. Some people, like Henderson, got chatty and retreated into humor. Some people, like my manager, became practically catatonic.

There was no predicting those reactions beforehand either. The toughest son of a bitch might start weeping on the spot. A delicate seven-year-old might come off as cool as a Navy SEAL. I'd seen it all, so Steve's response, as blustery and dictatorial as he was under normal circumstances, didn't surprise me.

"That—that's right," Steve said. "She was running all over the place down there ... like ... like ..." He shook his head.

"Like she was looking for the killer?" Shaw offered.

"Yes. Like that."

"For how long?"

"Um. Until the cop got here. The first guy. The one who threw up in the parking lot."

"Deputy Hicks," Henderson said helpfully. "He got here about eight minutes after the call. Hicks is pretty green, just out of the academy, and he hasn't seen ... hasn't seen ..." He trailed off when Shaw frowned at him. That frown was something else. I wondered if she'd gone to Catholic school. I couldn't picture it, but I'd briefly attended a Catholic school when Dad was assigned to Hanscom in Bedford, Massachusetts, and some of the nuns frowned like that. She might have learned from the best. "Anyway," Henderson said with a nervous chuckle, "it was Hicks. I feel sorry for the guy, being first on the scene with this one."

Shaw looked back at me. "Until Hicks got here. That's a long time to look for a possible murder suspect if you're not even sure it's a murder."

"I'm confused," I said. "Am I being accused of something?"

"Accused?"

"You're treating me like a suspect."

"Well, that's interesting. *Should* you be a suspect? I thought you said you were sure it was a suicide."

"I didn't say I was sure."

"Oh, so now you *do* think it was a murder?"

"I didn't say that either."

"But you said I'm treating you like a suspect. That tells me you *still* think this was a murder situation."

"No, it doesn't. It just says that's the way you're treating me."

"Then why do you keep glancing out the patio doors?"

"Sorry?"

"You keep looking at the patio doors. Like maybe you think somebody's going to be out there. The killer, maybe."

"It's a nice view, that's all. I enjoy the view."

"Oh, is that all it is?"

Now it was my turn to lean back in my wingback chair. I'd been too flippant. She'd rattled me with that comment about me looking out the patio doors, and it annoyed me that she'd managed to do that. Detective Maya Shaw didn't miss much, I had to give her that. She'd sensed I was hiding something—she had that instinct, the same instinct I had—but she hadn't known for sure until I got flippant. Now she knew. It was what I would have thought had I been in her position. Which I had been, once upon a time.

She stared at me, doing her best to wait me out again. Her gray denim jeans hugged her legs and hips, the fit tight enough that she'd obviously done it on purpose. A lot of women in law enforcement played down their sexuality, even their femininity, doing their best to dress in a way that may not have been masculine but certainly was androgynous. It was as if they were afraid they wouldn't be taken seriously if they didn't.

Not Detective Shaw. She may have been wearing a lightweight blue cotton blazer over a simple V-neck white blouse, certainly professional attire in her line of work, but everything fit her just right. The V-neck was low enough, and revealing enough, that she was practically daring people to look at her cleavage. I wondered if it was a coincidence that her side holster was also clearly in view.

I heard the high-pitched wine of an electric leaf blower in the parking lot, which seemed oddly out of place with the bloody mess next door, but then life at the Orcadia went on. I regretted telling Steve there'd been a murder in 1109 as soon as the words had left my mouth, but that had been in the heat of the moment, when I still thought the killer was nearby. Of course, I *did* think there'd been a murder in 1109, but I was privy to a lot more information than I was willing to reveal.

Shaw sighed and flipped her notebook open again, and I took some pleasure in the fact that I hadn't been the first one to break the silence.

"Let's go back to earlier in the morning," she said, looking down at the notes she'd written. "You said when you went in to clean Mr. Welk's room, that he was in there."

"I did. He was."

"And he still wanted you to clean? Didn't that seem odd,

somebody who was planning on committing suicide wanted his room cleaned?"

I shrugged.

"And you didn't talk with him?" Shaw asked.

"Just briefly. About the weather, you know. He was writing something on his legal pad. He seemed very focused."

"And you didn't see what was on the pad?"

"No. What was it, a suicide note?"

"Bingo," Henderson said, with another chuckle.

Shaw shot him a look that could have frozen over Cascade Bay. He stopped chuckling. I found the presence of a suicide note interesting. Once I'd discovered Welk in the bathroom, I'd never looked back at the legal pad on the folding table, but I'd seen that it was there. I'd been too intent on catching the killer. There were a lot of questions I wanted to ask about that note, but of course I couldn't, not without suggesting I thought this wasn't a suicide.

"Interesting that you would jump right to that conclusion," Shaw said. "That what he was writing was a suicide note."

"Is it really? Don't a lot of people who commit suicide leave a note? I think I read somewhere that it's about a third or so."

"Hmm. You *read* somewhere."

"What's that supposed to mean?"

She sighed. "Ms. Pantelli, please. Let's stop playing dumb, okay? You have to admit, if you were in my shoes, your presence at the Orcadia does raise questions. It's a strange coincidence."

This was enough to get Steve, swimming in his catatonic fog, to surface again. "Her—her presence? What?"

Shaw gave me the long smoldering silence again. I returned it in kind. I didn't like where this was going, but it was inevitable. All it took was a little bit of Googling—something Steve, in his desperation to hire a housekeeper when it was tough to hire anyone for menial jobs on Orcas Island, hadn't done. Oddly, though, I'd found this lack of cursory online checking to be more the norm for the types of odd jobs I'd been working since I left the Bureau. As long as I didn't have a criminal history, which I didn't, I was usually good to go. Heck, half of them never even called my references, which were always exemplary. Nobody outworked me, that was for sure.

"I really don't know what you're talking about," I said. "I'm just a hotel maid."

"Ah, yes, *just* a hotel maid," Shaw said. "Why did you leave the FBI, Ms. Pantelli?"

"Come on, who's playing dumb now? That doesn't have anything to do with me being here."

"The FBI?" Steve said.

"Oh, you didn't tell your new boss about your previous life?" Shaw looked at him with unmistakable disdain, and her tone, if it was even possible, became even more icy. "Mr. Murray, you're telling me you really didn't know anything about her time in the FBI?"

"I don't—I don't understand—"

"How she was a hot-stuff special agent until accidentally shooting a thirteen-year-old girl in a meth house in Boise? How even though she's worked random shit jobs in lots of places since then, she still somehow finds trouble wherever she goes? You're *really* telling me you didn't know any of that, Mr. Murray?"

The pink in Steve's nose spread to the rest of his face. I felt my own face getting warm. In my previous life, as she'd called it, I'd run into the occasional cop who hated the FBI out of general principle, but contrary to what most people saw in the movies, the Bureau's presence was usually welcomed by local law enforcement. However, the stereotype of the overbearing FBI special agent had been around so long that some cops ironically actually *did* act hostile to us because of what they'd seen on TV. I wondered if she was one of those or if she was just trying to get under my skin.

My bet was the latter, so I reminded myself to stay calm. Say nothing. Wait her out.

"For the job Karen was applying for," Steve said, his mustachioed lips pressed so tightly together that it was any wonder he could speak at all, "nothing but ... but her relevant work experience mattered."

"Relevant," Shaw said, nodding. "All right, sure. Didn't matter if she'd killed someone if all she was doing was scrubbing toilets, right?"

In the span of a few seconds, Steve's face went from pink to the same color as the ketchup bottles at the marina burger stand. He rose abruptly. "Excuse me, I, uh, I … need to check on some work issues."

Just like that, he was gone. I glowered at Shaw. She glowered at me. Henderson's radio crackled. He answered the call on his way to the door. I heard something about the crime scene tech needing some assistance, and then he was outside, leaving me and Ms. Frowny Pants alone with the humming mini fridge, the afternoon light lancing off the emerald waters of the bay.

"I'm trying to figure out what your play is here," I said.

Her eyebrows arched. They were so perfectly shaped that she must have plucked them this morning. "My play?"

"You think that I'm suddenly going to get more cooperative if you get me fired? That's your brilliant strategy?"

"I'm not trying to get you fired."

"Well, it certainly looks like—"

"And what do you mean, *more* cooperative? You're telling me you're not cooperative right now?"

"Listen, Detective—"

"Is there a *reason* you're not being cooperative? Do you have something to hide, Ms. Pantelli?"

"I think we're done here," I said. "There's really nothing more I can add. I told you everything. So unless—"

"Did you, though?"

"—you want to hold me as a material witness to a suicide, something I'm sure won't float with any decent—"

"You don't think it's a suicide."

That stopped my little speech cold. It was the shift in tone as much as what she said. It wasn't confrontational. She'd spoken the words gently, almost empathetically, like a doctor delivering a grim diagnosis.

"I'm trying to help you," she added.

"Oh, really?" I said. "By dragging up my past in front of my manager? How was that helping me?"

"I wanted us alone. I couldn't very well ask your boss to leave, not unless you asked for a lawyer, which you hadn't. I knew Sergeant Henderson would be called out momentarily. And you know as well as I do that after today, *somebody* was bound to tell Mr. Mustache that Karen Pantelli was no ordinary housekeeper. This is a small island. The deputies stationed here know who you are now. People talk."

"I'm still trying to figure out how this is you doing me a favor."

"The *favor* is that I'm giving you a chance to level with me one on one, off the record. You must have a good reason for not wanting to say what's really going on here, but I don't like being kept in the dark. Whatever you tell me now, you can even deny later if you want. I know this is highly unusual, but I figure it's better to work with off-the-record information than no information at all."

"You're serious?"

"Absolutely. I was only doing the bad-cop routine so Henderson didn't think I was giving you preferential treatment. The truth is, I respect you, Ms. Pantelli. What you did in Houston in particular—the world owes you a big thanks. I don't get why you live the way you do, but that's your business. It's obvious you like keeping a low profile. A *very* low profile. I can't help you do that unless you also help me."

If the situation hadn't been so serious, I might have smiled. It was a good move, presenting herself as my ally. Was it genuine, though, or was she simply trying a softer approach because being gruff and confrontational hadn't worked? The way our wicker chairs were turned toward one another, in the stillness of the room, we could have been therapist and patient. She leaned back, pressing her palms together over her lips and gazing at me over the tops of her fingers. More in the sun now, her dark skin had a bronze luster to it.

I thought about the note from Welk in my back pocket. I thought about what she might make of that list of names and the story that went along with it. She wouldn't believe it, and I wouldn't blame her. I still didn't believe it myself, and I didn't want to spend my time convincing her when I still had to convince me. Plus I didn't trust her. I found myself liking Detective Maya Shaw more than I did a few minutes ago despite my rising frustration and impatience, but I didn't trust her.

Yet I *might* need her help at some point, and the least I could do was let her know that her instincts weren't totally off.

"You want to help me?" I said. "Don't release my name to the press. Don't release my name to anybody. It's even more important than ever that I keep my name out of the news."

"Why?"

"I can't tell you that."

"Really? That's all you're going to give me?"

"That's all I *can* give you. Until I know more."

"Uh huh. And when you *do* know more, you'll loop me in?"

I hesitated. "Maybe. If it's safe to do so."

Her well-honed frown made an encore appearance. She shifted in her seat, the wicker crackling, and I saw enough of her sidearm to recognize it as a Beretta 92FS. Interesting. Few cops carried Berettas anymore—mostly it was Glocks, S&Ws, and the occasional Sig. I wondered what it said about her that this was her gun of choice. It was a big handgun, one of the heaviest, lots of metal. "I don't like this," she said. "You're asking me to trust you on blind faith."

"Weren't you just basically asking the same thing?"

She chuckled. It was a very faint laugh, but it was good to know that she was at least *capable* of laughter. "Fair enough," she said. "But you're not the one whose career could get torpedoed by whatever this thing is with Colin Welk. Your job here doesn't mean as much—no offense."

"None taken," I replied. "It's obvious I wasn't exactly on the fast track at the Orcadia."

She didn't laugh, but there was a twinkle in her eyes, a glimmer of her real self, and I thought I saw something else too, a kind of hurt often hidden behind humor. Some people joked because they wanted to laugh and to have people laugh with them. Others joked because it was the only way they could live with the pain. I was in the latter category. I sensed Detective Shaw was probably the same.

I also found the comment about her career interesting. It suggested she had ambition beyond working as a detective for the San Juan County Sheriff's Office. I would have liked to know what that ambition was, and I thought about asking her, but then Henderson returned, and she put her frown back on. Ah, so it was a sort of mask then. I see you, Detective Shaw. You don't think I see you, but I do.

Henderson said the crime scene tech was done, the coroner had done what he could on site, and he was ready to load up the body if Detective Shaw was okay with it. Henderson also wanted to know if he could notify next of kin or if Shaw wanted him to hold off a bit longer. Apparently he was getting heat from Sheriff McKinley, who didn't want relatives to read about this in the news.

Shaw looked at me, pursing her lips. Moment of truth. How was she going to play this? I thought about Welk's son, Isaac. I wondered how old he was and whether he had other family around to take care of him.

"Go ahead load him up," she said to Henderson. "We have what we need for now, and there's no evidence to suggest this wasn't a suicide. And yes, let's notify next of kin."

When Henderson left, the two of us once again alone in the hotel room, Shaw flipped open her notebook.

"What's your current address?" she asked. "And a phone number where you can be reached?"

I told her. She wrote it down. Then she turned to a blank page and scribbled her own number on it, which she tore off and handed to me.

"All right," she said. "You think of anything relevant, you call me night or day, okay? And don't leave the island until I give my say so, all right?"

I hesitated. She looked up, arching an eyebrow.

"Really?" she said. "You can't even promise me that?"

"All I can say is, I'll do my best. And if I learn anything I think will blow back on you, I'll let you know."

She slapped her notebook closed. "You know, you're really not making this easy for me, Karen."

I smiled.

"What?" she said.

"You used my first name. I guess that means we're becoming friends, huh?"

She frowned. "Don't get ahead of yourself. I still don't trust you."

"Well," I said, "that means we already have something in common ... Maya."

4

Steve didn't officially fire me, but it amounted to the same thing. He told me to take tomorrow off as a "courtesy because of the trauma of the situation," as if he was doing me a favor. I told him I wasn't feeling particularly traumatized, but he insisted. When I talked to him in his office, I could see that he had a Google search open on his computer, all the results having some variation of my name. His eyes were bloodshot, his breath smelled of Altoids, and I was guessing that the magic water bottle next to his monitor was empty.

I may not have been feeling traumatized, but apparently he was.

Since I wasn't scheduled to work another shift until Wednesday, it was a good bet that all my hours would be reassigned in the meantime. It was just as well. I wasn't sure I'd be coming back anyway, though it would have been nice to have the option.

By the time I headed for my car, it was half past three, so I was surprised to find Elena smoking a cigarette on one of the wooden benches near the marina. Both of our shifts ended at three. While it wasn't unusual to find her taking a smoke break on one of these benches—the marina, and the adjoining boardwalk in front of it where the benches were, was the only place where smoking was allowed at the resort—it *was* unusual after she was finished for the day. She was usually in a hurry to help with the dinner shift at Buena Comida, her son's Mexican restaurant in Eastsound. Unlike a lot of the Orcadia employees, seasonal workers who returned to the mainland at the end of the summer, Elena was a permanent resident.

"Oh, *mi amiga*," she said, "I so sorry, what happen? You okay? *Eso fue horrible.*" Elena, who'd only immigrated to the US from Mexico ten years ago, had a habit of shifting back and forth from English to Spanish without realizing it. "I stay, make sure you *estas bien.*"

I shifted my backpack on my shoulders and glanced back at the Amovar. The cops were gone. The only sign that something terrible had happened earlier were the shell-shocked attendees of the math conference consoling each other on the mansion's front steps. "I'm all right," I said. "I just feel bad that a guest would, you know, do that."

She shook her head and blew smoke out of the side of her mouth. In the afternoon sun, her skin was roughly the same honey-oak hue as the bench, with the same shiny-but-tough lacquer sheen. That was how I thought of Elena: shiny but tough. Her gray hair was up in a bun, but lots of individual hairs had sprung loose and fluttered in the breeze. The smell of barbecued halibut wafted over from a thirty-foot catamaran tied up on one of the farthest slips, where tendrils of smoke floated over the gleaming hull.

I was impatient to get back to my place and figure out my next move, but I didn't know when I would see Elena again. She was one of the few people I'd told about my search for my mother. Although she didn't have information that could help, she'd eagerly pointed me toward people on the island who might.

"*Sí, sí, muy mala.* I stay a little. You talk? It no good, you have no one talk."

"That's very kind of you. I'm fine, though."

She eyed my backpack. "You come back, *sí?* Work again?"

"Well, I sure …" I was going to say "hope so." I liked Elena too much to lie to her, especially since I didn't know if I'd ever see her again. Even if Steve *didn't* fire me, would I come back to the Orcadia? No. Would I even stay on Orcas Island much longer? Probably not, if Welk was telling the truth about Mom. I almost never came back anywhere. It was my modus operandi. I was the dead-eyed drifter, after all, the woman who didn't put down roots, who didn't need anyone, not really, at least not for long, and yet I felt a clench of sadness at the thought of never sharing another conversation with shiny-but-tough Elena. The least I could do was be honest with her. "Actually, I'm not really sure. My hunch is … probably not."

She shook her head again and peered around me at the mansion. "He not nice, that one. But he not worst either. I see lots bad. The last was *pinchador de trasero.*"

"*Trasero?*"

"Oh, how you say? Someone who, um … " She leaned to one side and pinched her bottom.

I chuckled. Her polo, once black like mine, was now a faded charcoal and spotted with black marker where she'd inked over the places she'd accidentally gotten bleach on it, an occupational hazard. Just another reason to hate Steve. He was too cheap to buy his employees more than one shirt.

"Yes," I said, "I've had a few bosses like that. They usually live to regret it, though. I'm tougher than I look."

She smiled. One of her incisors was missing, leaving a gaping hole, but she never seemed self-conscious about it. "You look very strong to me. *Una dama dura.*"

"Thanks. I think."

"It true? What they say?"

"What's that?"

"You police?"

"Ah. That."

"It true then?"

"Once upon a time, yes. FBI, actually. That was a different life."

"Why you ... no do?"

I shrugged. "Just time to do something different."

"You smart. *Corajuda.* Probably good police. You should do police again if you good. Better than this. Much better. Where I come from, many police no good. Always *dejarse sobornar.*"

"What's that?"

"Oh, you know," she said, turning her palm over and miming putting dollar bills into it.

I chuckled. "That happens in the States too. They're just sneakier about it here."

"Hmm. Sneaky. *Sí.* Sometimes I think the people who most pretend be good are ones most bad."

This made me smile. "That's very insightful of you, Elena."

"What's this, full of sight?"

"Insightful. It means *mucho* smart."

She turned bashful, giving me a dismissive wave, a little red appearing in her bronze cheeks. "Oh, *eres tan tonta.* I no smart. Just live long. See things. You live long, not much surprise."

"Hmm. Well, I guess it just goes to show you can't trust anybody, huh?"

"Oh! No, you must trust. No trust, no friends, *sí?* Very lonely. Not good. Need people. People *is* life."

Now I felt my own face getting warm. "Elena, I want to be just like you when I grow up."

"Ah! Stop. *Eres una niña muy tonta!*"

It was the kind of conversation I was going to miss, even the overbearing motherly concern, maybe *especially* the overbearing motherly concern, but Elena's earlier comment also got me thinking about Colin Welk. *People who most pretend be good are ones most bad.* I wasn't so sure it was a good idea to trust people too readily, but maybe if I'd trusted Welk a little more, giving his story just a bit more credence, I would have been more alert to potential danger instead of assuming Welk was crazy. And maybe, if I'd been more alert, Welk would still be alive. That was on me.

"Elena," I said, "did you talk to him at all? Professor Welk?"

She looked up at the Bayshore building, which we could see from the balcony side. We were both familiar enough with the rooms to know which patio was his. There was nothing there now, not a hint of life inside. The slider was dark. "The one who …?" she began.

"Yes. Him."

"No."

"Nothing seemed unusual about him? Nothing out of the ordinary or different?"

"He in wheelchair."

"Other than that, I mean."

She smiled sadly. "You be like police now?"

"Just curious, that's all. Did you see him at breakfast maybe or talking to his colleagues? How did he seem?"

She thought about it. "See outside on his patio in morning, in wheelchair. I was here, on break. He on phone. I hear him say, 'Please be patient. I'll be home soon.' I wonder who waits for him. I wonder why he say he be home soon, if he …" She teared up. "Maybe if I talk to him. Maybe …"

"Hey, none of that," I said. "I didn't mean to imply that we could have … Believe me when I tell you there's nothing you could have said or done that would have stopped this from happening."

She nodded, but I could see that she didn't believe me. I wondered who Welk had been talking to. His son Isaac? I wondered if Isaac had gotten the news by now. I had a feeling I was going to be talking to Isaac before long. Maybe soon if I came to the conclusion he was really in danger.

"Well," I said, "I better get going." I was not a touchy-feely person, but I gave Elena's shoulder a squeeze. "I just want you to know how much I appreciate you, okay? You're the best."

Her eyes teared up again. "If you no work here, what you do now?"

"I don't know. Something else."

"Police?"

"No, not that. Never again." I chuckled. "I'm something of a dead-eyed drifter now. I'll just drift somewhere else."

"What you say? Dead eyes?"

"Never mind. Just trying to make a joke."

"You have very nice eyes. Like the sea."

"Thank you. I wasn't … Well, that's very nice of you."

"You still no boyfriend?"

"No. Not right now."

"Many men, they see your eyes, they fall in love."

I laughed. "I wish that was true."

"It is, it is. You just have to stop long enough time so they see."

"Right."

She took another drag of her cigarette, then stubbed it out in the concrete ashtray next to the bench. "This no good, you by yourself so much."

"I promise, I'll be all right."

"If you want, you come stay with me. Marco no mind. He like you."

This offer probably shouldn't have surprised me, knowing Elena, but it still did, enough that I actually felt what might have been tears in my own eyes. Not that I ever would have admitted it to anyone. "That's very kind of you, Elena. I actually have a good place to stay for the moment. I trade a bit of housekeeping for free rent, so, um, that's all squared away."

"Oh."

"But I, uh … I really appreciate it. I'll be seeing you, okay?" I turned to go, wanting to get out of there before I made a fool of myself. What would the boys at the Bureau think of Killer Karen, the nickname they'd once given me, getting all weepy just because somebody had been nice to her? That wouldn't do. That wouldn't do at all. "You keep being kind, okay? The world needs more people like you."

Now Elena *was* crying. "You are sweet. Oh! Wait. That make remember." She unzipped her purse and rifled through it. "One good thing on bad day. Got big tip! One hundred dollar! Say I should share it with others, so I give you. Huh. I only have ten other dollar. Can you change?"

"Wow, that's great. See, it pays to be kind. A little silver lining."

She looked up from her purse. "Silver what?"

"Never mind. You keep my share."

"What? No, no. I get change from—"

"I insist, Elena. Use it on those cute grandkids of yours if nothing else."

"You sure?"

"Please. Or treat yourself to something nice. You deserve it. Just don't spend it all in one place."

"Why? Probably spend it at grocery. Food *very* expensive."

I laughed. "I didn't mean … Never mind. You keep being nice, okay? I'm serious about that one. That's the reason you get the best tips, you know? You always find a reason to be nice to people, no matter what. Even if they don't deserve it."

Unable to speak, she offered me a misty-eyed nod. I took that as my cue to escape. I walked slowly, the heaviness of the goodbye weighing me down. The Smokercraft parked in the slip nearest us roared to life, covering the sound of my footsteps on the board-walk. If I'd been a little bit faster, or if the boat's engine had been a little bit louder, I might not have heard Elena, but somehow I did.

"Choose one person a week," she said.

I froze. I was still on the boardwalk, about a dozen paces away, looking right at the Bayshore room where I'd found Colin Welk's lifeless body only hours earlier. With the room dark, the white Adirondack chairs on the patio reflected back in the glass.

I turned around. Elena, tugging another cigarette out of the pack, paused when she saw me gaping at her.

"What did you say?" I asked.

"Perdón?"

I edged my way back toward her, keeping my movements slow and my voice calm, not wanting to alarm her. "What you just said. Did I hear you correctly? You said … *Choose one person a week?"*

"Ah! *No pensé que estaba hablando en voz alta. Sí,* it remind me."

I took a few more cautious steps toward her, feeling my heart shift into a higher gear. "It reminds you of what?"

"Oh! The tip, the hundred dollar. It was on the note."

"What note?"

"He left a note. Very sweet. He say how much—"

"Do you have it?"

"What?"

"The note, do you have it?"

"Sí. I was going to ask Marco to explain since it has many words I don't—"

"Can I see it? I'll translate it if you want."

"What's wrong?"

"Nothing, nothing, I'd just like to read it.

With a shrug, she unzipped her purse and pulled out a sheet of Orcadia stationary that had been folded into quarters. When I opened it up, I found a handwritten note, a loopy script in blue ballpoint ink that was probably from one of the pens that the hotel provided:

HERE's a little something extra for you and your fellow housekeepers. I appreciate your hard work! All I ask is that you try to do a random act of good for the world. My principle has always been to choose one person a week. —H. A. P.

I DIDN'T WANT Elena to know how alarmed I was, but some reactions are hard to hide. This was a message from Professor Welk's killer—there was no doubt about it—and it was a message directed at me. It wasn't just the note, which was bad enough. It was the initials, which obviously weren't the killer's. They were initials I knew almost as well as my own.

Hope Allison Pantelli.

My sister. She went by Salwell now, her husband's last name, but the initials couldn't have referred to anyone else. From the training I'd gotten in the FBI, I could tell by the cross-strokes on the t's that they'd been made right to left and that the o's had probably been done counterclockwise, both typical of lefthanders. Was Mr. Grim left-handed? Only about 10 percent of people were.

"Karen?" Elena said.

I looked at her, feigning a smile, but it was too late. Elena grasped my left hand, which had gone ice cold. Her own fingers felt as rough as the scouring brushes we sometimes used to scrub grime off the bottoms of the tubs.

"You sick?" she asked. *"Te ves blanca como un fantasma."*

"I'm okay," I said. "I just … Well, never mind. Can I keep this?"

"What wrong?"

"Nothing. Nothing, I just want to keep the note."

"You want part money?"

"No, no, it's not that. There's just …" I trailed off, debating how much to tell her, and quickly decided I couldn't tell her much. I couldn't put her at risk. But I also needed information that Elena might have. "The guest who wrote this, do you know his name?"

"Um, no. Old man. Gray hair. Wife very nice too."

"He came with his wife?"

"Yes. Sweet lady. *Su cabello estaba teñido muy rojo.* Oh! They come big family. You know, all week. Everybody go today."

"The Monroe reunion."

"Sí, Sí, that one."

I studied the note again. The Monroe reunion was a big family affair that had blocked out a dozen rooms, most of them from Washington state but some from as far as Wisconsin. I knew the group because while some, like the couple she'd described, were staying up in the Hillside rooms, most were down in Bayshore. I could even picture the couple she was talking about, frail but good-natured, always smiling, always at the center of any of the family dinners. "You're *sure* this was from them?"

"Sí. Very sure."

"Do you remember their room number?"

"2103. Why, problem?"

"No, it's fine. Really. It just ... Never mind, sorry I'm so distracted. Still dealing with what happened today, I guess. But you take care, okay? I want to talk to the front desk real quick about something I just remembered, but I'll talk to you soon."

She gave my hand another squeeze. "Okay. But come to Buena Comida, *sí?* One time."

I told her I would try and hustled back to the Amovar. Cady, a summer hire from Longview, was on duty at the front desk, but there were no guests, and she was busy folding brochures at the back counter, leaving the computer station free. I asked her if I could use the computer to look up a few things, and she said it was no problem, not really looking at me. I heard her sniffling, undoubtedly because of what had happened in 1109, but I didn't have the time or the headspace to comfort her. She was better off anyway. People usually ended up *more* upset when I tried to comfort them.

Using a blank sheet of printer paper, I jotted down the names and cell numbers of not only the occupants of 2103 but also people staying in nearby rooms as well, three on each side, above and below. I didn't actually think the sweet old couple in 2103—who were John and Madeline Rowe, it turned out—had anything to do with Colin Welk's death, but I wanted to at least rule them out. If they didn't leave a note for the housekeeper, there was a good chance that Welk's killer had snuck into to the room after they'd departed and left the note so it would look like it was coming from them.

I would have liked to have gotten the names and numbers of *everyone* staying at the Orcadia last night, but I heard Steve down the hall talking to Dana, the restaurant manager, so I made a quick retreat.

Besides, I already sensed that nothing would be gained from talking to John and Madeline Rowe. If Mr. Grim had gone to such elaborate lengths to deliver this warning to me, knowing full well there was a good chance I'd never see it, I doubted he would be so sloppy as to leave any clues. On the way to my Honda, with the sun bright in my eyes and a stiff breeze rippling the sails of the boats on Cascade Bay, I eyed every person I saw with great suspicion. I could understand how easily Colin Welk had become paranoid. Mr. Grim could have been anybody.

It was clear I was already playing a dangerous game, a game I'd never wanted to play in the first place.

5

Twenty minutes later, at Moran State Park, I slouched in the duct-taped seat of my '98 Honda Civic, staring at the cell phone in my lap. It had taken me only five minutes to reach the day use area at Cascade Lake. I'd spent the rest of the time with my finger hovering over the name Ben Wilde in the two-person list of contacts I'd bothered to save on my Cricket phone. I'd picked up this one in Cheyenne after accidentally leaving the last one in a gas station restroom outside Nashville.

Or maybe it was St. Louis. It was hard to say. Losing my phone was a regular thing with me.

Past my car's dented white hood, the sun glittered out on the water like gold confetti. A man and a woman paddled a canoe. A pregnant woman and a toddler in matching yellow swimsuits built a sandcastle. At the Sugar Shack, an old man in a button-adorned fishing cap poured creamer into a steaming paper cup. With my window rolled down, I smelled popcorn. I sometimes stopped at the Sugar Shack after my shifts and treated myself to a bag of popcorn, slowly munching away on the buttery goodness while watching people having fun at the lake. Not today, though. Today was not a day for popcorn. Probably not tomorrow either. Probably not for a long time.

I called Ben, but it went to voicemail. I left a message. I'd barely put the phone back in my lap when it rang.

"Karen?" he said before I could even get out a hello. I may have had misgivings about calling my former partner—we'd shared an awkward kiss last time I'd seen him in person, and I had mixed feelings about it—but it was still good to hear that deep baritone. "Jesus!" he went on. "It's been weeks. Is this your new number? I'm so relieved that—"

"Yes," I said, "it's me."

"Thank God! You know, even a simple text would be nice. Where are you?"

"Orcas Island. You?"

"At work." He sighed.

I heard him typing and imagined him in that swanky new office in the J. Edgar Hoover Building in DC. He hadn't quite made it to the seventh floor—that was shorthand in the FBI for the highest levels of leadership—but he was getting closer. Working on a Saturday was proof enough of that. "Orcas ... Right! I *thought* that was in the Sun Juan Islands, but I couldn't remember for sure. What the heck are you doing there? The last time we chatted, you were in Florida. Is this about your mother?"

I debated about what to tell him. The couple in the canoe were awkwardly trying to take a selfie, the boat rocking violently, and they were laughing about it. I tried to imagine Ben and I in a canoe and couldn't picture it. A bank shoot-out in Omaha, maybe, but not a canoe. I flashed to the kiss we'd shared in Houston, remembering the feel of his lips pressing against mine, and forced the thought out of my mind.

"Listen," I said. "I need a favor. It's a big one, and you have to trust me because I can't tell you much right now."

I heard him drum his fingers on his desk. "I'm already leery. What is it?"

"I need my sister put under FBI protection."

There was a pause long enough that I could just make out

someone talking in the hall outside his office, then Ben laughed. When I didn't join him, he cleared his throat.

"You're serious?" he said.

"Absolutely."

I heard the creak of his chair, then the click of the door closing. "Okay, what has Hope done now? She go off her meds and do something stupid? Or is it that abusive husband of hers? Did she finally get smart and—"

"No, no, it's nothing like that. I'd never ask this of you if that's all it was." I'd helped Hope leave Ronnie once only to have her boomerang back to him. Ever since, we'd barely been on speaking terms. Still, she was the other name in my contact list, and I'd go on looking out for her no matter what she thought of me. "It's much bigger than that, Ben. She really could be in serious danger."

"What kind of danger?"

"I ... can't tell you that."

"Karen, come on."

"I told you that you have to trust me. I'll tell you more when I can, but right now it's extremely important that you not tell a single soul about this."

"What?"

"Whoever protects her, they can't know why they're protecting her, and they certainly can't tell anyone."

He groaned. "This is your weird sense of humor again, right?"

"Nope."

"A practical joke."

"I'm dead serious. I know the proper channels you would have had to go through under normal circumstances, but I need you to short-circuit that process somehow."

"Let me get this straight. You want me to arrange FBI protection for your sister, but you can't tell me why, and you also want to make sure that nobody finds out about it."

"That's the short of it, yes."

"Well, why didn't you just say so! No problem, I'll just hit the big red button here on my desk that makes all that happen!"

"Ben."

"Oh, and this other button here makes giant green butterflies fly out of my ass. I've got buttons for everything!"

"Ben, I'd tell you more if I could."

"Would you, though? Really? Because, you know, history suggests otherwise. You don't tell me jack shit until you have no other choice."

I sighed. I'd doubted this wasn't going to be easy, but I'd somehow hoped he'd take my word on faith. "Look," I said, feeling my throat constrict and my face grow warm, "I know I … I haven't exactly been a great friend to you. I'm sorry about that. I'm dealing with some stuff, okay? But you know me, Ben. You know I'd never mess with you on something like this. You know … you know how hard it is for me to ask for help."

The line was silent. I didn't hear anyone talking out in the hall on his end. I didn't hear anything.

"I need you on this one," I said. "I'll tell you more when I can. I *will.* And I'll make it up to you somehow."

He replied with a long exhale of resignation. It wasn't exactly a yes, but I knew from that sound alone that he was going to help me. "You don't have to make up anything," he said.

"How about tickets to the next Kenny G concert in DC?"

"Stop."

"What, you over Kenny G now?"

"At least my musical taste doesn't start and stop with Fleetwood Mac."

"Ha! See, there's the Ben Wilde I know."

"Well, the Ben Wilde *you* know is sitting here trying to figure out just how in the hell I'm going to arrange around-the-clock protection for your sister without giving anyone a reason why."

"You're smart. You'll figure it out."

"Well, I can think of *one* way. I'll do it myself."

"What? No."

"It's probably the only option, Karen."

"Bullshit. I'm not letting you——"

"Look, you want my help or not? I can hop a flight tonight,

rent a van, and be monitoring your sister's place in Atlanta before midnight. It's the best way to keep this thing tight. How long are we talking? Gary has been pressing me to take a few days off, but there's some stuff going on with the task force that will make it hard for me to be gone long."

I shook my head, not wanting to agree with him but knowing that Ben was right. He had to do this himself. I'd known it before I'd even called, which was part of the reason I'd been so reluctant. Gary was Gary Harding, the assistant director of the Counterintelligence Division and Ben's direct supervisor since Ben's promotion to lead liaison of the Joint Terrorism Task Force. That Ben had used Gary's name so casually was a sign of just how important my old partner had become.

I felt a pang of jealousy at that, and the feeling surprised me. I'd thought my career ambitions had gone the way of the FBI badge, department-issued Glock, and gold gross necklace I'd tossed into the Delaware River once upon a time.

"What's going on with the task force?" I asked.

"Oh, I see," Ben said, "you get to ask me questions, but it doesn't work the other way around?"

"I just don't want you to do anything that hurts your career, that's all."

He let out a bigger sigh this time. "Just some bullshit political stuff, okay? Homeland Security has been throwing sharp elbows, wanting to treat every redneck with an expired hunting license as a possible domestic terrorist. I've had to do some push-back before we trample all over people's civil rights. But it's fine. I can get away for a few days. Longer than that becomes an issue."

"I really appreciate it."

"You really can't tell me *anything*?"

"I wish I could."

"It's hard for me to know how to protect Hope if I don't even—"

"I can tell you it's a single operator. That's all. And even that's probably too much."

"All right, that helps a little at least. Does your sister know she's in danger?"

"No. And she can't. If she changes her routine at all, even in the slightest way—"

"I get it, I get it. I'll be a fly on the wall. Or in this case, the fly on the windshield of a rental car."

"It's very important that you not tell a single soul about this."

"Yes, you've made that abundantly clear."

"I really, really appreciate it."

"You've made that clear too."

The undercurrent of bitterness was hard to miss. I didn't want to leave it this way. Ben Wilde had been a mentor, friend, the only person who stood by me after the shit went down in Boise, and more importantly, as I tore apart my own life piece by piece, there had always been the possibility of something more between us. Only the possibility, yes, but over the last year I'd gone from outright rejecting that possibility to feeling ambivalent to … actually fantasizing about something more. Sometimes quite vividly.

Only occasionally. But it was there. I couldn't deny that the attraction was real, but it didn't mean I wanted to act on it. At least not yet.

"I'm serious about those Kenny G tickets," I said.

"All right."

"Next time I'm in town—scratch that. When this thing is done, I'm coming to DC."

"Hmm."

"How's it going, by the way? The new position?"

"Oh, you know."

"Come on, Ben. I'm trying here."

He chuckled. "I know. I just enjoy hearing you squirm. You serious about coming to DC?"

"Absolutely." And as I said that, I felt what could only be described as butterflies in my stomach. Dear God, what was I, some starry-eyed teenager? Then, like an idiot, I followed up with a couple of sentences loaded with all kinds of innuendo. "We'll paint the town red and party all night—you know, the whole deal. It's a date."

This time he replied with one of his patented, deep-seated laughs, whether it was from embarrassment or delight I couldn't tell, before quickly changing the subject. "All right, well, as to the new position, I'm getting the feeling that my presence is a diversity thing. You know, it's nice to have a black man on stage when the task force talks to the press."

"Screw that," I said. "Just do your job and do it well, and the rest will take care of itself."

"Uh huh. I think that's the same advice I gave *you* when you complained about not being treated fairly in the Bureau because of your gender."

"Yeah, and it was good advice then, and it's good advice now."

"I suppose so. Say, Karen?"

"Yes?"

He didn't answer for a second, and I found myself feeling two things simultaneously: one, I hoped that he *wouldn't* say something heartfelt and awkward, not when I had much bigger things to worry about, and two, I hoped that he actually *would*.

"Be careful," he said.

I felt a mixture of disappointment and relief, but I did my best to keep all that out of my voice by forcing a laugh.

"Well, you know me."

"Yeah," he said. "That's the problem."

6

Months ago, after I'd gotten the tip that Mom once worked at the Orcadia, the first thing I'd done was use Google Earth to bring up Orcas Island. I'd never been there. When seen from space, the fifty-seven-square-mile land mass in the sea north of Puget Sound vaguely resembled an M, with the middle section separating the appropriately named West Sound and East Sound. The Orcadia Resort was halfway up East Sound, on a spit big enough to create Cascade Bay.

Thomas Amovar, the rich, nineteenth-century timber baron who'd built the mansion that eventually became the heart of the Orcadia Resort, had certainly chosen a great spot for his "summer residence," as he'd called it, with Cascade Lake nearby and Mt. Constitution, the highest point in the San Juans at 2,400 feet above sea level, just minutes away. In my experience, half of first-time visitors complained about it being too cold and never came back. The other half picked up real estate brochures. I may have spent the bulk of my formative years in Tucson, but I knew the moment I drove off the ferry from Anacortes that if I was going to put down roots anywhere—and I still had no plans to do so—it would be here.

Deer Harbor. Moran State Park. Turtleback Mountain Preserve. The rocky beaches. The way the fog hugged the Douglas firs and lodgepole pines that crowded the hilly landscape. Orcas Island had a lot going for it. There were plenty of places to stay right there in the hills near Cascade Bay, if a person could afford it, but for my money the most perfect spot on Orcas Island was the tiny community of Olga.

Located five miles to the south of the Orcadia Resort, Olga was barely big enough to be called a hamlet and certainly had no business associating itself with words like "city" or "town." That was part of the reason I loved it. Look it up online, and not much comes up other than that it was named after the wife of the island's first postmaster. Maybe fifty houses nestled among the firs and oaks that border the rocky shoreline of tiny Buck Bay, many vacation rentals and second homes but also dozens of quirky permanent residents, few of whom were as unique as the woman who'd hired me to oversee her two Airbnb cottages.

Our first meeting happened because of one of those chance encounters that made me wonder if there was actually a higher power after all—maybe not an all-knowing, all-powerful deity staging an elaborate marionette show but at least a part-time god who occasionally liked to meddle. For some reason, heading home on that Saturday after Colin Welk died, maybe because I already knew on some level that I wouldn't be on Orcas Island much longer, I thought about that chance encounter as I rounded the last bend and Orcas Island Artworks Gallery came into view.

This was a month ago, in late May. Just like today, the sky was an unblemished blue, and the Douglas firs crowding the serpentine two-lane Olga Road were a verdant green, which shouldn't have been remarkable but was since most days in between had been overcast. On *this* Saturday, cars packed the gravel lot outside the Artworks building, no surprise in late June, but on a Tuesday in May my Civic was one of only three cars when I parked outside Catkin Café, a bistro attached to the gallery. I'd just been hired at the Orcadia—I started the next day—and was doing a quick tour of the island. I spotted the sandwich board that read

Coffee and Pastries and thought I could use a pick-me-up before continuing.

If I hadn't been so tired, I may not have been in the mood for an Americano. If the bistro had been any busier, I might have passed it in hopes of finding something less crowded. If the parking lot had been any fuller, I might not have seen the woman with purple hair. If she hadn't gotten a call from her sister ten minutes earlier while on her usual morning hike on the Coho Preserve Trail just up the hill, she might not have been crying when I saw her. And if she hadn't been crying, I doubted I would have said anything to her.

If.

So many conditions, so many twists and turns in both our lives had to go *just so* for us to meet in that moment. If our meeting had only led me to a place to stay, I might have attributed it to simple good luck, but there was more than that. A lot more, it turned out.

I was locking the Civic, turned toward the smell of coffee wafting from the bistro, when I caught a rainbow flash from the corner of my eye. I looked over the top of the car and saw a stout woman walking along the road. She was just emerging from an oak tree's dappled shade, and in the golden light her plume of curly hair was the same rich purple as the camas wildflowers. Her choice of hair color, not even close to natural, was bold indeed, but it was probably the *least* bold thing about her.

She was barefoot. The lack of footwear, her curly hair, and her short, burly frame all made me think of Tolkien's hobbits—if a hobbit had just stepped off a bus from Berkeley to Burning Man. She wore a tie-dye dress so colorful that I actually winced and so long that it dragged across the asphalt behind her like a psychedelic wedding gown. She wore a leather tunic, the kind popular at Renaissance fairs, and the straps pushed up her bosom, barely containing her mammoth breasts. Her skin was like polished suede. Her deeply-lined face, and the white at the roots of her hair, made me guess that she was in her late sixties. I found out later that I'd underestimated by ten years.

She held a phone limply at her side—one with a tie-dye case

—and she was openly sobbing. The tear tracks down her tan face made me think of rain in a desert. I got the feeling this woman didn't cry often.

Turned out I was wrong about that one too. She cried all the time. Just not out of sadness.

"Ma'am?" I said. "You okay?"

She flinched at my voice. In the umbrella of her hair, her gold hoop earrings swung wildly, glinting in the bright sun. It wasn't until I stepped around the Honda that I noticed that she had a dog with her, a toy poodle wearing what could only be called a tie-dye skirt with ruffled yellow lace circling its hind end. It wasn't leashed. When I came into view, it yipped at me.

"Oh, hush now, Peanut," she said. There was a touch of a southern accent, but only a touch. She wiped her eyes with the back of her hand and offered me an apologetic smile. "Sorry about that. He's very protective of me. Vicious beast, as you can see."

"No need to apologize," I said, taking a few steps toward her so we weren't speaking across a parking lot. "Just wanted to make sure you're okay."

"Oh! Thank you. I'm … Well, I don't know what I am. Just got some distressing news." She chuckled. "You thought it was a harmless little bunny."

"Excuse me?"

"What?"

"You said something about a bunny?"

"Oh! Yes. Sorry, I didn't know I said that aloud. Monty Python. Do you know Monty Python? It was from the *Holy Grail* movie, I think. Or maybe it was from *Life of Brian*? Holly would know better—better than me."

At the hitch in her voice, she teared up again, but then she gave her head a powerful shake.

"Oh my," she said, "I don't know what's come over me. I'm really fine. Sorry for, you know, acting like this."

"It's all right," I said. This woman may have been many things, but she was definitely not all right. "Do you need to sit down?" I nodded toward the chairs on the deck outside the bistro. "Do you want something? A water? I'd be happy to buy you a cup of coffee."

"Oh!" the woman said. The hand came to her breast again. "That's so ... so sweet of you. The kindness of a stranger. But you don't need to do that. I'm sure you have places to be."

"Nope," I said. "I'm just seeing the island today. No agenda."

Peanut yipped again, but it was a half-hearted yip, and as I approached, the little dog actually cowered behind the woman's dress, peeking out like a performer from behind a theater curtain. I squatted on the gravel and extended my hand. Peanut blinked a few times—its eyes were milky white—then trotted out to sniff me. It licked my fingers. Up close, I saw that its tan fur was patchy and thin. Old, old dog.

"Well, will you look at that," the woman said. "She never warms up to people that fast. Do you have a dog?"

"No. I've never ..." And then I remembered a long-buried memory, when I was five years old and my father brought home a mangy cocker spaniel he'd found in Davis-Monthan's boneyard, sleeping in the cockpit of a rusty F-16 Fighting Falcon. How the dog got up there nobody could figure out, but my sister and I both begged our mother to let us keep it. She steadfastly refused, and Dad reluctantly took it to the pound. I never knew what happened to it. "I mean," I said finally, "I—I don't have one now, but I always thought I'd have one ... you know, eventually."

"Is something wrong, dearie?"

"No, just ... just remembering. How about that coffee? Tea? Espresso? My treat."

"Oh, that's sweet of you, but I actually have a pot waiting at the house. It would be a shame to dump it out. I always have my first cup before my walk, then come home for a second. And a third. And a fourth." She laughed, but her eyes turned sad. "A bit of a caffeine addict, I'm afraid. Another thing I have in common with Holly."

"All right," I said. "You sure you're okay, though?"

She gave my shoulder a squeeze. It was probably meant to be

gentle, but she had the grip of a dock worker. "Thank you! Thank you again. That's so nice. But yes, I'll be fine. Enjoy your tour. Orcas is heaven, as far as I'm concerned. Just don't tell anyone that. We don't want the place overrun—we've got enough tourists as it is. Present company excluded, of course." She chuckled.

"Your secret is safe with me," I said.

"I don't doubt it! Peanut is an *excellent* judge of character." She pursed her lips and stared at me for so long that I grew uncomfortable.

"Ma'am?" I said.

"You know, you actually look familiar. Sound familiar too. Did you say this is your *first* time here?"

"Yes."

"Are you from Seattle? I lived there for decades before I moved here in the eighties."

"No. Tucson, actually. Mostly, anyway, since my family moved around a bunch. Never lived west of Arizona, though."

"Ah. Never even been to Tucson. There is something, though. You really do look familiar. I'm not usually wrong about this sort of thing."

"Maybe I just have one of those faces?"

"Maybe so. Well, thanks for your kindness, dearie. I don't want to keep you any longer." She tapped her phone against her thigh. "And I do have to get home and figure some things out. Enjoy your vacation."

"I will," I said.

We exchanged furtive smiles. A white Chevy Volt coasted down the hill behind her, its electric engine making it a silent predator. I worried about little Peanut, but the woman snatched up the poodle as if she had a sixth sense about it. After the car passed, she barefooted it across the road and toward a street at the bend, carrying the dog the whole way. If the loose rocks on the shoulder bothered her, she didn't show it.

"I'm actually not here on a vacation," I called after her.

She turned, purple hair vibrant in the sun, the little dog

pressed so tightly against her bosom that it was almost swallowed in the fold between her breasts. "What's that?"

I didn't know why I'd said it. It just felt like I should. We were still close enough that I didn't have to shout but far enough away that it felt awkward. I stepped closer, to the edge of the road. The double yellow line, which had been recently painted, glowed like neon.

"Sorry," I said. "That sounded strange. I just … I'm not here on vacation."

"Oh?"

"I just got a job at the Orcadia."

"Oh! How lovely."

"Yeah. Just a housekeeping gig, and pays squat, but it's all I need." I glanced at the yellow lines, squinting at how bright they were, then looked back at her. "So, um, this is going to sound strange, but I'm actually here on Orcas looking for my mother. You said you've been here since the eighties, and I thought, hey, maybe there's a chance you met her. It's not that big of an island."

"Oh. Well, maybe. You never know."

"She was about my build, and her hair was pretty much the same, maybe a little lighter, though I think that's because she dyed it. Her name was Karen Pantelli. Same as me. We, uh … we have the same name."

She furrowed her brow, but I couldn't tell if it was because she was considering my question or because she was concerned about my state of mind. I wouldn't blame her for being concerned. My voice sounded strange even to me. I'd been asking people about my mother for months, but even after all that time my throat still tightened up and my face got flushed when I did. It annoyed me that talking about Mom could *still*, after all these years, have that kind of effect on me.

"Ah," she said. "Well, I can't say the name rings any bells, I'm afraid."

"That's all right."

"It sounds like there's quite a story there."

"There is."

She nodded but was wise enough not to ask for details, and I wasn't going to volunteer any. She started to turn away, then stopped and looked at me abruptly. Peanut squinted at me with similar intensity.

"Wait," she said, "where did you say you were from again?"

She took a few steps into the road. There was no traffic. The breeze, stirring the tops of the fir trees, had grown still.

"Tucson," I said. "Originally, anyway. Lately, I've been I've been kind of—"

"And you got a job at the Orcadia?"

"That's right."

"Did your Mom work there too? Back in '93?"

Now it was my turn to stare. "How did you know that?"

She adjusted Peanut in her arms, staring at me, saying nothing. The dog stared at me too. Everybody was staring. Behind them, I saw a thriving vegetable garden and a greenhouse overgrown with ivy, and, glimpsed through the oak trees at the rear of the garden, a white, colonial-style house. I didn't know it yet, but most of Olga was nestled back there, a couple blocks of houses, a long-dormant general store in the process of being restored into a community center, and a tiny county park with a public dock for the smaller boats that could manage mooring in the shallow waters of Buck Bay.

She nodded toward the road just off to the left. "I think you better come with me," she said. "I have plenty of coffee ... and a story to tell you."

———

HER FULL NAME was Beverly Ann Braun, but she told me most folks called her Bev. A few of her best friends called her Babs because of her initials. I could take my pick. I went with Bev because I didn't want to presume we'd end up friends, though I already liked her quite a bit. And that was before she told me about her encounter with Mom. After that, I liked her even more.

Except for Peanut, Bev lived alone in a two-bedroom wood-shake cottage on First Street. It looked like something out of a fairy tale, surrounded by wildflowers barely contained by a white picket fence. Since we'd passed Fourth Street on the way in and the streets counted down from there, I assumed that was it for the thriving metropolis of Olga. A hand-painted driftwood sign on the gate read COZY CABINS. A gravel path led to the right around the perimeter of the fence and to the back of the property. On our way into the house, she told me she had a pair of one-bedroom cabins she rented via Airbnb.

"Theo actually built them before he passed," she said. The front door was unlocked, which probably shouldn't have surprised me but still did. "I really didn't want them at the time, but now I'm glad he did. Not just for the money but because it gave me something to focus on. After he was gone, you know."

Inside it smelled strongly of freshly brewed coffee and faintly of Indian food. So many pictures of Theo, the spitting image of Ernest Hemmingway in his silver-bearded years, adorned the mantle of the white brick fireplace that I couldn't even see all of them. Her place was small and made smaller still by how packed it was with furniture and decor, a quirky mix of coastal kitsch and psychedelic sixties. The east-facing windows overlooked Buck Bay. The blackberry bushes at the rear of the property were so over-grown that I could only see the end of the public dock, like a wooden finger jutting out into the water.

Standing at the slider that looked out on her newly stained deck, I could see more: a wild, grassy patch of yard crowded with hand-painted birdhouses and, bordering the yard, two cabins with similar wood-shake siding as the main house. Beyond both the yard and the cabins, since the angle was different now, I saw a bit more dock and some sailboat masts. The view over the top of the blackberry bushes was spectacular, a rippling, gray-blue ocean between various islands and land masses, hazy and yet somehow distinct at the same time, places whose names I did not yet know but would become intimately familiar with soon enough. Hazy and yet distinct. Those words could have also described my memories of Mom. They were hazy, but they were still distinctly real to me.

The slider was cracked open, and I heard water lapping against the rocks as rhythmic and soothing as a lullaby.

"It's a little piece of heaven, isn't it?" Bev asked behind me.

I swallowed. "It is."

"Came here on vacation forty years ago and never left. Got a job in one of the shops in Eastsound and met Theo a few weeks later. He was running fishing junkets for corporate clients, and he'd just bought this place. Cream?"

"What's that?"

"Do you take cream with your coffee?"

Finally prying myself from the view, I turned to look at her. She stood behind a yellow tile counter, two ceramic mugs steaming in front of her. Looking at me, eyebrows raised, she held a miniature metal carafe poised over one of the mugs.

"Ah," I said. "No, just black."

"You sure? I make it pretty strong."

"The stronger the better."

"I see. A strong woman who likes her coffee the same way."

"Oh, I don't know about that."

She chuckled. "I think you do. You don't strike me as some-body who lacks for self-confidence. Peace of mind, maybe, but not self-confidence. I'm the opposite. I have a lot of peace of mind but hardly any self-confidence."

I didn't know what to make of this, so I said nothing. We sat at the pedestal table near the slider. The tablecloth was patterned with seashells and fringed with lace. The salt and pepper shakers were miniatures of Jerry Garcia. My coffee was still too hot to drink. It was always a judgment call when it was safe to take that first sip of hot coffee without burning one's tongue, and I often jumped the gun. I didn't know if I lacked peace of mind, but I definitely lacked patience.

Outside, the first cabin appeared dark and empty, but the second, closer to the blackberry bushes and with the better view, had sand-caked Nikes on the bristled doormat. I could just make out part of the deck on the other side as well as the back of a cheap white plastic lawn chair, the kind that can be bought at any Walmart in America and which, I remembered now, a *Wall Street Journal* opinion writer had once dubbed a symbol of America's decline. Too much plastic and too much leisure, he'd written.

I wondered, if I were sitting in that chair right now, if I'd worry much about America's decline. Probably not. I could imagine spending a whole life in that chair. It was not quite a desire to do so, but there *was* a hint of longing, and the feeling surprised me. In the years since I'd left the FBI, I'd barely thought about my future much less longed for a particular one.

While I was looking, an old man in Bermuda shorts and flip-flops sat in the chair and unfolded a newspaper. The bamboo windchime cast its shadow on the back of his bald head.

"That's Frank," Bev said. "He's a nice estate lawyer from Bellevue. Been coming here this week every year for ... Oh, gosh, a decade, I guess. The guests in the other cabin checked out this morning. I've got a young couple from Portland showing up tomorrow for a five-day stretch. Both places are pretty booked this summer, the norm."

I nodded, but I didn't ask any follow-ups, because I was eager to hear what she had to say about Mom. Patience, Karen, patience. Bev took a sip of her coffee, which had so much cream in it that the color was beige bordering on white. Peanut jumped into the rocker, curling up on the cushion and ignoring both of us.

"Have you been up Mt. Constitution yet?" Bev asked.

"No. I saw the sign, though. For the road that goes up that way."

"You should. It's the best view in the San Juans."

"Okay."

She turned the mug gently in her hands. Other than the sea lapping against the rocks, it was so quiet that I could hear Frank turning the pages of his newspaper.

"I think that's where I met your mother," Bev said. "I can't say for sure since she never told me her name, but the time frame seems right. 1993. That's the same year Theo died, you see."

"Oh, I'm sorry."

She gave me a little shrug as if it was no big deal, but her misty eyes betrayed her. "A long time ago. We had ten good years. *Very* good years if I'm judging by the standards of my first husband, Mr. Piece of Shit." She looked up. "Sorry. There isn't much bitterness anymore, but the insults are habit."

"Profanity doesn't bother me. In fact, I usually curse like a sailor unless I restrain myself."

"Well, don't restrain yourself on *my* part." She laughed. "You would have got along great with Theo. He not only cursed like a sailor, he *was* a sailor, and a good one. I never worried about him on the water, strange as that may sound. No, it was on land where he got himself into trouble. He actually died in Bellevue, of all places. In a car accident. He was there visiting Clay, his brother. Clay was a piece of shit too, but Theo wasn't like me. He could never give up on anybody." She sighed. "Sorry, I'm going off on a tangent, aren't I?"

"It's fine."

"Liar. I can tell you're chomping at that bit, and I won't make you wait. The reason I remember your mom is because I was in a pretty sad state of mind just like she was. After Theo died, I used to go up to Mt. Constitution and just perch myself on the stone wall for hours. I went up there early on Mother's Day—real early, I think it was just after dawn. Honestly, I didn't even realize it was Mother's Day until your mother told me. I don't think I would have even been able to tell you what day of the week it was."

She got up and retrieved the pitcher from the Mr. Coffee, refilling her mug and absent-mindedly adding extra to mine even though I hadn't taken a sip. Now I'd have to wait again. Too hot. Life was not kind to us straight-black coffee drinkers.

"She was the only one there," Bev said, taking a seat again. "A blonde woman about your height and size, wearing one of those short-sleeved green polos the employees used to wear at the Orcadia back then. I remember being surprised that she wasn't wearing a sweatshirt since it was chilly—wet and chilly. Not rainy, but the fog was so thick that morning it might as well have been rain for how damp the air was. By the time I walked from the parking lot to the wall, I was already wiping water out of my eyes. Your mother—sorry, I shouldn't say that since we don't know for sure. And it's doubtful we'll ever know."

"It's all right," I said, eager for her to go on. "Let's just assume it was."

"Yes, well, your mother was leaning against the wall and staring east, toward the mainland, but of course there wasn't much to see. I could barely see Lummi Island, much less Bellingham, but it was still pretty. There's always something so peaceful about those really foggy days, the way the tops of the islands seem to float in the clouds. I planned to give your mother distance—there was plenty of room for both of us—but I could hear her crying."

"Crying?"

"Yeah. I asked her if she was all right. And when she turned and looked at me, with eyes just as green as yours, I saw that it wasn't just the fog wetting her face. It's strange, isn't it? You stopped me a little while ago because I was crying. And I did the same thing with your mother. Maybe we were meant to meet on the road today."

Bev sipped her coffee. I finally got brave and tried mine. It was hot enough that I winced but not so hot I burned my mouth. It was good too, strong with notes of chocolate.

"When I asked if she was all right," Bev continued, "she didn't answer. I asked her if there was anything I could do—call somebody, get her anything—and she shook her head and said she was trying to make up her mind about something. I probably should have left her alone at that point, but I could tell she was in pain, and it's true what they say about how misery loves company. It somehow makes you feel less alone when you're with somebody who's also suffering. I guess that's not news, huh? Pretty much every support group has that idea as its foundation."

"I guess so," I said.

Bev raised her eyebrows. "Not one for support groups? Or is it just support at all?"

"Maybe both."

"Huh. Well, they've helped me from time to time. Your mother and I, we stood there side by side and stared out at the fog. She said the weather was sure a lot different from where she was from. I asked her where and she said, 'Arizona—originally.' She asked me if I was from Orcas. I said no, I was from Alabama, of all places, and then I started talking about Theo. How much I missed him. It wasn't long before we were both crying. All that from a comment about the weather. People are always knocking small talk, but I've often thought small talk is like a small door on a big house. It's just a way inside."

Bev peered down into her coffee, the light from the window teasing out all the groves and lines in her face. On the deck to his cabin, Frank snapped to the next page of his newspaper. Out on the bay, a two-masted sailboat cruised past, and not far behind it, two guys in an aluminum boat motored across the sailboat's gentle wake.

"And with both of us crying, your mother said, 'I'm trying to decide something. If I should go back. To Arizona. I've left a couple kids behind. It was a rotten thing to do, but I thought it was for the best. They have a good father, and I wasn't good for them. I wanted to be, but I wasn't.' It was a pretty bold thing to say to a stranger, but maybe she could see that I was just as raw emotionally as she was. Or maybe she just had to tell *somebody*."

Bev sipped her coffee, looking not at me but at the window. I couldn't tell what she was looking at. Maybe it was Frank Collins's bald head, the overgrown blackberry bushes, or the glittering surface of Buck Bay. Or maybe she was looking into her past, seeing my mother in her green polo shirt, seeing the fog, seeing all the bad choices people make and the lives they leave behind.

"I told your mother I wasn't going to tell her what to do," Bev said. "I didn't have kids myself, so I couldn't speak to that. I told her I'd made so many bad choices in my life I was in no position to advise her. I just told her to trust her heart. If she listened to it, it would tell her what to do. She thought about this for a while, then she said, 'I just decided. I'm going to go back for them. Just not yet. I have to figure something out about me first. But I'm going to go back.' And then she gave me a big ol' bear hug. I think the camp hosts walked by then and saw us, then turned right back around, seeing these two ladies alone at the wall, crying and hugging one another."

Bev, still looking out the window, sighed. "Your mother told me that it was okay to be sad. She told me I was strong, she could tell, and I'd find a life for myself after Theo. She told me how much she appreciated talking to me, and then when we went our separate ways. I never saw her again. Maybe I should have encouraged her to go back to you. I should have pushed harder. I'm sorry I didn't."

"It's not your fault," I said, and my voice sounded strange. "It's good to know that she ... she at least wanted to. On some level."

Finally, Bev looked at me again, her eyes lighting up with concern. She squeezed my hand. "Oh, honey."

"What?"

"You're crying."

"I am?"

She nodded. I touched my face, surprised to discover that my fingers were wet.

"Will you look at that," I said. "Guess I'm not so strong after all, huh?"

Bev smiled. "No, honey, that just means you're human."

7

We talked a little more about Mom—or at least I did since Bev didn't have much more to tell—and then I got into the long, strange journey that had brought me to Orcas Island. Bev's eyes lit up when I talked about my past. A huge fan of all the crime shows, she asked a lot of questions about how the FBI worked. People were usually disappointed to discover that most of a special agent's job was performed behind a desk, as it was with just about any member of law enforcement, but Bev listened with genuine interest no matter what I said.

She made me want to talk, which was really saying something for me. I talked so much that my voice grew hoarse. I might have gotten loud too because Frank slapped his newspaper closed and returned to his cabin. When I was done, Bev picked up her phone, texted something, then placed it back on the tablecloth with a sigh.

"Well, that settles it," she said.

"Settles what?"

"You told me you're looking for a place to stay, right?"

"Well, yes, but Steve said there's some apartments in East-sound that might—"

"Don't bother. You're staying here."

"What? No, no, that's very nice of you. But I couldn't possibly afford—"

"I'm not going to charge you." And when I began to protest, she held up her hand. "It's not going to be free either. See, that call I got earlier was … was from my sister's husband. Holly is … Well, she's decided to stop her cancer treatments. Stage four breast cancer, already had a double mastectomy, but I guess … Well, I need to go see her."

"Oh, Bev," I said, "I'm so sorry. And here I was, rambling on when—"

"Are you kidding? You let me focus on somebody else's troubles for a few minutes. Gave me time to just sit with the news. I didn't—I didn't even know Holly had cancer, you see. We've been estranged."

"Oh, hell, I'm sorry."

"We're very different. She chose to stay in Birmingham—that life, the church. Me, I couldn't get away from all that fast enough. But I've got guests booked for the summer, and there's no telling how long I'll be in Alabama. You can stay in the house rent free so long as you look after the guests. It shouldn't be too hard. I'll be taking Peanut, so you won't have to worry about the dog. "

"Bev, I'm just not—"

"Don't say no. Just get your things and put them in the spare bedroom. And when I come back, so long as we both think it's a good idea, you can stay on if you want. I'm getting too old to do this by myself. Besides, I just texted Allen I'm coming."

"Allen?"

"Holly's husband." She smiled. "So you'll really put me in a bind if you say no."

I was touched by her generosity. She took a sip of her coffee, looking at me intently over the top of the mug.

"Well," I said, "I guess I wouldn't want to put you in a bind."

———

THAT FIRST MEETING with Bev may have been barely four weeks ago, but on that Saturday in June, as I parked the Honda on the gravel next to her white picket fence, it amazed me how much her place felt like home. I'd forgotten what that felt like. After what had happened at the Orcadia, I wasn't sure I'd be staying much longer either, but maybe that was why it felt like home more than ever. A place didn't really feel like home until you were thinking about leaving it.

Bev's purple '62 Volkswagen Beetle, coated with a layer of dust and pine needles, was parked in the single driveway in the shadow of a sprawling laurel. The leafy green bush was coated with grime too, a sign of how little rain the island had gotten lately. There were no guest cars. The Morhalls, a couple from Wisconsin, had headed home that morning in their blue Kia Soul. I didn't have anyone showing up for the waterside cabin until Monday. No red Toyota Camry either. The two retired high school teachers staying in the garden cabin had gone to Friday Harbor for the day.

For a little while, at least, I had the whole property to myself. I breathed out a sigh of relief. I'd have no distractions while I focused on what I was going to do next.

After a quick search of the house, the cabins, and the yard— and finding nothing amiss—I grabbed my Rand McNally atlas from under the seat and brought it inside. The house, full of golden, gauzy light, felt stuffy from being closed up. I opened the slider to let in the breeze off the bay. My stomach gnawed at me —I seldom ate breakfast, and with everything that had happened, I'd missed lunch too—so I cracked open a can of chicken noodle soup.

Comfort food. Mom used to make it for me when I was sick. She said I could have as much chicken soup as I wanted, no questions asked. I remembered those words specifically. *No questions asked.* Funny how I hadn't thought of that in years. I didn't have many memories of her being kind, but there were a few. Just a few. Enough to convince me that she wasn't all bad.

While the soup warmed on the stove, I set the atlas on the table, then unfolded the list of names and the note from Mr.

Grim. Out on the water, the ferry from Anacortes, a white square so far out that I could have covered it with my thumb, passed out of sight. Blakely, Lopez, Decatur, Shaw—I could see all the surrounding islands vividly today. It didn't take long for the breeze, rippling across Buck Bay, to cool the room.

I studied the list of names, twenty-five in all, dating back to the first of the year. I didn't know any of the people personally, nor did any of the names seem familiar. A mix of ethnicities. I didn't see any cities east of Louisville, Kentucky, so that was something. The cities were a mix of big and small. The day of the week varied. Sometimes the deaths occurred close to one another sequentially: Roswell, New Mexico, followed by Amarillo, Texas, one week later. But sometimes they jumped across vast distances: Columbus in Mississippi one week and Reno the next.

Seeing no obvious patterns, I grabbed a felt tip marker from the roll-top desk, then followed Welk's instructions, marking each of the cities with a black dot. The first dozen or so, I saw no pattern at all, just random dots ruining a perfectly good atlas. This one might have been wrinkled, ripped, and coffee-stained, but it had served me well since I'd picked it up at a 7-Eleven in Baltimore.

Yet it soon became quite clear what the pattern was. It didn't take a genius to see it either, just someone who could read a simple three-letter word:

GOD

So Mr. Grim literally had a God complex. Big shock. Most serial killers did. It was as if he were saying, "I'm God. I literally get to choose who lives and who dies." What *was* a surprise was that he was shouting it in such an obvious way. Wouldn't someone of genius-level intelligence come up with a more sophisticated pattern?

But maybe not. Maybe the pattern being simple was part of the point. It was a way of daring someone to catch him. A worthy opponent, as Welk had said. "Look at what I'm getting away with," he seemed to be saying. "You know the pattern, and you still can't stop me."

It was hubris, plain and simple. And it might be a way to catch him.

I examined the list again. Welk had said that Mr. Grim essentially repeated this pattern every year. It was only June. Since the word "GOD" was already obvious, I wondered what would happen the second half of the year. Would he spell out a different word? I doubted it. A few dots already seemed superfluous, hugging close to other dots, so my hunch was that Mr. Grim just thickened his letters. It was another way of flaunting what he was doing. Or to put it in a more biblical sense, knowing the *word* of God didn't mean knowing the mind of God.

If Mr. Grim wanted to frustrate me, he was already succeeding. Welk had promised to give me more information Sunday to help narrow my search, but now I'd never hear it. I looked at the three upcoming names to see if they offered any clues:

BUTTE, Montana … Zhao Chen
   Casper, Wyoming … Tom Shelby
   Phoenix, Arizona … J. Doe

IN THIS CASE, the locations proceeded west to east. The cities were listed alphabetically … but not the states. I couldn't see any other commonalities. It looked random. My frustration growing, I set the list down and examined the letter Elena had given me. Other than the "one act a week" remark and my sister's initials, I couldn't see any other clues buried within it. It was obviously a message for me, though. That was unsettling enough.

He *knew*. He knew Welk had told me about him, and he was letting me know that he knew. That meant the element of surprise

Welk had been counting on was gone. The letter wasn't just a message then. It was a warning: *Leave this alone or your sister dies.* Perhaps, as Welk had believed, Mr. Grim wanted a worthy opponent, but he didn't see me as it. He could have tried to kill me too, but that would have raised more questions than Welk's suicide by itself.

Besides, my fingerprints were all over that room. People had seen me go inside right before Welk had died. Mr. Grim could have framed me for murder rather than make it look like a suicide. And even now, if I raised that possibility, I was only pointing the finger at myself as the chief suspect. It was another way Mr. Grim had boxed me in.

He was giving me one way out.

Should I take that out? I couldn't just let him go on killing. That wasn't an option, at least for me. I could just turn over everything I knew to Detective Shaw, but if I did, I'd be putting Hope's life at risk. Maybe forever. I couldn't do that either. And what proof could I actually give the police anyway? Maybe Welk *had* committed suicide. Maybe the "one act a week" note to Elena, including my sister's initials, was just a coincidence.

The first thing I had to do was confirm that these names were real victims. I went to the bedroom, unzipped the duffel bag I kept under the bed, and grabbed the cheap Chromebook I'd picked up at a pawnshop in Miami, bringing it back to the table.

Then, as I was powering it on, I remembered Welk's warning.

He'd specifically said to be careful about going online.

It seemed absurd, worrying that Mr. Grim could monitor this scuffed old Chromebook in this quaint cottage in this sleepy hamlet on a remote island that had to make the list of the most out-the-way places in the world ... but then, Professor Welk was dead, wasn't he? He'd known what Mr. Grim was capable of in the most personal way possible, taken every precaution, but he'd still paid the ultimate price.

Was it really paranoid to believe that Mr. Grim was watching me even now?

I stood and walked to the slider, the ocean breeze through the screen cool on my face. The sailboat I'd seen earlier was gone. Over the top of the blackberry bushes, I saw two fishermen at the edge of the dock, tying up an aluminum boat, their jovial laughter rising above the sound of the water lapping against the rocky shore. There were three other boats docked below, a smaller sailboat and two jet boats, no activity. On a separate dock to the right, a private one belonging to a Boeing executive, the forty-foot Catalina yacht was tied up where it always was since Mr. Quentin, Bev had told me, hadn't taken it out since his wife had passed away three years earlier.

There was no one I trusted more than Ben Wilde to keep Hope and her family safe. Until I was confident that what Welk had told me was true, I couldn't decide what to do next. Plus Mr. Grim may or may not have still been on the island, but he couldn't have gotten to Atlanta already. That bought me some time.

I spooned up a bowl of chicken soup and returned to the laptop. The soup was on the salty side, but it was warm and filling. I searched the first name on my list, David Farris in Columbus, Mississippi. Even with the state and city added to my Google search, another David Farris dominated the search results, a state senator from New Mexico who'd apparently gotten himself into trouble with a drunken hit-and-run traffic accident. His career may have been ruined, but he appeared to be alive.

I added the words "obituary" and "death," and eventually, on the second page of results, found a brief article in Columbus's local newspaper, *The Commercial Dispatch,* about eighty-two-year-old David Mathew Farris, discovered deceased in his home on 8th Street after a neighbor grew concerned about Mr. Farris's absence and called the police to do a welfare check. Mr. Farris was discovered at the bottom of his stairs in his pajamas, having apparently fallen and broken his neck. Mr. Farris's wife, Coleen Farris, had passed away ten years earlier. Their son, Tommy Farris, had died while serving in Iraq in 2004.

No mention of other family. Nothing came up as far as obituaries or funeral services. That was it, as far as David Farris of Columbus, Mississippi, was concerned, a life summed up in a couple paragraphs—and not even long paragraphs at that. I felt gloomy thinking about him in his pajamas, this old widower alone in his house, lying dead at the bottom of his stairs.

Finishing my first bowl of soup and going back for seconds, I confirmed the first dozen deaths. A truck driver who'd stopped for the night in Casper, Wyoming, was found dead in his Hampton Suites room, having overdosed on OxyContin. A homeless woman in Salt Lake City had died of "natural causes" in an encampment near I-15; no other details were forthcoming. At least half the victims appeared homeless. The most brutal so far was a woman in Reno, arrested multiple times in the past for prostitution, who'd been discovered naked, gagged, and with her throat cut in an abandoned Ford Escort.

Most of the deaths had flown under the radar but not all. Four months ago, a small-town sheriff on the Texas-Mexico border had been killed by a car bomb. I remembered hearing about that one on CNN. The prevailing theory had been that it had been the work of a drug cartel. If it really was the work of Mr. Grim instead, it showed that he was not immune to going after victims that would get a little more publicity.

My mood solemn, and satisfied that this was a list of real victims even if I still couldn't say for certain it was the work of a serial killer, I turned my attention to Colin Welk. How much of the good professor's story was true?

His bio on the University of Washington website confirmed his position as a full professor of mathematics. His picture was obviously from early on in his career. He had the same woolly beard, but his face was thinner, and the lines around his eyes were less pronounced. Given the green plaid shirt, his fashion choices hadn't changed much. He had a fairly active Twitter feed, but there was nothing on it about Mr. Grim. There were lots of links to scholarly research on computational analysis.

I found an obituary for his wife, Mona, who had indeed died thirteen years ago in an unfortunate accident while hiking alone in Olympic National Forest. She'd also been a professor at the University of Washington, though in the College of Education.

The black-and-white photo accompanying the obituary was grainy, but her youthful beauty still radiated from her eyes.

There was another picture of her from the UW alumni magazine, this one of her whole family at some kind of Fourth of July celebration: her, Colin, and their six-year-old son, Isaac, who shared his father's curly red hair and his mother's remarkable green eyes. Colin was standing on his own two feet, which made me wonder about the car accident that put him in a wheelchair.

An article titled "Professors that Inspire Us" from a year ago in the *Daily*, the UW's student newspaper, had a full-page write-up on Colin Welk. It pictured him in a wheelchair writing a math equation on a chalkboard. The article detailed how the hit-and-run car accident on New Year's Eve three years earlier that had left him paralyzed from the waist down hadn't slowed him down or dampened his enthusiasm for his students. That would have put his accident nine years after his wife's death.

Hit and run. Mr. Grim's handiwork? A fate worse than death, Welk had said. Was that what he was talking about? I couldn't find much on Isaac Welk. No social media. No news. I found enough online to verify that he was nineteen but not much else. He should have graduated from high school by now, but no amount of searching brought up anything other than that he was related to Colin and Mona.

Then I found something—in *Chess Times*, of all places, where Colin was interviewed after winning the Northwest Invitational three years ago. Most of the interview was about the intricacies of his tournament strategy, but at the end he encouraged everyone to donate to TBI research.

TBI. Traumatic brain injury. Was Isaac involved in the same car accident that paralyzed his father? Maybe the fate worse than death wasn't about Colin but about the son. I found a couple of addresses for the Welks, the most recent a house in Seattle's Fremont neighborhood. Google Street View showed a blue-and-white craftsman with a single-car garage under the right half of the house. A silver Chevy van with a wheelchair lift was parked in the driveway. I used King County's online property research site to confirm that it belonged to Colin and Mona Welk. I jotted down the address.

The next thing I did was search for Zhao Chen in Butte, Montana. There was only one, a professor of geological engineering at Montana Technological University. Since Mr. Grim could already be on his way to Butte, I debated about calling Professor Chen, but I was reluctant to tip off Mr. Grim that I had a list of his potential victims. And what would Chen make of my warning? I'd sound like a crackpot.

I gazed out at Buck Bay in the evening light. The water, calm and still, looked like green glass. The firs crowding the banks cast long shadows. Already a plan of action was forming. It was a ten-hour drive from the ferry terminal in Anacortes to Butte, Montana. I'd drive it as fast as I could. I'd protect Chen without letting him know, at least not until I had no other choice. I was using him as a kind of bait, and that went against almost every instinct I had, but Chen might have been my best chance at catching Mr. Grim.

If it came down to it, though, saving Mr. Chen would take priority. I wouldn't sacrifice him. That might have been something Welk could live with but not me.

However, I'd make a pitstop in Seattle. It was risky because if Mr. Grim was monitoring the Welk place, going there would strongly suggest that I was on the hunt for him. I couldn't pass it up, though. Welk had said that he had handwritten research locked in a safe. If something in there could give me an edge, I needed to see it. Plus I hoped to find more information about my mother. I might not be able to go looking for her for a while, but I didn't want to lose my chance. How, exactly, I was going to get into a locked safe was something I'd have to figure out once I got there.

When should I go?

Soon. Tonight, if possible. The digital clock on the microwave read 7:58 p.m. According to Google Maps, it would take two hours to drive to the Welk house once I rolled off the ferry. The next ferry left Orcas at 8:50 p.m. The terminal was on the other side of the island, a half-hour drive, but I could make it if I left in the next fifteen minutes.

It was crazy to think that I'd woken that morning with no plans other than to continue cleaning rooms at the Orcadia, and here I was about to set out to stop a serial killer, but I didn't see any way around it.

Fortunately, part of being a dead-eyed drifter was traveling light. Everything inside the house that was mine fit into my one fraying duffel bag, zipped up and ready to go in seven minutes. Weirdly, the shoulder strap was missing, but I didn't have time to do more than a cursory search under the bed for it. I tried not to think of it as a symbol that my life was always falling apart.

I'd call Bev from the ferry. I hated leaving her in a lurch, but Gwen Nichols, a neighbor who rented out her bottom floor as an Airbnb, would occasionally cover for Bev, and vice versa, so I hoped Gwen would do so again on short notice. I was already dreading talking to Bev. I wouldn't be able to give her any details, and I liked her too much to lie. How would I resolve that? I had no idea. I usually didn't care what anyone thought of me, but I hated the idea of Bev being disappointed in me.

After locking the house, I left a key under the mat, tossed my duffel on the passenger seat, and was about to climb into the Honda when a familiar voice spoke from the street.

"Going somewhere?"

It was Detective Maya Shaw.

8

Detective Maya Shaw stood alone at the end of the driveway. The sun, low in the sky, showed up twice in her mirrored sunglasses. She was still dressed in the white cotton blouse and the gray denim pants, but gone was the blue blazer and the side holster. A more casual look. Trying to put me at ease? If so, it was not a part she played well. Maybe if she'd let out that tightly-braided ponytail, it would have helped, but I doubted it. If tension could have been harnessed as an energy source, the island could just plug itself into Detective Maya Shaw and call it good.

I didn't see a car, but I imagined it was down the street. That had to be deliberate. I had a decision to make: admit I was leaving and raise her suspicions or lie and likely miss the 8:50 ferry, costing me valuable time. Neither option was good, but admitting I was leaving might prompt her to retain me as a material witness. I couldn't risk that. And there was one last ferry at 10:50 p.m.

"No, just forgot my phone in my car," I said. I grabbed it from the passenger seat and held it up for her to see. "Found it."

"Uh huh."

Up the road, I heard a motorcycle roar past and, even farther away, the whine of a leaf blower, but otherwise Olga was quiet. I shut the Honda's door and shoved the phone in my back pocket, hoping she didn't see the duffel on the passenger seat. For once, I was glad I was perpetually bad at washing my car. The dirty windows would make it hard for her to see inside.

"What can I do for you, Detective Shaw?" I asked.

She eyed me suspiciously. "Oh, you know, just thought I'd stop by. We got off on the wrong foot at the Orcadia, and I felt bad about it. This isn't police business. More of a social call."

"Ah."

"Not buying it?"

"Well, most people who stop by on a social call don't actually use the term 'social call.' Not unless you're in a Jane Austen novel, anyway."

Her gaze turned stony, but then she surprised me with a faint chuckle. Those faint chuckles really were her specialty. I wondered if I'd ever hear outright laughter from her. "Okay," she said, "you got me there. I obviously suck at the personal stuff."

"Well, don't take lessons from me," I said. "I'm barely functional as a normal person myself."

"Duly noted. However, I wasn't completely lying. I do feel bad. I know I can come off as a raging SOB even under normal circumstances, and in a situation like that, I get a lot worse. I wanted you to know it wasn't personal. I really do respect you."

I nodded, weighing my response, wondering what I could say that would get rid of her quickly without making it look like I was trying to get rid of her quickly. I still wasn't sure if she was playing me. The clock was ticking on that 8:50 ferry, though. It was still better if I made it.

"I appreciate that," I said. "And I respect you too. I can't even imagine how hard it is to do what you do as a ... as a ..."

"As a black lady with the personality of an iceberg?"

"Well, I wouldn't have put it *quite* like that."

"You don't need to mince words with me, Karen. I'm not going to take offense. The truth is, I just choose not to dwell on that stuff much. Or let it stop me. What if I'd been born two hundred years ago? I'm from Virginia originally. I would have been a slave, so it's all relative."

I smiled. Maya Shaw may have thought of herself as an iceberg, but I already liked her. Maybe it was because I was an iceberg myself. "That's a healthy attitude."

"Is it? I half don't know myself these days. If I hadn't ..." She shook her head. "Well, that's all water under the bridge. Or through the sound, as it were. No sense dredging that stuff up. Geez, I'm really going all in with the water metaphors, aren't I?"

"Maybe, but I get your ... drift."

"Nice."

We both laughed. Or I laughed. She gave me another faint chuckle. The first blush of orange splashed into the blue sky. If this was just a social call, she'd say her goodbyes and go. I'd still make the 8:50 ferry. If there was something more ...

She took off her sunglasses, slipping them into the front pocket of her shirt. "Well, there is a little something I wanted to talk to you about."

Drat. "Oh yeah?"

"Yes, some new information has come to light. I wanted your take on it. See if it changes your mind about ... well, what you said at the Orcadia."

"I see."

"Can we go inside?"

"Sure," I said, then hesitated. I didn't want her to see my bag —or the pristine state of Bev's house. "Actually, I was about to walk down to the public dock to stretch my legs. You want to come?"

"Well, it is sort of a sensitive matter. As long as you don't think anybody will hear—"

"Oh, there's nobody down there now. I just looked from the dining room."

She shrugged. I led her up the driveway and to the left. The sun peeked over the tops of the oaks. The entrance to the public dock was one house over at the tiny county park, a couple picnic tables in a grassy area already browning in the summer sun. We passed some hanging potted red geraniums and a hand-carved Use at Your Own Risk sign, our shoes crunching on the hard-packed gravel until we reached the weathered boardwalk.

She didn't say anything until we reached the end of the railings, the breeze cool on our faces, the dock undulating beneath us, the sun a yellow ribbon on the rippling water. Nobody was there. It smelled like fish and diesel. Well beyond the mouth of Buck Bay but not so far into the channel that he would be a nuisance to passing boats, a man in a jet boat sat under his covered cockpit reading a newspaper. He was too far away to make out, especially since he wore a straw hat that shadowed his face. Beyond him, I saw the ferry on its way to the terminal. My ferry. The one I was going to miss.

The dock was wider at the end, where the boats were tied up, and we stopped there. There were wooden dinghies turned upside down but no place to sit. I'd chosen the spot on purpose. If we stood, maybe our conversation would go faster. She gazed out at the water. In the low, bright sun, her skin looked more brown than black, like polished mahogany.

"It never gets old, does it?" she said.

"The view? No. Not to me anyway." I looked out at the passing ferry. I decided to just let it go. There was time. Not a lot, but I didn't need to feel rushed. Then I surprised myself by making a personal confession. "It was even starting to feel like home."

"Really? Wow."

"Not the same for you, huh?"

"No, Seattle is more my style. I want to get back eventually."

"I thought you were from Virginia?"

"I was. Originally. I moved from Roanoke to Seattle when I was sixteen. To live with my Aunt Regina."

"Oh. That must have been tough. I moved a lot as a kid, so I know how hard moving can be, especially for a teenager."

She faced me. "No, it was a blessing. My mother was a raging drunk, and my stepfather was getting a little ... well, too handsy, if you know what I mean."

"Oh. I guess it's great your Aunt Regina was there for you then."

She gave me another one of her chuckles, but there wasn't even a hint of warmth this time. "She was—at first. Then her new boyfriend, who was a drug dealer, got her hooked on meth."

"Geez, I'm sorry."

Maya shrugged. "Life has taught me to expect the worst. I would have ended up on the streets if it hadn't been this woman cop who kind of took me under her wing." She shook her head. "Well, we don't need to get into all that. I want you to know I talked to Colin Welk's son. Isaac. I had to … well, you know."

"Give him the bad news," I said. "Yeah, not a fun part of the job."

"No, it isn't. He got very upset."

"Well, I can imagine."

"No, that's just the thing. You can't. This wasn't a normal upset. Isaac started screaming profanities, got hysterical to the point he was, you know, hyperventilating. I think he was even going to throw the phone against the wall but his caretaker wrestled it away from him."

"His caretaker?"

"Yeah. Guy named Jared Whallen. He came on, introduced himself, and told me he'd call back when he had Isaac calmed down. He was a little upset himself. When he did call back, he explained that Isaac had already been through a lot in life. Lost his mother in a freak hiking accident. Then he and his father were in a bad car accident, one that put Professor Welk in a wheelchair and Jared in a coma for six weeks. When he came out of it, he was more prone to these … violent mood swings. I guess he can't really regulate his emotions. Can't concentrate on much either. Short term memory is shot."

"That's terrible," I said. None of it surprised me, based on what I'd already learned, but for some reason it still hit me hard. Maybe it was because I always felt extra sympathy when kids were involved. *A fate worse than death.* "And now he's lost his father. That's a lot of tragedy for one person let alone a boy."

"He's nineteen. Not really a boy anymore."

"Yeah. But it sounds like he's always going to be a boy, right?"

"I guess you're right."

"What's going to happen to him? Are they going to stay at the house, or is there, you know, another relative who will take him in?"

Maya shook her head sadly. "I don't know. And it wasn't my place to ask. Like I said, even Mr. Whallen was upset, so I didn't want to press him. He'd already told me something else interesting, though."

"Oh yeah?"

"I asked if Professor Welk had ever mentioned you."

"You did what?"

"Oh, come on, Karen. You would have done the same thing. Whallen said he'd never heard the name Karen Pantelli before."

"Well, there you go. I don't know why you'd think—"

"Not so fast. He also said he came down to the Welk's basement office last week and overheard him talking on the phone. It was something about a woman working at the Orcadia."

"Well, that could be any—"

"I'm not saying he was talking about you. In fact, I'm pretty sure he wasn't. He said Professor Welk clammed up when he saw Whallen and even got after him for coming downstairs unannounced, but Whallen definitely heard the question, 'So when exactly did she stop working at the Orcadia?' Now, that couldn't be about you, could it?"

"I have no idea."

"Don't you?"

"No. Maybe he was just doing his due diligence. He was the conference organizer, after all."

"By asking about a particular employee? That's getting pretty far down in the weeds."

"Sure. He's a math guy. The nitty gritty details matter to guys like him."

Maya pursed her lips. "Maybe so, but I'm pretty sure it was about something more than the conference. Because I learned one other thing that puts Professor Welk's so-called suicide in a whole new light. Something I think you'd really like to know."

"And that is?"

Maya shook her head. "Oh no, not until you tell me the truth about what happened with Welk. Quid pro quo, Karen."

"We've been over this. I'll tell you everything when it's safe."

"And you can't even tell me what the danger is?"

"No."

"Even if I told you this piece of information, this thing I learned, might help you solve a mystery you've been trying to solve for a very long time?"

I hesitated. Was this information about Mom? If I even asked that question, it would confirm I was not only at the Orcadia with an ulterior motive but that Welk had known what that motive was. If Maya already suspected this much, however, what was the harm in telling her more? Maybe not all of it but enough to get her off my back.

"Look," I said, "if you can promise me that—"

Her cell phone rang.

Grimacing at the interruption, she pulled the cell phone from her back pocket. She squinted at the screen—I could see that it was an unknown number—then answered it with a sharp hello. She listened, forehead furrowing, then covered her free ear with her other hand.

"I'm sorry," she said, "what's that? Speak up. I couldn't hear you."

The sun chose just that moment to duck behind the oaks and firs to the west, the yellow ribbon vanishing off the water. Maya had her back to the bay. The breeze rippled a single loose strand of her hair. Something caught my eye out there, a flash, and I looked past her. The jet boat was still there, the one with the man in the straw hat, but he was no longer reading his newspaper. He stood at the edge of the cockpit, half in shadow, but I could see very clearly that he held a cell phone to his ear.

"Hello?" Maya said again. "Anyone there?"

She tilted her head to the side, looking not at me but at the weathered gray planks. Feeling my heart beating all the way up in my throat, I stared at the man in the straw hat. He lowered his cell phone. He was tall but not that tall. Thin but not that thin. He could have been anyone.

"Huh," Maya said, looking at the screen. "Well, whoever it was, he just clicked off. Weird, though."

I swallowed. "Did he say anything?"

"Well, I thought ... Nah, probably just the wind. It was just one word."

"What word?"

"He just said 'God' and hung up." She shoved her phone back in her pocket. "Probably just a wrong number. What were you about to say?"

As she refocused on me, I forced myself to look back at her so it wasn't obvious what I was really paying attention to, but I kept my peripheral vision fixed on the man in the straw hat. He'd already disappeared into the cockpit. I had a decision to make and only seconds to make it. If I told her the man in the straw hat might be Colin Welk's killer, there was a chance that we could catch him. She could call for help. They could get a boat out here.

But what if they *did* catch him? Was there any actual evidence that tied him to Colin Welk's death? And what would happen if he got away? He was toying with me, testing me, seeing how I'd react. I didn't mind if he knew I was leaving Orcas Island. He'd probably guessed that Welk had told me about Mom, which meant there was no reason for me to stay. But I didn't want him to think I was coming after him or that I was on to his overall pattern.

"Karen?" Maya said. "Earth to Karen, hello?"

"Sorry," I said, blinking. "Just lost in thought for a second."

"Uh huh. Back to our conversation before we were interrupted. I have a feeling you were about to tell me something important. What was it?"

The jet boat kicked up a plume of white waves, the high-pitched whine of the motor reaching me a split second later. Without quite looking at it, I watched the boat make a hard turn, toward us, coming closer, and I tensed, thinking he might do something truly insane like ram the dock, but then he banked again and sped away.

He was still quite a ways out, and he was hidden inside the cockpit, but he reached his free hand behind him in a casual but deliberate wave.

9

The motorboat sped away from Buck Bay, the wake thick and frothy until the hull planed above the water. The whine of the outboard motor receded as he angled left toward Anacortes or Bellingham or who knew where. Away from here. I knew the chances of getting him before he reached shore were disappearing by the second, but I felt helpless to do more than just watch him from the corner of my eye.

My little bit of deception must not have been enough to fool Detective Maya Shaw because she glanced over her shoulder. "What are you looking at?" she asked.

"Nothing," I said. "I was just … lost in thought."

She looked back at me and shook her head. "Whatever. What did you want to tell me?"

I shrugged. "It was nothing important."

"Really? You started asking if I could promise you something. If I could promise you what?"

"Yeah. I was just going to say … if you could promise to let me handle things, I won't let anything blow back on you."

"That's it?"

"That's it."

"Well, how kind of you. Looking out for me like that."

"Maya—"

"Let's stick with Detective Shaw, all right? If that's how it's going to be, fine, but you can forget about me offering up any more information about Colin Welk. Or about anything else."

"I understand."

"Do you? I really hope you know what you're doing, Ms. Pantelli."

I was going to offer some apologetic words, but she brushed past me. I turned and watched her go, then looked back at the bay. The jet boat was gone.

———

WITH A LITTLE EXTRA TIME, I went back inside and called Bev. I'd been dreading telling her that I was leaving, but as I probably should have guessed, she was more concerned than hurt. Was I all right? Was there anything she could do? I told her it was an urgent matter that couldn't be delayed. The explanation was so vague that it wasn't really a lie, but I still felt horrible. I could barely keep it together when she made me promise I'd come back as her guest after whatever I had to do was done, even as I knew that I wouldn't.

Was it a lie to say something you desperately wanted to be true even though you knew it wouldn't be?

After I got off the phone, I went into the backyard. The sky, full of splashes of red and gold a few minutes earlier, had turned gray and hazy. The breeze stirred the tops of the blackberry bushes. I smelled barbecued chicken. I heard muted laughter. I didn't see the jet boat again.

The garden cabin renters showed up, having returned on the 8:50 ferry, all laughter and smiles, their faces tan from the sun and their noses pink from the wine I smelled on their breaths. I gave them Bev's number and explained that I had to leave unexpectedly, which saved me from having to write them a note. Then, with the sky fully dark, it was time to go.

The drive was uneventful, my windows rolled down to take in the smell of the firs, and when I parked in one of the loading lanes I had an hour to kill. I got out and walked. There was something Scandinavian about all the white buildings and red roofs. The windows in Orcas Hotel, a converted colonial house that overlooked the bay, glowed gauzy yellow. Everything in town was closed, even the little store next to the terminal, but it still smelled like cooked salmon from the hotel restaurant. I felt tense, expecting Mr. Grim to pop out from any corner.

He didn't. I watched the ferry, lit up like a birthday cake for a centenarian, float into the dock. Boarding was a meticulous and methodical production of being directed around the road, down the ramp, and eventually onto the ferry itself, some cars up, some down, all the exhaust-spitting vehicles packed into the tunnels like cigars in a tin box.

Once I'd parked and killed the engine, I was free to go upstairs, so I did, squeezing between my driver side door and the bulwark. Anything to get out of the gas-smelling tomb for a few minutes. The two floors above, with their diner-style booths, red-and-white striped tiled floor, and rows of identical vinyl chairs felt like a Greyhound Station on steroids. The boat was sparsely occupied. I went out on deck and leaned against the rail as the ferry departed. The few scattered lights along the boardwalk made the little town of Orcas seem even more remote in the darkness than it looked during the day. Lonely and forlorn.

Just like I felt. As we started to sail down the Salish Sea, the breeze turned into a biting wind, so I headed back inside. While the galley was closed, there were a couple drink machines next to all the pamphlets, so I slid in a five dollar bill and was rewarded with a cup of coffee that tasted like motor oil but was at least hot. I decided to go back to the Honda.

When I emerged from the stairwell, I saw that someone was sitting in my passenger seat.

I froze. I hadn't locked it. Stupid. The roar of the ferry's wake and the churn of the big engine reverberated off all the metal. I was approaching from the rear. With an F-150 partially blocking my view, I couldn't make out much more than a person in a baseball cap. A collar turned up. The strip of lights high above, thin and harsh, created shadows everywhere.

Mr. Grim? If so, it seemed stupid and bold of him to make a move against me this way. It turned out I didn't need to be so worried. As I peered over the hood of the F-150—nobody was in the truck—I saw that the person sitting in my passenger seat was Detective Maya Shaw. She wore a Seattle Mariners cap and a black trench coat. She had the window rolled down, and she looked at me at the same time I looked at her.

"Surprise!" she said, raising her voice to be heard over the noise.

"No," I said.

She eyed my coffee. "None for me?"

"You can't be here."

She smirked. "A little late for that now. I don't think the captain will turn around."

"I'm serious. This is a bad idea."

"Why is it a bad idea, Ms. Pantelli? That's what I would like to know. By the look on your face, you thought I might be someone else, right? Who?"

The cup was so hot that I had to shift it to my other hand, but I felt like tossing it at her instead. "I don't know why you can't just leave me alone. I told you I'd loop you in when I can. You're just making things worse."

"Hey, this is just a happy coincidence, that's all. I decided to spend a night in Anacortes for fun. Saw your car and thought, 'Hey, that's Karen Pantelli's Honda Civic. I was pretty sure I asked her to stay on the island. She must have a pretty good reason for leaving.'"

"Just doing some shopping on the mainland, that's all."

"On the last ferry?"

"It was a spur of the moment decision."

"Is that so? Then why was your duffel bag on your passenger seat when I stopped by in Olga?"

So she *had* seen my bag. "What's with the baseball cap? You supposed to be in disguise?"

"Sort of. I didn't want you to recognize me. I wanted to see if someone was with you first."

"Who would be with me?"

"Are you going to get in or not?"

"I think you need to get out."

"I'm not going anywhere until I get some answers. Otherwise, you have a permanent passenger, sweetheart. Wherever you're going, I'm going too."

"You're serious?"

"One hundred percent. I got a whole bunch of vacation time built up, and Sheriff McKinley has practically been begging me to use some of it. Now get in so we don't have to shout to hear each other."

Cursing, I swept over to the driver side. The paper cup had a plastic lid, but coffee still sloshed out and scalded my hand. As I got in, I pretended not to notice the steaming brown liquid on my skin, but Maya did.

"Ouch," she said. "Got any napkins?"

"I'm fine."

"How about in the glove box?" She opened it, releasing all the maps, guidebooks, receipts, and other crap that had been stuffed inside. "Holy moly, you've got your whole life packed into this—"

"Will you stop?" I licked the coffee off my hand. "See, it's gone? I'm fine."

"Your skin looks red. You want me to go find you some ice?"

"Dear God, what are you, my mother?"

She closed the glove box and rolled up her window, muting, at least somewhat, the rumble outside. "No, just trying to be helpful. If we're going to be partners on this thing, we need to look out for each other."

"We're *not* going to be partners."

"If I were you, I wouldn't drink that yet. Probably burn your tongue."

I glared at her. I almost took a drink out of pure spite. Instead

I fished the gum wrappers and loose change out of the drink holder and slid my cup inside. "You're way over the line, Detective. Unless you want to arrest me—and I'd like to know on what grounds—you have no right to an illegal search of my vehicle."

She raised her finely-trimmed eyebrows. "An illegal search?"

"Would you like me to call Sheriff McKinley and explain to him what's happening here?"

"Now hold on—"

"Either you get out, or I file a complaint with your boss. You're just going to have to trust me on this, Maya."

Her eyes turned hard. "I learned a long time ago never to trust anyone. You trust people, you get burned."

"What was all that stuff about being partners then?"

"If you want to play hardball, fine. I'll leave. But then I'll call Sheriff McKinley myself and tell him about how you came to the Orcadia looking for information about your mother, who worked there back in the nineties. And that Colin Welk was for some reason interested in your mother as well. Right now, nobody knows all that but me, but wow, does that raise a lot of questions. So why don't you just level with me for once, okay?"

I glared. She glared. When I got tired of nothing but glaring, I took a sip of my coffee. It was still hot but not enough to burn my tongue. Since it tasted like motor oil, maybe burning my tongue would have been an improvement. Because I was a glutton for punishment, I took another sip and stared out the front window. I didn't see anyone in the cars ahead of us. I looked backward and didn't see anyone in the ones behind us either.

"Okay, look," I said, "if I tell you everything and you're satisfied that there's really nothing you can do that won't make things worse—and you will be convinced of that, I guarantee you—will you promise to let me go? I'll call you when I can."

"I can't make that promise."

"Then we're at a dead end. I'll go back to Orcas with you, and a whole bunch of people are going to die."

"What the hell are you talking about?"

I took another sip of my coffee. Winced at the taste. Waited her out. Waited some more. Finally, she took off her baseball cap and sighed.

"Fine," she said, "I'll go back to Orcas if I can't help you. But I want the truth, Karen. All of it."

Bringing Detective Maya Shaw into the loop wasn't what I wanted to do, but I didn't see any way around it. While we churned across the Salish Sea, I sipped my coffee and told her everything. She was too sharp to hold anything back. We stopped at Lopez, some cars got off and some got on, then the ferry rumbled toward Anacortes. Between the islands, the sea was so dark that it felt as if we were in outer space; the scattering of house lights were like distant stars.

She wanted to see Welk's list and the letter from Mr. Grim. I gave them to her. She studied both for a long time before handing them back to me. The captain announced that we'd be disembarking in Anacortes at 11:55 p.m. The lights of the terminal came into view like an awaiting space station.

"So now you get it, right?" I said. "You come with me, you'd just be putting both our lives at risk."

She nodded. "I see your predicament."

"And you believe me?"

"Strange as it is, yeah. I do."

"All right. Then you agree that the best thing is for you is to stay in Anacortes until—"

"But I'm still going with you."

"What? But you just said—"

"I said I believe you. I didn't say I think you're better off on your own."

I pounded the top of the steering wheel with both fists. "Damn it, Maya. You promised, if I told you everything—"

"I promised that I'd go back to Orcas Island if I couldn't help you. That's it. I never said if you told me everything I'd stay out. I think you need my help more than ever."

"But—"

"And I think you're overstating the danger, Karen. We're talking about one person. This isn't some superhuman. You and I, it's two against one. I can watch your back, and you can watch mine. And while I believe you, I'm not sure Colin Welk was being completely on the level. I can help you figure out what he might have been hiding. I have access to resources you won't have. You need me."

I felt like throwing her off the ferry. All around us, people streamed back to their cars. I did the opposite. I hopped out and slammed the door. A guy with a walrus mustache shouldered past me. When I was crossing in front of the Honda, Maya rolled down her window. With all the noise—people talking, car doors slamming, water churning as the ferry moved into position—she had to raise her voice to be heard.

"What are you going to do," she shouted, "abandon your Honda?"

I stopped and glared at her. "No, I'm just going to hit the head. Too much damn coffee. You want to come with me for that too?"

"I'll still be here when you get back," she said sweetly.

"Oh, believe me, I know!"

She said something else, but I was already gone. I had to swim against the tide of people in the narrow stairwell, enduring lots of annoyed glaring and irritable muttering. If people knew what I was capable of, they wouldn't have been so cavalier. I was more than happy to practice my particular blend of judo, karate, and FBI training on whoever wanted to get first in line.

Despite my desire to get as far away from Detective Maya Shaw as possible, I was pushing open the swinging restroom door when I sensed something was wrong.

I got a whiff of whatever lemon-scented cleaner they'd used on the tile floor, but that was as far as I went inside. I didn't know what set off my intuition, but it was strong enough that I actually felt the hairs on the back of my neck rise.

I whirled around and saw a boy in a denim jacket helping an old lady in a white shawl toward the stairwell.

The boy was probably eight. Unless the old lady was going to hit me with her cane, I doubted she was a threat either. But I'd learned never to ignore this feeling. It didn't happen often, but it usually meant my subconscious had picked up on something. A detail. A smell, a sound, something I spotted from the corner of my eye that tripped my internal alarm.

I raced back into the stairwell, bounding down the stairs until I reached the remaining throng of people.

I forced my way through them. This time, I was approaching my Honda from the front, and it wasn't long before I could make out Maya Shaw in my passenger seat—chin down, her cap casting her face partly in darkness, hard to make out with all the people passing in front of her, but she seemed fine. The overhead fluorescents, high above, cast her shadow on the headrest behind her.

I was about to breathe a sigh of relief when I realized that it wasn't Maya's shadow.

Someone crouched behind her in the car.

———

10

The person behind Maya was visible only as a dark shape. A hoodie, pulled low. Or a pullover ski mask. Maybe both. I was fifty feet away with a black Mercedes, a tan Subaru Impreza, and a young couple in matching University of Washington sweatshirts between us, but I could clearly see that this person was leaning close to Maya's ear. Maya wasn't moving, as if she was listening intently to what he was saying.

Then I saw the rope around her neck.

"Hey!"

My shout rang through the bay, echoing off concrete and steel, loud enough to rise above the cacophony. The person's hood tilted upward. There was a fraction of a second when we both froze, but then he threw open the back door. The rope around Maya's neck fell forward.

He was a man of average height and build, dressed in a navy blue windbreaker, blue jeans, and gray Nikes. As he clambered out of the Honda, he turned away from me, so I didn't get a good look at his face, but I was right about the pullover ski mask. Gray. Knitted. Judging by how fast he sprang out of the vehicle and sprinted in the other direction, he must have been fit.

I ran.

We were both in the same narrow alley between the bulkhead and the cars, an alley not more than three feet wide. He was fast, but I was faster. I might have been able to grab him before he reached the far set of stairs, his obvious destination, if not for two things. The first was the young couple in UW sweatshirts, turning at my shout, who blocked my way. The second was my concern for Maya, who still had her chin down and wasn't moving.

Struggling past the UW couple, I shouted, "Stop that man! Stop him!" But there was no one between him and the stairs, at least no one out of their vehicles, and he dodged into the stairwell and disappeared.

I had to let him go.

The Honda's passenger side window was still rolled down, so I didn't need to open the door to get to Maya. Her eyes were closed and her chin was down. I put my finger under her nose, and there was breath, thank God. I opened the door. She would have fallen out if I hadn't caught her.

"Is she all right?" the UW woman behind me asked.

"What happened?" her male companion asked. "I didn't see—"

"*Wassis? Sombee ... t'ere ...*"

It was Maya, mumbling. Her eyelids fluttered. I saw a faint red line around her neck. If she'd been choked for long, she would have been coughing violently, so I'd gotten to her just in time. But why was she so incoherent then?

"Maya," I said, giving her shoulder a little shake. "Maya, wake up. It's me, Karen."

She mumbled again, coughing a little. I spotted a red dot on the left side of her neck, a tiny one obscured by the faint mark from the rope. A pinprick from a needle maybe. I suspected that she'd been injected with a sedative, which would have been easy enough to do with the window rolled down. He'd injected her when nobody was looking, then climbed calmly into the back seat if he were just a regular passenger.

Looking down, I also saw something else. It wasn't a rope in her lap, but a gray strap.

My strap, the one that had gone missing from my duffel bag.

Something cold slid into the pit of my stomach. My fingerprints were all over that strap. The bruising from the rope would have obscured the mark from the syringe.

If I'd shown up even one minute later, I would have returned to find a very dead Maya Shaw, with plenty of people in the surrounding cars who'd witnessed us arguing earlier. A full autopsy *might* have revealed that she'd been drugged before being choked, but even then, would that have been enough to clear me? Probably not. He would have killed Maya and framed me for her murder all in one brilliant stroke.

Brazen, even reckless, but brilliant.

"Should we get help?" the woman behind me asked.

I felt Maya's wrist. Her pulse was steady. Could I risk leaving her behind to go hunt for Mr. Grim? If he came back, she was defenseless. Plus she might have been stable for the moment, but she definitely needed to see a doctor. I could have an ambulance meet us at the terminal. If I acted quickly, perhaps the ferry's captain could even keep everyone onboard, preventing Mr. Grim from escaping.

This thought had no more crossed my mind than a woman announced over the loudspeaker that disembarking was commencing. Pedestrians were free to walk off the ship, she explained, with vehicles to follow shortly.

Too late.

Mr. Grim had timed this perfectly. While the nice UW couple regarded me with grave concern, I could picture Mr. Grim strolling off the ferry at this very moment, the pullover ski mask and navy blue windbreaker discarded in a restroom upstairs. Would he have been spotted on a security camera? I doubted he would have been so careless.

I changed my mind about what to do. If I made a ruckus now, I'd be raising questions I didn't want to answer. Maya's condition was stable, and it would take time for an ambulance to get to the terminal. The best course of action would be to drive her myself to the hospital in Anacortes.

"She's okay," I said, then forced a chuckle. "Just drank too much. We had a girl's weekend, lots of tequilas. I shouldn't have left her alone. I think that guy was trying to steal her purse, but I'm not sure what we can do now. We're disembarking."

The woman looked skeptical. "Are you sure she's all right?"

A few cars up the ramp started their engines. A cascade of taillights, one after another, glowed red. I told the woman it was fine. The man, gesturing with his iPhone, asked if I wanted him to call the police. I told him since it didn't look like anything was stolen, I wasn't sure there was much point.

They shuffled away, climbing into an Impala. The Ford Mustang in front of me began to move. Maya groaned. I buckled her seatbelt across her. Her head still slumped forward, but at least she was firmly in the seat. The F-150 behind me honked. I gave him a friendly wave and hopped in the Honda's driver's seat.

"Hang tight, Maya," I said, starting up the car. "I'm taking you straight to the ER."

Rumbling up the ramp and onto the pavement, I scanned the sidewalks beyond the chain-link fences and around the terminal. In the darkness, at such a late hour, there wasn't much to see. Only a handful of people milled about, most in the short-term parking area, some hugging, some already headed for cars. I didn't know what I was looking for, but I kept thinking Mr. Grim had to be among them.

Watching me.

———

BY THE TIME I parked outside the emergency room at Island Health, the dashboard clock in my Honda Civic read 12:37 a.m. The drive had only taken fifteen minutes. It would have gone even faster if not for the ferry traffic clogging WA-20.

"Where—" she said, blinking at me when I opened the

passenger door. She'd been coming out of her stupor the last few minutes. "Where, um, where are we?"

"Getting you help," I said.

The EMERGENCY sign above my head glowed red in the thick, wet air. She squinted at it. "No," she said.

"It's not up for debate," I said.

"Wha … wha happen …" She touched her neck, which still bore the red line, albeit even more faintly, then she looked up at me sharply.

"Yes, it was him," I said. "I think he injected you with something first, but I stopped him before he could choke you. Come on now. I need to get you inside."

Something changed in her eyes. There was real fear there. Limping through the sliding ER doors with her, I felt sad. And, strangely, lonely. I'd thought I'd seen a reflection of myself in the stony-faced Maya Shaw, but there might have been a bigger gulf between us than I'd realized. I wasn't afraid. Frustrated, certainly. Embarrassed that Mr. Grim was one step ahead of me? A little. But I wasn't afraid.

I was angry, though. Oh yes. And I was going to use that anger to make sure I caught the bastard.

Inside, as we staggered over the tan-and-white tiles, nobody rushed to greet us, probably because the lobby was filled with people in even more dire need than Maya. Lots of coughing, lots of bandages, lots of concerned partners or parents. The air was thick with bad body odors and disinfectant, smells that should have canceled each other out but didn't.

When I reached the counter, a nurse handed us both surgical masks under the plastic partition and asked us the nature of our medical emergency. I told the clerk this was Detective Maya Shaw and that someone had apparently drugged her against her wishes —spiked her drink, most likely. She should call the San Juan County Sheriff's Office immediately.

With the nurse still barking questions at me, I lowered Maya into one of the few remaining chairs, the vinyl cushion whooshing when Maya slumped into it. I put the mask over her face. Her fingernails dug into my arm through my windbreaker.

"Don't leave me," she pleaded.

"You're going to be okay. This is for the best."

I yanked my arm away and headed for the door. With the blue surgical mask blocking most of her face, the desperation in Maya's eyes looked all the more stark. The nurse was rounding the desk to talk to me, but I didn't stay for her either.

I was back in the Honda in seconds, roaring out of there before the sliding glass doors even closed. It was good I rushed. I'd only made it a few blocks when I heard an approaching siren. It was a little unusual for the police to turn on their sirens in this kind of situation, but then, the way I'd dropped off a San Juan County detective in the ER was more than a little unusual too.

Hearing the sirens made me feel both relieved and sad. I was relieved that help was on its way, an extra level of protection for Maya in case Mr. Grim came back, but also sad that I was leaving her behind. It was true that I hadn't wanted her involved and that she was a pain in the ass of the first order, but at least part of me was warming to the idea of having a partner again. For a little while anyway. As Maya had said, to have someone watch my back while I watched theirs.

With that possibility gone, it made me acutely aware of how exposed I was trying to go after Mr. Grim by myself.

I was back where I'd started.

Alone.

11

———————

Under the bone-white glow of a crescent moon, the Honda roared over a barren Highway 20 until I finally connected with Interstate 5, heading south toward Seattle along with a somber procession of long-haul semis. I weaved in and out of the boxy beasts like a rabbit racing through a herd of stampeding buffalo. My speedometer kept bouncing over eighty until I realized that getting pulled over wouldn't help, and I forced myself to stay under the speed limit.

It might have been well past one in the morning, but I wasn't tired. Coming face-to-face with a serial killer had a way of waking a person up.

Increasingly paranoid, I powered my phone completely off. Then I took a couple random exits, hopping on and off the freeway and parking alongside rural roads for long spells until I was sure nobody was trailing me. Still not convinced, I stopped at a Shell station in Conway. The Honda's tank was still half full, but I filled it up anyway, then bought a flashlight, some batteries, and a Snickers bar from the mini-mart, using cash for all of it, before cruising a few blocks to an empty gravel lot next to the train tracks.

I parked next to a stack of wooden palettes, killed the engine, and sat there munching my candy bar with the windows rolled down, my engine ticking, and the farmer's field across from me gray and desolate in the moonlight. Nothing happened. It smelled like dry grass and manure. I heard a train to the south approaching. Crickets. The pulsing hum of the interstate.

It felt odd not to hear the water gently lapping against the rocky shore, my constant nightly companion these past few months. I didn't realize how much I'd gotten used to it until the sound was gone.

After a freight train finally roared past, rocking the Honda, I did a thorough search of the vehicle. Twenty years ago, I never would have thought a lone operator on the move could be making use of a tracking device, but they were so common these days—all someone needed was twenty bucks and a smart phone—that I couldn't rule it out.

With the dust cloud from the passing train stinging my eyes, I searched all the obvious places—under the bumper, in the wheel well, under the hood—and didn't find anything. I gritted my teeth and went to work on the interior. My duffel bag was easy enough to search, as was the glove box and under the seats, but the problem was that I had so much other random crap. A few years ago, working as a housekeeper in Des Moines, Iowa, I'd removed the Civic's rear seats, and now it was filled with all kinds of junk: a Dyson vacuum, mops, brooms, plastic buckets full of cleaning supplies, sleeping bags, a tent, a cooler, a lantern that needed no batteries, a tool kit, and two giant plastic totes crammed with so much random garbage that the lids bulged. Everything smelled musty and felt grimy.

My whole life had been reduced to what was in the car. It hadn't seemed like much until I had to search through it. Now I felt like I should have been on a new show: *Hoarders on Wheels*. What was I thinking, keeping all this stuff? How many Swiss Army knives did one person need?

Frustrated, dripping with sweat, I slumped into the driver's seat. It was possible there was no tracking device on the car, of course. Mr. Grim could have simply been monitoring the ferry terminal on Orcas Island, knowing that if I was going to leave, that would have been the way. Yet I didn't think he'd leave something like that to chance.

Where would I put a tracking device, if I were him? He probably wouldn't hide it so much as put it right in the open, camouflaging it just enough that I'd never notice it, mocking me—almost the same way he'd been mocking me when he'd called Maya from that sailboat on Buck Bay.

I searched the glovebox again and came up empty. I looked in the toolkit and found nothing in the plastic case but the tools that should have been there: various screwdrivers, a hammer, measuring tape, and the like. I checked the first aid kit. Nothing. I checked the makeup bag. I almost never wore makeup, but every now and then it came in handy for job interviews. No dice. I did, however, manage to fill the air with Maybelline foundation when I dropped the case.

Wiping the tan powder off my windbreaker, I cursed my stupidity. Enough. Enough of this foolishness. I put the key in the ignition, then stopped. I thought about the toolkit again.

I opened the case and took out the measuring tape. When I tugged on the metal sticking out of the opening, it refused to budge. There was a seam down the middle of the plastic. Examining it closely with the help of the flashlight, I saw translucent glue sticking out in a few places along the seam, not noticeable unless it was right up to the eye.

Heart pounding, I took the hammer and the flathead screwdriver out of the case, then got down on my knees on the gravel. Blinking the sweat out of my eyes, I used the tools to crack the seam, then I pried open the case.

And there it was.

A black plastic square rested inside, unremarkable except for a gray GP logo. I recognized it. *GeoPulse.* It was one of the most popular consumer GPS tracking devices on the market.

I grabbed the hammer and lifted it over the device, intending to destroy it with one savage blow. This was the moment when Mr.

Grim stopped being one step ahead of me. A far-off train whistle pierced the stillness. A dog barked down the road, a lonely call in the darkness. I let my anger cool, realizing there was another option. It wasn't enough that Mr. Grim would no longer be one step ahead of me.

I needed to be one step ahead of him.

———

NINETY MILES SOUTH ON I-5, I pulled into a Love's Travel Stop just outside Tacoma. It was one of those massive gas station complexes that was practically a mini mall, with not only a market big enough to be a small-town grocery store but also a Subway, a Godfather's Pizza, and a Chester's. Even at 3:44 a.m., it was a bustling place, most of the pumps in use, people coming and going through the double glass doors under the yellow-glowing Love's heart on the tan brick facade.

I parked outside the market, bought a bottle of water and a packaged blueberry muffin, and went outside into the crisp night air that smelled of diesel and garlic pizza. I leaned against the Honda's warm hood, waiting, eating my muffin and pretending it didn't taste like a wet sponge, until I finally settled on a good candidate: a big guy in a Hawaiian shirt, as wide and low to the ground as his eighteen-wheeler. As he approached the market, he yanked up his stained blue jeans.

"Still a ways to go tonight?" I said to him.

The guy grunted, barely pausing on his way to the doors. "Just San Fran. No biggee."

"Seems plenty far to me. I don't know how you guys drive all night. I couldn't do it."

He gave this a dismissive wave as the doors swung shut behind him. Chatty fellow. I waited until I saw him head toward the bathroom, then when I was sure nobody was watching, I used the duct tape I'd had in my car to fix the GP tracker under his bumper.

I was on the road before he'd even come out of the restroom.

12

Ten minutes later, I'd backtracked on I-5 to the SeaTac rest area. With traffic so light, I was tempted to drive straight to Seattle, maybe find a place to hunker down in the Fremont area so I didn't have to fight morning traffic, but fatigue finally caught up with me.

The promise of sunrise was already on the horizon, a strip of lavender in the sky over the brick restroom building and through the fir trees. I squeezed into a parking space between a station wagon with a blue tarp for a rear window and a crinkled Winnebago adorned with travel stickers. A handful of people passed under the yellow cones of light like silent wraiths. Most folks were in their cars. Despite the sign prohibiting overnight camping, I suspected many were transients living out of their vehicles.

I locked my doors. I cracked open my windows. I reclined my seat. As exhausted as I was, my mind wouldn't stop racing. I thought about all the nights I'd spent in my car the past few years. Rest areas like this one. Little city parks. Walmarts. Logging roads. Cornfields. New subdivisions. I'd even spent one night in a junkyard, my Honda Civic sadly having no problem blending in with all the other beat-up jalopies.

I still wasn't sure how I was going to get access to Welk's safe, but I hoped the tracker would at least make Mr. Grim believe I was on my way to California. Searching for clues about Mom, maybe, but heeding his warning and giving up on going after him. I still had to assume Mr. Grim was watching the Welk place, though. I needed a plan, but my thoughts were too fuzzy to think of one. Sleep. I needed sleep, at least an hour or two, or my mind wouldn't be sharp tomorrow.

A breeze smelling of dry grass and fir flitted through the cracked-open window. The intermittent hum of traffic started to lull me to sleep, but there was something about the noise, the rise and fall of rushing air, that conjured up a memory. After Mom left us, I used to lie awake for hours, listening to my three-year-old sister breathing. Hope used to have nightmares almost every night, and I waited, waited for her breathing to get quick and ragged, waited for that inevitable cry in the dark, knowing I'd have to comfort her. Which I did. Soothing words. *It's okay, it's going to be okay, I'm here.*

It helped, but just when I'd thought she'd gone back to sleep, I'd hear her dainty feet on the carpet. Pad down the hall. Crawl into our parents' bed. For a whole year, she did this. I'd find her there in the morning, clinging to Mom's pillow the way someone lost at sea clings to a life raft.

It made me jealous, but I was six, a big kid in my mind, and big kids didn't do stuff like that. Then during a bad thunderstorm, one of those Tucson deluges that floods the streets and fills the desert with lakes that linger for weeks, I didn't feel like a big kid. I felt lonely and afraid. I climbed out of bed. My parents' room smelled of beer, sweat, and the jet fuel used at Davis-Monthan Air Force Base, the scents I most associated with Dad in those days.

As usual, Hope was already there, so tiny she could have been a cat. Before I could crawl in beside her, Dad rolled over in bed.

"Not you," he said.

It was too dark to see his eyes, but his head floated over me like a dark balloon. I stood there stupidly for a long time, then I did something I almost never did, even back then, even at six years old. I started to cry. He held up a finger.

"Nope, no tears either. Go back to your own bed. There are a lot of Hopes in the world, kiddo, and they need people like us. Strong people. You understand?"

I didn't. Not then. I was only six, after all, and I thought he was being cruel, but I didn't argue either. I just went back to my room. I lay there for hours hating him. Hating Mom. Hating myself most of all, for being whiny and weak. I didn't think I'd ever sleep.

But I did.

And in the morning, I vowed never to be so weak again.

———

I WOKE to someone tapping on my driver side window.

Sunlight glinted off a gold badge. It was a cop, a baby-faced young man with blond curly hair as compact as a dish sponge. Too young to be wearing that uniform. It had to be a costume. His lips moved, and words came out of them, but still feeling groggy, and with a truck roaring to life in the parking lot behind him, I didn't catch it.

"I'm sorry, officer, is there a problem?" I said. At least, that was what I intended to say. The mumble that came out was more akin to, "*Srryosserzerepobem?*"

He gestured for me to roll down my window. I fumbled for the button, blinking, and finally got it.

"I'm afraid you can't camp here, ma'am," the cop said. He even sounded fourteen.

The gears in my brain were just starting to turn. The traffic on the interstate was much louder than last night, a steady roar. My shirt was drenched with sweat and stuck to my chest. I looked at the dashboard, but with the Honda off, so was the clock. "Um, what time is it?"

He glanced at his wristwatch, a massive stainless steel thing he probably could have used to deflect bullets. "8:43, ma'am. Now, I'm afraid you have to move along. There's free coffee in that building. If you'd like the name of a shelter, I can give you one. It's going to get hot today."

I swallowed. The grass behind the cop was brown and parched, and that was how my mouth felt. Like water-starved grass. The Winnebago and the station wagon were gone, as were most of the other vehicles parked at the rest area last night. I'd never intended to sleep so long. Mr. Grim was on the move. I couldn't afford to just sit around.

"I was just, you know, napping for a moment," I protested feebly. "I'm not homeless. I mean, I am—temporarily. But it's by choice."

He shrugged. "Okay."

"I don't need a shelter."

"Nobody can force you to go there, ma'am. But a lot of people find them helpful." It was subtle, but I saw him lean forward and inhale through his nose. "And you know, if you need help getting clean, they can help with that too. It's hard to do that on your own."

I wondered what he smelled. It wasn't booze, not unless there was a rotten apple in my car starting to ferment, always a possibility. I was wide-awake now, irritated at his assumption. All his assumptions.

"I'm not on drugs," I said.

"All right."

"I'm not homeless."

"You said that."

"I was in law enforcement myself once, you know."

"Oh?"

"FBI, actually."

He nodded. I could see that he didn't believe me, and for some reason I felt desperate that he believe me. I didn't know why. I didn't usually feel like I had anything to prove to anyone. I seldom told anyone about my past life, and I especially didn't tell strangers.

"Well," he said, "you still can't camp here."

"I'm not camping."

"Ma'am—"

"And I'm really more of a drifter. It's a choice." I could see he didn't believe me, and my annoyance with him swelled like a bruise. "There's a difference, you know. When you choose not to have a home. It's not the same thing. Maybe I just like being a drifter, okay? Maybe I don't want a home."

I detected a flicker of sympathy in his sad smile. "Most of the homeless say the same thing to me. Most of them say they live this way because they like the lifestyle."

I wanted to keep arguing, but what could I say? He was right. I'd talked to plenty of homeless people in my travels, and while many were mentally ill, drug addicts, or both, almost all of them claimed they lived on the streets by choice. Sometimes I even believed them. Mostly, though, I saw their defiance at the word *homeless* as a desperate attempt to try to get some measure of agency over their lives.

While I was sitting there mulling this over, he took out a business card and handed it to me through the crack in the window.

It was the name of a shelter in Seattle.

"Thank you," I said.

———

As irritating as he was, the cop actually gave me an idea about how to visit Professor Welk's house even if Mr. Grim was watching. I'd thought the cop had looked like a kid playing dress-up. Like he was wearing a costume.

That was what I needed. A costume.

After I'd helped myself to some of that free coffee, I freshened up in the rest area bathroom and changed into the nicest outfit I owned: a white blouse, a pleated gray skirt, and black leather pumps with low heels, something I'd bought for an ill-fated stint as an attorney's receptionist. I even put on makeup and panty hose,

God help me. I almost wished that cop were still hanging around. Who looks homeless now, pal?

When I'd gussied myself up enough, I headed into Seattle. Traffic was lighter than I expected, and I wondered if it was because of the weather. On the radio, the DJ said it might hit a hundred degrees Fahrenheit, approaching record territory for the emerald city, and I could certainly believe it. The sun already beat down like a mallet on my windshield, straining the limits of my Honda's rattling air conditioner.

My first stop was a Target just north of the rest area, where I picked up a pair of J.Crew sunglasses and a pay-as-you go Tracfone. I texted Ben from the parking lot, telling him this was my new number and asking if everything was all right in Atlanta. He replied that he was in position and everything was fine. I texted back that I'd call him when I thought it was okay to do so and that I really appreciated him helping me.

Next, I stopped at Wired, a coffeehouse in the Fremont area that had internet and computers. While sipping an Americano and nibbling on a cranberry scone, I looked up the Welks' address on Google Earth to get a sense of the neighborhood. No way was I risking a drive-by in my distinctive white Honda Civic. The house was just a few blocks off busy Aurora Avenue on a cracked-pavement street adorned with telephone poles and draped with powerlines mixed in with other old homes and newer condo complexes. It was the kind of neighborhood where cars lined the streets, so I'd have no problem parking a few blocks away without drawing attention.

I picked up a dozen roses and a sympathy card from a nearby florist, then made a final stop at Harp's Costume Shop, where I bought a blonde wig. When I put it on in the car and checked myself in the rearview mirror, I thought I was unrecognizable, especially with the sunglasses on. Perfect. Maybe it was my ego, but I even thought I looked a little like Marilyn Monroe.

Careful to take a circuitous route that steered clear of the Welk house, I parked a few blocks over under the shadow of a big-leaf maple. By this time, it was closing in on noon. Noon was good. Noon meant I could be doing this on my lunch hour. Walking to the house, the sun glaring off the sidewalk, I didn't see anyone. The driveway was empty. The Chevy van with the wheelchair lift was undoubtedly still back on Orcas Island, but a yellow Nissan Leaf was parked on the street in front of the house. Jared Whallen's? It had a Black Lives Matter bumper sticker.

I ascended the steps to the front door. The curtains in the bay window were drawn. No light or movement. On the stoop was an Amazon package, about the size of a shoe box, addressed to Colin Welk. I pressed the doorbell and heard it ring inside.

A bald black man in a fraying yellow bathrobe opened the door. His bloodshot eyes were magnified by the thick lenses in his black-framed glasses. The robe's sash wasn't tied. Underneath he wore baggy gray sweatpants and a white Jay-Z T-shirt, his pot belly distorting Jay-Z's face, making it wider, longer. In the unforgiving sunlight, his scalp looked like a bruised plum. The smell of cigarettes hit me like a shove to the chest.

"Hi, I'm Coleen Grant," I said. "I was a student of Professor Welk's. I just came by to express my condolences."

He blinked—slow, steady blinks, as if each one were a conscious act. Blink, blink, blink. He was a couple inches shorter than me but probably outweighed me by a hundred pounds. His fleece-lined moccasin slippers were coming apart at the seams. His big toe poked out of the left one. "Oh," he said, "that's … that's nice of you. We're—we're, um, still kinda in shock. I'm Jared. I … I help around here."

I handed him the roses. "I'm sorry to intrude," I said, "but is there any chance I can come in? I'm having car problems. I can call my husband from the car, but it's getting kind of hot already."

"Oh," he said.

"I know, it's really forward of me to ask—"

"No, no, that's all right. Please. Please, come in."

He opened the door wider and started to step aside, then noticed the Amazon package. He snatched it up with his free hand, giving me a peek of his hairy belly, then cupped the box under his arm. I stepped into a dimly lit foyer with orange terra cotta tiles, a high ceiling, and a tear drop chandelier that was off. The light came from narrow windows along the roofline. A staircase with an oak rail and white spindles led to a landing with three closed doors. Heavy metal music thumped inside one of them. Behind Jared was an opening to a kitchen. Green marble countertops. To the left, carpeted stairs descended into darkness.

"Do you, um, want me to put those in water?" I asked.

He looked at the flowers as if noticing them for the first time. "Oh," he said. "No, that's okay. Do you, um, want a glass of lemonade or—"

"No, no, I'm fine, thanks." I didn't see any security cameras. No Google or Alexa devices. Nothing obvious that would allow Mr. Grim to monitor us. He could still be watching, of course, but what was I going to do? Pretend to be Coleen Grant forever? My getup felt silly now that I was inside. It was time to come clean. "Is Isaac here?"

"He's ... he's not in a good place. Probably not good to talk to him right now. It's still so fresh, you know?"

"Yeah. Well ... I'll start with you, and you can decide how you want to loop him in."

"I'm sorry?"

I took off my sunglasses. I thought about taking off the wig too, but it'd been hard to get it on just right, and I was going to need to wear it when I left. "I'm not Colleen Grant. I'm sorry for lying, but I'm ... being careful. My name is Karen Pantelli, and I was at the Orcadia when Professor Welk was ... well, when he died. It's vitally important that I talk to you. This is going to come as a shock, but it's pretty clear that Colin Welk's death wasn't a suicide."

He looked at me so long that I wasn't sure he'd heard me. The thumping bass filled the stillness.

"I'm sorry," I said, "I know this all seems—"

"Let's go to his office," Jared said. He gestured with the flowers toward the staircase that led downstairs.

"You're not surprised by what I just said?"

"Not really. Professor Welk, he, uh, told me something like this might happen."

"He told you what he was working on?"

"No . . . not exactly." He lowered his voice. "I guess I just assumed it was something top secret for the government. He was always so weird and paranoid, hiding stuff in that safe of his, and he's such a genius with numbers, you know. Figured he was doing something for the CIA."

"I'm not CIA."

"Oh. Well, let's go where we can talk in private. I don't really want . . . well, he's already so upset."

"I understand," I said.

A door upstairs creaked. We both looked up. A gangly young man stared down at us from the landing. I *assumed* he was staring because I couldn't see his eyes. They were hidden by a curtain of oily red hair as long in front as it was in back. In his white tank top, his shoulders looked as sharp as razor blades.

"Hey, Isaac," Jared said. "This is, um, this is a former student of your dad's. She just wanted to say how sorry she was."

Isaac said nothing, leaning against the rail like an abandoned mop, not much of his face visible except for a pimply chin. He wore green plaid pajama bottoms. Jared started to say something else, but Isaac retreated into his room, slamming his door so hard that dust rained down on us.

Jared sighed. "Sorry."

"It's okay," I said. "You can tell him everything later. When he's ready."

He led me downstairs, flicking on the light switch with his elbow, trailing cigarette fumes. The staircase doubled back on itself, narrow enough that his shoulders brushed against clamshell walls. I wondered why he was taking the flowers instead of leaving them in the kitchen. The guy definitely wasn't in his right mind.

We ended up in a daylight basement with a glass slider that looked out on a patch of grass and a crumbling wooden fence. Jared shuffled across the tiles in his slippers, past a wood stove and a green microfiber couch, to a door with a plain pine finish. Early eighties decor. There was an elevator just past the stairwell, behind a glass door, which explained how a man in a wheelchair could get down here.

However, for a man in a wheelchair, the actual office was a fairly tiny room. The same tiled floor. Two curtained windows. Mahogany bookshelves jam-packed with books. A big oak monster of a desk that faced the door. There was no desk chair, of course, and plenty of room to navigate around the desk. It smelled faintly of mold. Paper, binders, and spiral notebooks littered the top of the desk as well as a few math textbooks.

There were two external monitors, and a docking station where he obviously plugged in his laptop, but no other computers. I spotted math exams marked up with red ink. There were also a couple of Seattle Seahawks posters, which seemed an odd fit for the scholarly professor. I wouldn't have thought him into football. Then again, people were often more complicated than initial stereotypes would lead us to believe.

It was the one thing that gave me hope about humanity in general. We didn't all fit into tidy little boxes.

If I'd been expecting a CSI-like control room for a man tracking a serial killer, this wasn't it. No maps on the walls. No messy marker boards. No grainy photos of possible suspects. I knew Welk would never be so obvious about what he was doing, but I still found myself disappointed.

There was, however, a safe—a big, black, cast iron one with a combination lock.

Jared placed the Amazon box on the desk, balancing it precariously amid all the paper flotsam, then closed the office door most of the way. He listened at the gap for a moment, then shook his head. "I just got him calmed down. He was . . . well, he pretty much destroyed his room last night. I'm kinda surprised his stereo even works."

"I'm really sorry to hear that," I said, which sounded lame. It *was* lame. I was never great at offering sympathy.

Jared nodded solemnly, biting down on his lower lip, waiting. I told him everything. I didn't see any reason to hold back. Maybe I was putting him at risk even being here, and I told him so, but I also told him that I didn't see any way around it. If we were going to stop this guy, I needed whatever edge I could get. If he knew something, anything, about this Mr. Grim that might help me catch him, he should tell me. If he could get me access to whatever research Professor Welk might have on this guy—I nodded toward the safe—I needed it now.

Jared kept chewing his lip, nodding now and then, but otherwise said nothing until I finished.

"So I guess you want the combination, huh?" he asked.

"Do you know it?"

He nodded. "Right before he left for Orcas, when I was in the other room, he mumbled it to himself when he was opening it. I tried it on Friday, and it worked. I probably shouldn't have, you know, but . . ." He shrugged.

"So that's why you're not surprised by everything I told you? You already looked at all his research?"

He shrugged. "It was mostly a lot of numbers and formulas, so it didn't make much sense to me. Try 23-6-9. That's, uh, what worked last time."

I bent down on my knees in front of the safe, which actually wasn't all that easy in the skirt. I tried the combination. It didn't work. I tried it again. Still no dice.

"Are you sure it was—" I began, turning to look at Jared, but the rest died in my throat.

He was pointing a gun at me.

13

————

The revolver in Jared Whallen's trembling hand was a make and model I knew quite well, mostly because I'd seen one recently. As in yesterday morning.

It was a S&W .38 Special, a black, snub-nose revolver with a walnut grip, identical to the one I'd seen in Colin Welk's much steadier hand at the Orcadia. It was so like the good professor to own a backup. Based on the way the books on the shelf behind Jared were pushed aside haphazardly, I figured that was where the revolver had been stored, hidden but still easily accessible if Welk ever needed it.

"You know," I said, "I'm getting *very* tired of people pointing guns at me."

Jared chewed on his bottom lip with vicious intensity. I thought the chances of Jared being Mr. Grim himself were almost zero, but nervous people were impulsive and trigger-happy. I was still squatting on the floor. He was several paces behind me. I was not in a position to disarm him even if I'd wanted to go that route.

"Jared," I said, "I really am here to help. Otherwise, what would be the point of me even talking to you?"

"Now—now—now, we're just going to be, you know, calm here," he said.

"I'd feel more calm if you put that gun down."

He fumbled in the right front pocket of his bathrobe, finding it difficult because he was doing it with his left hand, and fished out a cell phone. "I'm not going to shoot unless you do something stupid. I'm just—just going to call the detective."

"Detective? What detective? Maya Shaw?"

"Don't move! I mean it!"

"Jared, I'm just standing up, okay? Real slow. Please. Tell me who you're calling."

"Guy named Henderson, okay? He's come to Seattle to arrest you, for what you did to his partner. For almost choking her to death. He said if I don't help him, you'd get away."

"Henderson? He's a uniformed cop, not a detective. And he's not Maya's partner." Jared's thumb hovered over the phone's screen, but so far he hadn't actually made the call. There was still hope. The police showing up was a hell of a lot better than getting shot, but something else was going on here, and I already had a creeping sense of what it was. "What exactly did this person say to you? Please. It's important."

"He said—he said you'd want to get into the professor's safe. It's why you killed him. He said to keep you in here until he got here if I could. You're a killer. I read about you. You even killed a kid once."

I ignored this broadside. "Look, Jared, you want to call the police, fine, but do it directly, okay? I don't think that was Henderson. It was probably Mr. Grim."

"Mister who?"

"Professor Welk's killer. It was actually Welk's name for the guy. *That* was what he was working on—a serial killer. One he'd been tracking for years. Mr. Grim killed Welk's wife. It's actually why he's in a wheelchair too. Why Isaac is the way he is. Mr. Grim came after him for getting too close. It's why he's so secretive about his research."

"He said you'd come up with crazy stuff like that. He said—he said it's part of your MO."

"Call the San Juan County Sheriff's Office directly then. Ask for Henderson. He'll have no idea what you're talking about."

"Shut up! You're—you're not tricking me."

"Jared, if you call the number Mr. Grim gave you, you're putting all of us in great—"

Danger. I didn't finish the word because the office door opened. Jared swung his gun toward the door, giving me an opportunity to lunge for it, but then I saw who was entering and gave up on the idea.

Isaac.

If I tried to grab the gun, the kid might end up getting shot. While Isaac was still barefoot, dressed in the tank top and green pajama bottoms, he wasn't shuffling around like a zombie anymore. He stood ramrod straight, his bright green eyes blinking in and out from behind the wall of red hair.

"Who killed Dad?" he said.

"Isaac, stay back," Jared said. He redirected his gun back toward me. "She's dangerous. She's the one who killed your father."

"I did no such thing," I insisted. "Your dad wanted my help. I'm sorry about what happened on Orcas, that I couldn't save him, but—"

"Help with what?"

"With catching Mr. Grim. A serial killer. *He's* the one who killed your dad. I'm so sorry."

"Stop!" Jared said. "Don't listen to a word—"

"Why do you have a gun?"

"Isaac, she's dangerous. I'm just going to call—"

"Nobody would want to kill Dad." He'd gotten louder but not in an angry way. It was more like someone had turned up his volume knob. "It doesn't make sense."

Jared, who'd hit a few buttons on his phone, paused. "Isaac, remember what we talked about? When you get upset, just take deep breaths and—"

"Nobody would want to kill Dad. He was *nice.*"

"Isaac, listen to me. Go sit on the couch in the family room. Do it now."

"I want the Amazon box."

"What?"

"Maybe it was a present for me. Sometimes Dad would buy things on Amazon for me."

Jared blocked him with his arm. "We can do that later. This isn't the—"

"No, now! *Now, now, now!*"

While Isaac had gotten increasingly louder, these last three words were delivered in a jarring shriek. He clenched and unclenched his fists. His face, what I could see of it, turned the same color as his hair. Ruby red. Even with that .38 Special pointed at me, I felt for the kid. I'd only been in his presence a few minutes, but it was already obvious that the car accident that had crippled his father had also robbed Isaac of a normal future. Maybe forever.

With Jared blocking Isaac with his phone hand, it meant he couldn't finish his call. That bought myself a few more seconds to plead my case.

"Look," I said, "just give him the box, okay? Let him open it, if it makes him happy. Just don't make that call, okay? Not yet. Hear me out. It was important to Professor Welk—to your dad, Isaac—that Mr. Grim not know I'm after him. Let's talk. Let's talk about ... about why ..."

It came to me then, exactly what Mr. Grim was trying to do. I may never have figured it out if Isaac hadn't been so fixated on the Amazon box. Why did that package show up this morning? Was it really just a coincidence? I remembered something I'd read yesterday about one of Mr. Grim's victims. The small-town sheriff in Texas.

"We have to leave," I said.

"What?" Jared said.

"Now. We have to get out of this house."

"What are you *talking*—"

"That Amazon box. I think there might be a bomb inside. Mr. Grim has used them before. And it's probably booby-trapped, so don't open it."

I started toward the door, but Jared wasn't having any of it. He jabbed the .38 at me.

"Come on!" I said. "Don't you see? Mr. Grim can't get into that safe, so he's going to blow it up instead. Destroy all the research. And he was hoping I might show up so he could kill me at the same time. That was why he wanted you to call. But he might not wait. He might do it at any moment. And it's got to be a powerful bomb, to take out that safe."

"That's crazy," Jared said. "You're just—you're just trying to trick me."

"Please. Let's go out the back."

"I'm going to call Henderson. We're all just going to stay put and I'm going to call him.

"If you do that, we're all dead."

"You're lying."

"Look," I said, "I'm going to walk out of here right now. Slow. Not running. You follow. Point the gun at me. I don't care. Just leave the Amazon box, okay? We can talk about this out back. What's the harm?"

"If you take a step," Jared said, "I'm pulling the trigger."

"I'm putting my hands up, okay? Look, I'm putting my hands up over my head."

"Don't," Jared warned.

"I'm going to walk slowly past you and I'm not going to do anything. I just want to leave."

"I'll block you."

"Jared! Come on! At least give me a chance to answer all your questions before you do something stupid."

"You're insane," Jared said.

He punched a final button and held the phone to his ear. Was I insane? Maybe there was nothing in that Amazon box but new jockey shorts. Maybe it really was Henderson who would answer. Maybe, if I tried to escape, I was just going to get myself killed.

But I didn't think so.

"Hello?" Jared said.

I heard a voice on the other end, a man's. People have a natural inclination to look down or away when they speak on the phone, and Jared was no exception. There was an instant when his gaze turned to the floor. It gave me an opening. He was probably expecting me to charge him, so I didn't do that. I delivered a hard, brutal front kick underneath his right hand. His gun hand.

It was no easy feat in a skirt . The .38 went flying. So did his phone. The revolver thunked against the shelves. The phone spun toward the hardwood. My right shoe also joined the fun, the black leather pump bouncing off the ceiling like a wayward missile.

It was a lot of chaos, which worked to my advantage. Knowing that Mr. Grim would probably figure out what was happening, I needed to put as much distance between me and that Amazon package as possible. Jared made it easy for me. I was fully intent on plowing through him, but he lunged to his right, for the revolver, which gave me just enough of a gap to squeeze by him.

My elbow raked against his terrycloth robe. Isaac stood there gaping at me. I couldn't stop. To stop would be death.

"Come on!" I shouted.

A mistake. I knew as soon as the words were out of my mouth that I was already confirming my presence to Mr. Grim. Now there was nothing to do but run. Run for the back slider—past the wood stove, the green microfiber couch, everything a blur. One of my pumps was missing. The orange tile was cool against my bare foot.

I prayed that the slider was unlocked. It was. I threw it open, and the glass cracked. On my first step, my bare foot touched down on rough concrete. Second step, my other pump skidded across weed-infested grass. All barefoot now. I was scaling the fence—weathered boards that dug into my hands—when I saw Isaac beside me.

Thank God. My skirt, catching the edge of a board, ripped up my thigh. I was afforded one last glimpse of the open slider behind me, with no one standing there, before I fell into what turned out to be the neighbor's prized rose bushes.

I thrashed my way through the thorny vines and was back on my feet before I even felt the hot trickle of blood on my calf. The neighbor's curtains were all drawn. A dog barked inside. Isaac was luckier than me, touching down in a child's sandbox, just a little stumble before he was up and running beside me, both of us slamming against the chain-link gate to the right of the house at the same time, gasping for breath.

We stared at each other like two escapees from a mental asylum. Maybe we *were* insane? If so, I'd ruined a rosebush and scratched myself to hell for nothing.

I could see that Isaac was thinking this very thing. I could see it because for once his hair, sweaty and sticking to his scalp, was pushed aside enough to fully expose his eyes. Bright green eyes. Eyes like his father's.

"Maybe it wasn't really a bom—" he began before his house exploded.

14

—————

"Hello?"

An hour later, I'd barely punched the last digit of Maya's personal cell phone number, the number she'd given me back on Orcas, when she answered. As beat-up, bruised, and shell-shocked as I was, I still cringed at the hoarseness of her voice. It was a reminder of what had happened last night on the ferry. A reminder of my failure.

Another failure.

I finally managed to rustle up a hello in return. She said nothing for a while. A male news anchor droned in the background, loudly enough that I could actually hear that he was talking about the house exploding in Seattle's Fremont neighborhood. I wondered if it was local or national news. Probably national. The strangeness of Professor Welk's place blowing up a day after he'd supposedly committed suicide on Orcas Island was the kind of thing twenty-four-hour news channels feasted on.

"Where are you?" Maya asked finally.

I thought about how to answer that. My right ear was still ringing, so I shifted the phone to my left. Isaac, sullen and unresponsive, crouching low in the Honda's passenger seat, sported a thick white bandage on his neck courtesy of the fence shard that had grazed his skin like a bullet. If that piece of fence had veered just a bit more to the left, he'd be dead now. Dead like Jared Whallen. Dead like his father. The bodies were piling up.

The sun beat down on the Honda's hood, intense even through my sunglasses. Or maybe my eyes, like my ears, were just feeling the effects of the explosion. A Target sign loomed over us, as vividly red as my car was white, the traffic from the busy boulevard buzzing past just ten feet from my front bumper. The packaging from the new Tracfone I'd bought in the store lay crumpled at my feet. I wasn't taking any chances even turning in the old one. We were miles from the Welk place, and I could no longer make out any sirens, but I still found myself looking over my shoulder for cop cars.

The trench coat I'd thrown over my shredded and bloodstained blouse felt heavy and suffocating, even with the air conditioning cranked up to max, but I knew I'd draw more attention if I took it off. The bloodspots were superficial, but they looked garish on the white blouse. They were even more garish when I let myself linger on the fact that the blood probably wasn't mine.

"I'll get to where I am in a second," I said. "Did anyone else get hurt?"

"What?"

"In the neighborhood. People nearby."

"So that *was* you."

"It's not what you think," I said.

"I don't know what I'm thinking."

"You're thinking I caused it somehow."

"Did you?"

"For God's sake, no! It was Mr. Grim. Of course it was Mr. Grim. Now please tell me. Did any of the neighbors get hurt?"

"No. And the fire department has managed to contain the blaze. They haven't said if they've found any victims yet. Was anyone in the house?"

"Yes," I said, looking at Isaac. "Jared Whallen was inside—or at least, he was standing right at the back patio door."

Maya was silent. Isaac, slumped into the duct-taped vinyl seat as if he wanted to dissolve into it, didn't react. He was turned slightly toward the window, his hair clinging to his skin like a headscarf and hiding his eyes. He'd draped the pink Minnie Mouse sweatshirt I'd dug out of the back over his T-shirt—spotted with even more blood than mine—but he hadn't put it on as I'd suggested. It was hard to blame him, and not just because of how girlish the sweatshirt was. The air blowing out of the dashboard vents was barely cool, and across the street the US Bank's digital sign read 98F.

Maya finally let out a long, ragged sigh. "Tell me everything. Tell me what happened."

"I will, but are you okay? Are you back at home?"

"Don't worry about me, for God's sake. Tell me everything right now, or I swear—"

"All right, all right," I said. A store employee pushing a train of carts across the parking lot shot me a suspicious look, and I waited until he'd passed, then caught Maya up on everything starting from when I'd cajoled my way into the Welk place in disguise.

"Jesus," she said when I was finished. "And this kid? He's with you in the car."

"He is," I said.

"And what the hell are you going to do about *that?*"

A bead of sweat rolled down my temple, and I wiped it away with the back of my hand. We couldn't stay in this greenhouse on wheels much longer, and it wasn't just because of my crappy air conditioning. It was also the smell. The kid stank like a basketball team's jersey hamper. "Well," I said, "that's the main reason I'm calling. I need your help."

"Oh, *now* you want my help," she said.

"Are you still at the hospital?"

"No, I'm not at the fucking hospital. Jesus."

"Home then?"

"Yes, home. I know—I know I said some things, at the hospital, but it was just … That's passed. I didn't say anything about Grim. About any of that stuff. If that's what you're worried about."

"I wasn't—"

"Sure you were. You want me to keep a lid on that stuff, and I am. For now, at least. It's costing me because McKinley is starting to wonder about my personal life, because of what you told the hospital about someone trying to date rape me and because I told him I couldn't say who it was definitely, just any of a number of guys who happened to be at the bar Saturday night. Thanks so much for that."

"I'm sorry, I didn't know what else to—"

"Save it. I still haven't said boo. I just told him you were a friendly waitress who took me to the hospital. And I'm fine. Sheriff McKinley wants me to take a couple days off, just to get my head straight, but sitting around isn't helping me one bit. I have a b-bruise on my neck, so what, I'll wear a scarf. I look good in scarves."

"Okay." I didn't like the hitch in her voice when she said the word "bruise," but I didn't see the point in pushing this any further —except to sincerely apologize, which I did. "I mean it. I'm *really* sorry. About what happened. And about leaving."

Maya sighed. "What do you want, Karen?"

I looked at Isaac again, considering. I'd tried to talk to him, but he'd been practically comatose. After the explosion, I'd made the split decision to flee the scene, not the most courageous act, but I knew that nothing could be done for Jared and that the longer we hung around the fire, the more likely we'd end up ensnared by the police or, worse, killed by Mr. Grim. If he was even in Seattle. There was no way to know.

I'd thought about dropping the kid off with a relative or family friend, but even if I could coax a suggestion out of Isaac, I felt uncomfortable leaving him exposed like that. Mr. Grim might come for him. I'd not only be putting Isaac at risk, I'd be putting whoever was watching him at risk too.

There was only one person who came to mind for such a task, and I said as much to Maya.

"You want *me* to protect Isaac?" she said.

"In so many words, yes."

She was quiet. We hadn't been talking long, but the phone already felt hot against my ear. A Safeway truck rumbled past. A man dressed in layers of grimy coats stumbled down the sidewalk, gesticulating wildly, yelling at every passing car. For a brief moment, I saw my own future if I couldn't get Mr. Grim out of my head. A crazy person screaming at traffic.

"I can't," she said finally.

"Maya, come on."

"I'm sorry." She sounded small, not at all like the Maya I'd already come to know. "That's just not something I can … No. No, that's not going to work."

"I really need your help," I begged. "I don't know what else to do. He needs round-the-clock protection."

"No," Isaac said.

I looked at him. I hadn't realized until now that he'd been staring at the side of my face. It was the first thing he'd said since we'd jumped in the Honda. He was still looking at me. Waiting.

"Take him straight to the Seattle police station," Maya said. I doubted she'd heard Isaac's voice since he'd spoken so softly. "That's much safer than me acting as some sort of bodyguard."

I was still looking at Isaac, weighing how to deal with what he said. He went on staring at me. Since he rarely made eye contact, it was unnerving when he did. "You know I can't do that," I said to Maya.

"If you don't want to go in yourself, drop him off at the front door. He can ask for help. I could make a call, maybe help that process in a roundabout way without, you know, revealing too much."

"No," Isaac said again, louder this time, his eyes like green lasers, boring into me. I wasn't even sure he'd blinked.

"Was that him?" Maya said.

"Yes," I said.

"He doesn't want to go to the police?"

"Apparently not."

"Well, what *does* he want?"

"That's a good question." I raised my eyebrows at him. "What *do* you want, kid?"

He looked at me for a second, then turned and leaned his forehead against his window. I should never have put him on the spot like that, but I was feeling frustrated and still more than a little shell-shocked. But if *I* was feeling that way? This kid had not only just lost his father yesterday but his caretaker today. Even someone *without* a traumatic brain injury would have had trouble absorbing all that without turning into a gibbering mess. And all that recent tragedy was piled on top of growing up without his mother.

All he knew was that he was sitting in a crappy Honda on a hot summer day with some woman who may or may not have been partly responsible for all the terrible things that had just happened. It should have been no surprise then, what he said next.

"I want to go home," he mumbled.

His breath misted on the glass, instantly evaporating in the heat. It took me a moment before I could speak. I may have just had a bomb blow up in front of me, but his words hit me with far more force.

"He says—" I began.

"I heard him," Maya said. Her voice was very small, like a sigh into my ear. "What am I supposed to do? If I bring him here, I'm just putting him at risk."

"I know," I said.

"I'm supposed to go hole up in the mountains somewhere? I just—I just can't do that right now. Not after ..."

"I get it," I said.

"You don't sound like you get it. You sound pissed."

"Well, Maya, what do you expect from me? I mean, you know what it's like to be ..."

"To be what?"

I didn't want to go there, but she was right. I *was* pissed. I didn't ask for any of this either, but here I was. I was sorry that Mr. Grim had gotten his hands around her neck, but she was still alive, and I needed her. So did Isaac. "To be alone," I said. "To be all alone. When you came to Seattle—"

"That's not fair," she said.

"When you came to Seattle, you were in a bad situation, and somebody took you under her wing. Helped you out. Otherwise you would have ended up on the street."

"Stop."

"Who was it, Maya? It was a cop, right? That's what you said. What was her name?"

"It's not—It's not the same."

"Who is she? Maybe I should go talk to her. Maybe she'd help me out. Seems like she's the sort who would."

"Now you're being an asshole. And Jo isn't even around here anymore. She's like some sort of small-town police chief on the Oregon coast."

"Jo?"

"Never mind. You're not going to manipulate me here. I'm not stupid. I'm not falling for that."

"I'm not trying to manipulate you."

"Like hell!"

"Look," I said, "I'm sorry about what happened on the ferry. I really am. But you've got to shake that off and get on with things. Seriously. Otherwise it'll sink you. Trust me, I know. I let some stuff from my past sink me, and I'm still trying to get back up for air. Now, are you going to help me out or not?"

"Take Isaac to the police station," Maya said. "That's your only choice here, Karen. It's the only thing that makes sense."

"Fine, forget it. I've got to go. I can't stay in this parking lot any longer."

"Wait. What are you going to do with Isaac?"

I looked at the kid again, who hadn't moved since he'd turned to the window. "Well, I guess he's coming with me."

"You can't be serious," Maya said.

Isaac didn't react, not even a twitch, but he didn't say no

either. I hadn't known what I was going to do until I said the words aloud, but it really was my best option. Right now, there was nobody who could protect him better than me. I was mobile. I was highly motivated to prevent Mr. Grim from finding him. And nobody knew the kind of danger Isaac was in better than I did.

"As long as he's okay with it," I said, "yes, I'm serious."

"Where are you going?" Maya asked.

"You don't seriously expect me to tell you that, do you?"

"Really? You *still* can't trust me?"

"It's not about trust. I just don't want to put you in any more danger. And I was wrong to call you in the first place. I get that now."

"Don't say that. For God's sake, don't say that. Just tell me what you're going to do, Karen. Somebody out here should know. Are you going to hunt down the other people on that list you showed me? Try to protect them or something?"

"Goodbye, Maya."

"Karen, wait, don't—"

I hung up on her.

———

She called back. I let it go to voicemail. She tried again, and I turned off the phone, tossing the damn thing into the chaos behind me. Even this didn't get a reaction from the redheaded boy wonder.

Baking under the glass, sweating through my trench coat, I debated my next move. Where *was* I going? Both of us needed to get cleaned up, and Isaac needed something to wear other than pajamas, but those were immediate concerns, and I needed an overall plan. After the disappointment of Maya's refusal to help me began to fade, I started to feel something else.

Rage.

I hated Mr. Grim. I may have hated him before, but I felt it viscerally now, the anger like an ulcer burning a hole in my stomach. I hated what he'd done to people—Maya, Isaac, Colin Welk, and maybe my mother—but also the thousands of strangers left in his murderous wake, the innocent victims who'd never see another tomorrow simply because they'd had the misfortune to cross paths with a psychopath. Rage could be dangerous. Rage could cloud your judgment, make you impulsive, and cause you to make stupid mistakes when a bit more level-headed consideration could steer you onto a better path.

But rage could also be useful. It could serve as motivating fuel, the kerosene mixed into your blood that could get you moving when frustration, despair, or fear gummed up the engine of your will. I didn't like giving the wheel over to anger, but I sensed that those other three bogeymen, especially frustration, were starting to wear me down. I couldn't let that happen. Mr. Grim may have won this round—as he'd won all the rounds to this point—but that was about to change.

It was Sunday. The beginning of a new week. According to Professor Welk, Mr. Grim would claim another victim in the next seven days. He might claim more, but he would at least claim one, most likely someone selected to fit his pattern. I didn't have Welk's research, but I did have the list he had given me. The next person up was Zhao Chen in Butte, Montana. An eight-hour drive. If we left now, we could be there before midnight.

If Mr. Grim didn't know about the list—and I prayed he didn't—I still had a chance to catch him. Not much of one maybe. Certainly not enough to hang all my hopes on, but it was all I had.

I turned the ignition, bringing my old rust bucket rumbling to life. Isaac finally turned in my direction. His face was as pale and lifeless as concrete, but that only added fuel to the fury burning within me. Mr. Grim had made Isaac this way. And Mr. Grim would pay for it, as he would pay for everything else he had done. Oh, yes, rage could be useful. I just hoped it would be as useful for Isaac as it was for me.

"How would you like to come with me while I catch the guy who killed your father?" I asked.

He barely did more than blink, but there was something in his eyes, a little glimmer of anger, a flash within that concrete mask, that could be a sign that rage could work its handiwork on this kid just like it was doing for me.

That was all the answer I needed. I put the Honda in gear and we headed for Montana.

15

Isaac Welk may have been nineteen years old, an adult in the eyes of the law, but it still felt like I was a parent running off with a child in the middle of a messy custody battle. It wasn't just that he was mentally impaired to the point where he probably couldn't be trusted to make decisions concerning his own welfare or that he was dressed in a skimpy T-shirt and pajama bottoms, like an oversized toddler who'd wandered too far from home. It was because I knew it wouldn't be long before the world was looking for him.

As soon as the Seattle Fire Department determined that Jared Whallen was the only person who'd died in that fiery inferno, people would realize that Isaac Welk was missing. CNN, Fox News, and all the rest would pounce on this thing like wolves on a wounded deer, transforming Isaac Welk from a sympathetic victim to a menacing villain in less time than it took me to squirt Arby's sauce on my roast beef sandwich. And even though it might upset him, I finally decided I had to tell Isaac so.

"I have to be honest," I said, wiping some of said Arby sauce from the corner of my mouth with a paper napkin. "There's a decent chance they're going to think *you* blew up the house."

He paused, mid-bite, and looked at me over the top of the wrapper. He'd pushed his hair behind his ears, so I could at least see his eyes. Not that I saw much reaction there. It was like looking at a pair of dull green marbles.

While he was staring at me, he managed to drip some Arby's sauce on the Miami Dolphins T-shirt I'd given him, a brand new one that had still been wrapped in plastic when I'd fished it out of Hoarders Central in the back of the Honda. It wouldn't have bothered me except that the stain looked like blood, and actual bloodstains were why we'd tossed his tank top in the gas station restroom just down the road. He'd at least replaced the bandage on his neck with a fresh one as well as cleaned up the minor cuts on his cheek, but he still looked too conspicuous to take out in public even *before* his face inevitably got plastered all over the news. After that happened, I wasn't sure what I was going to do.

I fished another napkin out of the bag and handed it to him. "See what you can do about that," I said, nodding toward the stain. "Don't wipe. Just lay it on the stain, very lightly, barely touching the shirt, so the napkin absorbs most of the liquid instead of spreading it. A little trick I learned from working at a dry cleaners."

He looked down at his shirt. Even though it was closer to eighty degrees in Ellensburg than the ninety it was in Seattle, and even though both our windows were rolled down, letting in a breeze that smelled of sage and dirt, it was starting to heat up in our little tin box on wheels. Behind Isaac, the red-and-white CASINO sign, mounted on a pole fifty feet high, loomed over the mostly empty parking lot.

Three o'clock on a Sunday, I didn't really think the Wild Goose Casino would be bursting with cars, but I expected more than a Dodge Dakota hauling a trailer full of ATVs, a red Subaru Impreza with GORE FOR PRESIDENT bumper sticker, and, weirdly, a rusted-out school bus parked at the back, where the parking lot abutted a field of scrub bush and the occasional oak stretching to the sandy brown foothills of the Cascade Range. Even though this little casino was just a two-minute drive from I-90, it still felt like a long way from anywhere—which was why I'd decided to eat our lunch there. Or dinner? At three o'clock, it could really go either way.

The whole time I was thinking this, Isaac went on staring intensely at his shirt. Was he pondering that stain or mulling what I'd said about people thinking he'd burned down his own house? Both? Neither? The kid was a cipher. He'd barely said a word on the hour-and-a-half-drive from Seattle.

"Isaac?" I said. "Did you hear me?"

He finally looked at me, roast beef in one hand, napkin in the other, but he didn't say anything. He didn't make a move to clean up the mess on his shirt either. A seventies-era Oldsmobile, a blue one with a copper-colored hood, rolled into the lot and parked near the school bus. Inside the Oldsmobile, two teenage boys lit up cigarettes, ignoring us. I was about to take another bite of roast beef when Isaac burst into tears.

"Oh shit," I said.

There was no warning. No building up to it. One second his face was as placid as a mannequin's; the next he was engaging in what my sister Hope called a good old-fashioned ugly cry.

"I'm s-s-sorry," he sputtered.

"Don't worry about it."

"I'm so sorry. I suck. I suck so much."

"Hey, hey, now—"

"I'm such a fucking klutz. I ruined your shirt. I'm s-s-sorry."

"Hey, man, it's all right, " I said. "Really. Hey, hey, take it easy now, really. It was just a T-shirt that some dude who was hitting on me gave to me. This pro football player in Miami. I didn't care for it all that much. Or this guy. He was a real jerk. It was why it was still in the plastic. Figured I'd use it as a paint shirt someday maybe. You know, while I was repainting a house. If I ever own a house. Probably not likely, at this point. Or give it away at Christmas to somebody I don't like. Hey, Isaac. Really, it's okay. There's—there's a box of tissues in the glove box. If you need them."

I was babbling. It was often what I did when people cried in my presence. I wasn't a crier myself. Other than tearing up when Bev told me about Mom, I couldn't remember the last time I'd cried. Maybe when Dad died, and how long ago was that? Five years? Six? I didn't remember crying when we spread his ashes near Cape Canaveral, as he'd requested, but it felt as if I had. I should have cried anyway. Hope certainly did. She'd cried the whole drive from Atlanta, and I didn't blame her, not at all. He'd confessed to us on his deathbed that he'd tried repeatedly to get into the NASA program, his career as an Air Force pilot only meant to be a stepping stone to fulfilling his dream of becoming an astronaut. Never happened for him.

He hadn't cried about it, though. Or about anything else. Not once. Not ever. Not even when he was dying of cancer and there was nothing we could do to save him.

Isaac's ugly cry went on for so long that I wanted to crawl out of my skin. I'd dealt with a difficult, taciturn teenager a couple years ago, a girl who'd jumped out of the back of a van in Denver fleeing something horrible, but Isaac was different. More unpredictable. More volcanic. I glanced at the teenagers in the Oldsmobile and saw that they were staring at us, plumes of smoke billowing out of their cracked-open windows.

Great. Suspicious eyes on us was all we needed right now. I started to reach for the glove box, partly to get the tissues, partly to just give myself something to do, when Isaac spoke.

"What position?" he asked.

Just like that, the crying stopped. His hair had fallen partly in front of his eyes, blocking one of them from view, but the other was bloodshot, the skin around it puffy and swollen. Otherwise, though, he might have just stepped off the bus from school, tired, bored, but earnestly looking forward to whatever I might say.

"Excuse me?" I said.

"His position," he said. "The football player. What position did he play?"

"Oh. I don't know. He was a big dude. A linebacker, probably. He came into this bar in Miami I used to—"

"When was this?"

"Huh?"

"When did he give you the T-shirt?"

"Oh … I guess it was, what, three months ago? It wasn't long before I came to Orcas. Isaac, are you sure you're—"

"Was he black?"

"Black? No. What does that have to do with—"

"Was he a blond guy with long hair, kind of curly? Six foot four? Two hundred and forty-three pounds? Had a tattoo of an alligator on his neck?"

I blinked at him. "How did you know that?"

"His name is Vince Schumacher. He's the only white line-backer that played for the Miami Dolphins last year. Third year. Picked in the fifth round, out of Wisconsin, where he was third-team All-Big Ten. He had two sacks and an interception just last year. Good player."

"Wow," I said, "you're a real fountain of knowledge about … What was his name?"

"Vince Schumacher."

"Right, good old Vince. Tried to squeeze my … Well, never mind. He didn't do it again after I twisted his arm behind his back and put him on the ground. He was a good sport about it, though. He actually gave me that T-shirt *after* I did that to him. Are you a huge Miami Dolphins fan?"

Isaac shrugged. I could already see the light going out of his eyes. I didn't want to lose him.

"Or just football in general?" I said.

"Just football," he said, his voice getting softer. "American foot-ball. Not soccer."

"And you remember everything about the game, huh?"

Another shrug. This time he turned and gazed out his passenger side window.

"Do you have a photographic memory?"

"No."

"Do you remember things about other sports or—"

"Just football," he said even more quietly.

"I see." I remembered the posters in Professor Welk's office. "Was your dad a Seattle Seahawks fan?"

"Yeah."

"Did you guys used to go to any games? Or watch them together on TV?"

He shrugged again. He wasn't crying, so that was good, but I was losing my connection. It was like listening to a radio signal fade into static. He'd said more to me in this one conversation than he'd said in the past two hours. I didn't want him to climb back into his shell. Other than trying to get all the way to Butte rather than stop somewhere along the way—we still had more than seven hours of driving to go—I didn't have plans about what to do when we got there other than to find Chen and protect him, covertly if possible. Since I'd failed to get into Welk's safe, I wondered if Isaac knew things that might help me. Even if Welk hadn't confided in him about Mr. Grim, the kid obviously noticed things, maybe more than his father was aware.

"I'm really sorry about what happened," I said.

He shrugged.

"If you want to talk about it—"

"No!"

In the enclosed Honda, his *no* was like a hammer hitting a nail. He hadn't even looked at me, nor did he do so now.

"No problem," I said. "We don't have to go there. But we can, you know, if you want to. Just saying."

He was so close to the window that each breath formed a white ring that quickly faded. So talking about his feelings was out. Okay then. Football might be different, though, a gateway to talk about other things. Unfortunately, while I was familiar enough with the game to understand it, even enjoy it a little if it was on TV when I walked into a room, I was no expert. I knew the last couple NFL champions and might be able to name an MVP or two from the last decade, but that was as far as my knowledge of American football went. For all sports, really. I'd played Boys & Girls Club basketball in the summers through elementary school because Dad made me do *something* other than ride my bike all over town, plus I'd run a couple years of track in high school, mostly to meet boys because at least track was coed, but sports weren't really my thing.

Still, as we cruised back onto I-90, into the vast swaths of semi-arid steppe desert east of the Cascades, I gamely did my best. I asked Isaac what his favorite position was. I told him I was partial to the kicker because it was the one position I could imagine myself playing—coming in at the end to save the day, destined to be the hero or the goat. I never minded the pressure. I thrived on it. It was all the team player stuff I hated.

I talked and talked. The problem was, he didn't talk back. Not a word. I asked him about the last time he'd watched a game. I asked him who he thought would win the Superbowl, whether the league should expand, and if he'd played himself. Nada. He leaned his head against the window, jostling when we passed over a divot or when I gunned it to pass an RV, but otherwise he could have been asleep. I knew he wasn't, because I could just make out his blinking eyelashes, but he didn't make a sound.

The road hum beneath our feet was our constant companion. I cracked open my window; even the smell of dry dirt and diesel exhaust was a relief from the kid's locker room stench. Plus the wind noise was at least *something* to listen to other than my own voice. We passed over Wanapum Lake. I ran out of things to say about football around the thriving metropolis of George, population 823, according to the sign. The city's name, when I connected it to the state we were now in, drew a chuckle out of me.

"George, Washington," I said. "I guess they were huge fans of our first president, huh? Living in a state named after him wasn't enough. They had to name their city after him too."

I looked at him. Not even a flicker. Still, I talked on, hoping *something* would pique his interest. I talked about the stupid stuff Hope and I got into back in Tucson. I talked about growing up as an Air Force brat. I told him stories about my old partner, getting myself to laugh about how Ben would drink his cappuccinos— never straight coffee, it always had to be a cappuccino, an espresso, or, as a last resort, an Americano—with his pinky finger extended like some sort of British aristocrat.

Nothing got Isaac to so much as twitch. I probably would have given up, but there was something about the emptiness outside, full of grassy hills already browning under the relentless sun, that kept me talking. It was like I was trying to fill the emptiness with my voice. Except for the electrical poles poking out of the parched earth like the spiked back of a buried beast, and the very occasional ranch house on a lonely hill, we were passing through an empty void.

The car's shadow stretched ahead of us on the blacktop, growing longer as the sun moved behind us. The void was broken up briefly around Moses Lake, which adjoined a decent-sized city of the same name, but then it was back to brown nothingness. An hour passed. Then another. I finally lapsed into silence. I think I might have muttered something like "You win, kid, you'll have to give me pointers on how to give somebody the silent treatment," but I might have imagined it. I tried to think of another way to reach him. I came up empty. Maybe empty was better. We were in a land of emptiness, after all, so we might as well be empty inside too.

We were closing in on Spokane, and I was reaching for the radio dial to catch some local news, when Isaac spoke.

"I count to ten," he said. "That's how I win. I count to ten."

At first, I thought it was a non sequitur, maybe something about counting cars, the ponderosa pines, or even the overpasses, all of which had gotten more numerous on either side of I-90 as we descended toward the city in the distance. Then I realized that he was actually responding to what I'd said earlier, as if the ensuing minutes never happened.

"Oh, the silent treatment," I said. "Right. That's how you win. Do you count your breaths or … ?"

"No," he said, "I just count. I learned it when I was little, at Montessori school. To be quiet, we were supposed to count to ten."

"Ah."

"It helped kids calm down. It worked really well."

"I see."

"You asked for pointers," he said. "That's how I do it. It probably would have worked when your sister would get really upset. Like that time she lost one of her rollerblades. Just count to ten."

I realized a couple things then. The first was that Isaac obviously existed in his own time continuum, moving at his own pace, no matter what the world did. The second was that even when I didn't think he'd heard me, he probably had; otherwise he never would have commented about Hope's rollerblades. That was one anecdote in a stream of anecdotes.

However, the most important insight I gleaned from his comment had nothing to do with his actual advice, not exactly, but that he'd noted I'd asked for pointers.

He was trying to be helpful.

Of course. *That* was why he'd identified the NFL player who'd given me that T-shirt. It wasn't to impress me. It was also why he was telling me to count to ten. I'd asked for pointers on how to keep quiet, and he'd interpreted that to mean I needed help controlling my emotional outbursts, just as he did, so he'd offered up a strategy that worked for him.

"So when you and your dad used to watch football together," I said, "did he sometimes ask you questions about, you know, certain players?"

"Sure," he said.

"Like their stats and that sort of thing?"

He nodded.

"And you always knew the answers?" I said.

"Not always."

"But most of the time?"

Another nod.

He was still with me. He hadn't pulled his turtle act and retreated into his shell even though the conversation had veered back toward what was obviously an emotionally fraught subject. I pondered this as we made our way into the thick of Spokane, bumper to bumper. The five-o'clock traffic was nothing compared to Seattle's, but it was still annoying.

"Look," I said, "I really need your advice. I'm not sure if we should stop for dinner in Idaho or if we should push on to Montana. We've got almost five hours of driving ahead of us, and I really think we need to get to Butte tonight. I'll need to fuel up at some point, so I figured we'd just double up then, you know? Fuel the car, fuel us." I chuckled. "What do you think?

He shrugged. His hair had fallen in front of his eyes again, so I couldn't read them.

"So push on then?" I asked.

He turned to the window. Why would he give me advice before but not now? I thought about this as we slowed amid a symphony of brake lights in three lanes. The sun, low in the west, glared in my rearview mirror. A white Toyota Sienna crept past us in the right lane. A man in a blue jersey and baseball cap was talking to three boys behind him, all wearing similar jerseys. Isaac perked up.

When the sun shifted, I saw that there was a woman in the passenger seat, also wearing one of the jerseys. Big red curly hair. Like Isaac's hair. Was that why he'd perked up? There was a goofy white doodle in the backseat. White van. White dog. Look how picture-perfect they were. They even had one of those bumper stickers with the stick figure family: Mom, Dad, three boys, a dog. On the other side of the bumper, they also had a Gonzaga University Faculty/Staff parking permit.

Somebody in the van must have said something funny because the boys were all laughing. I felt sad and lonely, seeing them laugh, and then I felt bad for feeling that way. A happy family shouldn't provoke that kind of reaction from me, but it did. I'd never been part of a family like that. Neither had Isaac, for that matter.

The van moved ahead. Then we were back in the lead. Again and again, we swapped places, and I kept hoping that they'd take the next exit or the next, but no, this laughing, smiling, lucky, yes, oh so lucky, perfect family seemed destined to torture us with their utter perfectness forever. Finally they veered off, thank God. Off to the big game, with metal bleachers, juice packs, and even more perfect kids and even more perfect parents who would all revel in their perfect lives. They'd preach effort and sportsmanship and teamwork ...

Teamwork.

That word was enough to jolt me out of my caustic inner monologue. Even when I'd been in the FBI, I'd never been much of a team player. At first, I hadn't even liked having a partner, but I'd gotten lucky with Ben. I missed him. We'd worked well together. He'd balanced out my headstrong nature with a more measured approach. I felt that loss acutely now, feeling overmatched against a foe playing me like a puppet.

I didn't have Ben, but I did have Isaac. I looked at him, this gangly kid with a mop of red hair who'd lost everything and everyone who'd been important to him. Given the magnitude of his loss, it seemed unfair to ask much of him. I didn't like asking for help. It made me feel weak. Yet I sensed that if I wasn't absolutely genuine, Isaac would see right through me.

I'd asked him if he'd wanted to come with me while I tried to catch the guy who'd killed his father. What I hadn't asked for was his help. Not really.

"Isaac," I said.

He didn't move. We were crossing a bridge over the Spokane River, all the tan and brick buildings lined up along the banks like a little city that wanted to be more than it was. I felt a kinship with it. I was trying to be more than I was too.

"Look," I said, "I really could use your advice with ... catching this guy. Mr. Grim. I know it's not fair to put you in this situation, given ... given what you've just—you know, with your dad. I'm sorry about that. I am." My face felt warm. My throat was tight. This was even harder than I thought it would be. "But I do need your advice. I really do."

Isaac straightened his back. He still wasn't looking at me, but I had his attention. I hadn't gone all in, though, and he knew it. It was one thing to ask where to stop for dinner. It was another to ask for help catching a serial killer. It wasn't just the asking either.

It was the *why.* I had to be nakedly honest in a way I almost never was. It was the only way Isaac would know I meant it.

"Look," I said, "Isaac ... I'm saying ... Look, I'm ... Man, I'm saying 'look' a lot, aren't I? Geez, I'm making a mess of this whole thing. What I'm saying is ... What I'm saying ..."

He finally looked at me, a glimmer of green through a tapestry of red. Getting his attention was what I'd wanted, but it didn't make it any easier to say what was on my mind. In the end, I just forced it out.

"He scares me," I said.

Isaac blinked, but that was it. I pushed on anyway.

"I don't scare easily, you know?" I said. "Yeah, yeah, that sounds all macho, but it's true. I've never scared easily. And I've faced down some seriously depraved people. Deviants with no sense of right or wrong. You can't even call them animals because I've never seen an animal that kills just because."

Isaac leaned toward me. It was almost imperceptible, but it was there.

"Your dad," I said, "he didn't deserve to die like that. Nobody does. And we have to catch this guy. We *have* to, you know? But I'm like ... I don't know. I'm scared. How else can I put it? It's hard for me to say, but I am. It's like he's one step ahead of me. It's like he's manipulating me, playing me for a fool, and I can't stand that. I hate ... feeling powerless. And I guess the thing that we hate most is also what scares us the most, right? I guess that's it. And here's the thing, Isaac. Here's the thing. I don't know if I can do this alone. I need your help. I really do. Your dad—he talked about how this Mr. Grim just killed random people, but it doesn't feel that way now. It feels like this is an elaborate game, just for me. And if more people die, it's my fault. *My* fault. Can you help me? Can you help me catch him?"

Isaac kept looking at me. This time, I decided to wait him out. We raced toward the Idaho border, the city of Spokane shrinking in my rearview mirror.

"Okay," he said.

"Okay?"

He nodded.

"You'll help me?"

"Yeah."

"Great," I said. "Well, then. Let's, um, let's start by——"

"Tell me everything," he said. "Tell me everything you know and maybe I can help."

———

THAT ACTUALLY TURNED out to be the easy part. I thought it would be hard, talking about the serial killer who'd killed his father, but Isaac was hungry for information. Maybe it was a way to distract himself from his own sorrow, or maybe it was because deep down he'd always known there had to be an explanation for why he'd suffered so much tragedy.

I talked as we crossed Idaho's panhandle, rising to five thousand feet above sea level. Firs, pines, and spruces clung to the steep hillsides on the other side of the concrete barrier as we moved through Montana's Bitteroot Range. We passed the Lookout Pass Ski Recreation Area. No snow this time of year. Not even a hint.

The sun perched like a gold coin on the mountains behind us, and the light was already fading. Our gas gauge was ticking just above empty. When I pulled into the Conoco station in Superior, Isaac was looking at me intently, but he hadn't said a word.

"Well?" I said, killing the engine. "Any advice yet? Any reason why I'm feeling the way I do? You know, that he's got it out for me? Am I just ... crazy?"

He didn't answer. I wondered if this was all for nothing. Even if he hadn't been aware of what had been in his father's safe, I'd hoped it would jostle loose a memory, something his father had said or did that would give us a clue. Oh well. I would have liked to say that talking through everything again made me feel better, a little cheap therapy, but it hadn't.

I was reaching for the door handle when he spoke.

"Maybe he's scared too," he said.

16

Fifteen minutes later, we slouched in a vinyl booth at Rough Rider Bar & Grill across the street from the Conoco, both of us munching on badly charred cheeseburgers.

The burgers were lathered up with so much tangy barbecue sauce that I could barely taste the meat anyway. It was food. It would do. The light through the blinds was a dusky mix of purple and orange. According to the buffalo clock above the saloon doors, it was 9:25 p.m. It had taken five hours to get here from Ellensburg, but we'd also lost an hour when we'd crossed into the Mountain Time Zone.

It was a tiny town, so small that the market attached to the Conoco probably doubled as the grocery store. Manufactured homes were mixed with single-story ranches. Twenty-year-old cars baked in the weeds. Not many sidewalks. Only a few cars were parked in front of the Big Sky Motel down the street. It would have been a decent place to hunker down for the night, but we still had miles to go before we reached Butte, and I didn't want to give Mr. Grim any more of an edge than he already had.

Plus I had another problem. So far, I'd been buying fuel, food, and other things with my spare cash—mostly tip money from the

Orcadia—but that was almost gone, which left me with the 167 dollars in my checking account. Even if I'd wanted to stay the night, I couldn't afford it. I had no idea what I'd do when the money ran out. I drew the line at bank robbery, but only slightly less appealing was the prospect of asking someone to loan me money. Maybe I could settle for petty theft?

Plus I didn't want to use my bank card anyway. I didn't want to do anything that could potentially tip off Mr. Grim where I was.

While I chewed on my grizzled burger, I thought about what Isaac had said, that Mr. Grim was scared. When I'd asked him to elaborate back at the gas station, he'd only shrugged. Typical. I'd figured Mr. Grim for pissed, of course—pissed that Colin Welk, aided by his extraordinary power of computational analysis, was onto him. Pissed that Welk had roped me into helping. Pissed that he wasn't being left to his own devices, free to hunt and kill with abandon.

But scared? Ben used to say that anger was just fear by another name because people who were scared inside were the ones most likely to lash out, but I never quite agreed with him. Fear may have been anger's second cousin, but it was its own thing. Fear made a person weak. Anger made a person strong. It was not something people liked to admit, but it was true. Anger also tended to make people reckless and fear cautious, less likely to give into their rashest impulses, but there was no question that anger could be a powerful motivating force.

It certainly was for me right now.

And Mr. Grim, from what I knew of him so far, had not struck me as a particularly fearful person. Fearful people did not methodically hunt and kill over a thousand people over thirty years. And right now? He was certainly not being cautious, trying to strangle Maya on the ferry in front of all those witnesses. That was reckless to the extreme, which made me think he was angry, very angry, so angry he was finally losing his control.

That could work to my advantage—if I could figure out how to lay a trap for him in Butte.

After wiping barbecue sauce off my face, I said as much to Isaac. We were in a back booth, far from other people, but I still kept my voice low. Isaac paused with the burger inches from his mouth, a strand of onion sliding out and landing on his curly fries.

"Maybe he's angry too," he said, "but I think he's mostly scared. Scared people can also do stupid stuff."

I cringed at how loud he was even if I was glad he was talking. "It's not going to help if other people overhear us, okay?"

He shrugged, but the next time he talked he was quieter. The orange Budweiser sign in the window tinted his hair with a neon sheen. He was still wearing pajama bottoms, but so were a couple of teenage girls going into the gas station market across the street, so apparently it could also be a fashion choice. That made me feel old. My dad never would have let me leave the house in pajama bottoms. Two Harleys roared out of the parking lot, both of the riders sporting American flags on the backs of their leather jackets. Beyond the saloon doors, Elton John was singing about a candle in the wind.

"But scared of what exactly?" I asked. "Of getting caught? If things had gone just a little differently on the ferry, I probably *would* have caught him."

Isaac shrugged. "Maybe he's not scared of getting caught, or at least not that that much anymore. Maybe he's scared of something else."

"Like what?"

He shrugged and took another bite of his burger. A waitress was busing a booth across the room, so I leaned forward, lowering my voice even more.

"He's obviously not scared of *me*," I said. "If he was scared of me, he could have put a bomb on my car instead of a GPS tracker. He's proven he knows his way around explosives." I realized, when I said this, that it could come off as particularly callous, so I rushed ahead. "That's why I feel like he's playing with me. He could have killed me back in Orcadia, but he didn't. Why?"

Another shrug. He'd finished his burger and was starting on

his fries. He slathered so much ketchup on them that I doubted he could even taste the fries themselves. He'd started to retreat behind his curtain of hair again, and I wondered if it was because he was thinking about his father. Or Jared. His life in Seattle. Maybe I was pushing him too much.

"We don't have to talk about this stuff right now, you know," I said. "We can talk about something else."

"No, it's okay. I want to help. I just ... didn't want to make you upset."

"Make *me* upset? How?"

"I don't think he's scared of you."

"Oh."

He talked more hurriedly. "Like, I think I'm a pretty good Magic player, you know, so I don't like it when people say I'm not very good. I don't usually win tournaments, but I usually come in second or third. You seem ... pretty tough. Like, you know, maybe you could be in an action movie. So I didn't want you to think I thought you were ... you know, weak ass or something."

"Magic?" I asked. "You mean, like card tricks?"

"No, it's a game. A card game. Magic the Gathering."

"Oh, *that* card game."

"Yeah, it's fun."

"So I've heard." I grinned. "Weak ass. Okay."

"You're not, though. Weak ass."

"I get it. I'm not offended."

"I'm kinda weak ass, and I know it. You're not."

"No, Isaac, you're not—"

"But you could be like, Dwayne Johnson, and maybe he *still* wouldn't be scared of you, you know. That's all I'm saying. If he was scared in the usual way, he never would have killed all those people."

"Shh. Yeah, that's my point. He's mad, maybe, but not—"

"No," Isaac said, "I mean he's not scared in the *usual* way."

I munched on a french fry, enjoying its salty, ketchup-free taste, as I pondered this. "The usual way," I repeated.

"Yeah. Like, you know … afraid of the dark, afraid of spiders, afraid of dying. You know, the usual."

"Right. So what's *not* the usual way?"

He shrugged.

"Afraid of aliens from space?" I asked. "Zombies trying to eat our brains?"

"Nah. That's just made-up stuff."

"Okay, what then?"

He munched on his french fries, saying nothing. Maybe Isaac didn't know exactly what he meant, but I thought he was onto something. I wasn't really scared of the usual things either. Death. Taxes. Dating. Maybe dating, just a little. I'd already admitted that Mr. Grim scared me, but I'd also admitted that that was because I didn't like feeling powerless. I knew where that fear came from too. It came from watching Mom on one of her bipolar tornadoes, hyped up and talking a mile a minute, painting psychedelic murals on our living room walls, or cutting the sleeves off all her shirts because she'd suddenly decided that sleeves were choking her creative spirit—watching all this and waiting for the inevitable crash, the screaming, the dishes thrown against the wall, and knowing there was absolutely nothing I could do to stop it.

I wondered if Mr. Grim wasn't so different from me in that regard. Not afraid of being powerless, maybe, but something similar.

"Maybe he's … afraid of losing control?" I said. "Like he's, I don't know, afraid somebody might mess up his great masterpiece? I told you he's weirdly spelling the word 'God' on a map with each victim."

Isaac swallowed his last french fry, then pushed his plate away. He looked at me, eyes invisible behind those tangled bangs but definitely looking at me, and I waited, expecting him to say something. He didn't. I worried again that I was making a mistake bringing him along. It was true that helping me was distracting him from what he'd just been through, but that was a short-term fix. He'd have to face his trauma sooner or later.

"Look," I said, "I want you to know something. I appreciate

your help. I do. But you don't have to come with me. It could be dangerous, and if that scares you—"

"Can I have a milkshake?"

I don't know what I expected him to say, but that wasn't it.

"Excuse me?"

"A milkshake. Can I have a milkshake?"

"Oh, sure. When the waitress comes back, I'll—"

"A chocolate one."

"Sure. She's over there with another customer, but I'll flag her down. Like I was saying, though, I want you to know that if you're worried at all about coming with me on this—"

"Not strawberry," he said. "I hate strawberry."

"Okay, that's fine."

"I *really* hate it. Vanilla is a little better, but I like chocolate best."

"Okay, Isaac, I get it." I signaled to the waitress, who was heading back to the kitchen, and she changed course. "Look, she's coming now. One chocolate milkshake coming right—"

He burst into tears.

———

IT WAS QUITE A SCENE, not just a few tears but as if the water mane had burst and the whole town was flooding. I told him it was no problem, we'd get him a milkshake, two if he really wanted them, but I'm not sure he heard me over the howling. I tried to console him, tried to ask him what was wrong, tried to offer him a wad of napkins, but the crying only got louder.

When nothing would get Isaac to stop—he was starting to hyperventilate, clutching at his throat—I got up and barked that we needed to leave. *Now.*

I didn't know if this would work, but it did. He left willingly, though he continued to cry. People stared. We didn't need this. We didn't need this at all. I dropped some bills on the table for our check and ushered him to the Honda, then peeled out of the parking lot before a cop could show up and start asking questions.

We hadn't been back on I-90 for more than thirty seconds, roaring east toward the Rocky Mountains in the purple twilight, when Isaac flipped his emotional switch again. Just like that, all the waterworks stopped, and he was back to his usual routine, staring out the window.

The silence was so abrupt that I found it as shocking as the original outburst.

"What was *that* about?" I asked.

His shoulders moved up and down in a subtle shrug. I clenched the steering wheel, trying to stay calm, but I was having a really hard time of it. Across the grassy median, a semi barreled past, pushing a wall of air that shook the Honda. The truck's headlights gave Isaac's face—what I could see of it anyway—a ghostly pallor.

"Talk to me, Isaac," I said. "Tell me what upset you."

Still no answer. I tapped the steering wheel, debating. Trying to catch Mr. Grim was going to be hard enough without worrying that there was a stick of dynamite in the passenger seat that might explode at any moment. Ten minutes later, I took the exit for the Quartz Flats Rest Area.

"What are you doing?" he asked,

"Stopping."

"Why?"

Now it was my turn to give him the silent treatment. In the last gasp of twilight, I took a spot far from other vehicles, closer to one of the covered picnic areas than the restroom building in the center. If he was going to have another outburst, I wanted him to be as far from everyone as I could.

Not that many people were around. A few semis, U-Haul trucks, and RVs were in the bigger spots, but only a handful of cars were parked near the restroom building and the covered picnic areas. Ponderosa pines towered over well-trimmed grass. The streetlamps were already aglow. I got out of the car, slammed the door behind me, and headed for the restroom. We needed to have a talk, but I couldn't do it yet.

Over the pulse of interstate traffic, I could just make out

some chirping crickets. The thin, crisp air smelled like freshly cut grass. When I was about to round the corner of the brick building, I glanced back at Isaac. It was only meant to be a glance, just to make sure he was still in the Honda, but I froze. Half his body was cast in shadow from the streetlamp, the other half hazy and indistinct, but there was still no mistaking his expression.

Utter terror.

The fear was so palpable that at first I assumed somebody lurked behind me. I whirled around, but there was no one there. I trotted back to the Honda. The glare from the streetlamp on the windshield hid his face momentarily, so I was a little surprised when I opened the driver side door and found that whatever I'd seen on his face was gone. Mr. Blank had returned.

"Are you okay?" I asked.

He didn't answer. He didn't look at me either. Was I losing my mind? I slipped into the driver seat and closed the door. I couldn't see his eyes, but now that I was looking at him more closely, I saw that his hair was … vibrating. He was trembling. So I *hadn't* imagined it.

"What is it, Isaac? What's got you so scared?"

"I'm not scared."

"When I looked at you a second ago—"

"I'm not scared," he insisted.

I decided not to push him on the fear thing, but I couldn't completely let it go either. Too much was at risk. "Look," I said, "we're going to be in Butte in a couple hours. When we get there, I'm going to find a way to do a sort of stakeout—watch Zhao Chen *very* closely. If your dad was right about who Mr. Grim's next victims are—"

"He was right," Isaac said. "Dad was never wrong."

"Okay, well, it's all on us, see? We can't go to the cops. They'll just think we're crazy, and it will tip off Mr. Grim that we're onto him. And if we tell Mr. Chen? He'll probably think we're nuts too. Even if he doesn't, he'll probably act differently, get all paranoid and tip off Mr. Grim that way."

Isaac stared out the window. Was he even listening? I reminded myself to double down on the helping thing.

"I can't do this without you," I said. "I can't watch him all the time. I've got to sleep too. That's where you come in. You'll have to watch him some of the time too."

He glanced at me, then looked at the empty grass outside. It was only a glance, but it was encouraging.

"We're definitely putting Chen at risk," I continued, "but I don't see any way around it. We have to use him a little like … bait. The good of the many, you know? I hate to admit it, but your dad was kind of right about that—to a point, anyway. I will save Chen over catching Mr. Grim if it comes to that, but weighing Mr. Chen's safety against all those possible future victims? It's a risk we have to take."

"What if Mr. Grim already knows?" Isaac asked. "I mean, what if he already knows you have this list?"

Isaac still didn't look at me, but his hair wasn't vibrating anymore. This was good. He was talking, not focusing on whatever had gotten him so rattled. "Then unless Mr. Grim is a really stubborn SOB," I said, "Mr. Chen is probably fine. But it will also mean we're screwed. He'll change who he's going after, and we'll have to find some other way to catch him. But if he *hasn't* figured out we have this list, then this is our best shot at stopping him, right?"

Isaac replied with the faintest of nods.

"Good," I said. "Because here's the deal. I'm going to level with you. I know you want to help, I get that, but I *have* to be able to count on you. We can't have any more outbursts like what happened at the restaurant. Chen's life is going to be at risk. Our lives will be at risk. And all the people Mr. Grim might kill in the future—*their* lives are at risk too. No more making a scene, you get me?"

It was back to radio silence. Not even a blink. I was about to speak again when he piped up.

"Okay," he said.

"Okay?"

"Yeah. I won't … make a scene. But let's go."

"I can count on you?"

He nodded. It wasn't much, but it would have to do. Whatever his fear was, it was too big for him to talk about. I just hoped it wouldn't blow up in our faces later.

17

Monday. Technically, anyway. While the dashboard clock read 12:01 a.m. as I turned onto Alabama Street, a few blocks from Montana State Technical University, it didn't feel like Monday. It didn't even feel like Sunday. It still felt like Saturday, as if it had been one long continuous day since I'd walked into room 1109 at the Orcadia and found Colin Welk in his wheelchair, waiting for me.

A lot had happened in that forty-hour period. Welk murdered. Maya barely surviving Mr. Grim herself. A house exploding, with Jared Whallen claimed as another victim. Seven hundred and fifty miles put on my Honda, the bulk of it spent with the nineteen-year-old enigma sitting next to me. Despite all that, I felt wired and wide-awake.

The kid next to me was another matter. He'd fallen asleep immediately after we pulled out of Quartz Flats Rest Area. He didn't stir for the next two and a half hours, the passing headlights lighting up his face through his veil of hair. He kept on sleeping as I cruised into the neighborhood where Chen lived, the streetlamps revealing an old street wide enough for cars to park on both sides, telephone wires drooping over cracked asphalt, and a towering trapezoidal metal structure at the end of the road lit up from below like a rocket tower. I learned later that this was the defunct Anselmo Mine.

A pothole finally jostled him awake. "Hmph?" he said. "Wha —What's happening ..."

I steadied him with a hand on his shoulder. "It's okay. We're in Butte, that's all. See that green house up there, the one with the porch and the little wrought iron fence?"

Wiping slobber off his chin, he blinked out into the darkness. As wide as the street was, the houses were still packed in as tightly together as railroad cars. A rare few, boxy and plain, even looked like railroad cars, but the majority were actually quite nice, restored Victorian, craftsman, and turn-of-the century homes, some obviously occupied by a single owner, others turned into multi-unit dwellings by the looks of the doors and mailboxes. It was an odd mix, to be sure, but somehow it all worked.

If it weren't for how few trees there were, the street could have been plucked from Seattle's Fremont area. The biggest difference were the cars—more trucks than mid-sized SUVs, though even there it was just a matter of degree. I even passed a Prius. Only one, though. In Seattle, they were everywhere.

"That's where Zhao Chen lives," I said. "We're going to do a drive-by first. I don't think Mr. Grim could have gotten here before us, but if he did, well, we're going to chance it. Just keep your eyes peeled, okay?"

"What do I look for?"

"Anything. Signs of life. Signs things are off. Hell, they could be on vacation for all we know."

Isaac chewed on his bottom lip. A decrepit Dodge Dakota passed in front of us on the cross street, but otherwise the neighborhood was still. The house mostly matched what I'd seen on Google Earth—a glorified cottage with a gabled roof, a covered porch with decorative lattice, and a painted brick punch-out with arched windows on all three sides—but there were differences too. A wheelchair ramp had been added next to the wooden steps. And the patch of grass, which had looked lush and green online, was now festooned with weeds that reached nearly as high as the wrought iron fence.

The porch light was on, a brass lantern that mimicked the flickering pulse of a candle, but all the windows were dark. The curtains were drawn. A white Honda Odyssey was parked in the narrow alley to the right of the house—it was the kind of neighborhood that was full of narrow alleys—and the van's side door was very low to the ground. Outfitted for a wheelchair, most likely.

Something cold slid into the pit of my stomach. Was I too late? Had Mr. Grim crippled Chen like he'd crippled Welk? Yet if that was the case, it was something that had happened months ago—years, maybe, judging by the weathered, gray railing next to the wheelchair ramp. An orange tabby scampered out from under the porch and darted under the van, but otherwise all was still.

"See anything?" I asked Isaac. "Other than that cat?"

He shook his head.

"Okay," I said. "We'll circle around and park a few houses up the street. I'm going to get out and ring his doorbell. See if we can get him to come to the door."

"I thought you weren't going to tell him what's going on?"

"I'm not. I'm going to walk up a block and hide behind that old trailer, the one with all the brush in it. I'll be able to see the alley and his front porch—most of it, anyway. You'll be able to see the rest."

"I want to go with you," Isaac said.

"No, I need you to watch from the car. You'll see the windows on the other side of the house. Even if he doesn't open the door, hopefully he'll at least peer out one of the windows. Remember: Chinese guy, short black hair, probably five foot eight, thick glasses —that's who we're looking for, but I'm interested in anyone in that house. I'm counting on you, okay? No matter what happens, stay put. If he comes out of his house, make sure you duck low so he can't see you."

Circling around, I heard a police siren a few blocks over, and I tensed, but the sound receded from us. When I finally parked in front of a brick four-plex, killing the engine, the street was just as still as before. There wasn't even a cat this time.

I got out and started walking. The night was warm but dry, the air wicking away the sweat on my arms. It smelled like grass, dusty earth, and something faintly metallic, maybe from all the truck beds that had baked under the sun all day. I passed next to a buzzing electrical transformer and around an orange barricade where the city had dug up a section of concrete, making as if I was to zip right past the Chen house, then abruptly darted through his wrought iron gate and up the ramp. The screen door was almost all mesh in front of a door painted a darker green than the exterior. The doorbell button glowed like a lit cigarette.

When I punched the button, however, I didn't hear anything inside. I punched it twice more, then reluctantly banged on the screen door. Too hard. The whole neighborhood might hear that one.

Before I'd gotten back to the sidewalk, I heard the door rattling open behind me.

"Hey!" a man shouted.

I leaped over the gate. I was fortunate there were no street-lamps nearby; once I got beyond the reach of his porch light, I was swamped with darkness. I heard the creak of the screen door.

Sprinting up the sidewalk, I chanced a backward glance. Lit by the porchlight above him, much of his face was shrouded by shadow, but the bespectacled Asian man in the white T-shirt and gray exercise shorts was definitely the same man I'd seen in the MTU faculty photo. Thinner. Face more gaunt. Short-cropped hair more white than black now. But definitely Chen.

He shouted at me again, louder. Across the street, a window brightened. Just ahead, an alley veered to the right, a dark corridor of single garages, garbage cans, and chain-link fences. I ducked into it, kicking into a higher gear, running practically blind until I made it to the next street. I hot footed it up another block to an auto body shop on the corner, closed up for the night. The street was deserted. Some dogs barked in my wake, but that was it. No sirens.

I took my time making my way back to the Honda, walking a few blocks one way then another, ending up at a Cenex Station on Excelsior Avenue, a major thoroughfare. The adjoining Zip Trip mini-mart was an island of light surrounded by an ocean of darkness. A man was filling up a Jeep Cherokee, one hand on the nozzle, the other holding his phone. He didn't look at me.

It was nearly twenty minutes before I slipped into the driver's seat of the Honda. Chen's front door was closed, but a golden halo now ringed one of the curtained windows.

"What did he do after I ran?" I asked.

"He came out and looked around," Isaac said, "like he was sort of seeing if anything was missing. Then he went back inside. What now? Just sit here and watch him?"

"No, we have to be smarter than that. And we can't live in this car for days on end." I tapped the steering wheel, gazing at all the dark houses around us. "Maybe one of the neighbors will let us crash on a couch?"

"You think they will?"

"I was joking, Isaac."

"Oh." He pointed at a brick four-plex up the way a bit. "There's a place for rent up there. I saw a sign when we drove past."

I looked. He was right. I saw the red-and-white placard in an upstairs window. "Good eye, kid, but I'm not sure I have the money for that. And that would probably take a long time to set up anyway—references, background checks, that sort of thing, none of which would be good for us."

"Oh yeah."

While I was pondering, a sedan turned onto Alabama, its headlights sweeping in our direction. Both of us ducked out of view. The car rumbled past but didn't stop.

For some reason, I was reminded of the time Ben and I staked out a cocaine dealer's ranch house in southeast Baltimore, looking for proof he was working with a major Mexican drug cartel. A rival cartel had driven right up to the house in a Mini Cooper—we'd ducked out of sight that time too, not knowing what was coming—and used their AK-47s to turn the front of the house into a cheese grater before we could even call for backup. It had led to lots of jokes about how much easier our jobs would be if we didn't have to follow the law. Just show up and start shooting.

Plus what kind of cartel has a Mini Cooper?

That memory made me think about the apartment for rent in a new way. I wasn't in the Bureau, but I was still thinking like an FBI agent who had to operate within the confines of the law. If I wanted to catch Mr. Grim, I couldn't afford such limitations.

To a point, anyway.

I studied the four-plex again, seeing all the dark windows, thinking about the kind of people who might live there.

———

"How about the neighbors?" I asked. "Are they very rowdy?"

A few minutes after ten the next morning, my voice bounced off all the bare white walls and empty vinyl countertops in the vacant one-bedroom apartment. Standing at the kitchen window, the glass water-spotted and speckled with dirt, I peered at the Chen house across the street. No activity. As far as I knew, Chen hadn't left his house since I'd rang his doorbell.

The landlord, who'd introduced himself as Miles Trusk, stood behind me. "Well," he said, "the lady downstairs is deafer than diddly, and the kid next door is gone for the summer—home with his folks in California."

I turned as he was speaking, watching as he screwed up his face and said the last word in four distinct syllables, *Cal-i-for-nia,* as if he was saying *for-ni-ca-tion* instead. His woolly gray mustache dwarfed his lower lip. His head was roughly the same color and shape as a pumpkin. He'd hooked his thumbs under the straps of his grease-stained denim overalls. The musky smell of him filled the room.

"All summer, huh?" I said.

He shrugged, and I could actually feel it. The floorboards

were so bouncy that anytime either of us moved, they wobbled beneath me.

"Yeah, well," he said, "that's college kids these days, right? You know what my dad did when I turned eighteen? Handed me a Greyhound schedule and one of his old suitcases, a hundred bucks inside. He told me I had to be out of the house before dinner. I hated his guts at the time, but it sure did force me to grow up quick. More kids could use that tough love approach. Look at how it turned out for me. I may have started out in the copper mine, but now all these smart aleck college kids are paying *me* rent."

"You sure showed them," I said.

"What?" He took a step toward me, which jangled the ring of keys attached to one of his belt loops. He had a lot of keys. "I'm sorry, I didn't catch—"

"Never mind." I held up the application he'd given me; some of the toner had rubbed off on my fingers. "I like the apartment, but there are a couple other places I need to look at, just to make sure. Where can I drop this off? Do you live close by or—?"

"No, no, I live on Milner, other side of town, address on the bottom there. This one won't last long, you know. Got a bunch of people looked at it just the last few days. Where you work?"

I doubted that if he'd had that many people looking at it he would have had to print out an application that morning, but I kept this thought to myself. "Actually," I said, "I'm still lining up a job. Got a couple leads, though."

"Oh." His eyes might have looked like tiny black buttons, but they shrank even more. "Well, I've rented to folks who've just started jobs, but you have to actually have a job. And I need first, last, and deposit, just keep that in mind."

I turned back to the kitchen window. "Oh, one other thing, I guess. That green house, the one with the ramp. I lived next to somebody with a ramp like that a few years ago, and they were running a group home for seniors with disabilities. I mean, it wasn't really a big deal, but one had Tourette's and—"

"What house now?" As Trusk sidled up to the window, I got smacked by a wave of garlic, sweat, and other unpleasantness.

"Oh, that one, yeah. Chinese guy. I think it's his wife in the wheel-chair. Seen him pushing her around the neighborhood. She kinda got that droopy face, you know. Probably a stroke. They won't bother you none."

It took all the willpower I had not to wince at the man's smell. I drifted toward the front door. "Okay, good to know. I'll get this to you soon as I can."

"I didn't see your car, by the way. You do have a way to get around, right? Hard to get a job without a car."

"It's parked a few blocks over."

"Uh huh. Where'd you say you'd moved from again?"

"Thanks for your time, Mr. Trusk. I've gotten the information I need."

I was smiling as I closed the door. Then, hustling, I took the keys I'd unhooked from Trusk's belt loop to the apartment next door. The landing was covered but exposed to the crisp morning air. It took about ten seconds to find the right key, but it was there, and I had the door unlocked and the whole mess of keys deposited on the floor outside the empty apartment, the one Trusk was in, before I even heard him cursing inside.

I was down on the sidewalk when I heard a door open back in the alcove.

"Well, shit, there they are," Trusk said. "Musta dropped them."

18

An hour later, Isaac and I sipped the tomato soup we'd filched from California College Kid's cupboard—his real name was Tim Laver, according to his junk mail—and peered out the kitchen window. So far, there'd been no activity at Chen's house, not even a rustle of the closed curtains. There'd been plenty of Monday morning activity elsewhere on the street, but I would have assumed the Chen house was unoccupied if I hadn't seen the man himself last night.

Isaac blew on the spoonful of soup. Bits of saltine crackers floated in the steaming orange liquid. "So what would you have done if you couldn't get the key? Like, would you have beat up that landlord guy so we could stay here?"

I laughed, thinking Isaac was joking, but he stared at me with utter seriousness. He'd brushed his hair and tucked it behind his ears, so for once his face was completely exposed. It was good to see his face. In the morning light, his eyes were roughly the same emerald green as the cotton hoodie he was wearing, also courtesy of Mr. Laver. It fit him about as well as a banquet tablecloth on a stop sign, but I didn't blame him for choosing it over the pink Minnie Mouse one I'd offered him earlier.

Thinking how best to handle his odd question, I braved another sip myself, my eyes watering as the soup scalded my tongue. It tasted burned too. Salty and burned. Hope used to joke that I couldn't even cook soup, and I hated that I was proving her right.

"I unlocked the bedroom window in the empty apartment while I was looking at it," I said. "We could have used that place if we had to, but this is much better. Or we would have spent another night with the Honda in the Walmart parking lot. But look, we may be doing a little trespassing, but I want to make a few things clear. That soup you're eating, and those clothes you're wearing, I'll mail the guy money for those things eventually, okay? I'm not a thief. And more importantly, I don't hurt *anybody* unless I have no choice, and even then, only bad people."

"Bad people," Isaac said, nodding.

"Yeah, and only bad people who deserve it. I'm not some random vigilante with a cape, okay?"

"A cape?"

"You know, like a superhero."

"Right. Capes are kind of silly anyway. In real life, they'd just get in the way. Plus they'd just get torn all the time."

I laughed. "I guess you're right."

"Shouldn't you have a gun or something?"

"I'm not really big on guns anymore."

"But what if Mr. Grim has a gun?"

"Then I'll improvise." I could see that he didn't like this answer. "Look, I'll use a gun if I have to, but only if I have to."

"Why is that?"

I shrugged. I'd finally gotten him talking, but that wasn't really a topic I wanted to get into with him, at least not now.

"I couldn't do it," he said.

"What, use a gun?"

"No, I mean, do what you do."

"I'm not following. Are you talking about breaking in like this? I told you, it's a last resort."

Isaac sipped his soup. I felt weirdly agitated by his silence this time. I didn't know why it was so critical that he understand my point, but it seemed of vital importance. What was my point anyway? It had something to do with how I saw myself. I may have left the FBI, but there was still something about my years in the Bureau that was core to my identity. I was one of the good people. I may have skirted the edges of the law occasionally for a greater good, but I never forgot which side of the line I belonged on.

"I mean it," I said. "I never hurt people on purpose. Or break the law unless there's no way around it."

He sipped more soup. He might have nodded, but I couldn't tell. I didn't like that I couldn't tell. The one-bedroom apartment was crowded with secondhand IKEA furniture and cheap, pressboard bookshelves full of World of Warcraft knick-knacks. We could hardly turn around without bumping into something. It made even the silence feel crowded. Sounds that would have passed unnoticed grew louder, agitating me. The *plunk-plunk* of the leaky bathroom sink down the hall. The rhythmic ticking of the Snoopy clock mounted above the kitchen sink. The distant whir of someone's leaf blower.

What was wrong with rakes anyway? A rake was cheap. A rake didn't need to be recharged. A rake provided good exercise. People were always opting for the shiny new thing, the gizmo or gadget that would make life easier for themselves, but all they were doing was making life more complicated and more expensive. So what if I lived out of my car? It was my choice, wasn't it? I wanted to keep life simple. I wanted to live on my own terms.

"I live this way because I want to, you know," I said. "It's not like I'm poor. I don't break into places because I don't have choices. This isn't an ordinary thing for me."

Isaac paused, tendrils of steam rising from the spoonful of soup held before his lips. I had no idea how I'd leaped from thinking about leaf blowers to defending my vagabond lifestyle. I was about to tell Isaac to forget it when he surprised me.

"I get it," he said. "The more people try to make you live a regular life, the more you don't want to do it. And just because you don't have the kind of life that most people have doesn't mean you're not a good person. You can still make a difference with things. Maybe even a bigger difference, right? Because you're so unattached."

I was so floored by his insightfulness that I didn't know quite what to say. "Right," I said dumbly. "That's it exactly."

"It's cool," he said.

"Okay."

"I wish I could do that. Just, you know, live on my own. Even have a regular life. That would be okay too. But I probably won't."

He dropped this comment the way he'd crumbled crackers into his soup, as if it was no big deal, and went back to sipping. For me, though, it was heartbreaking. He hadn't been talking about being a vigilante, breaking into an apartment, or anything along those lines. When he'd said, "I couldn't do it," he was just talking about being self-sufficient. Here I was getting defensive about my life choices, and he was just talking about something as simple as being able to live without someone looking after him.

I was trying to think of *something* to say when Isaac dropped his spoon with a clatter.

"There he is!" he said.

I looked. There he was, indeed—or at least the backside of him. Zhao Chen stood in the doorway, facing inside his house, the screen door propped open. He wore a billowy yellow polo, saggy tan khakis, and Birkenstock sandals. Thick glasses, black frames. In his faculty photo, he'd had plenty of hair, but most of it was gone now. In the bright sunlight, the top of his head was as white as a rice cracker.

He was guiding a wheelchair out of the house. I hadn't seen a photo of Chen's wife, so I didn't know what I was expecting, but the smiling, rosy-cheeked blonde wasn't it. It wasn't until he turned her wheelchair around that I saw that her smile turned into a sneer on the right side of her face. The sneer wouldn't have been so jarring except for how it contrasted with the rest of her— a warm, radiating goodness I detected even a story up and across the street.

While his clothes were loose and wrinkled, like he'd grabbed them off the floor, she looked like she was ready for a photo shoot for AARP magazine. Her green suede coat and yellow silk scarf were flawless. Her tan pants were nicely creased. Her black pumps gleamed as if recently buffed. Pearl necklace. Diamond earrings. She may not have been dressed like a fashion icon for today's youth—the clothes looked more J. C. Penny than J.Crew—but she did look great.

I noted that he hadn't locked the door. Forgetfulness? Or just the sense of security that came from living in a small town? It bothered me, how easily Mr. Grim could walk in there. It also gave us the same opportunity. We watched the two of them make their way east down Alabama.

"Are we going to follow them?" Isaac asked.

When they reached the end of the block, they turned left. A man in muddy overalls, hoeing in the garden of the white craftsman on the corner, gave her a friendly wave, and she waved back with her left hand. Her right stayed firmly in her lap. It was a small gesture, but it made me smile. I'd only gotten a glimpse of the Chens, but I already liked them. And I didn't like leaving them exposed.

Zhao Chen and his wife soon passed out of sight. Isaac started to rise, and I put my hand on his arm.

"Sit," I said.

"But—"

"Sit down, Isaac. Seriously."

For a second, I thought he might have another meltdown, but he slumped back into the kitchen chair. I realized that up until this moment, I'd been deluding myself. Yes, I was going to try to use Zhao Chen to catch Mr. Grim, but I'd told myself that I could fully protect him at the same time. Now that I was watching Chen disappear around the corner with his wheelchair-bound wife, I couldn't hold those two contradictory goals in my head at the same.

"We'll do our best to protect them," I said, my voice pinched and my face warm. "But the most important thing is catching Mr. Grim. It has to be."

"So we're not even going to follow him? Not at all?"

"If we can do it without being seen, yes. Otherwise, no."

Isaac looked down the street again. They were already gone. They might even be already dead, for all I knew. I hated what I was doing. When Isaac looked back at me, I saw the disappointment in his eyes, and I hated what I was doing even more. How would my father look at me right now? What would he think? This wasn't me.

You have to stay strong, kiddo. The world needs strong people. There's a lot of Hopes in the world, and they need people like you and me. You understand?

I put my bowl in the sink. I turned the faucet to warm, letting the water heat up, and squirted some Dawn on the sponge sitting there on the grimy metal. "The good of the many," I said. "That's what's important right now. The good of the many."

Isaac said nothing, but I could feel the weight of his disappointment against my back like an avalanche barreling down a mountain.

———

To our great relief, Zhao Chen and his lovely wife returned to their house twenty minutes later.

While Isaac spent the rest of that morning channel surfing on the 50 inch HD television—it was the nicest thing in the apartment—I hopped on the Google Chromebook I found under Tim Laver's bed. He must have had a laptop too since there were a mess of cables on the folding table that served as his desk, and that made me hopeful that he had Wi-Fi in the apartment.

He did. *LaverLair* was the first network listed. He must not have used the Chromebook in a while, because it prompted me for a password. Fortunately he'd jotted "LaverLair/MrCa$hman" on a 3x5 card he'd tacked to the bulletin board behind the folding table. I was surprised to see *ZCOnline* as the second network listed, with two bars. Zhao Chen? Most likely.

Sitting at the kitchen table so I could better monitor the Chen house, the first thing I did was scan a dozen different news sites, both national and local, to get a sense of how much heat might be on Isaac and I. CNN had one article about Welk on their front online page, provocatively titled "House Explosion and Missing Son Raise Questions About Suicide of Respected UW Professor," along with both Isaac's school picture and Welk's faculty photo, but there was nothing in it about me, Mr. Grim, or Maya's brush with death on the ferry.

Unfortunately, as I'd feared, the leading theory seemed to be that Isaac might be the one responsible for the house bomb. Why would he have disappeared otherwise? If somebody we'd come across in the past two days called the police—a waitress, gas station attendant, or somebody just driving along next to us on the interstate—our situation might get a lot more complicated in a hurry. Not just because the police would have a better sense of where we were. It might also suggest to Mr. Grim that we had a good idea who his next victim was going to be.

The local news had a bit more about both Colin and Isaac Welk, especially about the tragic death of Mona Welk, but nothing really newsworthy. There was a bland quote from Sheriff McKinley in the *Island Sounder* that "all appropriate measures were being taken in the investigation of Colin Welk's death at the Orcadia" but nothing that would give the reader the sense that perhaps the worst serial killer the world had ever seen was responsible.

The next thing I did was research the Chens. Janice Stout-Chen, Zhao Chen's wife, had a Facebook account partially open to the public. Using that and some posts she'd made on Heart-Hub, an online support group for all the maladies that might befall the heart, I determined that she'd suffered a severe stroke three years ago. They had no kids. She'd worked as an administrative assistant at MTU until her stroke. She mentioned in one of the forums that while she'd worked just across campus from Zhao for years, she didn't actually meet him until he accidentally bumped into her cart at Safeway.

Zhao had taken early retirement two years ago to care for her. Her forum posts were nearly always cheerful, her Facebook full of amusing stories, funny GIFs, and reposts of local events in Butte. Zhao had a WordPress blog called "The World of Geoengineering" that had a few posts after his retirement announcement but nothing in over a year.

The last thing I did, partly to take my mind off my own agitation regarding the Chens, was look for information about my mother. I searched for any reports of Jane Does that had turned up dead along that stretch of I-5 during the weeks and months after she left the Orcadia. I found a couple old articles in local papers about unsolved murder cases, as well a few tantalizing posts in Reddit true crime forums, but there wasn't much more I could do without more time and better resources. It was probably just as well.

Right now, I had to focus on catching Mr. Grim.

The Chens didn't leave for the rest of the day. A Safeway van parked in their driveway about three in the afternoon, and I tensed until a middle-aged woman in a black fleece vest started unloading white grocery bags from the back. The postman delivered mail. An Amazon driver placed a shoebox-sized package on their front porch. Remembering what had happened back in Seattle, the Amazon package made me especially nervous. I watched Chen open the door, wave to the purple van as it pulled out of his driveway, then disappear with the box inside his house. If there was a bomb in that box, there was absolutely nothing I was going to be able to do to save him, not unless I ran over there right now and …

And what? Told him everything? Go on the run? The four of us would pile into that van of theirs and hit the road for an extended road trip. How extended? Days, weeks, a lifetime?

No bomb exploded that day, but the Amazon package did give me an idea. What if I made my own delivery to the Chens?

Just before nine o'clock that night, Isaac turned off the

M*A*S*H rerun and shuffled to the kitchen table, where I was still nursing the hot cocoa I'd made us. We'd made the decision to split up the night shift to give each of us a decent chance of getting a good night's rest, him taking the 9:00 p.m. to 3:00 a.m. shift because he was more of a night owl, and me, being more of an early bird, covering the 3:00 a.m. to 9:00 a.m. block. When he sat across from me, I told him what kind of delivery I had in mind.

"A video baby monitor?" he said.

"Yeah," I said. "My sister had one when her kids were little, and they've only gotten better since. I was looking it up on the computer, and I can get one at Walmart."

"You have cash for that? I thought you didn't want to use your bank card. You know, in case Mr. Grim—"

"I'm not using the card. I actually found a birthday card to Tim from his parents. It was under the bed, must have fallen back there. There was a hundred dollar bill inside."

Isaac frowned.

"I know," I said. "But I'll pay him back for that too. Here's what I'm thinking. I put that baby monitor somewhere in the house, hopefully pointed at a high traffic area, that might give us the edge over Mr. Grim we need."

He chewed on his bottom lip. "Don't you need a really good phone for that?"

"Actually, the one I'm looking at also allows you to use Wi-Fi. When I got on the Chromebook, I could see Chen's network from here."

"You can't use his network. He might see that you've logged into it. He's a science guy. He's probably pretty good with tech. And if Mr. Grim has tapped into Chen's network—"

"Oh, I know. I'm just hoping that if I can see Chen's network, that the reverse is true, which means I might be able to hook up the baby monitor to our friend Mr. Laver's network even from across the street. Signal might be weaker, but I'm hoping it works."

Isaac nodded, looking at me steadily. The more comfortable he got with me, the more eye contact he made. "Smart," he said.

"Thank you. Every now and then I have a decent idea. So I should only be gone an hour or so, okay?"

Isaac swallowed. "You're going *now?* I thought you were going to sleep. You'll be really tired if you—"

"I'll be fine. I need to move the car anyway. Don't want Walmart to think I abandoned it."

"But what if Mr. Grim comes while you're gone? What am I supposed to do? I don't have a phone. I can't even call you."

"I'll leave the phone with you. If Mr. Grim *does* show up, and he's real obvious about it, call the police, okay? Even if you have to tell them who you are, call the police. I don't think he'll be obvious about it, though, and the reason I'm going tonight is odds are he's not even in town yet. Anything we want to do to set a trap for him, we better do it right away."

"So you'll break into Chen's house tonight?"

"Too risky. Hopefully, they'll go on a walk tomorrow, and I'll do it then."

"But—"

"Isaac, what's the problem? You just said it was a good idea."

This whole time he'd been looking right at me, a duration of steady, direct eye contact that would have been unnerving even for a normal person and was even more unnerving considering it was Isaac. "It is," he said. "It is a good idea."

"Then what is it? What's wrong?"

He finally looked down at the table. "Nothing."

"It doesn't sound like nothing."

He shrugged, the turtle retreating into his shell again. Outside, the shadows were long, and the sky, though it was not yet sunset, was already graying.

"I'm counting on you," I said.

"I know."

"You know, when I'm at Walmart, I can get us some snacks. If there's anything you want—"

"I don't want anything."

"You sure? How about a Snicker's bar? Reese's Pieces? You've got to have a favorite—"

"I don't want anything!"

If somebody had been walking by on the sidewalk below, they surely would have heard him. Fortunately, nobody was. I raised my hands in a gesture of surrender. Isaac shook his head and looked out the window, his anger disappearing as quickly as it had arrived. I knew we needed to get to the bottom of whatever his issue was but decided to put it off for now.

That turned out to be a mistake, a really big one.

19

Whatever had gotten under Isaac's skin, he was fine when I got back from my sojourn to Walmart a little before eleven. It was easy enough to move on because soon we were both focused on the large white box I removed from the Walmart bag: the Jarcom Video Monitoring System, which pretty much wiped out my remaining cash.

He offered to test it while I slept. I told him that was fine as long as he promised to be very careful. He sounded downright giddy to get his hands on it—as giddy as Isaac got, anyway.

Taking his change in attitude as a good sign, I headed off to bed, shutting the bedroom door so his fussing with the packaging didn't disturb me. The walls were plastered with movie posters —*World War Z, Pacific Rim, Lord of the Rings*. The room had a dusky, dank smell with a whiff of citrus, most likely from the incense sticks atop the dresser. The king bed dominated the room with a thick mattress so comfortable I figured I'd be asleep in minutes.

I wasn't. I kept thinking about Hope and the girls. I thought about Ben, staked out in his rental car in the dark, watching her house. I was lying atop the bedspread, using clean sheets I'd found in the hall cabinet, and I wrestled with those sheets for nearly an hour before finally reaching for my phone. I had a new phone. Ben had a new phone. There was no way Mr. Grim could be eavesdropping on us, so I decided touching bases with him was worth the risk, especially since we hadn't talked since Saturday. He answered right away.

"Hey, it's me," I said.

"Karen! Is everything all right? You told me you wouldn't call unless—"

"It's fine. Sorry, I know it's almost three in the morning there, but is everything okay on your end? Hope and the kids …?"

"Yeah, they're fine. Followed them to Denny's Saturday night. Followed them to church yesterday. She and the girls didn't go anywhere today, making it easy for me, but Ronnie left for his job at UPS and didn't come back until after midnight." Ben cleared his throat. It was good to hear that deep baritone of his, but there was a raspy, nasal quality to it that worried me. "Based on how he tripped and staggered his way to the door," he continued, "I'm thinking he was out drinking at a bar. He even belched so loud he got the neighbor's dog barking."

"Nice. Ever the gentleman, that Ronnie."

You told me to stick with Hope and the girls, so that's what I did. It does mean he was, you know, more exposed."

"No, that's perfect. You okay, Ben?"

"Yeah, yeah, just picked up a head cold, that's all. I'll be all right."

"Well, you sound like shit."

He chuckled, which started him coughing again. "Don't beat around the bush, Karen. Just tell me what you really think."

"Are you getting any sleep at all?"

"Cat naps. I'll be fine."

"God, now I feel even more guilty. I know you can't keep doing this by yourself much longer."

"I said I'll be fine." He undermined his own statement with another series of coughs, which boomed like gunshots in the enclosed car. "How are things on your end? Any luck with, you know, getting on top of this thing? You getting any sleep yourself? It's what, about a quarter to one there?"

I sighed. "No luck so far, but I'm setting a little trap that I hope will … Wait a second, how did you know that?"

"Sorry?"

"About the time. You said it was a quarter to one here. If you thought I was still on Pacific time, you would have said a quarter to midnight."

"Oh, right. I guess my math was off, that's all."

"Bullshit. You know where I am, don't you? How did you know that? When you said, 'getting on top of this thing,' you were about to say something else, weren't you?"

"Karen—"

"God damn it, Ben. I thought I told you how important it was that I keep this secret!"

"Karen, if you'll just—"

"Maya. It had to be her." I kicked off the sheets and hopped out of bed. "I haven't told anyone else! I showed her the list of potential victims, so she must have figured out where I'd be from that. Christ, I can't believe she called you! Do you have any idea what kind of danger she's putting us all in by doing that?"

"Will you calm down? Take a breath, for God's sake. All right, fine. Yes, she called me."

"That bitch."

"Will you *stop?* She's just trying to help. She didn't know I was here in Atlanta, not at first."

"At first? What's that supposed to mean?"

"She called my FBI number and left a message saying she wanted to talk to me about a case she was working on, but I ignored it. I figured it could wait. Then she must have called the district office this morning, and they told her I was out on vacation because then she leaves me *another* message saying she really needed to talk to me about that case when I got a moment, adding that she could still get me those Atlanta Braves tickets if I was interested. I just needed to let her know ASAP."

I snorted. "Was that supposed to be a code? Because you're in

Atlanta? Jesus, she might as well have put out a message for Mr. Grim in neon lights."

"Is that what you're calling him?"

"Oh, she didn't tell you that part, huh? I figured she would have emailed you a fifty-page report complete with footnotes. She really is trying to get me killed, isn't she?"

"Come on, Karen. She's actually worried about you."

"That's a funny way of showing it."

"What was she supposed to do? You wouldn't answer her calls. She said she felt bad, not doing more to help, but she also knew she couldn't go to Butte. She didn't want to mess up your stakeout. That *is* where you are, right? And you have the Welk kid with you?"

I simmered quietly, saying nothing.

"I'll take that as a yes."

"Look, I need to go. We can talk later."

"Hold on, will you? We were careful. She didn't use her own line to call me."

"Oh, I'm so glad you were careful. I hope you were careful enough that Mr. Grim doesn't try to come back and finish the job with her."

"What are you talking about?"

"Oh, she didn't tell you that part, huh? I'm not surprised. Yeah, he tried to strangle her, Ben. And he was about five seconds away from succeeding if I hadn't stopped him."

"What? How did this happen?"

I told him about the ferry. It turned into an overall update on everything that had happened since that fateful morning at the Orcadia, and Ben listened quietly through all of it. "So you see why I'm a little skeptical of her motives," I said. "If all she wanted to do was help, she could have at least taken Isaac off my hands. Making a risky phone call and getting my old partner riled up is not my idea of help. That's just ... meddling from a distance for no good reason."

Ben said nothing, though he was so congested that I could hear him breathing through his nose. On my end, the apartment was as still as a mausoleum; I could just make out the hum of the refrigerator in the other room. I couldn't even hear Isaac tinkering around at the table. The silence with Ben stretched so long that I knew there was something he wanted to say but was debating whether to say it.

"What?" I said. "Spit it out, whatever it is."

"Well," he said, "this is probably going to piss you off big-time, but she's doing a lot more than meddling from a distance. She's actually on her way here right now."

"She's *what?*"

"She hopped a red-eye from SeaTac a couple hours ago. Then she's renting a car and joining me."

"Why the hell would she—"

"I didn't ask her to do this, Karen. But like I said, she's pretty smart. She said there was no way I could provide 24-7 protection to Hope and her kids by myself. She wouldn't take no for an answer. Pretty stubborn woman, if you ask me. Reminds me of someone else I know."

"I can't believe she would do that!"

"You said it yourself, Karen, I can't keep doing this myself much longer—and I'm doing a pretty piss-poor job of it anyway. It's not just the lack of sleep. There's only so many drive-bys and walk-bys I can do without a nosy neighbor calling the police on me. I'm already pushing my luck."

I didn't know what to say to this. I knew he was right, but I still didn't like Maya doing it. "If she wanted to help, why didn't she come get Isaac for me? That was the kind of help I needed!"

"I don't know. Once she realized I needed help, she kind of fixated on that."

I was about to lay into him a bit more when I heard a clatter in the other room, like glass smashing to pieces. A cup dropped in the kitchen maybe. In the strip of pale-blue light under my door, I saw a movement of shadows. I covered the phone and called Isaac's name. He mumbled something about everything being fine, but it still wasn't good.

"Shit, I gotta go," I said to Ben.

"Look, I understand if you're angry—"

"It's not that, Ben. I just heard a noise—I think he dropped something."

"Wait, tell me what's—"

Clicking off, I threw open the door. It was dark out there except for the umbrella of light over the kitchen table where the Jarcom system looked fully assembled, packaging strewn all over the vinyl floor. Isaac wasn't there. He wasn't in the bathroom off to the left either, where the door was open and a nightlight revealed that the room was empty.

But then I spotted movement to my right. He squatted on his knees in front of the love seat, his back to me, his dark sweatshirt and dark jeans making him almost invisible.

"What happened?" I asked.

"It's okay," he said.

His voice sounded thick. I stepped beside him and saw that he was picking up black-and-white ceramic shards. Stepping closer, I recognized the shards as the Mickey Mouse piggy bank that had been sitting next to the big screen TV.

"What did you do," I said, laughing, "throw it against the wall?"

I meant it as a joke, but when he didn't say anything, I realized that this was exactly what had happened.

"But why? Christ, you're bleeding."

"I'm fine."

"Stop. We can get that later." I reached for his hands. "I'm more worried about—"

"I said I'm fine!" he shouted.

He jerked away from me. I raised my hands and backed away. He picked up a few more shards, then stopped, shoulders sagging. I heard him breathing.

"Was it setting up the camera?" I said. "Was it frustrating?"

"No. That was fine."

"Okay."

"It's working great. I think it will be great."

"Oh. That's good, right?"

He didn't answer. I grabbed the plastic garbage bin next to the TV and placed it next to him. When he was done putting the shards in the basket, I grabbed some tissues and pressed them into his bleeding palm. His hand felt warm and unyielding, like concrete on a blistering hot day.

He stood so close to me that I smelled the tomato soup on his breath. He finally looked at me, his pupils so dark that even with only the kitchen light I saw my vague reflection in them. I realized then that I was standing there in nothing but black panties and a loose white T-shirt.

In my alarm at the noise, it hadn't even occurred to me to put on clothes. It also hadn't occurred to me—although it really should have—that as immature as Isaac sometimes acted, I was still dealing with a full-grown man. He swallowed. It actually made a noise, a kind of *glump,* and it was such a cartoonish sound that I would have laughed if I wasn't afraid that such a reaction might deeply wound him.

"Hold it like this for a while to stop the bleeding," I said. "Then, um, go get cleaned up in the bathroom, okay? I'm sure … I'm sure there's bandages in there. You might not even need them. The cuts are, um, pretty small."

I dropped my hand away. He kept staring at me with deep soulful eyes. He wasn't bad-looking. Down the road, some girl could definitely lose herself in those eyes.

"Okay then," I said, heading back to the bedroom. "Okay, I better get some sleep. I'll relieve you in a couple hours."

I regretted my choice of words. *Relieve you.* God, when sex was on the brain, everything sounded dirty. As I shut the door behind me, he was still looking at me, eyes wide as ever, one hand pressed on top of the other as if he were cupping something precious between them rather than just a bloody ball of tissues.

———

WHEN I SHUFFLED zombie-like out to the kitchen at 3:00 a.m., Isaac didn't mention our awkward moment. Too tired to think straight, I decided that the best thing would be to just focus on watching Zhao Chen unless Isaac wanted to clear the air.

Which he didn't. That was no surprise, but what *was* a surprise was that he presented me with a detailed log of the past six hours using a college-ruled notebook he'd found in the kitchen. *White cat darts under Ford Bronco up the street ... Car alarm a few blocks over ... Green Datsun pickup drives by, bad muffler.*

That he managed to maintain that level of vigilance while fully testing the video security system—which he explained in painstaking detail—was certainly impressive, yet the deep bags under his eyes told me another story, so I ushered him off to bed. At the time it felt like maybe our ship was sailing into smoother waters.

It was too for a bit. While I needed to make three cups of the Folgers instant coffee I found in the cupboard to keep my eyes open until Isaac returned at 9:00 a.m. to relieve me, a quick nap gave me enough of a boost when Isaac woke me an hour later because the Chens had just headed out for another "walk and roll." Those were Isaac's words, and he even laughed when he said them. It was the first time I remembered him laughing at anything.

Having monitored the neighborhood for a day now, we were relatively confident that Mr. Grim wasn't hiding nearby, but I still stuffed my hair into a gray wool hat and wore one of Tim Laver's baggy plaid shirts to hide my figure. There was still a risk, no way around it, but I thought getting that video system into the Chen house was worth it.

Just as earlier, it didn't look like the Chens had locked their front door. I hoped that was true, or I'd have to improvise. As I crossed the street in the bright sunlight carrying the video system in the Walmart bag, I was already sweating under the hat, and it itched like crazy. I glanced at our kitchen window. I'd told Isaac to pull down the shade if he saw anything suspicious as a signal to me, but it was open. So far, so good.

I kept my distance as a middle-aged man in a gray tracksuit jogged past, huffing and puffing and leaving a musky odor in his wake. He didn't stop. I was still very conscious that Mr. Grim could be anyone. It was risky for me to walk straight into their house in broad daylight, but I figured if I acted like I belonged, nobody would bother me. It was a strategy that usually worked.

It worked this time too, at least so far. A floral scent hit me as soon as I was inside, and the source was right there, incense sticks in a crystal vase. Except for the continuous rumble of their air conditioner, the house was still. In my current getup, the cool air was a welcome relief. Based on their weed-infested yard, I expected a similar state within, but it wasn't like that at all. The overhead entryway light had been left on, so even with the living room curtains closed, I had no trouble seeing the faux hardwood vinyl floor, the brown microfiber furniture, or the watercolors of Rocky Mountain sunrises, everything bright and new and well-cared for.

Pushing deeper, however, I saw that the living room was something of an exception. In the kitchen, the dishes were piled in the sink, and the glass-top oven was coated with grime. The dining room was filled with so many Amazon boxes, Safeway bags, and other junk that I could barely see the table. As for the bedrooms and bathrooms? I didn't dare put the camera in there for fear it might be crushed in an avalanche.

I was standing in the doorway to her warzone of a bedroom, wondering if Janice Stout-Chen's cheerful demeanor was, like her house, hiding a much messier interior, when something brushed against my leg.

I looked down and saw an orange tabby, a cat so fluffy that it looked like it had just come out of the dryer. It blinked big green eyes at me.

"Hello, kitty," I said. "You're not going to make life difficult, are you?"

He meowed.

Now I had to get down to business. Where to put the camera? The white dome wasn't much bigger than a softball, but it would still stand out if I put it out in the open. I found my solution in that hoarder's heaven of a dining room. There were so many boxes that I doubted they even used the room. There was an outlet behind a sewing machine that I didn't even know was there until I moved some boxes, and the camera was completely camouflaged when I plugged it in and put the boxes back.

The orange tabby, who had taken to following me around the house, brushed up against my leg again, offering up a much louder meow this time. A looking-for-a-tuna-handout kind of meow.

"You're really not helping," I said.

I plugged in the camera. The bead-sized light on top started blinking, a good sign, but it needed to turn solid blue if it was connected to Tim Laver's Wi-Fi. It kept blinking blue for a good two minutes, so I unplugged it and plugged it back in, starting over the cycle. Still no luck, just a lot of blinking.

I was contemplating moving the camera to another location when I heard the front door opening.

20

"Hello?" a woman said. "Jan? Zee? It's just me—dropping off the fruit basket you ordered."

I froze. She sounded older, her voice husky and rough, like a lifelong smoker. I was out of view of the front door, but there were no good escape routes. The back slider was off the kitchen, and the only way to the kitchen—without moving the mountain of cardboard boxes blocking the passage from the dining room to the kitchen—would take me right past the front entryway. Same problem with the door to the garage. It would take me right past her. There were no windows I could climb through anywhere close.

I heard the click of heels on the faux hardwood. I prayed that she'd just drop the fruit basket and leave. A close friend? A relative? Maybe she was Jan's mother since she hadn't knocked. I hadn't heard a car, which meant she probably lived close.

The door slammed, which got my hopes up, but then she passed me on her way to the kitchen. She didn't look my way, but I got a good look at her, a stocky blonde in a blue denim jacket, her face roughly the same shiny, weathered tan as the suede purse slung over shoulder. She carried a wicker basket piled high with apples, oranges, and other fruit. She could have been anywhere from forty to seventy, but her shoulder-length hair was so yellow that it must have been dyed, her forehead so smooth that she must have had Botox injections. Probably on the upper end of that age range then.

She set the basket on the counter. I heard a cabinet door creak. What was she *doing?* The Jarcom's light finally turned solid blue. Oh, *now* the device finally cooperates. The woman opened the fridge. Liquid splashed into a glass. It was so still in the house that I could actually make out the *glump-glump* of her swallowing.

I was debating about just making a dash for it when the orange tabby appeared in the doorway to the living room.

It stared at me intently, its eyes like plastic green buttons, its body a fuzzy blockade impeding my escape. Try to hop over it and it might dart under my shoes. I made a sweeping motion at it, trying to shoo it out of the way, but it responded with a loud, piercing meow.

"Garfield?" the woman said. "Where are you, honey? Here kitty, kitty."

Garfield? Really? The owners got zero points for originality. I heard the clicking of her heels on the vinyl kitchen floor. The cat *still* didn't move. I pulled down my wool hat, trying to hide as much of my face as I could, and prepared to make a run for it, cat be damned.

Then the doorbell rang.

Garfield darted under some boxes. I actually got a glimpse of the woman's hand—that was how close she was—before she reversed course, muttering under her breath. Could this be Mr. Grim? I didn't think he'd ever be so obvious, but anything was possible.

Heart pounding, I crept toward the living room and saw her open the front door. A rectangle of sunlight spilled into the foyer. From my vantage point, I couldn't see who was there, but I could make out the side of her face, enough to see the wariness.

I started to take a step when I heard a familiar voice.

"Sorry to bother you, ma'am," Isaac said, "but I thought you should know your dog got out."

"What?" the woman said.

"He's on the side of the house."

"Dog? We don't have—"

"A little brown-and-white Jack Russell terrier?"

"No, we don't—I mean, my daughter, she's the one who lives here—she doesn't have a dog."

"Oh. Well, I'm just afraid he might get hit by a car. I was walking by, and this woman in a Volvo, she almost got him."

"Heavens! All right, I better come look."

She closed the door behind them. I heard their voices moving along the front of the house. I slipped out the back slider.

———

I JUMPED the chain-link fence behind the house, squeezed through a wall of arbor vitae, and managed to sneak past another glass slider, where an elderly woman was watching *The Price Is Right* in a La-Z-Boy, then circled around a few blocks on the baking sidewalk. By the time I got back to our apartment, sweaty and flush-faced, Isaac was already there, grinning like the kid who'd eaten a whole package of Oreos. He explained that he told the woman that the dog must have run off already.

Suppressing my desire to tear into him for taking such a risk, I complimented him on his quick thinking and told him he was very brave. I laid it on pretty thick, but I could tell he needed it. He soaked it up like a sponge that had never been used.

The Chens returned. Miraculously, the camera worked. The audio feed was strong, even through the Chromebook's tiny speakers, but the video was pixelated, blinking in and out, and we couldn't see much except the middle of the living room. Still, that was significant because it was a heavily trafficked area whether somebody used the front door or the hall to the bedrooms. The biggest disappointment was that the Chromebook's hard drive was too small to record anything. We had a live feed and nothing else.

That aside, having a set of eyes and ears right inside the house was a huge improvement.

The rest of Tuesday, both Isaac and I perched over that Chromebook at the kitchen table, absorbing every bit of information we could about Zhao, Janice, and Peg, which turned out to be Janice's mother's name. Peg relayed the mystery of the stray dog with breathless enthusiasm. Janice, speaking out of one side of her mouth in a soft mumble, said she didn't know of anyone nearby with a Jack Russell terrier, but she'd post about it on Nextdoor. Zhao offered up the opinion that the missing dog was probably a scam of some sort, adding that a strange-looking woman had rang the doorbell last night but ran off.

Strange-*looking* woman? It was hard not to be offended. I may have been strange, but I didn't think I was strange-*looking*.

As the conversation shifted to more mundane matters, we learned that Janice, who'd indeed suffered a stroke two years ago, had recently started a new physical therapy program. We learned that Zhao, who'd been on sabbatical last year, was teaching one online course for MTU this summer, but otherwise he didn't have to go to campus. We learned that Janice's sister, Mary, who lived in Topeka, was dating somebody new, but Peg didn't expect it to last. After Peg left, we learned that Zhao wasn't too keen on his mother-in-law letting herself into the house when they were gone.

They had lunch. Janice watched TV down the hall, the sound too low for us to make out more than the canned laughter. Judging by the clicking of a keyboard, Zhao worked on a laptop in the kitchen. If there was some reason why Mr. Grim would want to target these two rather ordinary people, neither Isaac nor I could see it. But then, according to Welk, it would have been a surprise if that *wasn't* the case. Mr. Grim greatly preferred to kill random people so long as they fit his overall "God" pattern on the map.

For the next two days, Isaac and I settled into a nice routine, continuing to split the shifts. I moved the Honda each night—to a busy Best Western parking lot, then back to the Walmart. Isaac continued his meticulous log. I told him that it wasn't really necessary, but he insisted that if we had a record of everything normal, even the boring stuff, then maybe the out-of-the-ordinary stuff would jump out at us. I couldn't fault his reasoning even if I suspected that if we had any hope of saving the Chens, it would be a split-second opportunity that happened because we stayed constantly vigilant.

If nothing else, though, the log gave Isaac something to do other than focus on the depth of his loss. As the hours passed, my doubts about our stakeout increased. Was this all a waste of time? I had nothing to go on but Welk's list. To distract myself, I tried to do some more digging for anything I could find about Mom, but that search was even more frustrating. The most obvious thing to do was call Anne Lambert, Marv Friedman's former secretary, just to see if she remembered anything else about Mom's appointment with the Hollywood agent, but I didn't dare do that right now.

The days may have been starting to blur together, but Welk's theory about what Mr. Grim wanted was still fresh in my mind: *a worthy opponent.*

I didn't feel worthy.

What was I doing, sneaking around in broad daylight, hopping neighbor fences, and only narrowly avoiding disaster with the help of an erratic teenager who really should have been with relatives, friends, or at least a good therapist right now. Did I really think a baby monitor I bought at Walmart was going to help me catch one of the worst serial killers the world had ever seen?

And was Mr. Grim even a serial killer? I only had Welk's word on that. If the week passed and Mr. Grim didn't make a move against Zhao Chen, what would I do then? Assuming Colin Welk had been on the level, that would mean that all his research, everything he'd sacrificed, including, in the end, his own life, would be for nothing. Isaac being fatherless would be for nothing.

I checked in with Ben on Wednesday night. He had nothing new to report, but then Maya, who was in the car with him, chimed in to say not unless they counted the argument two neighbors had over who, exactly, had the right to trim the bordering eucalyptus tree. This got them both to laugh. I didn't like that laughter. It reminded me of all the times that Ben and I laughed on our various stakeouts over the years.

Was I jealous? I told myself I wasn't. I'd already made it clear to Ben that I wasn't interested in pursuing a relationship, so what was the problem?

I also researched the next two victims on my list—or at least the next one since Welk didn't know anything about "Jane Doe" except that she was a woman in Phoenix. It wasn't hard to find information about Tom Shelby in Casper, Wyoming. He was something of a minor celebrity, the author of the *Fur and Fang* series about anthropomorphized animals, most of whom had various disabilities to overcome. A cat with three legs. A dog with no smell. A hawk who couldn't fly. The three dozen books weren't bestsellers, by any means, but he appeared to have a sizable and enthusiastic audience that had allowed him to make a living as an author for decades. It was all the more impressive considering the hardships Shelby himself had to overcome.

According to a couple write-ups in *The Star-Tribune,* Casper's local newspaper, Shelby suffered from early onset macular degeneration. His vision had started to blur in his early teens and had only gotten progressively worse. The first article, from decades earlier, pictured him in his late twenties wearing glasses with thick lenses and thick black frames. He was smiling, though, and he had an everyman, good-looking-neighbor, Tom Hanks or Jimmy Stewart sort of appearance. The article had come out shortly after his first book was published in the late 90s and had a positive, triumphant tone: the inspiring story of the writer who'd overcome challenges just as the animals in his stories had.

The most recent article in *The Star-Tribune,* published five years ago, was more somber. For a man who would have been forty-four when the accompanying photo was taken, he'd aged well. His dark-brown hair was streaked with silver, and his face, already lean, was more gaunt, but he was still quite the handsome fellow. This was especially true because he wasn't wearing those ridiculously large glasses. The reason he wasn't wearing the glasses, though, was the same reason the article had been written. It turned out that the most recent *Fur and Fang* book would probably be his last since he was now almost completely blind. "I have no interest in learning to write through dictation," he was quoted as saying. "It's time to dedicate myself to other pursuits." For one, he wanted to spend a lot more time playing the piano, another great love of his.

He told people not to feel sorry for him because just like the characters he wrote about, sometimes it was important to find new goals when the old ones just didn't suit you anymore.

He didn't have any kind of social media presence—he was actually quoted in an interview on a children's book review blog that the less out there about him personally, the better—but there was still enough that I was able to flesh out his biography a bit. Married in his twenties, but currently single. No kids. Before his books took off, he'd worked for a few years as an English teacher on the Wind River Reservation. He'd moved for the job, having actually grown up in rural Massachusetts, but fell in love with Wyoming and decided to stay even when he could move anywhere. I managed to find a current address and even a phone number, the latter of which came courtesy of the semi-annual newsletter of Casper's Southside Neighborhood Association. His phone number was listed because he was collecting books for the Casper Library Annual Fundraiser. Typing his address in Google Earth brought up an old Victorian house shadowed by cotton-wood trees.

Shelby was good to his word. After publishing two books a year for almost two decades, he hadn't published anything in the last five. I pictured him alone in that old Victorian house, sitting in the dark because he had no need to turn on the lights, the haunting notes of his piano filling all those empty rooms.

I went to sleep Wednesday night more determined than ever to stop Mr. Grim.

———

BEN and I are sitting in a black Ford Mustang, an unmarked police vehicle on loan from the BPD. I'm in the driver seat. Ben's smoking. The vents roar out a steady stream of cool air in a hopeless battle against the relentless Boise sun making war on our windshield. The air conditioning can only keep the car so cool because we've got the windows cracked open for my benefit. I hate the smell of smoke.

We're arguing about whether we should listen to a jazz or oldies station. Ben reaches out and flicks off the radio, killing Miles Davis's trumpet in the middle of a long high note. He takes a puff of his Marlboro Red—this was before he smoked e-cigarettes—and blows the smoke out the side of his mouth, toward his cracked-open window.

"Well," he says, "are we going to do this thing or not?"

I look out the window at the meth house—the flaking green paint, the bowing roof. It makes me think of a slapdash cake baking in the oven. Like a child made it. Or maybe the child is in the cake. They're in the cake and they're in the oven. They need to get out of the oven. Somebody has to get them out of the oven.

"Not yet," I say, and my throat is so tight that it feels as if someone has got their hands around it. Choking me. Choking the life out of me. "Maybe they're not in there. Maybe—maybe this is the wrong place."

I hear him grinding out his cigarette in the ash tray. "I'm not talking about that," he says. "I'm talking about us."

"Us?"

"Come on, Karen. Don't play dumb. Hey. Hey, look at me."

But I can't look at him. I just keep staring at the house, thinking about what awaits me inside. "Maybe it will go differently this time," I say.

"It won't," he says, closer.

"I could save her."

"You can't." I feel his breath on my neck, warm and seductive. "But you can save yourself."

"Ben."

"You don't have to be alone all the time."

"I'm fine. I'm fine being alone."

"No, you're not. Look at me."

"I don't need anyone."

"Please, just turn around."

I know that when I finally look at him, when I look at those big brown eyes, my resistance will probably crumble, but I turn anyway. We're so close that I see all the tiny lines in his lips, like cracks in the ice.

"Karen—" he says.

I kiss him. It feels right. For once, it feels right. I cup my hand behind his head, feeling the stubble of his short-cropped hair, pressing closer. His hands slide to my hips, fingers slipping under the waistband of my jeans, fingernails raking across my flesh.

"You know," he murmurs, "you actually … look a lot like her."

"Mmm. What's that?"

"Your mother. Except for the hair, the resemblance is quite remarkable."

The voice—it's different, and I realize it isn't Ben. It's Colin Welk. I jerk away, expecting to be looking at Welk, but it's still Ben. He looks wounded.

"What?" he says.

But then, as I pull back a bit more, I spot something in the passenger window, a spot of red. I lean left and see redheaded Colin Welk, smiling at me through his thick beard. He's sitting in his wheelchair just outside the car.

"If you need me," Welk says, "I'll be in the bathroom."

———

MY EYES SPRANG OPEN, my heart thundering in my ears. It was dark. As the fog of the dream cleared, I remembered where I was. Butte, Montana. Mr. Grim. All of it.

Yet the sensation of the hand on my hip didn't fade. That wasn't all. A slender body spooned against my own, bare legs warm against my bare legs, something firm pressing into the crack between my buttocks, straining against the thin cotton underwear providing interference.

I whirled out of bed, sheets and bedspread flying, and crashed against the dresser. My elbow landed a direct hit on one of the metal knobs, and pain jolted up my arm.

"Ben!" I shouted. "What the fuck!"

Through the crack in the blinds, a faint glow from the neighbor's porch light spilled across the bed. A spindly figure sprawled on the top sheet, the gaps in his ribcage like a grate over a storm drain.

"I'm not Ben," Isaac said.

"What?"

"Ben," he said. "You called me Ben."

"Get the fuck out!"

"What?"

"Get the fuck out of my bed! Now!"

"Why did you call me Ben?"

I lunged for the switch by the door, flooding the room with light. I was dressed in a threadbare T-shirt and panties, but he was completely naked, his engorged penis amid that red cloud of pubic hair pointing right at me.

"Where are your pants?" I said.

"What?"

"Your pants! Your pants! Put some pants on, for God's sake!"

I spotted his rumpled sweatpants in the doorway and flung them at him. He got his hand up just in time, blinking at me, his bottom lip quivering, whatever dream he'd had about what was going to happen crumbling down around him.

"I'm sorry," he said.

"Don't," I said.

"I'm so sorry. Please—please don't leave me behind."

"Leave you behind? What are you *talking* about? I've dragged you along with me across half the country! Don't do this, Isaac! Don't you *dare* have a meltdown on me!"

I saw it happening, his eyes squinting into slits, his face reddening from top to bottom, but all I could do was march out of

the room. It was either that or strangle him. He'd left the bedroom
door open, and it was dark in the living room too, dark everywhere except the light over the kitchen sink, a pale glow on the
vinyl floor.

Behind me, I heard Issacs's meltdown commencing, the blub-
bering and sobbing, the pounding and thrashing about on the
bed, and I realized something I should have probably realized
before.

He'd been afraid of being abandoned.

Of being alone.

That was it. That was the big fear he'd refused to talk about.
Every time I'd even hinted that he probably hated being with me,
it was another reminder that I might disappear out of his life. My
anger fading, I thought about going back, trying to calm him
down, when another light caught my attention.

The video monitor.

It sat on the kitchen table, a gray glow because the image itself
was dark. I was gripped with dread. How long had Isaac been
lying next to me? Twenty minutes? An hour? Leaving the Chen
house unobserved for even five minutes would have been too long.
The microwave clock showed it to be 3:12 a.m.

I stepped closer. The camera was positioned so that it revealed
the dining room, the doorway to the kitchen, the front entryway,
and enough of the living room that we could make out the couch
and the back of the love seat, everything hazy and muted, the
barest amount of ambient light coming from the kitchen and the
nightlight in the bathroom. Nothing seemed amiss.

It was only when I crouched over the screen that I saw what
my eyes must have skipped over at first glance.

The Chen's front door was wide open.

21

A mistake. It had to be a mistake. I could only see part of the front door on the monitor, and none of the screen door, so maybe the Chens had simply forgotten to close their main door when they'd gone to bed. It was summer, after all. Lots of people cooled down their houses in the evening by making use of their screen doors.

Not the Chens, though. In the split second I took in the image on the monitor, that was what the little nagging voice in the back of my mind told me. In the days that we'd been watching them, the Chens hadn't used their screen door that way. Not at night. Not during the day. Not even once. Isaac had never mentioned them doing it during his shifts either. I'd read his logs every time I took over for him. He would have mentioned it too. He certainly mentioned the precise time they locked the front door each night.

They also had air conditioning. I remembered it from when I was in the house.

Back in the bedroom, Isaac's sobbing had become a steady, droning moan, but it sounded as if it was coming from a distant shore, so very far away. My heart had never really slowed down since I'd awoken, and it kicked into an even higher gear now. I cracked open the closed kitchen blinds with my fingers, peering through the gap, half-expecting to see Mr. Grim standing on the Chen's porch.

He wasn't. The screen door was closed, and the mesh, with no light behind it, was an opaque black surface. It was almost all screen, so it was a lot of black. The light over the front door showed no one on the concrete porch, the wheelchair ramp, or anywhere close to the house. I didn't even see a cat. Nothing was amiss. Nothing was out there that shouldn't have been out there at two in the morning—quiet houses, still cars, the pock-marked asphalt lit up under the streetlamps like the surface of the moon.

Maybe the Chens really had left the front door open by mistake?

Then a shadow appeared in the black mesh.

It was the silhouette of a person, on the other side of the screen door, one who'd just leaned close enough to the mesh to be seen—broad shoulders, bulky. He was wearing some kind of hat. The silhouette appeared only briefly, like something floating to the surface of a pond before sinking away, but there was no mistaking that it was a person.

No, no, no. That was what I heard in my head, but it was the sound my heart was making too—a fierce and steady pounding, *no, no, no*, booming deep in my ribcage. Not now. Not after all this. I whirled back to the monitor and saw, on the screen, a man in a gray trench coat, gray fedora, and black leather gloves float like a wraith across the entryway and veer right, down the hall. It was too dark, and his chin was bent too low, to make out his face, but I did see something else just as he disappeared from view—a glint of metal.

He was holding a knife.

A hunting knife, a big one, with a serrated blade. The firm way he gripped it in his gloved hand, there was no doubt what his intentions were.

I was running then, sprinting for the apartment's front door. Charging after a serial killer unarmed, barefoot, and dressed in nothing but underwear and a skimpy T-shirt was not ideal, but I couldn't spare even five seconds to slip on my shoes. In five seconds, the Chens might be dead.

Barreling out our front door, crashing down the stairs, powering across the warm asphalt in my bare feet—I did all this without even taking a breath. I always knew when I was being impulsive, but that never stopped me. I could live with being too stupid. I couldn't live with being too indecisive.

No one stood on the porch. I saw no shadow in the screen. The dry air slipped across my bare skin, smelling of grass and dirt. As I got closer, I could see into the house, if only a little, and there was no one there, not at the screen, not in the entryway.

I leaped onto the porch and slammed against the screen door, my right hand tearing partially through the mesh.

"Hey!" I shouted into the house. "Hey now! I saw you!"

I hoped that would be enough to throw Mr. Grim off course, make him worry more about his own escape than carrying out his plan, but leaning against the mesh, gasping for breath, I didn't hear anything.

I jerked the handle and leaped inside, the bottom of the screen door clipping my shin. I slipped on the cold tiles but didn't go down. Fists up, ready for anything, I took in big gulps of air, scanning the darkness. Other than the rumbling air conditioner, I heard nothing. The porch light spilled into the foyer, cutting a yellow rectangle across the tiles to the carpet beyond.

"Help."

The whispered plea came from down the hall. A black umbrella, a tall one with an oak handle, jutted out of a copper vase by the door. I grabbed it and brandished it like a sword, then made my way toward the hall in a wide circle, fearing Mr. Grim might be standing right there.

He wasn't. I flipped the switch, and light flooded a short, carpeted hall with three open doorways—a bathroom with a blue pastel counter to the left, two bedrooms on the end. All the rooms were dark. I knew the master was on the right.

"Help ... please help."

It was Janice, in the master, and she was in pain. Keeping the umbrella up, I approached the doorway on the right. I saw a fitted sheet tucked into the mattress, lacey white trim around the box frame, and a pair of plush pink slippers partly sticking out from under the bed.

No Mr. Grim. Staying alert, vigilant of what might be behind me as well as what might be in front, I reached around the threshold and flipped the switch. A free-standing brass lamp in the corner flooded the room with garish light, an LED bulb that would have been more fitting for a morgue than a bedroom. But it wasn't a morgue I saw.

It was worse.

Blood. Blood on the bed. The bedspread was gone, and I saw more red than white on the sheet. The smell hit me then, a rust-like odor that sprang out to greet me as if it had been waiting for me to enter the room. There was so much blood that for a moment I had a hard time even seeing the body in the middle of it—Zhao Chen. He was naked except for his blue-striped boxers, eyes gazing at the ceiling but seeing nothing, hands at his neck where his jugular had obviously been cut.

He wasn't moving. The blood flowing from his neck was a trickle, not a river; his heart had stopped a while ago. There was nothing I could do for him. The way the blood pooled around his neck and head, with few splatters and smears elsewhere, it didn't even look like he'd fought back. This didn't just happen, not since I'd first spotted Mr. Grim, anyway. Ten minutes ago, maybe, but not two.

Mr. Grim hadn't been heading down the hall to kill Zhao Chen. He'd already done that. Why go back inside, then? Why not just leave?

And where was Janice?

I stepped to the right and saw her quivering in the corner, between the end table and the wall, one leg tucked up so her knee was under her chin, the other leg jutting at an awkward angle. Her blue-and-white polka-dotted pajamas were smeared and spotted with blood. She blinked at me through blood-soaked hands. I crept toward her, mindful that Mr. Grim could still be close by, and she flinched away from me.

"I'm here to help," I said. "Are you hurt?"

It took her a second to process my question, but eventually she shook her head no. When I advanced toward her again, she whimpered and raised her bloody hands as if to ward off blows. A mostly naked stranger stood in her bedroom holding one of her umbrellas as if it was Excalibur, so I didn't blame her for not trusting me, especially after what she'd just been through.

She didn't appear to be cut anywhere. The blood must have been her husband's. I looked over my shoulder, listening. "Where is he?"

"He grabbed—grabbed my hand."

"What?"

"I woke up and he was grabbing my hand. Then I heard Zee. He—he was making ... the most awful sounds ..."

She buried her face in her blood-soaked hands. I spotted what was most likely the murder weapon: a carving knife to the right of the bed, both the oak handle and the serrated edge soaked in blood. I recognized it. It wasn't the one I'd seen in the video feed moments ago. It was from the Chen's kitchen set, and Mr. Grim had left it on Janice's side of the bed, not more than three feet from where she now cowered on the floor, sobbing uncontrollably.

Now I understood.

When she'd said that someone had grabbed her hand, that was probably Mr. Grim, wearing his gloves, pressing the handle into her palm before he took it back to cut Zhao's throat. I could already see tomorrow's headline: DISABLED STROKE SURVIVOR KILLS HER HUSBAND.

I was debating what to do when I heard sirens.

Police sirens, fast approaching. They could have been headed elsewhere, but I doubted it. Judging by the sound, I had a minute or two until they arrived. Had someone seen me enter the house, or had Mr. Grim made the call himself? My bet was on the latter. But where was he? Did he go out the back?

I looked at Janice. I looked at the knife. If I got caught with it, it would go very badly for me, especially since I would be fleeing the scene of the crime, but I didn't want to leave it either. I had to give her at least a chance—muddy the waters of motive, gum up the gears of justice, and keep the cops from latching onto one theory at the exclusion of all others. The absence of the murder weapon, especially given Janice's handicap, would sow plenty of doubt, and that doubt would create the opening for another case to be made down the road when I could hopefully present other evidence to exonerate her.

Plus I wanted—no, *needed*—a victory over Mr. Grim. Even a small one.

I grabbed the knife.

"I'm sorry," I said to Janice. "I know this is hard to believe, but it's better that you don't tell them I was here. Tell them only that a man broke in and killed your husband, okay?"

"What? What … what are you—"

"I'm going to catch the guy who did this."

She was still talking as I fled the room. I wish I could have stayed, could have comforted her, but there was no time. I had little confidence that she'd do as I asked, but what of it? If she told the cops about me, that also created an alternative theory.

Of course, if I was caught, Montana was one of twenty-seven states that still had the death penalty. So there was that.

The sirens, even louder, bore down on the house. Neighborhood dogs barked their displeasure. Still wary that Mr. Grim lurked in the house, I slid into the living room along the wall, bloody knife held at the ready, the pebbled surface scraping against my bare back. No one was there, not in the room, not standing at the screen. Where was Mr. Grim? And why had he gone back to the bedroom when Chen was already dead?

Pushing that thought aside, I focused on my escape. I had only seconds until a police cruiser screeched to a stop in front of the house, so I couldn't go out the front. The back slider was my best option.

With no more need for the umbrella, I dragged the handle over the carpet a few times to remove the fingerprints, then returned it to the vase. I thought about leaving the video camera behind because it might make an outside stalker theory more believable, but the cops might trace the serial number back to my purchase at Walmart, where there very well could be security camera footage of me buying it.

I wanted to help Janice, but not if it put more heat on me. If I wasn't free to pursue Mr. Grim, we were both sunk.

Staying vigilant, I darted into the chaos of the dining room and snatched up the video camera, wading into the sea of cardboard for the power plug. Amid the wail of sirens just out front, I heard tires screech to a halt. It must have been reported as some sort of domestic violence situation, rather than a robbery in process, or they wouldn't have turned on their sirens, afraid they'd scare off the burglar before they had a chance to catch me. It was good for me because otherwise the cops might have been at the door before I'd had a chance to escape.

Even so, it was going to be close. I managed to retrieve the power cord just as I heard car doors slamming. Two vehicles, by the sound of it. The camera under my arm, I fled to the glass slider off the kitchen.

The door was unlocked.

Was it because the Chens hadn't locked it last night or because Mr. Grim had gone out that way? The slider had been out of view of the camera, so Isaac wouldn't have had a log of it, so I'd never know, but my hunch was this was how Grim had avoided me. There was no time to worry about it now, other than to be aware that he could be hiding outside, ready to jump me.

I heard boots on the concrete, coming up the walk. Would a cop come around the back straight off? I didn't think so, but then I didn't know what had been said on the 911 call. It was all darkness and shadows on the back patio, sandwiched, as it was, between the house and the wall of arbor vitae pressing against the chain-link fence, but I saw no sign of Mr. Grim. Still, I kept the knife up as I slid open the slider, using the side of my hand so I didn't leave fingerprints.

Warm night air hugged my bare torso. It smelled of bark dust and fir. I figured the cops probably wouldn't just barge in without ringing the bell first, not without probable cause, and not with so many prank 911 calls these days, but then Janice yelled from the bedroom.

"Help!" she called out, first in a weak voice, then trying again, louder. "Help! Please! I'm—I'm back here!"

It all happened even faster then, as if we'd just crested the top of the roller coaster and were on the last downhill *woosh*—cops barking at one another, the front screen door rattling open, Janice continuing to wail for help. Seeing a rusty shed and some plastic lawn furniture but no Mr. Grim and no cops, I jumped onto a crumbling concrete pad, a weed sprouting through a crack jabbing the heel of my right foot.

Hoping all that noise inside would provide some cover, I closed the slider, again with the side of my hand. It hadn't rattled before, but it rattled something fierce now. I scrambled over the rear chain-link fence, having a hell of a time scaling it in my bare feet, especially with my cargo in toe, but somehow I traversed it with only one scrape against my thigh.

I'd just landed on bark dust in the neighbor's yard when I heard the Chen's side gate rattle.

The cops.

I ran. I ran past a wooden garden box, hopped a boxwood hedge, and landed on a paver path on the side of the house. A bedroom window brightened, like a spotlight to my right, and I caught a blur of drapes and bedposts. I heard more sirens. Lots of sirens, coming from every direction.

My bare feet already throbbing, I dashed between a utility trailer and the garbage cans, staying low. A motion light at the peak of the roof illuminated. Other house lights were coming on now. Rather than turn left, toward Isaac and the apartment, I dashed across the street and along the side of the neighbor's house, where a Harley with tall handlebars was parked on a gravel pad.

I clipped the side mirror, invisible to me in the darkness, and went spinning into the gravel.

Jagged rocks scraped my palms and knees. A gash along my neck—a rosebush must have gotten me—pulsed, hot and bleeding. Several more sirens, quite distant, joined the others. More house lights came on around me.

In seconds, the whole neighborhood was going to be lit up like a big top circus, everybody lining up to see the crazy lady running around in her underwear, carrying a bloody carving knife and a baby monitor. Step right up, folks! Careful, she bites! Staggering to my feet, I gasped for breath and tried to think. I was safely obscured in the darkness, but that wouldn't last long.

What was my plan?

The first thing I needed to do was dump my cargo. In that regard, I lucked out: three garbage cans were lined up along the house. The first one was recycling. The second one was garbage, and I lifted out the top two bags, then opened the third. It reeked of curdled milk and rancid meat. After hastily wiping off as many possible prints as I could with my T-shirt, I tossed both the murder weapon and the camera inside, tied it off again, then deposited other bags on top of it.

With luck, the whole thing would end up at the dump, never to be seen again.

Now what? Try to get back to Isaac? That would probably be impossible with so many cops just across the street at the Chens. Nearby, a screen door banged open. I heard men's voices. More sirens joined the chorus; apparently the whole Butte police force was on its way, nobody wanting to miss out on what was probably the crime of the year in this Podunk mining town.

Cloaked in darkness, I was confident that nobody could see me for the moment, but I couldn't stay long. I shivered. The night was warm, but the sweat was cooling on my body. What I needed to do was hide—in a shed, a boat, a crawlspace, somewhere. Maybe I could sneak into a house when people were at work, find some clothes, maybe even borrow a car, find a way to get out of this. When things cooled down, I could make my way back to the apartment or at least the Honda. Retrieve Isaac. The longer I stayed where I was, the more difficult it would be to navigate my way out of this.

I didn't want to hide, but what other choice did I have? I was already thinking about Tom Shelby, the next victim on the list. Was Mr. Grim on his way there? Even breathing hard, my heart racing, the threat of being caught hardly allowing me to think of anything else, I still felt swamped by a tsunami of guilt. I'd used Zhao Chen as bait. I'd gone against all my instincts to do so, following Colin Welk's advice, and I'd failed. The greater good, Welk had said, but that only mattered if something good actually came out of their sacrifice. And it hadn't. Mr. Grim had gotten away.

More than that, I felt like he was mocking me. I had no proof yet that he knew I'd been watching the Chen house, but I felt it in my bones. *Look,* he seemed to be saying, *you know who I'm going to kill, and you still can't stop me. I'm God, Karen. Nothing can stop God. You tried to act like God yourself, using the Chens as pawns, and look where that got you.*

What would Dad think of me now, doing something like that? He'd taught me to be better. He'd taught me to be strong. The Chens had needed me to protect them. The shame of my failure was a vise that would never let me go. I already knew that it would be with me forever, just like the shame I felt at shooting that girl in the meth house in Boise.

"Fuck it," I whispered to myself. "I'm done using people as bait. I'm not sacrificing anybody ever again."

I didn't know yet what that vow meant for Tom Shelby, but I'd figure something out. I spotted an eighties F-150 across the street and two houses to the left, a truck with a topper on the back with tinted windows. The carpet of needles on the topper, from the overhanging pine tree, made me suspect that the truck hadn't been moved in a while. Perfect.

I was about to run for it when I heard a car approaching from down the street. No sirens, no lights. I pressed myself against the house, the rough wood siding and chipping paint digging into my back through my shirt.

The car crept along at barely a walking pace, tires crackling on the pavement. A cop on the lookout? I wondered what Janice Chen had told them. The car inched past without stopping, and I let out my breath. Then I recognized the shape of the car.

It was a Honda Civic.

My Honda Civic.

Dirt-caked. Chipping paint. Piles of junk in the back, no rear seats. Judging by the slender silhouette on the driver's side, it was Isaac at the wheel. I sprinted into the middle of the road, waving my arms wildly, hoping he'd see me in his rearview mirror.

There was a beat—long enough for another house window to come on to the left—and then Honda's brake lights glowed red.

My eyes blurred with sweat, my bare feet throbbed from all the abuse, and blood trickled from a cut on my neck, but all I felt in that moment was pure relief. I'd hopped into the passenger seat in seconds. He was more dressed than me, but not by much, a T-shirt, sweatpants, and tennis shoes without socks.

"Isaac," I gasped. "I didn't—I didn't even know you could drive."

It was a stupid thing to say, and I didn't know why I said it. Chalk it up to adrenaline. He put the car in gear, and we cruised away—not fast, drawing no attention, a real pro. No neighbors pointed at us. No cops showed up with guns drawn. I didn't think he was going to acknowledge my comment until we stopped at the next intersection, turned left, and sped away from the Chen house.

"Dad taught me," he said.

It was the kind of thing that should have gotten him all choked up, but it was my own voice that sounded tight when I offered my reply.

"He'd be proud of you," I said.

22

"Mmm? H-Hello?"

A groggy male voice, half awake.

"Yes," I said, "is this—is this Tom Shelby? I need to speak with you. Right now. It's urgent."

There was a pause. I had a hard time hearing anything over the Dodge Ram idling next to me, a forty-year-old truck with a muffler that probably stopped any pretense of muffling when Ross Perot was running for president. I adjusted the cell phone against my ear—thank God Isaac had grabbed it on his way out of the apartment—and prayed that Shelby wouldn't hang up. The shrillness of my voice didn't help, but then it was hard to speak calmly when a herd of mustangs was stampeding inside my chest.

"Um ... yes," he said finally. I thought I made out the slow rustle of sheets. Then, perhaps realizing that only someone with a true emergency would ring him up at 4:00 a.m. on a Thursday, he took on a more frantic tone: "Who is this? Did—did something happen to Darla?"

Darla. His ex-wife. I remembered it from my research. Shelby had a high, slightly pinched voice with a faint New England accent, his "Darla" coming out *"Daw-la."* He sounded a little like

John F. Kennedy, which surprised me since he lived in Wyoming. Then I remembered he'd grown up in rural Massachusetts.

I hesitated, trying to think of exactly what to say so he didn't dismiss me as a crank. From one of the totes in the back, I'd managed to toss on some grease-stained denim overalls and a fleece sweatshirt, too warm for the weather, but it would do for now. I was still in the passenger seat. Somehow we'd slipped through the swarm of police cruisers to find refuge at a twenty-four-hour Shell station just off I-90, where we were now parked.

The mini-mart's severe fluorescent lights, directly in front of us, whitened our faces like war paint. I felt exposed. The Honda was filled with the sweaty stink of us, as if we'd both just run a half marathon, which we pretty much had. On our way here, Isaac had explained that when he'd heard the first police siren, he'd assumed I'd head out the back of the Chen house and over the fence, escaping through the neighborhoods. He'd immediately dressed, slipped quietly out of the apartment, and run full tilt for the Honda parked at the Walmart.

"Hello?" Shelby said. "Are you still there?"

"Yes, sorry," I said, swallowing. My collar might have been soggy with sweat, but my mouth was dry. "Listen, this is going to sound crazy, but don't hang up on me, all right? Your life may depend on it."

"Who is this?"

"I'll get to that in a second, but if you're in your house, it's critical that you leave right now. You're not safe. I know you can't see well anymore, Mr. Shelby, but grab your wallet, go for a long walk, to a park, something, and call this number when—"

"I'm not going anywhere! Do you know what time it is? Glad you had some fun, mocking the blind guy! Good night!"

"Wait, don't hang—"

Up. He did, unfortunately. I dialed right back. It went to voicemail. I left a message, telling him my name was Karen, that I didn't want anything but to keep him safe, and to please, please call me back right away.

I didn't want to give Shelby too much information straight off for fear he might call the police. I didn't think the cops in Casper would immediately connect me to what had just happened in Butte, but I didn't want to take any chances. I didn't want to take any chances with Shelby either. While killing Tom Shelby so soon after killing Zhao Chen would be unusual for Mr. Grim, I wanted Shelby out of his house before Grim even got to town.

I cupped the phone in my lap, waiting. The phone didn't ring. Outside, a guy in army fatigues loitered near the propane tanks, mumbling to himself, gesticulating to nobody in particular. Over the concrete freeway barrier to the east, there was a softening in the darkness, a hint of the coming dawn.

I imagined Mr. Grim racing toward that dawn, heading to Casper, an hour's head start on me.

"Fuck that!" I screamed.

Isaac winced. Army fatigue guy jerked and looked at me. I called Shelby again, explaining who I was, first name, last name, the whole deal. I told him about Mr. Grim. I told him Grim had murdered Colin Welk and that I had Welk's son with me. I told him Grim had just killed Zhao Chen in Butte, Montana, gave him the exact address, and that if he Googled it in the next hour or so, there'd surely be something in the news. I told him to look me up.

I pleaded. I begged. I said he could call the police if he felt that was the only way to keep himself safe. If he told them everything I'd just said, the cops would probably come looking for me, but if that was the price I had to pay for his safety, so be it. I went on so long that the phone actually beeped and ended the call, but I'd said enough.

He didn't call back. A minute passed, then another. I looked at Isaac, the light from the mini-mart giving his face the smooth sheen of a ceramic mask. He'd dressed in sweatpants with holes in the knees, a Yellowstone sweatshirt he'd snatched from Tim Laver's closet, and the sneakers I'd picked up for him at Walmart.

At least he'd had the presence of mind to grab his running shoes. I was currently wearing flip-flops, the only footwear I could dig up in my totes on short notice. My feet throbbed as if I'd walked over hot coals.

"Do you think he'll call the cops?" Isaac asked.

"I don't know," I said. "But let's switch places while we wait."

We did, passing silently around the bumper, avoiding looking each other in the eyes. The night air, so warm before, even when I'd been racing around nearly naked, felt chilly against the sweat drying on my face. The darkness in the east softened by the moment. If Shelby didn't believe me, what could I do? A siren rose out of the stillness, the first in a while and probably not connected to what had happened at the Chens, but it was a reminder that we couldn't stay at the Shell station.

I turned the ignition. Even if Shelby didn't call me back, I still had to protect him. I had to try.

I put the Honda in gear, and we headed to I-90, the dawn, in a burst of fiery orange, making its full entrance as we ascended the ramp. Squinting into the glare, I accelerated past a Walmart truck, roaring over the blacktop. I may not have been able to floor it all the way to Casper, but I was going to do my best.

Traffic was light, making it easy to keep my foot heavy on the accelerator as we rose into the foothills of the Rocky Mountains. We drove for ten minutes, twenty, thirty. Inside the hills, the sun rarely bothered me. Was Shelby going to call back? It didn't look like it. With the excitement and despair of the last hour receding into the rearview mirror, I felt a wall of tension rise up between Isaac and I as real as the road noise filling the silence.

We hadn't spoken about what had happened in the bedroom. There hadn't been time, and more than that, I didn't know how to deal with it. In the end, he was the one who went there first.

"I'm sorry," he said.

I didn't answer. The road hummed beneath us.

"I know this is my fault," he said.

"It's not," I said, though I didn't completely believe it.

"I'll—I'll make it up to you."

"Isaac, no. We just move forward. I'm sorry if ... if I sent mixed signals."

He said nothing. I stole a quick glance and saw that he was staring out the passenger window, maybe at the guardrail flickering past. I realized there was something I could say that might make him feel better, and it helped that it was the truth.

"Let's focus on stopping Mr. Grim, okay?" I said. "I need your help, Isaac. I would have been caught for sure if it wasn't for you. And if we work as a team, I think we can catch him. But only if we're a team."

The phone rang, vibrating on the seat next to me. Glancing down, I saw that it was Shelby.

I answered it on speaker, hastily angling for the shoulder. In the process, I managed to send the phone tumbling, bouncing off Isaac's seat and thudding against his sneakers. I barked out a hello loud enough that Isaac, who was reaching for the phone, winced. He held it up so that the phone faced me.

There was only one car behind us, a distant pair of headlights. I managed to get the Honda stopped on the shoulder, a sheer cliff face looming to our right. It wasn't until the vehicle behind us—a U-Haul truck—roared past that Shelby finally spoke.

"I'm not saying I believe you," he said, "but I'm willing to listen."

———

I SPENT HALF an hour parked on the gravel shoulder of I-90, with the phone resting on the dashboard, trying to convince Shelby that he was in mortal danger. In the end, he still didn't sound entirely convinced, but he did say I'd been right about Zhao Chen. The news of his murder had just hit the internet. There wasn't a BOLO out on me in particular, thank God, but apparently the police *were* looking for a woman seen fleeing the house, one who'd been armed with a knife.

Score one for Janice Chen. I'd created a viable alternate suspect. Maybe I could keep her out of prison yet. It wasn't much, considering the depth of her loss, but it was something.

"I almost called the cops right there," Shelby said, "but I've always had a sort of ... I don't know, kind of an instinct about people. I don't know if I believe you yet, but I also don't think you're lying. I know that doesn't make any sense, but … well, that's why I decided to take a chance and call you."

"I'll be honest," I said. "If I were you, I don't know if I'd trust me either."

"Weirdly," he said, "that makes me want to trust you more." He laughed, but the warmth died quickly. "Karen, there is something else you should know. Maybe I'm stupid to tell you this, but I'll take a little leap of faith, just as you did. The police may not be looking for you yet, but they *are* looking for the kid that's with you —and not just because he's missing. He's now the prime suspect in the bomb that killed Jared Whallen."

"What?" I said, turning to Isaac. He'd been gazing out his window at the cliff face, not having piped up even once during the conversation, but now he turned and gaped at the phone. "What are you talking about?" I continued. "What's changed?"

"It just broke on CNN," Shelby said. "Apparently they found some stuff he wrote on Reddit on Sunday morning blaming his caretaker for his father's suicide."

"That's a lie!" Isaac protested. "I didn't write that! I do post on Reddit, but I'd never—I'd never—" He shook his head. "No! Never!"

"Is that you, Isaac?" Shelby said. "I'm really sorry, everything that happened to you."

"That wasn't me!"

"I'm sorry. But … but you should know, both of you should know, that's not even the worst of it. Apparently they found another thread where you—well, not you, but whoever was posting as you—was asking questions about the kind of homemade explosives used in Iraq."

"Shit," I said.

"I didn't write that!" Isaac screamed.

The kid was hyperventilating, on the verge of a full-on meltdown, so I had to take a minute to quiet him down, reassuring him it was all right, we'd find a way to fix this, all while I was thinking this was so like Mr. Grim. Covering his tracks. Pointing the finger of suspicion elsewhere.

It was certainly going to make it tough to take Isaac out in public, that was for sure. Our options were narrowing. It wouldn't be long before they'd be looking for me too. Why did I feel like a steer being chuted straight to the slaughterhouse?

Shelby didn't say anything until Isaac finally quieted down. "So this is the guy that's trying to kill me?" he said. "The same one framing Isaac for murder? I'm really the next one on his list?"

I sighed. "I can't say it with 100 percent certainty, but if I were you, I'd err on the side of caution."

"That's putting it mildly. Why me, though?"

"I wish I knew. Sometimes he kills random people, sometimes he kills people who are famous."

Shelby snorted. "I'm hardly famous."

"Well, by some standards you are, and the point is the same. It's like he wants to prove that God can strike *anybody* down, see?"

"Right. The pattern. He spells 'GOD' on a map of the United States. But it's got to be more than that, right? His system, I mean? It can't be totally random other than just spelling out that word, or Isaac's father—Professor Welk—he never would have been able to narrow it down?"

I looked at Isaac again, who'd gone back to staring out the window. This time he didn't even glance our way. "I wish we had Welk with us. He was obviously a brilliant man, but I'm afraid we're on our own. Even his research is gone."

Shelby sighed. "Right. But why can't we just go to the cops with everything you know? Isn't that the safer option? Maybe loop them in without letting them know where you are?"

A white delivery truck blew past, kicking up road dust that floated over the Honda. I knew we couldn't stay parked on the side of I-90 much longer. "Why would they believe us? Look, the important thing, right now, is to get you safe. You need to go somewhere no one would look for you. A hotel in another city. Pay cash. Tell no one. It needs to be a place with a landline because you don't want to use your cell phone, or even Wi-Fi, once you're on the road. You can call me from the place's landline when you get there. Or not. But please, just leave now."

He snorted. "You know, it's kind of difficult to do all that when you're almost blind."

In my excitement, I'd forgotten about his macular degeneration. "Jesus, I'm sorry. I know you can't drive. Okay, look, can you get a different phone, at a library or coffee shop, call a taxi or an Uber and—"

"I didn't say I couldn't drive."

"What? You just said—"

"I said I was *almost* blind. I can drive. If I go slow. And mostly stick to roads I know."

"Are you sure? How can you even know if someone isn't following you?"

"Look, Karen, I'm not sure I believe any of this stuff yet, so I've got to do this my way. And I have an idea where I can hide out until you get here. It's not a place that anybody would think to look for me. My friend has a cabin—used to be his dad's. It has a landline because Ri—" He stopped, catching himself. "Well, I'm not going to tell you his name, not just yet, but my friend is kind of old-school that way. He took the place off Airbnb because he wants to sell it, so there shouldn't be anyone there. He told me the combo to the lockbox a while back, said I could stay there any time, but of course … my eyes …" I could almost hear the shrug through the phone.

"How do you know your friend's not there?" I asked.

"He and his wife are in Cancún for their anniversary. They don't come back until Saturday. I'll go to the cabin now. When you get to Casper, call me on this line, and I'll tell you where it is—if I've decided to trust you. I'm not quite there yet."

"All right, but I'm not calling your cell. I actually want you to turn it off and leave it at your house."

"Is that really necessary?"

"Yes, damn it!"

"All right, all right," Shelby said, "I'll play it your way. I'll call you tomorrow morning from the cabin. But only if …"

"If you decide to trust me. Yes, I get it."

"Yes. Sometime after noon? Should give you enough time to

get to Casper, or at least close. And don't worry, I'll be armed. My dad taught me how to use a gun a long time ago. We used to hunt around Green Mountain when I was a kid. Even if I can't see much, I have Big Shot Bob."

"Big Shot Bob?"

"It's what I call my shotgun. Don't need much aim with Big Shot Bob. If anybody even tries to get close, I just have to point and pull the trigger. So I'll be ready for anything, trust me."

It sounded vaguely like a threat. "As long as you don't shoot *us*, I guess."

"Well, that will depend on how much I still believe you when you get here." When I didn't say anything, he chuckled. "That was a joke. Not a good one, I guess, but I admit you've got me rattled, Ms. Pantelli. And I'll level with you: I'll be doing some more research on you. If I have an inkling that you're lying to me …"

He trailed off, but I could fill in the blank. "You'll have a whole mess of cops waiting for me in Casper when we get there?"

"Something like that."

"That's fair. But I'm not lying."

"Well, as much as I might wish you *were* lying, I'm not sure if that would improve my situation. That would mean you're certifiably crazy and have some other motive in mind. And I've probably already told you too much about where this cabin is."

He was right about that. It also meant that Mr. Grim could probably also find it without too much trouble, but going to the cabin was better than him staying in the house.

"Look," I said, "if you want more proof, I have another idea. My old partner in the FBI, Ben Wilde, he'll vouch for me. I haven't told many people about what's going on, but I've told him. He's … well, I could give you his number?"

Shelby was silent. "And how would I know the person I'm calling is really Ben Wilde?"

"Hmm. Good point. I'll tell you what. Once you get to the cabin, call the DC district office and ask to be transferred. Leave a message for Ben with the cabin's number and … and give him some kind of code word, okay? So you'll know it's really him when he calls back. You come up with it. Will that do?"

"Well, it's a start."

"I just want to help you, Mr. Shelby. That's all."

"Tom. If we're going to be in cahoots together on this thing, I think we go by first names."

"Cahoots?"

"Sorry. I am a writer, you know. I guess my diction gets a little … weird when I'm nervous. Shit, I might as well admit it. I tell kids to own their feelings. I'm scared."

I laughed. "Now *shit*, that's a word I understand. Listen, it's going to be all right. I'll be there soon. Just get going and … and …" I was going to add that he should be extra vigilant, but I glanced in my rearview mirror.

Judging by the outline of the sedan just cresting the freeway behind us, a cop car was approaching.

"Crap, I gotta go," I said. "There's a … well, an unfortunate interruption that might pull in behind my car in just a second. Let's hope he hasn't seen CNN this morning."

"Oh no. Good luck."

"Same to you, Mr. Shelby."

"Tom. Go with Tom."

"All right. Tom. See you soon—hopefully."

I clicked off, then rifled through the back, searching for something for Isaac to wear that might disguise him. The best I could do was the Seattle Mariner's baseball cap Maya had left behind, which I tossed to him.

"Put this on," I said. "Tuck your hair up in it."

"What?"

"Quick! And then lean against the window and pretend you're asleep."

He did. Even with the sun rising over the hills ahead of us directly on his face, the shadow of the cap made it hard to see much. As I feared, the police cruiser, a black Crown Victoria with a crash bar that I could just make out through the glare of headlights, eased to a stop behind us.

For a long time, the cop sat in his car. With the sun bright on the Crown Victoria's windshield, I couldn't see him, but it was a good bet he was running our plates. Shit. Had someone in the Chen's neighborhood written down our license plate number? Had the San Juan County Sheriff's Office, despite Maya's assurance otherwise, finally decided that I was a person of interest in Welk's death?

Tapping the steering wheel, I waited. A log truck roared past, rocking the Honda and kicking up a cloud of dust. I grabbed the Rand McNally atlas, turned it to Montana, and opened it on my lap. Finally, the cruiser's driver side door swung open, and a cop in a cowboy hat, his gun belt riding under his belly, stepped out.

As he approached, hand on his holster, I rolled down the window. The cool morning air smelled of the log truck's diesel exhaust and dry grass sprouting on the rocky hillsides around us. When the cop bent down, he was wearing mirrored sunglasses, so I couldn't read his eyes. He wasn't smiling.

"Just needed to check the map, officer," I said, nodding down to the atlas. "I know this isn't a great place to park. I just—I get lost real easy, you know? And my boyfriend drove most of the night, so I didn't want to wake him. I'll be going in a second."

He kept looking, a round, ruddy face revealing nothing. Was he looking at me or Isaac? If this was it, it was it. I wasn't going to resist arrest. At least I'd gotten to warn Tom Shelby. At least I'd gotten to do that.

"Can I see your license and registration, please?" the cop asked.

I fished out both for him. He looked at them for a moment, then handed them back to me.

"I was hoping it was you," he said. "I couldn't believe my luck."

"Sorry?"

He chuckled and removed his sunglasses. "I mean, if someone had stolen your car, I could have gotten it back to you, I guess, and that would have been a story, but this is better."

I shook my head. "I'm afraid I'm still—"

"I read about how you helped bring down that dude in Vegas. I can tell you've tried real hard to keep your name out of the press, ma'am, and I get that, especially coming from Wyoming where most folks keep to themselves. So I don't mind you pretending to be all ditsy on me. But I just wanted you to know ... I'm a big fan, Ms. Pantelli. A big fan."

23

A little over seven hours later, after passing fully through the Rockies and onto the other side of the Continental Divide, then barreling south on I-25 across flat, barren plains on both sides of the interstate, we finally dropped into the shallow valley where Casper, Wyoming, rested in the western shadow of the Laramie Mountains.

The sun rode high in a paint-perfect blue sky that Thursday, but it was hard to appreciate the color when my eyes felt like dried glue. My back ached as if someone had been doing jumping jacks on it while dressed in cleats. I'd done a lot of driving the past few years, but rarely like that, so hardcore, so on edge after such a harrowing night. Shortly after our little run-in with the president of the Karen Pantelli Fan Club, we'd stopped on an isolated rural road in Three Forks to spend an hour searching the Honda—I explained to Isaac my fear that Mr. Grim had been watching us in Butte—and came up empty. Other than stopping briefly in Bozeman for gas and again at a truck stop in Sheridan to use the bathroom and put on better clothes, we'd driven as fast as we could without risking getting pulled over.

Or rather, I had. As much as I appreciated Isaac rescuing me back in Butte, and as much as I could have used a nap, I didn't feel comfortable sleeping while he was at the wheel. Just too unpredictable, especially after what had happened last night.

If I'd been in Casper before, I didn't remember it. While it appeared a decent size—I later learned it had a population of about fifty thousand—there was something quaint and provincial about it. Maybe, as we skirted the northern edge on I-25, it was because I didn't see any buildings taller than four or five stories, and even those buildings seemed smaller still when surrounded by towering mountains, many white-capped even in late June.

We were in the northern Rockies, where the mountains weren't nearly as impressive as the mountains south of us in Colorado, but that was kind of like saying the Empire State Building wasn't as impressive as the Shanghai Tower. Everything was relative. If the thin, mile-high summer air in our lungs was any indication, we were pretty damn high up even in the valley.

I took the Wyoming Boulevard exit, pulling into the Denny's next to a Holiday Inn Express. I parked at the back, the lot surprisingly crowded, the sun laser-white on all the dusty wind-shields. When I killed the ignition, the Honda let out a long, exhausted sigh. Almost like a death rattle. She'd been good to me so far, but I knew one of these days I'd turn the key and she'd just give me the finger.

The cell phone's clock read 12:14 p.m. Would Tom call? If not, I had no idea what the hell I was going to do. I couldn't keep dragging Isaac all over the country, especially when he was a wanted man. We needed another solution. He'd hardly said a word since we'd searched the Honda. I'd tried a couple times, mostly commenting on the scenery, but my efforts had gone nowhere.

"Hungry?" I said.

He shrugged.

"Well, I am," I said. "Let's go get some pancakes or something."

"I think we should wait. Mr. Shelby will call soon."

"Either way, we need to eat. Let's go."

He sunk lower in the seat, tugging the brim of his cap lower. "I'll wait here."

I slipped the cell into the front pocket of my jeans, a much better fit than the overalls I'd worn earlier. My white tank top with the spaghetti straps was a little skimpy, even considering the heat, but it was better than the fleece pullover. "Isaac, come on. With your hair up in the cap, nobody will recognize you. You can put on that Yellowstone hoodie if you're really worried about it. It will make you look bulkier. And we're close to Yellowstone, so you'll look like just another tourist."

He didn't like it, but he came with me after putting on the hoodie. We were a long way from Seattle, so I didn't think we had a lot to worry about, but then we passed the *USA Today* box on our way to the front door. I spotted his photo on the bottom right of the front page—a year or two younger, a little less gaunt, probably a high school photo. Same curly red hair, though. He saw it too.

"Oh shit," he said.

"It's all right," I whispered, reaching for the door handle. "Just act natural."

I almost added *for you* since natural for Isaac was still on the unusual side. I was afraid he might bolt right there, but maybe his grumbling stomach convinced him otherwise. If I hadn't been so punch drunk with exhaustion, I probably would have opted for a McDonald's drive-through instead, but we were here now.

Inside, amid the busy hubbub of the lunch crowd, nobody so much as gave us a second look. It took ten minutes to get seated, the smell of bacon in the air, John Denver singing "Take me Home, Country Roads" on the radio. Tom didn't call. Isaac, slouched across from me in the booth with his hoodie up and head bent low, kept rubbing his temples. I told him if the elevation was bothering him to drink lots of water. He shot me a dirty look. Good. Maybe if he thought of me more as a mom than a potential girlfriend, things would go better for us.

My stomach felt queasy, but I figured it was the lack of sleep. When the waitress showed up, I played it safe with a Cobb salad. Isaac ordered a cheeseburger. Still Tom didn't call. The food came. We ate. Then we waited some more, me nursing an iced tea, Isaac working on his second Dr Pepper. There were people waiting for tables, so I didn't want to hang out in the Denny's forever, but I didn't have a plan if Tom didn't call. I didn't know where to go. Stake out his house without him?

It might have been a combination of exhaustion and paranoia, but it felt as if people in other booths were glancing at us. A guy with a silver ponytail talked on his phone. Was he calling the cops? One way or another, our Bonnie and Clyde routine was going to end.

What was I even doing here? If Mr. Grim knew I had a list of his potential targets, he wouldn't go after Tom Shelby, would he? Or maybe he would. Maybe he'd known I was watching the Chen house all along. Not only that, maybe he'd been watching Isaac and I. Maybe he'd timed his kill for the very moment neither of us were watching that baby monitor.

If I hadn't been feeling queasy before, I was definitely queasy now. Once again, I suspected that Mr. Grim was manipulating me, playing some kind of game, directing me toward an outcome I couldn't see. My paranoia went into overdrive. What if he was in the Denny's right now? He could have been anyone. He could have been that guy with the ponytail.

I took out the phone and set it on the table. No missed calls. Signal was strong.

"What if he doesn't …?" Isaac began.

"He will," I said.

"But if he—"

"He *will.*"

Isaac chewed on his bottom lip. I wondered if he was still afraid I might abandon him. I knew we should probably talk about it, but I just couldn't, not yet. It was too raw. If Mr. Grim had been watching Tim Laver's apartment, it might not have been Isaac's fault; at some point, we would have dropped our guard.

He'd just timed it so it would cause friction between us.

"I still think Mr. Grim's scared," Isaac said.

"Shh. Don't talk about that now."

"I don't know of what, but that's why he's doing all this. Something's got him scared."

"Later," I said. And then, because I was mindful of the tension in my voice and I didn't want to let Mr. Grim drive a wedge between us, I whispered, "But keep thinking. We have to stick together on this, you hear me? You and me. We may not be able to trust anyone else, but we can trust each other. We have to be smarter than him."

He nodded. We went back to waiting. Finally, with the waitress giving me side-eye, we paid our tab and left. I was down to thirteen dollars and change. We were heading into the thin, warm air when the phone finally rang. I gestured to Isaac to keep walking toward the Honda. An old Winnebago as big as a manufactured home grumbled out of the parking lot, puffing out obscene clouds of black smoke that stung my eyes and choked my lungs.

"Tom?" I said.

"Yes," he said, "it's me. Are you in Casper?"

"I am."

"Good," he said. "I was worried, but you must have extricated yourself from that … uh, sticky situation."

"I did. Listen, hold on a second." We got in the Honda, where it was much easier to hear. "Are you at your friend's place? The connection sounds different."

"It wasn't easy, but yeah, I made it. I'm calling from the landline. I did everything else you asked even though I felt pretty silly, like I was pretending to be in a spy movie. *The Blind Spy*? Sorry, I know I probably shouldn't make jokes."

"No, joking's good. And if nothing happens, then it will just be a silly story you tell your friends someday."

"Hmm. Well, I don't have a lot of friends—most of them chose my ex-wife over me—but I get your point. Where are you?"

I hesitated, but if I didn't show some trust in him, I doubted he would show any trust in me. "The Denny's on Wyoming Boulevard," I said.

I didn't think my pause had been very long, but he must have picked up on it. "I didn't call the cops on you, if that's what you're wondering."

"Okay."

"But I did call your partner."

"Oh."

"Did what you said—left a message, explained what was going on without giving him any specific details, and told him to call me and say the word "Walt" as a code word so I knew it was him. He called back a couple hours later."

"Why Walt?"

"Oh, after Walt Longmire. Those Craig Johnson mysteries set in Wyoming. He's a favorite of mine. Anyway, Ben confirmed that you're not crazy. At least not *totally* crazy. Those were his words."

"Ah. So are you ready to give me the cabin's address?"

Tom fell silent. For the moment, at least, it was quiet enough outside that I could hear the murmur of traffic from I-25. I could hear my heart beating in my ears. I could hear Isaac, staring at the side of my face, breathing through his nose. I shifted in my seat, looking out at the parking lot, watching the way the air shimmered over the blacktop.

"It's hard for me to help you unless I'm there with you," I added.

Tom sighed. "Okay, then what? Once you're here, what's the next step? "

"We'll figure it out."

"Are we just going to hunker down here and ... what? Wait for this Mr. Grim to lose interest in me? I can't hide out here from the world forever, you know."

"It's only temporary."

"Is it? My ex-wife may not care what happens to me, but my neighbors might. My literary agent. The postman. I have an appointment with my ophthalmologist tomorrow morning. Should I call and cancel?"

"No. Don't call anybody yet."

"But won't people start to get, you know, worried? I was only partly serious when I said Darla took all my friends. I do have a few people who'd care what happens to me. My dad. He might call. He gets worried easy these days. Dementia setting in, you know. I—I hate to worry him. Massachusetts is so far away. My barber. He'd eventually wonder. That's—that's someone else."

I heard the growing anxiety in his voice, the worry threatening to bloom into outright fear. For a guy in the crosshairs of a serial killer, he'd done remarkably well so far, but everybody had their breaking point. "I know this is hard, Tom, but we'll figure out a game plan when I get there. This is not going to last forever, okay? One way or another, we're going to bring this guy down."

"I'm sure that's true, but my biggest concern is I don't want to go down with him."

"You won't. "

"Well, it's not your life on the line, is it? I'm sorry, that sounded unnecessarily blunt."

"Tom—"

"It's funny, you know. Going blind, it had gotten me pretty depressed. I don't mind being honest about that. But this, somehow ... Well, let's just say that the thought of dying has made me appreciate living in a way I didn't before, you know?"

It was such a frank admission that I didn't know quite what to say, and I felt for him, this man with darkness closing in from all sides, how vulnerable he must have felt, how scared, but then something clicked deep inside me, like a door to a hidden cache of resolve I didn't know I had.

"Listen," I said, "you're not alone in this, okay? I'm not leaving your side until I'm sure you're safe. Do you understand me? I mean that literally. Nobody's getting past me, Tom. *Nobody.* And unless you tell me to, I'm not leaving no matter how long this takes."

When I actually said those words aloud, I knew they were true. Maybe I couldn't stop Mr. Grim from killing some other random person, but I could stop him from killing Tom Shelby. I'd stay forever if it came to that. I was a dead-eyed drifter, after all. I didn't have anywhere I had to be.

Whatever else he thought about me, Shelby must have sensed my resolve. "Do you have a pen?" he asked. "The directions to the cabin are pretty straightforward, but it's still easy to get lost."

24

The cabin was up on Casper Mountain in the heart of Beartrap Meadow. This was a thirty-minute drive south through cattle ranches, gently rolling hills, and eventually up another twenty-five hundred feet into a high-altitude forest of aspen, ponderosa pine, and Douglas firs.

It wasn't a forest like the ones in the Pacific Northwest—mossy, damp, and full of dense underbrush—but it was as close as it got in Wyoming. Remote and removed. On the way in, however, as we passed signs for Beartrap Campground and I saw quite a few RVs and mid-sized SUVs loaded with camping gear, I worried that the cabin would be exposed to lots of possible threats.

Yet after only a few side turns, that concern faded. The cabin, situated on at least a dozen acres of its own, was plenty isolated. It was also a stretch calling it a cabin in the same way it was a stretch calling the Ritz-Carlton a boutique hotel. Not that we could tell this from the road. When we reached the turnoff for the drive, windows down, the crisp air fragrant with the smell of pine and fir, I couldn't even see the place. There might not have been much underbrush, and most of the trees might have been tall and slender-trunked, but they were packed so closely together that they blocked the view like a ten-foot fence. In winter, we might have gotten a glimpse of the cabin, but not in June, when the aspens, leafed out and green in the afternoon sun, provided even more privacy.

Privacy was good. The gravel drive would help too. We'd hear a car approaching. The address was handwritten in white paint on a wooden post at the end of the drive, and that was kind of what I expected the cabin to be like, rough and handcrafted, but once we finally wound our way through the trees, that's not what we found.

Yes, the sprawling log house had the *feel* of a cabin, but it was also huge, with a massive stone chimney, windows big enough for a buffalo to step through, and a wrap-around deck that could have hosted a wedding all by itself, everything larger than life, even the porch swings and log chairs, which would make adults look like children when they sat in them. The shed, built in the same log cabin style, tucked back in the shadows of some firs a good hundred feet from the house, was more what I was expecting, but even it was bigger than most suburban ranch houses.

If this place had been on Airbnb, it certainly would have been beyond my budget—which, granted, wasn't saying much.

The sun, approaching its zenith, filled the clearing with golden light. Even the bare, brown earth between patches of grass looked better in the bright sun. As we approached the house, tires crackling in the gravel and kicking up clouds of dust, I didn't see any cops lying in wait. One vehicle was parked out front, a silver-and-blue Subaru Impreza with a Wyoming license plate. Except for a solitary crow strutting along the top of the shed, I saw no movement. During the day, it would be hard for someone to sneak up on us. The night was another matter. With only one porch light I could see, a cast iron lamp next to the door, I imagined it got very dark out here.

As I parked next to the Subaru, Shelby came out the front door. The pictures I'd seen online hadn't done him justice. I'd known he had a handsome face, but he had the body to go with it, trim and fit in his red plaid shirt, blue jeans, and leather boots. Plus he'd sculpted his beard into a permanent five o'clock shadow, which might have seemed phony on someone else, a little too pretty boy, but it worked for him.

Or I should say it worked for *me*. I definitely felt a stirring of attraction, and I was picky that way. I never knew what I found attractive until I felt it, but his whole look—which an unkind critic might have dismissed as Hollywood's version of a mountain man rather than the genuine article—appealed to me. Maybe it was the black-framed glasses with the thick lenses. They added just the right quirky touch.

Medium build. Nice hands. His hair was thinner than what I'd seen online, quite a bit more silver mixed in with the brown, but I didn't mind a little seasoning on my steak. As I got out of the Honda, I told myself to settle down. It was probably just the thin mountain air making me feel light-headed. We were a mile and a half above sea level, after all.

"Karen?" he said.

It was a question. He didn't say the rest, but I heard it anyway: *Is that you?* That alone said a lot about how far, or rather how little, he could see.

"Yessir, the one and only," I said, and my voice sounded squeaky and schoolgirl nervous. "Got Isaac with me. Just the two of us."

"Good, good, nice to meet you. Um, I'd offer to help with your bags, but … that might prove challenging for me. Sorry." His New England accent flared up at odd times. The word "offer" came out *aw-faw.* He took a few tiny steps, tentative, reaching for the post. "I make a mean martini, though. Turns out my friend's liquor cabinet is fully stocked."

"My first suggestion?" I said. "Don't just walk out onto the porch unless you know for sure who's there, okay? If you're alone, stay inside with the door locked."

He winced. I hated that I'd made him wince, but we didn't have the luxury of pussyfooting around each other's feelings. This was life and death here.

"Right," he said. "That was stupid of me, wasn't it?"

"Just a little careless, but it's understandable. This is not a normal situation."

A normal situation? What was I, some kind of automaton? But Tom smiled and gestured toward the door. "That's the understatement of the year," he said. "Come in, come in, both of you. I've got hot water for tea. Richie also has both Dr Pepper and Budweiser in the fridge. I'm not usually a fan of either, but I didn't think you'd want me to stopping at Albertsons. Probably bring back the wrong thing anyway."

He laughed. He had a nice laugh, warm and rich. We followed him inside, Isaac with his hoodie still up, head downcast, and making even less eye contact than usual. The stone fireplace dominated a giant, central room with a high ceiling, the living area tastefully decorated with handcrafted furniture, Native American rugs, and a corner kitchen with gray quartz countertops. It was all one floor except for a loft, mostly obscured behind thick railing spindles shaped like totem poles reachable by a cast iron spiral staircase.

The room smelled of leather, wood, and mint tea. I spotted a green Lipton box on the kitchen counter and, at the end of a walnut dining table with a live edge, a steaming black mug. An HP laptop next to the mug was open to a blank Word document, everything blown up to ten times its normal size. The blinking cursor alone took up half the screen.

"You didn't go online, did you?" I asked.

"No, no, of course not," Tom said. "I followed your instructions. I just thought I'd journal about all this. It's not every day that you're hunted by a serial killer, you know." He smiled weakly.

"But have you been here before?"

"Um, yes. Once, two years ago. Why does that matter?"

"Back then, did you bring that laptop and use the Wi-Fi?"

Shelby saw where I was going. "Shit. It might have automatically jumped on. I didn't even … even think …"

He hurried to the laptop—too fast for his bad eyesight, it turned out—because his hip clipped the table corner, and he almost missed the chair as he grasped for it. Leaning so close to the laptop that his nose almost touched the screen, he brought up the network settings with the laptop's trackpad.

He sighed with relief. "No, it looks like it didn't jump on. Richie must have changed the password, thank God."

"Okay, good, "I said. "I know this whole cloak-and-dagger stuff might seem silly, but this guy *did* put a tracking device on my Honda, and we think he might have even been watching us all along while we were in Butte."

"Really?"

"Yes."

"As in, you think he, what, set a trap for you?"

"Well, we can't know for sure, but yeah."

"You didn't say anything about this on the phone. You said he was coming after me. That he mostly kills random people."

"He *is* mostly killing random people. Maybe "trap" is the wrong word. Maybe it's more like a test. He's seeing if I can get myself out of these situations. It's a game to him."

"But what game? And why is he doing it?"

"That I don't know. He's a sick asshole, right? It's hard to understand his motivations."

Tom swallowed. I could see he didn't like my answer. I didn't like it either. The way he was looking up at me, he seemed vulnerable. Behind those thick lenses, he had pretty blue eyes—more gray than blue, really, like a dusting of blue chalk on a cement floor. I didn't see anything wrong with his eyes, but then, I didn't know enough about macular degeneration to know what to look for.

"Look," I said, "the important thing is that we have to play it extra careful. How about your phone? Did you leave that behind?"

Tom nodded. "It was hell getting here without GPS, let me tell you. Sorry. I'm not trying to sound like some whiny wimp about this."

"Being brave is not the opposite of being scared!" Isaac piped up.

When we looked at him, the kid actually blushed, a real splash of red too. It was the first time I could remember him blushing since I'd met him. He looked at his shoes.

"Um, yes," I said. "I suppose that's—"

"Being brave is just telling yourself it's okay to be scared," Isaac mumbled, "and doing whatever makes you scared anyway. From *Mountain Heart. Fur and Fang* series, book twelve. I liked that one a lot."

"Oh, of course!" Tom said with a startled laugh. "My God, I'm so wound up I don't even recognize my own writing! In my defense, though, that was many books ago. So you read that one, huh?"

Isaac looked up, a furtive glance before staring at the floor again. He might have been taller than both of us, but with his hoodie up and hair jutting out the sides in oily red tangles, he reminded me of the stick dolls that Hope made for her friends in elementary school, ones fashioned from pipe cleaners, yarn, and cut-up rags. "Yes, sir," Isaac said. "Several times, sir. I liked them a lot. Except for *The Edge of Moon Canyon*. That one was kind of slow. Sorry. I probably shouldn't have said that. That was the only one I didn't like, though. The rest of them are awesome."

There was an awkward silence before Tom burst into laughter. Isaac looked up, surprised, and then the two of us joined in. The laughter may have had more to do with all the stress we were feeling than about what Isaac had said, but that was fine.

It was good to laugh. We all needed it.

———

I'D BEEN WORRIED that with all the windows in the cabin—and I decided to keep calling it a cabin since that was what Tom called it—that I'd feel like we were in a fishbowl, especially at night, but the grand nature of the place also included expensive curtains and blinds. That was my first order of business: I closed them all up and instructed Isaac and Tom to keep them that way. The windows high in the peak provided plenty of sunlight anyway.

Isaac and I fetched a few things out of the Honda—some

clothes, some toiletries, and some camping gear in case we needed to head into the woods on short notice. Tom, not wanting to deal with the stairs with his poor eyesight, had already claimed one of two downstairs bedrooms. I took the adjoining room, which left Isaac with the loft. He retreated to it almost immediately, once again back to being sulky and morose.

Tom handed me his Winchester shotgun, a 1920 Model 12 that had apparently been a gift from his father, which had in turn been a gift from his father. Pump action. Walnut stock. The magazine tube held six twenty-gauge shells loaded from the rear. The barrel had been cut down to eighteen and a quarter at some point, making the gun look like a prop from an old gangster movie.

We were in his bedroom. It was a decent-sized room even with a four post bed dominating it. We weren't even standing that close to another, but there was always something intimate about being in a bedroom when you're attracted to someone. Even holding a gun in my hands—for me, at least, the ultimate sexual buzzkill—didn't shake the feeling. With the curtains closed, the downy green bedspread looked soft and inviting in the yellow glow from the dresser lamp.

"I'm sorry about what happened," Tom said.

"What?"

"With that girl. In Boise."

"Ah."

"I just thought I should say that right away. The elephant in the room, you know. I read all about it. It sucks. What happened to you. I just wanted you to know."

I nodded, my throat tight, my face warm. The shotgun may not have changed my frisky mood, but bringing up what happened in Idaho certainly did. "I'd actually feel more comfortable if you keep it," I said, trying to hand the Winchester back to him. "As a last line of defense."

He opened the top drawer in the side dresser and gestured for me to look inside. There was a leather wallet, Subaru keys, and a Smith & Wesson M&P 40 semiautomatic pistol. Stainless steel with a black matte finish, it looked like it had never been fired.

"This is my last line of defense," he said. "I bought it a few years ago, after I got a couple weird letters from an overly zealous fan. And, um, after my initial diagnosis."

I leaned the Winchester in the corner and took out the pistol, ejecting the magazine. Loaded with ten rounds. I made sure the thumb safety was engaged before sliding the magazine back in and returning the gun to the drawer. I was leaning so close to him that I could smell his aftershave, a whiff of citrus. It got the engines of desire going for me again.

The way he looked at me, I didn't think I was the only one feeling it. "Okay, fair enough," I said, "but you barely need to aim with the shotgun. Even if your target's blurry, you'll hit it."

"Yeah, and that's the problem. I don't want to shoot something blurry. And I'm really rusty anyway, you know? I haven't shot in years. I might shoot …" He trailed off. It might have been my imagination, but I felt as if we'd moved closer.

"One of us?" I said.

"Yes. Or … or another innocent person."

"Okay. But, um, I'm not really innocent, you know." I laughed and backed toward the door. "I'll keep the shotgun. Big Shot Bob, right? Actually, we'll keep it in the living room, just behind the couch. That way any of us can—"

"Hey, look at what I found!"

It was Isaac, standing in the doorway. He looked back and forth between us, and there was something on his face, jealousy, confusion, that I might have paid more attention to if I hadn't been so irritated at him surprising me. I almost laid into him for startling somebody with a shotgun until I saw what was in his hands.

It was an old MacBook, one of the originals, its shiny white exterior coated in dust.

———

HE'D FOUND the laptop in a rolltop desk in the loft. Placing it on the dining room table, we hit the power button and found that it not only worked, but it had decent Wi-Fi. The battery didn't hold a charge, but it worked fine when plugged in. I complimented Isaac on his knack for finding random laptops. Since I doubted Mr. Grim could have anticipated that we'd be sequestered in this particular cabin, the computer meant we could now keep up with the world, as there was no way he could have put tracking software on it. It could also help us plan our next move.

What, exactly, *was* our next move?

That was a question I decided to put off until I had a chance to unwind, enjoy one of those Dr Peppers, and do some reconnaissance around the property. Isaac wanted to go with me, but I told them both to stay inside with the door locked and the shotgun close at hand. I tossed on the denim jacket I had in the Honda, taking the Smith & Wesson in the inside pocket. This might have been Wyoming, with more guns per capita than any state in the union, but a woman in the woods with a gun in plain view was still likely to raise questions. And the last thing we wanted was for anyone to be asking questions about us.

By the time I got outside, it was after five o'clock, and the air had cooled enough that I was glad I'd worn the jacket. The shadows of the ponderosas on the west side of the clearing stretched across the patchy grass like a giant's outstretched fingers. Circling the cabin, I could see quite a distance, not just across the clearing but well into the area of tall trunks in every direction.

There were windows on all sides of the cabin, so there were no real blind spots so long as we kept up a good vigil. The shed was locked. There was one window, facing the empty field, but the curtain was closed, and I couldn't see much around the edges except what might have been an axe. I got the barest whiff of gasoline. There was a lean-to off the back where firewood was stored. It was cooler there and smelled of damp fir. Judging by the moss on the top logs, I doubted anyone had chopped wood in a while.

I heard the distant rumble of a truck, but that was it; otherwise it was just me and the gentle rattle of the aspens in the crisp evening breeze. I did detect the faintest aromas of charcoal and barbecued hamburger, which led me to believe a neighbor was close.

Wrong. The nearest one was a solid ten-minute walk through the woods to the north, and there was no active barbecue. There wasn't anybody. The smell must have been coming from the campground. The modest two-level house with a daylight basement off the back, painted a similar green as the ponderosas so it practically disappeared into the forest, hadn't been used in weeks, maybe even months, judging by the buildup of pine needles on the front deck. There was no gravel drive, just a deeply rutted dirt road, and the only tracks were partial and broken, as if they'd endured plenty of storms since they'd been laid.

I heard the distant thumping bass of someone's stereo, farther to the north. Following the noise, I headed again through the forest over lumpy, uneven ground, far enough from the road that I only spotted it once, a strip of black that quickly vanished into a shimmery tapestry of green and brown. I heard laughter. The smell of barbecue got stronger. I glimpsed tents and RVs tucked back into the trees. Beartrap Campground. I was probably a mile from the cabin now.

The thin air and rough terrain had me breathing heavier. Doubling back, I veered toward Casper Road, the main one we'd come in on, then did a complete perimeter loop around Richie Rich's property. I doubted his name was Richie Rich, but I'd heard Tom refer to him as Richie, so that was what I was going with. The other neighbors were much farther away from the cabin, at least fifteen minutes on foot. Both houses looked occupied, so I didn't get too close.

Heading back, I felt good about hunkering down here. It was as good a place as any. I said so as I stepped inside, wiping the dirt off my sneakers on the floor mat. Tom, who'd let me in, said he was glad to hear it.

Isaac sat at the dining room table, studying the MacBook's screen intently. He had his hood down and even had his hair pushed back behind his ears. His expression looked serious. I wondered if he was reading news stories about himself. I wondered if that was good or bad.

"Sorry for not taking you along," I said to him, "but maybe we can go out together later, okay? I think we're pretty secure. The nearest neighbor is a good ten-minute walk, so it's not—"

"Oh, I know."

"You know? You know what?"

"That the nearest neighbor's about ten minutes away." Looking up from his computer, he must have taken note of my confused expression because he turned the computer around so I could see the screen. He was using Google Earth, and if I wasn't mistaken, it was currently showing a bird's eye view of the cabin.

"You know," he said, "you could have found all that out without taking a step outside."

"Smart aleck," I said.

He blinked. Once again, he'd just been stating the obvious. The humor was lost on him.

25

If someone wanted to approach the cabin without being seen, they'd definitely do it from the rear, and they'd most likely do it at night. There might have only been one porch light out front, but there were no lights out back, and only two windows faced that direction. The first was in the downstairs bath, but that was opaque glass, so it was impossible to see anything unless the window was open. The second was in the loft, which provided a pretty good sweeping view of the clearing behind the cabin during the day, but it would still be almost impossible to see anyone coming from that direction in the dark.

Still, as long as either Isaac or I was on watch patrolling the various windows—and maybe Tom, when he was awake, was in the living room with the windows cracked open to easily make out the sounds of someone approaching—I was fairly confident we could prevent anyone from sneaking up on us.

I said as much a half hour later when we gathered in the living room to form a plan and eat the chicken dumpling soup we'd found in Richie Rich's cupboard. I claimed the brown leather armchair. Isaac and Tom took the matching couch. It might have been half past six, but the sunset was still hours away, and even with the curtains closed the light streaming through the upper window made the room feel bright and airy. My hair, still wet from my quick shower, dribbled cool water down the back of my neck.

"It's still hard to believe Mr. Grim could ever look for us here," Tom said. His bowl, sitting on the glass coffee table, was still piping hot, steam rising in cascading waves. He reached for the spoon, then must have thought better of it because he massaged his temples instead. "Richie's not even that close of a friend. More of an acquaintance."

My own ceramic bowl felt plenty warm perched on my lap, but I thought it might be cool enough to drink. I was wrong. When I took a sip, it scalded the top of my mouth. Great. Now I'd be tasting chicken dumpling for the rest of the night.

"I've learned not to underestimate this guy," I said. "It's just safer for us to assume that he knows we're here."

"But how?"

"I guess he could have put a tracker on Mr. Shelby's car," Isaac said.

We both looked at him. He was slurping his soup as if the temperature didn't bother him. He didn't even look at us. For once, I was glad. He would have seen how embarrassed I was at this oversight. Tom must have read my expression because he shook his head.

"You can't think of everything, Karen," he said.

"I should have thought of *that.*"

Finally, Isaac stopped slurping to look at me. "Sorry. I just thought of it too."

"It's not your fault," I said. "I'm just glad you thought of it now. It makes me wonder if we should ditch Tom's car and head somewhere else."

"Jesus," Tom said, "Is that really necessary? You told me yourself you saw Mr. Grim just this morning, back in Butte. He couldn't have gotten here before I left my house. And you said you were extremely careful to make sure you weren't followed."

"He might have scouted you out ahead of time," I said. "We don't really know his methods, right?"

"Right, right. Sorry."

"Don't apologize. When I joined the FBI, Ben told me that the dumb questions you don't ask will lead to the dumb mistakes that get you killed, so it's better to be dumb and live."

Tom chuckled. "I'm really starting to like your old partner. He wanted to come out here, you know?"

"What?"

"When we talked on the phone, he said he had someone watching your sister, so he was free to come out and join us in Casper. He really wanted me to tell him where we were going."

My jaw felt tight. "Did you?"

"No. He was very insistent, though."

"That's Ben for you."

"He said you have a really hard time asking for help—even when you need it."

I shot Tom a withering look, and it must have been strong enough that he could see it even with his poor vision because he raised his hands in a placating gesture.

"Don't shoot the messenger," he said. "I have a hard time accepting help too. Part of why I've had such a tough time dealing with my … condition."

My sympathy melted my anger, but only a bit. "I *did* ask for help. I asked Ben to watch my sister. *That* was what I need him to do. But for some reason he keeps second guessing me."

"But that was for Hope," Isaac said. "It's easier for you to ask for help when it's for someone else."

I turned my withering stare toward Isaac. "What is this? Gang up on Karen day?"

Isaac put his bowl on the coffee table and shrunk back into the leather. "Sorry," he mumbled.

"Don't apologize!" I said. "Both of you need to stop apologizing so much! We don't have time for bullshit like apologies."

They gazed at me in silence. Now my face actually felt warm, a good sign I was blushing with embarrassment, which pissed me off even more. "Look, I'll search Tom's car when we're done eating. For now, let's assume I don't find anything, which means we're staying here at least a week. That gets us past Mr. Grim's … normal schedule. Is there enough food to last the three of us that long?"

Tom frowned. "It's pretty slim pickings, but there is a country store just—"

"We'll get food if we need to," I said, cutting him off, "but I'd rather not leave for this first week unless it's really necessary. Let's do an inventory of our rations after we're done eating. And other assets we might have."

Tom chuckled. "Rations. Assets. You make this sound like a military campaign."

"Well, it's probably better we think of it that way—like how we handle security, for example. Let's talk about that for a second. We need a game plan there too."

Sipping our soups, we agreed that I'd take the night shift, sleeping during the afternoon or evening, and that Isaac would be on guard during daylight hours. Tom would back us both up. Since he'd be sticking to his normal sleeping schedule, however this would mean he would be backing up Isaac more than me, which was what I wanted even though I didn't say that aloud, afraid I might bruise Isaac's feelings.

Our soups finished, we took our bowls to the kitchen and did a quick inventory of the food situation. Tom was right. It was slim pickings—most of what was in the fridge was bad, including the milk and the eggs—but there were cans of soup in the cupboard, a bag of frozen peas in the freezer, and enough other odds and ends that I suggested we could probably make it last a week if we stretched it.

"Stretch it," Tom said, shaking his head. He was rinsing his bowl in the sink, the hot water steaming up his glasses. "I didn't think I was going to have to go on a damn hunger strike. There's only so long I can survive on cocktail peanuts and saltine crackers, you know."

He might have meant this as a joke, but it came out laced with so much bitterness that I was momentarily taken aback. So was Isaac, apparently, who froze with the silverware drawer open. He'd been opening the drawers one by one in the vain hope that someone might have squirreled away some candy bars.

Tom must have realized how he'd sounded because he looked over at us—or rather, in our general direction. I could almost forget he was half-blind until I noticed his eye contact was a little off.

"Sorry," he said, "that came out wrong."

"What did I say about apologies?"

"Right, right."

"From this point on, I'm going to dock you one saltine cracker every time you say the word sorry."

Tom smiled, then turned to Isaac. "I think we better watch ourselves, kid. I'm pretty sure I can survive without the soup, but the crackers were the one thing I was actually looking forward to."

Isaac glanced back and forth between us. "I read in the *Guinness Book of World Records* about a guy who didn't eat for a whole year. He was really, really fat, though. And they had a bunch of doctors who monitored him and made sure he was, like, healthy and stuff."

Tom laughed. "Well, I don't know if I could make it a year, but I can definitely go a few days." He winced and rubbed his forehead.

"Are you okay?" I asked.

"Huh?"

"I've noticed you keep doing that. Rubbing your forehead."

"Oh. Just a headache … A combination of the elevation and my bad eyesight, I think. Oh, and maybe a touch of existential fear on top of it. That's not helping." He smiled. "So the plan is to stay a week and then reassess? That's it?"

"The plan is to keep you alive. That's enough."

"What if he just chooses somebody else?"

"Then he chooses somebody else. Right now, I can't do anything about that. I can do something about you."

He frowned. "And after a week? What then?"

"We'll figure that out in a week."

"I'd like to think a few people will miss me—my literary agent, if nobody else. Or maybe one of my neighbors. Most of them know about my poor eyesight. They'll get worried when I don't bring out my trash on Monday. What if someone files a missing person report?"

"Then they do. We'll deal with it when it happens."

"Karen—"

"Look, I know it's not much of a plan, okay? But at least we're showing Mr. Grim he isn't the all-powerful deity he thinks he is."

"But how are you going to catch him when you don't have any more names on the list? You said the next person is just 'Jane Doe' in Phoenix."

"You let me worry about that. We'll watch the news, see what develops, and adapt accordingly. Now how about I go search that Subaru? I think it's pretty damn unlikely he put a tracker on it, but none of us are going to sleep easy until that possibility is ruled out."

"I'll get the keys," Tom said, "but I'm going with you."

"I don't think that's a good idea."

"I don't care. I may not be able to see well, but I know all the nooks and crannies to search. And I refuse to let this guy dictate everything I do. I'll be careful, but I won't be a prisoner."

Reluctantly, I relented. Isaac came too. I didn't even try to refuse him. The sun perched just over the ponderosas, so bright on the Subaru's driver side window that I had to squint when I looked at it. I left Big Shot Bob nearby on the gravel, and we proceeded to search the car.

It hadn't been five minutes when Tom exclaimed in surprise.

We gathered around him, where he sat in the driver's seat holding a black plastic cup with slots for coins. That was in his right hand. In his left, he held a familiar-looking black plastic square between his thumb and forefinger. A gray GP logo was plainly visible.

"Shit," I said.

"It was inside," he said. "I had to unscrew the lid to get to it. Second place I looked."

"GeoPulse. Just like the one in my Honda." I started for the shotgun. "Shit, shit."

"Karen? What are we going to do?"

I snatched the gun, scanning the woods again. "We're leaving, that's what we're going to do. Both of you, back inside. Pack everything we have into the Honda. I'll stand watch, and then we'll get the hell out of here."

While Isaac started toward the door, Tom didn't move.

"No," he said, "I think we should stay."

26

———————

W hatever breeze had blown through the clearing must have stopped because I heard nothing, no rustle of leaves, no creaking of branches. Both Isaac and I, standing on the stairs to the porch, stared at Tom. He leaned out of the Honda, his eyes, magnified by his thick lenses, as large as cartoon eyes. I kept waiting for the punchline.

"Come again?" I said.

"I said I think we should stay. I think we should put the tracker back in the coin holder and pretend we never found it."

"Are you serious?"

"I'm deadly serious." He chuckled. "Maybe I shouldn't use the word "deadly," though, right?"

I stepped onto the gravel, the crunch the loudest sound in the clearing. Maybe that should have made me feel better because I didn't hear someone out there, but for some reason the absence of other noises heightened my dread. "Tom, don't joke. You know what this means, right? This tracker means he knows we're here."

"I know exactly what it means," he said, although his voice warbled this time.

"It means he was in Casper before we got here."

"I know."

"Maybe weeks before. Maybe months."

"I know."

"You wanted definitive proof he's had you targeted? This is as close as it gets!"

"I know! Believe me, I know!"

Our raised voices carried much farther. I didn't like it. I didn't like what he was saying to me either, nor did I understand it. The sun, finally dipping into the upper branches of the aspens, lanced the gravel with yellow, dust-filled beams. Just like that, it was darker in the clearing, the air hazier. It was a reminder that night was on its way. I didn't want to be here when it arrived.

I adjusted my grip on Big Shot Bob, pointing it off to the side, and took a few more steps toward him. I forced myself to speak calmly even as I could feel my heart beating up in my throat. "I don't get it," I said. "If we stay, we're sitting ducks."

Tom shook his head. "And how long am I supposed to hide from him? A month? A year? I'll always be worried he'll find me."

"It would never be that long. We'll get this guy one way or the other."

"How?"

"If we don't get him this week," I said, "then we'll move you someplace safe, somewhere he'll never find you. You don't have a lot keeping you in Wyoming anyway, right? We can get you a new identity. He'll lose interest."

Gripping the top of the Subaru door, Tom rose to his feet, a little unsteady, a little unsure. I was acutely aware of how exposed he was to danger, especially now, especially out in the open. I instinctively stepped toward him. He raised his hand.

"See," he said. "That's just the thing, isn't it? Are you always going to be there to help me?"

"I'll stay with you as long as it takes, I told you that."

He sighed. "Even if I believed that was possible, it's not just about me, Karen. Maybe he doesn't get me this week, but he'll kill someone else, right?"

"Those are just ... theoretical! You're the one I'm most concerned with right now."

"Fine, but I get a say, don't I?"

"Tom, if he knows we're here, he has a huge advantage!"

"But he doesn't *know* we know."

"Excuse me?"

"If we leave the tracker alone, he'll never know we found it. He'll assume we didn't. That means we have an advantage over him. We *know* he's coming. In a way, we're setting a trap for him."

"No."

"Karen, you said so yourself. We have to act as if Mr. Grim knows we're here, so what's the difference if he really does? It will make us even more vigilant. This might be your last, best shot at catching him."

"And use you as bait? No! I told you after what happened with the Chens that I would never do that again."

"They didn't have a choice in the matter. I do."

"I'm not sacrificing anybody!"

My voice boomed over the clearing. He winced. Without quite knowing it, I'd moved so that our faces were no more than a foot apart, close enough that the gray flecks in his blue irises looked like stepping stones across a pond. We had the door between us, a barrier of metal and glass, and it was a good thing because I felt like throttling him.

Or kissing him.

For even in my rage, I had to admire his bravery. It made him even more attractive, which made me even more desperate to protect him. When he didn't say anything, I groaned and stepped around the door to the back of the car, cradling the shotgun and surveying the trees under the first curtain call of dusk. Danger lurked behind every trunk, in every divot, inside every shadow, big and small.

"Karen," he said to my back. "Listen to me, okay? I'm not going to tell you I'm not scared. Because I am. No doubt. But you see why I have to do this, don't you? I can't live in fear the rest of my life. It's not just him. I'm going blind. It's going to be hard enough, losing the light. I can't—I can't be afraid of what's in the dark too."

I turned around. It was his face, even more than what he said, that got me. I expected to see fear there, and I did, but what I mostly saw was resolve. It was pure insanity, staying at the house when Mr. Grim knew we were there, but that didn't mean Tom was wrong. We might never get another chance to catch him.

"Look," he said, "I appreciate your help. God, do I. But I get it if you and Isaac need to leave. It's fine. It's not fair for you guys to take this risk. I'm *choosing* it. Maybe I didn't really believe he was real until this moment, but I do now. Boy, do I. And I'm drawing the line—"

"Will you shut up?" I said.

He blinked.

"Of course I'm staying," I said. "I still think it's stupid, but I'm staying. I can't speak for Isaac, though." I looked at him where he stood on the deck leaning against the post. He nodded. "Okay then," I said. "I guess that makes two of us."

"Thank you," Tom said, glancing back and forth between the two of us. "Really. Thank you."

I shook my head and pointed at the house. "Let's get inside and figure out how the hell we're going to catch this guy when he shows up—without getting killed first. You're being a stubborn, pigheaded buffoon, you know that?

As I approached, Tom smiled.

"It takes one to know one," he said.

———

Knowing that Mr. Grim was coming may have heightened my sense of dread, but it didn't change our plans all that much. What were we supposed to do, set out some steel traps in the patchy grass? Dig pits and cover them with aspen leaves? Bury landmines in the gravel?

No, our best option was to catch Mr. Grim in the act, which posed all kinds of additional risks, of course. For Tom, most of all.

Mostly, knowing that Mr. Grim was *definitely* showing up, rather than *possibly* showing up, just made us more jumpy and irritable.

As the light in the upper windows faded from rusty orange to a deep shade of violet, we talked about this in the living room, spelling out our security plan in more detail. I perched by the bay window, Big Shot Bob in my lap, the curtain parted just enough that I could see down the gravel drive. I'd cracked open the window. I heard the lonely howl of a coyote and not much else.

We decided that Isaac would take the noon-to-midnight shift. I'd cover midnight to noon. I'd usually catch some sleep after dinner. No matter what, Tom would get me up by 11:00 p.m. That way the only time one person was on watch—me—was after they went to bed and before either of them got up in the morning.

I didn't permit either of them to argue this point. I may have relented on staying at the cabin, but I was in no mood to debate minor details. I was in charge.

All windows and doors would remain locked. All curtains would stay closed. Whoever was on watch could crack open a window if they were stationed near it, but only then. Unless it was an emergency—as in, the cabin was on fire—neither of them should go outside without my permission. If someone *was* outside for some reason and wanted back in, they should announce themselves, then knock three times, plus, after a pause, three more. Tom put up a little fuss about this, arguing that even inmates on death row got a few minutes of fresh air in the prison yard every day, but he trailed off when I trained my icy stare on him.

"One shot from a sniper rifle," I said, "and your brains would be splattered all over that deck. That breath of fresh air might be the last you ever take."

He didn't put up a fuss about anything after that. I said that under no circumstances should anyone answer the landline. Everybody was free to go online with the MacBook, but under no circumstances should anyone email, post in a forum, or in any other way communicate with the outside world. I let my gaze linger on Isaac with that one, who, I worried, might feel compelled to clear his name on Reddit or other places.

Most of the time, Big Shot Bob would remain behind the couch near the front door. Tom would keep the handgun either on his person (only when we thought there was a threat that warranted it) or in his bedside drawer. Isaac told us he'd never even held a gun, and since Tom had already confessed to me that he was pretty rusty, I said I'd give them both lessons tomorrow.

We brainstormed a bit more, coming up with all kinds of crazy schemes for catching Mr. Grim, but as the night deepened and even the coyotes fell silent, our thinking got fuzzier and our eyelids heavier. When Isaac started rambling about using dirigibles wrapped in tin foil, I sent them both off to bed. It was closing in on midnight anyway.

There was half a can of Folgers in the pantry, so I brewed a pot of coffee and settled in for the long night. I made myself comfortable on the leather chair, Big Shot Bob lying on the floor in front of me like a loyal hound dog, the breeze flitting through the window growing cooler. I was on my second cup when Tom crept out of his bedroom, barefoot, hair mussed, and dressed in a short-sleeved white undershirt and gray sweatpants.

"Too wired to sleep," he said.

"Try. I need you both rested tomorrow."

He nodded. He was looking at me, but I couldn't tell if he was seeing me. There was something about how quiet it was that prompted us to whisper. There was something about whispering that made me think about hanky panky. I wondered if Tom was the sort of person who would ever call it hanky panky. I wondered if I was. I could never remember thinking of it as hanky panky before.

"I just wanted to say again how much I appreciate you doing this, Karen," he said.

"Okay."

"He's really coming, isn't he? No joke?"

I nodded. "And probably before next Wednesday. That's a week right?"

"A week." He chuckled. "What if he doesn't—"

"He will."

"But if he doesn't, do you think—"

"He will."

He bit down on his lower lip and looked at his bare toes. I knew I was coming off as pretty harsh, but I wanted him to get how serious I was. Mr. Grim would make his move in the next week, I was sure of it.

"You can still back out," I said. "We can pack up and go right now."

"No."

"There's no shame in it."

"No," he said more firmly, looking at me again. "At least, not until next Thursday. If he killed Zhao Chen Wednesday night, that's over a week, right?"

"A week is a long time."

"I'm staying."

"Fine."

He sighed. I heard something outside, a rustle or a flutter. When I leaned into the gap in the curtains, cupping my hands around my face, I saw the shape of what might have been an owl taking flight over the nearest ponderosa pine.

"You sure you don't want me to stay up with you a while?" Tom asked.

"I'm fine," I said.

"It's really no trouble. I'd just be tossing and—"

"I said I'm *fine.*"

I glared over my shoulder at him. Nodding mutely, he disappeared into his bedroom.

So much for hanky panky.

———

OTHER THAN BEING STARTLED around 2:00 a.m. by a pair of glowing eyes under the Honda that turned out to be a raccoon, the rest of that first night passed without incident. I moved from window to window, listening closely, but I never heard anything but the wind whispering through the aspens. I heard Isaac crying at one point, but when I headed up to the loft, I found him asleep in his clothes on top of the bed. Or at least pretending to be.

I drank so much coffee that my hands shook and my bladder quivered in agony. By the time Isaac emerged Friday morning, rubbing his red eyes, I was sitting with my legs tightly crossed in an effort to avoid pissing my pants. I'd been too afraid to leave my watch for even a minute. It was such a close call that I vowed to never do that again, whether someone was there to cover for me or not.

When nature calls, even serial killers sometimes had to wait.

Tom emerged a short while later, staring out at a vaporous fog that had settled into the clearing just after dawn. Was he mad? Let him be mad then. But after he brewed a new pot of coffee and whipped up some instant oatmeal for all of us that he'd found in the cupboard, he seemed more relaxed. He even told us a funny story about the disastrous weekend he took his ex-wife, then his girlfriend, tent camping for the first time. It was actually nearby at Beartrap Campground. Two things happened: one, they had the worst thunderstorm Casper had suffered in years; and two, she confessed that she hated camping but had been afraid to tell him so.

"I figured right then it was a sign I should propose," Tom said. The steam from the coffee misted the bottom of his glasses, but I could still see the playful glint in his eyes. "If she liked me enough to go camping even though she hated it, she was probably marriage material, right? But looking back now, I figure it was also a sign we'd eventually get divorced. I mean, she hated camping and I loved it, right?"

We all laughed at that one. Despite my exhaustion, I hardly slept Friday afternoon, not used to the firm mattress, not used to sleeping during the day, and constantly waking with a start, sure that Mr. Grim was in the house. Saturday went better, though the sleep was still fitful. Other than a family of deer, nobody ventured onto the property. I gave them both brief lessons on how to fire the shotgun and the pistol as well as how to load the spare ammunition Tom had brought.

We ate chicken noodle soup, microwave popcorn, and what-ever else we could scrounge. I exchanged a few texts with Ben; nothing was happening in Atlanta. We watched the news closely. No one reported Tom missing. No new leads regarding the investi-gations of Jared Whallen or Zhao Chen surfaced. Isaac was still considered the prime suspect.

A week. I told myself we just had to make it a week, which still left a lot of time to kill. While Shelby's friend had a full set of *Britannica's Great Books* in the loft, I was too restless for Plato's *Republic*, Darwin's *On the Origin of Species*, or even Twain's *Huckle-berry Finn*, leaving me with the piles of *National Graphic* and *Real Simple* magazines in the wicker basket next to the couch. And while the farming techniques of Australian Aboriginals and the fine art of decluttering one's master closet were interesting enough to pass the time for the average person, even they required too much concentration when I kept expecting to see a serial killer out my window.

So talking it was then. And since Isaac wasn't much of a talker, that meant mostly talking to Tom Shelby. In the first few days, we talked mostly about the mundane or the obvious. The weather. Where we were from. Current events. The one thing we *didn't* talk about was Mr. Grim. In Tom's case, talking about something other than the serial killer out to get him was probably a survival mechanism. For me, avoiding the topic was a way to sidestep my guilt for not being able to stop Mr. Grim so far.

The frost that had formed between us began to melt. It might have melted further if not for what happened Sunday. I woke around four o'clock in the afternoon, only about an hour after I'd gone to sleep, with an urgent need to empty my bladder. Heading back to the bedroom, it was so eerily quiet in the house that I popped my head in the living room just to make sure my room-mates were all right.

Isaac, his back to me, stood gazing out the gap in the blinds covering the kitchen window. His hair was still combed straight back from his shower this afternoon when I'd warned him that he would either bathe or we'd force him to sleep out on the wood pile. He wore a gray, zip-up hoodie he'd found in the downstairs closet, one he'd been living in for days, but at least he was clean. Storm clouds had blown in that morning, making the light gray and flat through the high peaked windows, but it was not yet raining.

"Where's Tom?" I asked.

Isaac jumped. When he turned around, I could tell by his sheepish expression that something was wrong. I stepped closer. Under my bare feet, the hardwood was peppered with cracker crumbs, already dirty after just a couple days.

"Isaac? What's going on?"

"He made me promise not to tell you," he said.

"He did what?"

"He likes to go for walks in the woods. He said he'd go insane if he didn't. He's usually only gone a few minutes."

"Jesus."

"He takes his handgun. He doesn't go far, just a little ways into the trees."

"I don't believe this. And I assume he waits until I'm fast asleep before he goes?"

Isaac didn't answer this. He wouldn't look me in the eyes either. While I patrolled the windows in a foul state of mind, he wisely sat his ass back down at the laptop to stay out of my way. It wasn't a few minutes. It was more like an hour, and those dark clouds threatening rain grew even darker, choking off the sun.

When I finally saw Tom tramping out of the firs, every divot and loose branch throwing him off-balance, the first raindrops speckled the Honda's windshield. When he actually reached the cabin, the storm took that as an invitation to start in earnest, a steady torrent on the deck.

He announced himself and knocked three times, then knocked three more. Isaac looked at me. I didn't move. Finally, Isaac got up and unlocked the door before scurrying back to the MacBook.

A draft of cool, wet air blew into the cabin as Tom opened and closed the door. I was leaning against the kitchen counter, arms crossed, glowering at him. His green North Face windbreaker was dotted with moisture, and the right front pocket sagged where he'd stowed the Smith & Wesson. His glasses instantly fogged, but I wasn't sure if he would have been able to see me anyway.

"Well," I said, "at least you didn't get caught in a thunderstorm."

He didn't jump as much as Isaac had, but it was close. Isaac, seated at the dining table, focused on the MacBook with laser-like intensity.

"Uh oh," Tom said, trying a feeble smile. "You sound just like my mom when I tried to sneak out after curfew."

"Don't even," I said.

He sighed. "Look, like I told Isaac—"

"You have a death wish? Is that it?"

"No, I just—"

"The safest place for us to be is in the cabin. Every time we stick our heads outside, we put ourselves at risk."

"But you're doing it," he said feebly.

"Yeah, but I'm ..." I trailed off, but Tom caught where I was going.

"Not blind," he said.

"I was going to say, I'm a former FBI agent who was trained for this sort of thing."

"Liar." He smiled playfully, but there was real hurt in his voice. "Right now, you're probably wondering if I'm going deaf as well as blind. Fine. I get it. It won't happen again. I just ... I get antsy, all right?"

"We can still leave, you know. We can leave at any time. "

"No," Tom said firmly.

"If we go someplace else—"

"No, Karen. I haven't changed my mind about that." He unzipped his jacket, then removed his glasses and wiped them on the black golf shirt he wore underneath. "We leave, we give up our best chance at catching this guy. I'm not doing that. And what if someone recognizes Isaac? It's too risky."

"But—" I began, but then Isaac interrupted me.

"It's not just me now," he said.

Tom and I looked at him. He was still hunched over the laptop, and he turned it so we could see the screen. It was the CNN home page. The first thing I saw was my face, the photo taken on my first day at the Bureau—a little younger, a little more youthful idealism in the eyes, and my hair tucked in a ponytail so tight that it raised my eyebrows.

The second thing I saw was the headline, the letters so large that even Tom could probably read them: FORMER FBI AGENT NOW CHIEF MURDER SUSPECT.

27

———————

I t was probably fitting that the light drizzle outside turned into a torrential downpour as I absorbed the news. The three of us huddled around the laptop. Since Tom couldn't read the actual article without sitting inches from the screen, I read it while squatting on the floor next to Isaac, then relayed the highlights.

"The headline pretty much sums it up," I said, shakily rising to my feet. "An anonymous email was sent to the *Butte Monitor*, but it got picked up by everybody else. Photos of me going into the Chen house. They clearly showed my face."

Tom swore under his breath. "But these days, that sort of thing could be faked, right? They can't just take it at face value, especially if it's anonymous."

"That wasn't all." My forehead felt as if someone had draped a hot washcloth across it. I tried to swallow the acid taste in my mouth, but it wouldn't go away. "There were also shots of me and Isaac going into the apartment across the street. The *Monitor* talked to people all over the neighborhood. Miles Trusk, that landlord guy, said he clearly remembered me. A door cam on the next street had a clear shot of my Honda, time-stamped with the license and everything—and with me climbing into the passenger seat. I need—I need to sit down."

I collapsed into the chair next to Isaac. I wasn't there long. As dazed as I felt, it only took a second for me to realize that none of us were watching the window, and then I sprang out of the chair and grabbed Big Shot Bob. I peered out the crack in the curtain, hoping he was out there, hoping he was stupid enough to show up when I was feeling this way.

There was no movement. The night looked darker. The breeze felt colder. The gun felt heavier in my hand.

"And you think he did this?" Tom asked.

I didn't turn around. Tom didn't have to say who *he* was. We all knew. I heard Isaac clicking the trackpad. I gripped the shotgun so tightly that the metal grinded against the bones in my left hand.

"It proves he was in Butte," I said. "Watching us the whole time. The *Monitor* hinted that the anonymous source was a local drug dealer who didn't want any trouble, but come on."

"But you already knew he was watching you."

"No, I *thought* so, but I didn't know it. Now I know. He's been manipulating me, moving me around, but why? He could have killed me there, but he didn't. I don't get it. He's playing some kind of game, but I don't know the rules."

"Maybe there are no rules," Tom said. "You said it yourself: he's a sick asshole."

"But there's a reason," I said. "I just don't know what it is yet. Maybe it's a twisted reason, but he's not doing this to me randomly."

Isaac groaned. "The *Seattle Times* just posted an article with an interview with a cop that remembered you sleeping in your car at the SeaTac rest area the same day that my house blew up. People are now saying we killed Dad together. That we—that we were in a relationship together."

"Of course," I said, still peering out the gap, still hoping Mr. Grim would be stupid enough to walk down the gravel drive right into my line of sight. "He's trying to pin the murders on us.

You just watch, other stuff will come out now. Forum posts between Isaac and me. Social media. Something." I shook my head. "I should never have gone to Seattle. I should have left it alone."

Behind me, Isaac rose so abruptly that his knees knocked against the bottom of the table. The look on his face, a mixture of betrayal and grief, was so gut wrenching that he was already out of the kitchen and up the stairs before I managed to speak.

"Isaac!" I said. "I only meant—I meant ..."

But what could I say? I'd only meant that maybe Mr. Grim wouldn't have blown up the house if I hadn't gone to Seattle, but I didn't know that, not really, and how would that make me sound anyway? In that one remark, I'd run the full gamut of self-centered, insensitive, oblivious, and—the home run of insults —cruel.

I shook my head. Our whole approach was wrong. I'd make amends with Isaac, but not now, not when I wasn't in the right headspace. I'd just find some way to hurt him again. That's what I did. In the end, I always hurt everyone I cared about. The people who were safest, both physically and emotionally, were the ones who stayed farthest from me.

"Talk to me, Karen," Tom said. "What are you thinking?"

"I'm thinking it's time to go."

"Now? In a rainstorm?"

"How much more proof do you need that he's setting us up for something?"

"But where would we go?"

"It doesn't matter. We'll figure that out on the road."

"It's going to be dark soon. Don't you think—"

"None of that matters, Tom!" He flinched. He may not have been able to read my expression, but his ears worked just fine. "Don't you see? All that matters is that we get the hell out of here. No more debate! Get your stuff! You and Isaac can load up what we have while I watch the—"

"No," Tom said.

"Excuse me?"

He crossed his arms. "No, I'm not leaving. Nothing's changed."

"Everything's changed! He's been making me dance like a puppet! I'm done."

"If we leave," Tom said, "innocent people will die. This is still our best chance to stop him. I understand if you and Isaac need to leave, but I'm staying."

"Damn it! He'll kill you!"

"I'm dead already."

That one hit me like a slap. "What? Come *on*. Because you're going blind?" When he didn't answer, I said, "That's not a death sentence. Not even close. You're a young man. You have many good years ahead of you."

He laughed, but it was a rueful laugh. "I'm not *that* young. And I wasn't talking about going blind."

"What?'

Tom shook his head. He'd handled my outburst with equanimity until now, but the anguish on his face was palpable. He started to say something, stopped, then stepped up next to me at the window. Gently, he pried Big Shot Bob from my fingers. "I haven't exactly been a nice person, okay? My ex-wife, when it got bad, she liked to say I cared more about my little animals than I cared about real people. She wasn't wrong."

"Tom—"

"No, listen to me. When I said I was dead already, I meant ..." He tapped his chest. The more he spoke, the rougher his voice got. "In here. I feel dead in *here*. Inside. I've felt that way a long time. "

"You don't have to—"

"Stop, Karen. Please, just stop. I'm not saying I *want* to die, okay? I'm just saying ... Hell, I don't know what I'm saying. I just know that I want to put other people first for once. That's worth it to me. I don't blame you for going, though."

"And leave you alone? Are you serious?"

"You both need to focus on clearing your names. That's got to be the priority for you."

"I don't believe this."

"I don't mean I'm not grateful! I am. I'm just saying that you and Isaac really should—"

"I'm not leaving you alone."

I reached for Big Shot Bob, but he held it away from me.

"You don't have to stay out of pity," he said. "I mean it. I understand if—"

"Will you shut the fuck up? "

For the second time, I made him flinch. I used his surprise as an opportunity to snatch the shotgun from him. When I looked up, there were only inches between us. We stood so close together that I could actually make out my own vague silhouette, a dark shape with little definition, both in the reflection of his glasses and, behind the lenses, in his pupils. That was how I felt. A dark shape with little definition. I was an outline without inward detail.

I related to what Tom was saying more than I wanted to admit. I may not have felt dead inside, but I did feel empty.

"Karen," he whispered, his breath warm on my nose. "You don't have to—"

"Shh."

"But—"

"Shh. "

Outside, the sun, hanging over the aspens, glared on the Honda's windshield. All was still. All was quiet inside the house too. His aftershave, that citrus scent I'd gotten so used to the past few days, was intoxicating. I was conscious of the cold barrel in my hands, the early evening light accentuating the silver in his hair, and the heat of him, his physical presence, so close.

I found myself staring at the tiny threads in his lips. I found myself leaning closer, then closer still.

"I want to stay too!"

It was Isaac, shouting at us from the loft, a blur of red hair off to my right. We both jerked back like a couple teenagers caught by a nosy parent. My heart was playing ragtime. My face felt like I'd just raced the hundred yard dash.

The way Isaac gripped the banister, his fingers white and

bony, made me think of a red-tailed hawk perched on a branch. His hair was parted just enough that I could see his eyes, and there was something hawk-like in his gaze too, penetrating and cold.

"Okay then," I said, swallowing away the lump in my throat. "Okay, I guess—I guess we're staying."

———

AND WE DID. For better and worse—and on that Sunday night, I was pretty convinced it was for the worse—we stayed. It wasn't long before I realized that Tom may have been right anyway. While it was true that we were setting ourselves up for Mr. Grim like two-dimensional pigeons at a county fair shooting booth, it was also true that even if Isaac and I left, Mr. Grim would never leave me alone. I felt that in my bones. He'd come after me sooner or later, and Isaac too.

At least this way, there was a chance that we could get the advantage over him.

Maybe.

———

IF THERE WAS one thing I didn't do well, it was *wait*. Even worse than waiting was feeling like I was doing nothing.

It was why I always gravitated toward menial jobs that kept me busy rather than ones that had me just sitting around. Waitresses. House cleaners. Yard workers. While I'd once worked the nightshift at a motel in Omaha, where if the phone rang even once it was a busy night, and patrolled as a security guard at a warehouse in New Jersey, where it was so quiet I could hear the mice breathing, these stints never lasted more than a few days before they drove me crazy.

I needed to be busy. I needed to be doing things. I needed action.

We kept up our routines as Sunday night turned into Monday and as Monday turned into Tuesday. The downpour turned into a drizzle, then back into a downpour again. The cloud cover was so dense and gray that it was hard to believe it was June. I did a daily reconnaissance walk, but I didn't know if Tom was staying indoors or not. I didn't want to ask. I figured if he was willing to risk his life by staying at the cabin, then it was up to him to manage that level of risk while we were here.

We talked. We watched the windows. We grew more stir crazy with each passing day, getting more curt, snapping at each other about stupid things, me especially. Our paltry food supply grew more dire, so we resorted to thinning the soups. We followed the news closely. As I'd feared, Tuesday afternoon more information came to light allegedly linking Isaac and I. It wasn't social media. It was worse.

Sheriff McKinley, Maya's boss, got a search warrant to search Bev's house and cottages because they knew I'd been staying there. They found a tin box full of good old-fashioned letters ostensibly from Isaac to me.

The police hadn't revealed the specific contents, but they were suggesting that not only did the letters indicate a romantic connection between us but also that *I* had staged Colin Welk's death with Isaac's help, making it look like a suicide. They also hinted that both of us had been indoctrinated into some sort of deep state conspiracy group that explained why we'd killed Jaren Whallen and Zhao Chen.

"So Mr. Grim tightens the screws even more," I said.

It was nearly five o'clock, but for once the sun was shining. Shafts of golden light painted gold medallions on the hardwood floor. Tom and I sat at the kitchen table, nursing our English breakfast teas. This time it was me at the computer, reading the *Seattle Times* aloud. Isaac was positioned at the bay window, peering out the gap. We'd run out of coffee yesterday and even our tea supply was running low.

"I'm sorry," Tom said.

"Well, it's not a surprise." I sighed. "I can't even imagine what Bev thinks of me now."

"Bev?"

"Beverly Ann Braun. My..." I was going to say "friend," but that seemed presumptuous after I'd left her in a lurch. "Landlord on Orcas. She owns the cottages."

"Well, she wasn't quoted, right? Maybe she doesn't believe it."

"Or maybe she's so pissed at me she can barely speak." The pain was so deep that it felt like a corkscrew drilling into my chest. I could handle most of the world thinking I was a murderer, but not Bev. I could barely handle her thinking bad of me. "Whatever. It's not like I was ever going back there anyway."

"Hey, don't say that. Who knows where life will take you after this. Maybe I'll even go with you."

That got me to chuckle, but when I looked at him, I could see that he was serious.

"Wow, really?" I said.

"Like you said, there's no reason I have to stay in Wyoming."

"There's no reason you have to go to Orcas either."

"Well ... I can think of one reason."

Without quite realizing it, I'd leaned closer. Or he'd leaned closer to me. I was trying to think of how to respond when Isaac piped up.

"The crackers are gone," he said.

We looked at him. He was still at the window, not in the kitchen, so it was an odd thing to say. Or maybe not so odd considering the unmistakable jealousy in his eyes. It wasn't just that. He was looking right at me, and I was so taken aback by his overall posture, the rigid jaw, the clenched fists, that I forgot what he'd even said.

I swallowed hard. "What's that?"

Just like that, Isaac's Jekyll and Hyde routine flipped. The smoldering intensity was gone. He shrugged and shoved his hands into the front pocket of his hoodie. "The Saltine crackers," he said, looking outside again. "I ate the rest of them. Sorry."

"That's all right," I said.

"We're pretty much out of food." His voice had become a whisper.

"I know. I was actually thinking about this. You know, I could scrounge some food from some of the homes around here. That green house to the north—it looked empty when I scouted it a few days ago."

"No," Tom said, "I don't want to steal."

I chuckled, thinking it was a joke, but he didn't laugh. "But we're eating Richie Rich's food right now?"

"Richie Rich?"

"Sorry. That's how I've come to think of your friend that owns this place."

"Oh." He laughed. "I guess that fits. Richie Rich. But that's different. I'll pay him back someday. I'm even going to pay him for using his place. Breaking into a stranger's house and taking their stuff? I don't want to cross that line."

"But we could just leave some money for—"

"No, Karen. I don't want to do that."

His tone had changed. It was sharper. Colder. I leaned back in my chair, raising my eyebrows at him.

"I'm not sure we have enough," I said. "What are we supposed to eat, ketchup packets?"

"We'll make it. It's just another few—" He winced, then reached for his temple.

"Are you all right?" I asked.

"I'm fine. Just the headaches again."

"Are you sure there isn't something more serious—"

"I said I'm fine!"

It was an outburst worthy of Isaac, who not only turned and looked at us but took a step in our direction. I raised my hands in a gesture of surrender. Tom glared at both of us, like a wounded animal backed up into a corner, then the fight went out of him. His shoulders sagged.

"Sorry," he said.

"It's okay," I said.

"No, it's not. I shouldn't—"

"It's okay, Tom. Seriously. We're all cranky." I rose from the table, parting with a curt wave. "And speaking of that, I should get some sleep. Don't let your guard down, now."

"Karen—"

But I was already gone.

———

It would not be true to say I slept like the dead because just like the night was defined by the day, sleeping was defined by the waking, and the dead do not wake. But I slept the deep, timeless sleep that I hadn't slept since we'd arrived at the cabin—really since Colin Welk pointed a gun at me at the Orcadia and maybe much longer ago than that—and I dreamed of Hope on a blue tricycle and Ben munching a Philly cheesesteak in DC and Tom walking barefoot on the narrow strip of sandy shore below Bev's cottages in Buck Bay.

I woke to a noise in the dark: something metallic, a click. I sprang upright in bed, heart pounding.

"What? What?" I said.

"Jesus," Tom said. "Sorry. I—I didn't mean to startle you. It was just the door."

The dream, the feel of cold sand still lingering between my toes, slipped away, reality reasserting its hold. It was so dark that I could only see him as an outline. I looked at the window, clutching the bedspread against my chest, each heartbeat hitting me like a sucker punch from the inside out. I'd left the window cracked open but locked. The air was fragrant with the smell of pine and damp gravel.

I was naked except for my underwear. The breeze was cool on my face, but the room was warm.

"Is it eleven already?" I asked.

"No," he said. "No. Not yet. Ten or so. I think."

"Okay. Is Isaac—?"

"He's fine. He's on watch. I just ... I thought I should apologize. For earlier."

We were both whispering. I heard a semi truck downshifting a long way away, miles maybe, and something about that distant sound made me relax. If I could hear that, I could hear Mr. Grim.

We were safe. For now. As I relaxed, I became conscious of how exposed I was under the sheets, the cotton rubbing against my bare skin.

"There's—there's no need," I said.

"I shouldn't have snapped at you like that."

"Don't worry about it."

"I appreciate everything you're doing."

"I know."

"I'm so grateful."

"Okay."

"I should, um, probably get out there. Back up Isaac. I kind of, you know, snuck in here. I tried to be … quiet."

Neither of us moved. We both knew what he was saying. We both knew what he was offering. I should have sent him away. It would have been the responsible thing to do, not just because of Mr. Grim, but because of Isaac, because of his feelings, but I was so wound up from all the restless days, with so much pent-up energy, that I craved what he was offering the same way someone lost on a desert island craved not just rescue but even the idea of rescue. The promise of it.

My eyes were beginning to adapt. I could see the glint of his glasses. The shape of his bearded jaw. His lips. I figured he could see me too. He might have been going blind, but he could see well enough. I let the bedspread fall away.

"Let's see how quiet we can be," I said.

———

WE WERE QUIET. We were oh so quiet. Like horny little mice, which was what Tom whispered in my ear at one point, which was such a silly thing to say that we had to hold back our laughter. We were both in a hurry too, everything frantic and rushed, not much foreplay, and even the desperate search for a condom—I actually had a few Trojans in my bag—carried out like two thieves hurriedly tossing a house with an alarm already ringing in our ears.

That was what we were. Not mice but thieves. We were stealing a moment that shouldn't have been ours, that was wrong to be ours given how fraught and dangerous our circumstances were—but damn it, we were taking it anyway, and to hell with the consequences. "Fast" and "sex" were not usually two words that went well together in my experience, but in this case it worked. It worked very well.

Tom was a good lover. He knew where to touch. He knew when to linger. In those desperate, frenetic moments in the darkness of my room, he *saw me* with his hands and his lips. He used every part of his body well, and when we both got to the place we were aiming for, we did it together, and it was satisfying in a way that it hadn't been with a man in so long that I'd forgotten just how good sex could be.

His body was lean and firm without being muscular, a few wrinkles, a little wear and tear, but he was like a well-worn saddle —comfortable and familiar without being old. When it was at its best, I actually had to clamp a hand over my own mouth, fearing that I was not only going to tip off Isaac about what was going on in my bedroom but maybe even people at Beartrap Campground.

That was something that never happened to me. I was usually the silent type, to the point where some of my more insecure partners asked me if I'd actually enjoyed myself. There was no doubt about it this time, and Tom, grinning at me foolishly as we lay next to each other on the sheets, knew it too.

"Well," he said.

"Yeah," I said.

"That was …"

"Oh yeah."

The moon must have broken free of the clouds because a sliver of moonlight sliced across both of us. His face was pink and glistening. The smell of us, that distinctive mix of sex and sweat, filled the room, but it was not an unpleasant smell. I lay with my head on his chest, our bodies pressed up against one another. His heartbeat was as steady as a metronome.

"I really should get a little more sleep," I said.

"Yeah."

"And you should be out there backing up Isaac."

"I know."

Neither of us moved. Then something moved.

"Or," I said, "we could do that again."

"Hmm. There doesn't seem to be anything wrong with *that* part of my body."

"There's really only one way to know for sure."

"You're not going to say seeing is believing, are you?"

I closed my eyes, leaning up close to his face even as I reached down below. "Tom," I breathed into his ear, "I don't need my eyes for what I'm about to do to you."

He groaned. Whether it was from what I was doing with my hand, the anticipation of what was to come, or both, I couldn't say, and I didn't care either because all I cared about was getting back to that place where I could stop thinking completely. Where the past and future didn't matter. Where I could feel alive and wanted and, if only for a few seconds, less lonely.

When he was ready, I climbed on top of him. Then we were moving together, and maybe I was a little too into it, and a little too loud, because it was quite a while before I heard the sound. It was even longer before I cared enough to figure out what that sound was.

"What was that?" I said, stopping.

"Huh?"

"I thought I heard something. Like …"

I was going to say "whimper," but there was no need because then I definitely heard a strangled sob outside my door. Then the thump of footsteps. The click of a deadbolt opening.

"Shit," I said.

As I slipped off Tom and onto the floor, the front door slammed hard enough to shake the house. I dashed naked to the window, throwing back the curtains just in time to see Isaac as he sprinted past the Honda, his gray hoodie flapping behind him, his tennis shoes crunching across the gravel. It was nearly a full moon, and for the first time in days, no clouds obscured it, so everything out there was bathed in a milky white glow.

I shouted his name but he didn't stop. The Honda momentarily blocked my view, so it wasn't until he was fully beyond the car that I saw the unmistakable shape of what was in his right hand.

The shotgun.

Tom, propping himself on his elbows, said something, but the words didn't register. I lunged for the light switch, got it on, and managed to scramble into my underwear, but my other clothes were nowhere to be found in the twisted tangle of sheets, at least not in the few seconds I searched, and I couldn't give it more than that. I had to go. I had to go now.

"Hey, hey," Tom said, reaching for my arm. "He'll come back. Give him a chance to—"

"No! He's got Big Shot Bob."

"It's fine. He just wanted protection. And we've got the handgun, so we ..." And then I saw understanding dawn in his eyes. "Oh. Oh, you're afraid he's going to ... to ..."

I yanked my arm away and sprinted out the door before he said the words, but they weren't words that needed to be said anyway. If we heard the sound of the shotgun, we both knew Isaac's target wouldn't be Mr. Grim.

28

For the second time in a week, I was sprinting outside nearly naked. Any sane person would agree that was twice too many, and this time I wasn't even wearing a bra, just a pair of Hanes black underwear. It was like a game of strip poker, and I was down to my last chips. Someone with my impulsive nature should probably reconsider whether it was really a good idea to sleep in so few clothes.

Yet in the moment, I wasn't thinking about any of that. If my breasts swung a little more freely, I barely noticed. If the gravel pierced the skin of my bare feet, drawing blood, it didn't register. If the night air chilled the sweat on all my exposed, sweaty flesh, it didn't matter.

All that mattered was getting to Isaac as fast as I could.

In the moonlight, I cleared the Honda, scanning the field, looking for him, and spotted him off to the left as he vanished into the shadows of ponderosas. I kicked into another gear, leaping the divots where the darkness pooled, pumping my arms, putting everything I had into it. Behind me, Tom yelled something, but I didn't stop.

If I stopped, I might lose my chance. If I stopped, I might regret it forever.

Stupid. So stupid. I should never have taught him how to use the shotgun. As I ran, I castigated myself for not foreseeing this, for not being more careful, for giving into my desires when it was obvious that Isaac would take it hard. He'd lost his mother, his father, and his caretaker. He'd thought he was losing me. From his point of view, what was left for him?

As the cabin receded behind me like a lighted atoll, darkness hugged me from all sides, the occasional strips of moonlight like white-crested waves on a vast sea. I stumbled. I staggered. I barely stayed upright, but I kept running. The wall of aspen and pines, with their tall, spindly trunks, loomed like the teeth of some ancient beast, everything beyond a foreboding darkness that threatened to swallow me whole.

I plunged into that darkness like Jonah into the whale. The wind on my face cooled, the smell of pine and fir stronger and mixed with the scent of moss and moldy leaves. I ran in the direction Isaac had gone, but I didn't see him. It was all shadows. A jagged rock cut into the arch of my right foot. A thorny weed raked across my left ankle. The pine needles littering the grounds sliced my skin like thousands of paper cuts.

Knowing that Mr. Grim could be lurking, I abandoned caution and yelled Isaac's name.

He didn't answer. The darkness grew deeper. I tripped over an invisible log, tumbling, scrapes and cuts everywhere, but was back on my feet before I even registered the blood trickling down my right calf. My eyes began to adjust, the aspen leaves on the ground like metal shavings, the lower branches like dusty old bones.

No Isaac in sight.

Unsure of which direction to go, I stopped to catch my breath at the edge of a clearing, leaning against a mammoth ponderosa pine. The bark was as rough as crumbling concrete. The moonlight, gauzy and diffuse, filtered from an opening in the canopy above, illuminating scattered rocks and tufts of grass. The clearing was maybe fifty feet across.

I held my breath for a moment, listening. Except for a far-off hoot of an owl, I heard nothing. I searched the ground, hoping to see footprints, anything, but I was disappointed there too. I stepped into the clearing, cupping my hands around my mouth to shout his name, when Isaac spoke before I got the chance.

"You're naked."

He said this as he stepped from behind a ponderosa pine on the other side of the clearing, the Winchester held loosely at his side. His face was awash in shadows, his eyes deep caverns. The moonlight washed out his gray hoodie, gave it a dusky, chalk-like appearance, making it almost as white as his tennis shoes.

I nodded, buying time. His finger wasn't on the trigger. Had he pumped a round into the chamber yet? There was no way to know. For the first time, I considered the possibility that he might actually shoot me rather than himself. "So," I said, trying to keep my tone light, "what's going on, buddy? A little late for quail hunting, isn't it?"

"You're naked," he said again.

"Yeah, I … I thought maybe we should start a nudist colony out here. What do you think?"

He didn't say anything. I couldn't see his eyes, but I could feel his leer. I'd clearly blown a fuse in his brain. Self-conscious, I started to cover my breasts but then stopped. I'd been trying to use humor to jolt him, but maybe I didn't need to work that hard. Maybe his hormones would do the trick for me.

I took a few more steps into the clearing, trying not to look like I was really walking in his direction at all. "We really should go back inside," I said. "It's not safe out here."

"You're naked," he said.

"Wow, you're like a broken record. You *have* seen a *Playboy* once or twice, haven't you?" I laughed. He didn't. I admonished myself for the joke, knowing he might feel belittled. "And I'm not *totally* naked. I've got underwear on, you know. That's something."

He said nothing. I looked at the sky, taking another step, watching the shotgun. It hadn't moved from his side.

"I think I see a few stars," I said. "Must be amazing on a really clear night, huh?"

Again, he didn't answer. I kept looking up, taking another step, wondering if I should just ask him for the shotgun and then quickly discarding the idea. The longer he didn't think about the gun, the better it was.

"You didn't even look at them." I laughed and took another step, fully conscious of the sway of my hips. "You sure are quiet, buddy. If there's something you want to—"

"Stop," he said.

"Isaac—"

"Not—not one more step."

I'd made it halfway across the clearing, lit up in the moonlight like a Broadway singer ready for her big solo. He was still too far away for me to make a play for the shotgun. "Okay. Okay, look, I've stopped. Just … Just keep talking, all right? What's wrong, Isaac?"

I was close enough now that when he shook his head, a violent shake, I could see the wet sheen in his eyes.

"Talk to me," I said.

"Go away. Leave me alone."

"I'm not leaving you."

"I fucking hate being here!"

I flinched. His shout wasn't the response I was hoping for, but his feeling of being trapped was a place to start. A way to reach him maybe. "I get that. I hate it too. And it will end soon."

"I don't mean *here*. I mean alive. I hate this!" This time the shotgun moved, an alarming thump against his thigh. "I'm—I'm broken! I don't want to be alive."

"Isaac, don't say that."

"It's true! Everything's messed up." With his left hand, he rapped the side of his skull three times. "In here! It's all messed up in here! I'll never be right again!"

"Hey, hey, I know it seems bad, but it's going to be okay. As soon as this if over—"

"You had sex with him, didn't you?"

It was a blunt question, embarrassing to answer standing there topless in the moonlight, but I saw no point in lying. "Um, yes. I did. It was a ..." I was going to say it was no big deal, but I didn't want to diminish it either, knowing Isaac was smart enough to see through any bullshit. "It just happened, okay?"

"I hate him! I hate Tom Shelby!"

"Isaac, you don't mean that. He's one of your favorite—"

"He's different! He's—he's mean!"

"He's mean? Why do you say that?"

"The way he looks at me! I can tell. It's like he wishes I weren't here! And—and—and he didn't even remember his own writing!"

"Come on, he's just scared. People act different when they're scared. And he's written a lot of books. He can't remember everything word for word. Come on. You've got to cut him a little slack."

Isaac took ragged, shuddery breaths, his nose running with abandon. I kept my gaze fixed on Big Shot Bob. Long and bulky, the shotgun was an ungainly weapon for committing suicide, even with a shortened barrel. The most obvious target, really the *only* target, was under the chin, and the easiest way to pull the trigger was with the thumb. That would require swinging the shotgun around and repositioning his hand, which would take time.

How much time? We were now separated by maybe twenty-five feet. On flat ground in good shoes, I could cover twenty-five feet in just over a second, but that was not from a full stop. Plus I was barefoot, and the ground was certainly not flat. Call it a second a half, and that was probably generous—if I even made it there at all. The shadowy minefield of lumpy ground meant I was just as likely to fall on my face as I was to get my hands on Big Shot Bob before Isaac pulled the trigger.

A second and a half may not have seemed like much, but I knew from experience that it was an eternity. If I had any hope, I needed to cut that time down by half. I shivered. After all the heart-pounding exertion of the last half hour—the sex, the running, and all the adrenaline that came with it—my body was finally noticing the chilly night air.

"You're cold," Isaac said.

"I'm all right."

"Do you want my sweatshirt?"

"No, that's—" I began, then realized that his offer was an opportunity. He was thinking about me. Not himself, not how depressed he was, not what he wanted to do with that shotgun. *Me*. "Sure," I said. "Yeah, that would be great, actually. That's very nice of you, Isaac. I appreciate it."

"Okay. I'll, uh, I'll toss it to you. But stay where you are, okay?"

I nodded, shivering again, this time deliberately. I watched him closely. I didn't want him thinking there was even the possibility that I was going to make a move. If he'd been wearing a pullover, he definitely would have had to put the shotgun down, but it had a zipper, and he was able to work the zipper down with his left hand.

At some point, though, he'd have to shift Big Shot Bob to the other hand, if only to pull the sweatshirt sleeve off his right arm. That was probably my best opportunity.

"God, I'm cold," I said. "Maybe a nudist colony at seven thousand feet elevation isn't such a great idea after all."

I didn't get a laugh, but I thought I saw a smile. It might have been a grimace, but anything that helped short-circuit a potential meltdown was a good thing. The plain T-shirt he wore underneath was so white that it glowed. Watching me the whole time, never once looking away, he'd managed to get the sweatshirt off his right shoulder with his left hand, his free hand.

As he worked the sleeve down his right arm, I leaned slightly forward. Almost there. So close.

Then it happened. With the sweatshirt balled up at his right wrist, he shifted the shotgun to his left hand. And, for the briefest of moments, he looked down.

I exploded into a run.

Traversing twenty-five feet was about the same as traversing two average bedrooms back to back. It should have been nothing, but almost all the energy was in the build up. The jagged twig I landed on with my first step, and the sunken cavity I landed in with my second, slowed me even more. If I'd been sprinting twice that far, the average speed would be a lot higher, but I barely covered half of it in the first second.

One thousand one ...

In the time it would take to say those words, Isaac looked up, gaped at me, then recovered enough to get the shotgun back to his right hand. If he'd wanted to shoot me instead of himself, that would have been all the time he needed. But he didn't really want to shoot me. That was part of what I'd been counting on. He did manage to raise the shotgun, even with the sweatshirt dangling from his right wrist, but there was hesitation. A pause. A blink.

It wasn't much, but it allowed me to tackle him.

I dipped my right shoulder and plowed into him. There was almost nothing to him, which should have been to my advantage, but he was so waif-like that his body went flying. As we tumbled in the darkness through dirt, dry grass, and pine needles, we separated. The shotgun skittered away.

Without a bigger body to slow me down, I careened far to the right, much farther than I'd intended. My head slammed into the trunk of the ponderosa pine he'd been near.

It was like an earthquake happened inside my skull. The impact stunned me senseless—but only for a second, and then all my senses flared at once. Pain radiated out to all my extremities. I tasted blood. My ears rang. I clung to consciousness the way a drowning sailor holds fast to a stray piece of wreckage, desperately to stay above water. I couldn't black out. Black out and I was dead. Or Isaac was.

I staggered and swayed to my feet. My vision remained hazy, but the moonlight lit up the shotgun's barrel like a beacon. I saw Isaac scrambling for it, so much closer than me. I took a step, but the world spun around me, whirling shadows, and then I was on the ground again, choking on dirt, an exposed root scraping my eyelid.

By the time I managed to raise my head, Isaac had the shotgun.

Pointed under his own chin.

"Stop!" he cried. "S-s-stop right there!

He was on his knees, sobbing. As my personal earthquake began to subside, I saw that his left thumb was on the trigger. He'd braced the butt of the Winchester on the ground and was holding the forestock with his right, leaning his chin on the muzzle. We were only separated by six or seven feet, but it might as well have been six or seven miles.

"Isaac, don't," I said, raising myself up onto my elbows. "Listen—"

"Stay there!"

"I'm not moving. See, I'm—I'm not moving."

"You tricked me!"

"I know. I'm sorry. I was only—"

"I was nice, and you tried to trick me!"

"I know! I shouldn't have done that. I just—I care about you. I don't want you to hurt yourself. Please put the gun down."

"Do you love him?"

"What?"

"Just tell me. Do you love him?"

"I just met him."

"But could you? Someday?"

His eyes were so shadowed that I couldn't read them, but his voice had changed, losing some of its hysterical edge. Flat on my stomach, looking at him across the gulf of shadows, I weighed my answer carefully. This was not a direction I expected the conversation to go, but now I could see how inevitable it was. I could also see what he was really asking, what he'd been afraid to ask.

He wasn't asking whether I loved Tom Shelby. He was asking if I loved *him*. And how could I answer? If I replied with even a whiff of bullshit, he would know. But I didn't think I needed to bullshit him, because I didn't think he wanted me to love him in a romantic way, not really. If I was wrong, he might pull that trigger, so I was banking his very life on my answer.

"I don't know if I could love him or not," I said. "I can't—I can't know that right now. But I know one thing. I don't want to lose you, Isaac. I care about you. And I'm never, *never* going to stop caring about you. Do you understand? I'm going to be there for you. I'll always be there for you … If you let me. If you want that."

He didn't move. In the agonizing wait that followed, I heard him breathing, but otherwise the woods were still. No wind. It was so quiet, in fact, that I thought I could just make out the distant rumble of a passenger jet as it crossed far above us, people on their way to Denver or Salt Lake City or some other place far away from here, a reminder that the world kept spinning and that life went on, good and bad. In our own little private universe of two broken souls, none of that mattered. All that mattered was whether Isaac would pull the trigger.

He put down the shotgun.

"Oh God," he said and buried his face in his hands. "Oh God. Oh God."

"It's all right," I said. "Isaac, it's going to be okay."

He might have been nineteen, but he cried the way a scared toddler cries—unconstrained, unselfconscious, like nothing and no one else in the world matters. I climbed onto my hands and knees, the top of my skull throbbing as if it had been hit with a hammer, my chest caked with dirt. Still afraid he might change his mind about the shotgun, I crept forward cautiously. He didn't look at me. I scanned the trees, seeing nothing but shadows.

I picked up Big Shot Bob. The barrel was warm where he'd held it. It felt heavier than a shotgun should feel, as if it was still holding the weight of what it could have done. On the ground next to me, so close I could feel his breath on my bare leg, Isaac went on sobbing. I wanted to comfort him, but the first order of business was to make sure I didn't have a loaded weapon within his reach.

I flipped over the shotgun to pop the shells out of the tube, but I hadn't so much as peered into the loading port before Isaac threw his arms around my legs. For a second, I thought he might have been tackling me in a desperate attempt to regain the weapon, but no, he was just hugging me. Hugging me hard enough that I almost went down right on top of him. Somehow I stayed up right, using my outstretched arm and Big Shot Bob as a counterbalance.

"I'm sorry," he said.

I couldn't hug him, not standing, so I patted the top of his head. "It's all right."

"Please—please don't leave me."

"I'm not leaving you."

He cried again. It was not so loud this time that anybody could hear it—nobody except Tom maybe. I let Isaac cry. I wanted him to get it out, all that loss and pain, as much as he could, because crying was a hell of a lot better than dying. While he unburdened himself, I looked at the shotgun and saw something that surprised me. The way the moonlight lanced through the canopy above us, it fell right on the loading port.

The tube was empty.

No shells were in the built-in magazine. Feeling truly cold for the first time even though I'd been naked, I held the shotgun closer to make sure, but there was no mistake. The Winchester Model 12 had a spring-loaded open receiver, so even in poor light it was clear enough. There was nothing in there. Taking my left hand off Isaac's head, I cycled the shotgun to make sure there wasn't a round in the chamber. There wasn't.

Big Shot Bob was unloaded.

The noise got Isaac's attention, and he stopped crying. I was so disturbed by my discovery that I barely noticed. The shotgun had been loaded the last I'd checked, which would have been yesterday at midnight when I'd started my last shift. Someone had removed the shells in the meantime. While Isaac could have unloaded it himself, his threat of suicide just an act, I discounted this possibility as soon as I thought it even though it was certainly possible.

I discounted it because something else came to me, a realization so startlingly clear that I knew it was true even if my rational mind hadn't caught up with all the supporting proof yet.

Tom Shelby was Mr. Grim.

29

———————

Like lightning before the thunder. That was what it felt like when the idea first came to me, when I first thought that Tom Shelby was Mr. Grim. The lightning of realization came first, but the thunder of supporting facts couldn't be far behind. I knew it was true. I knew it the way I knew the sun rose in the morning, that I'd done a terrible thing when I'd killed a girl in a meth house Boise, and that evil, real evil, the kind that feels no remorse, existed in the world and would always exist as long as good existed along with it.

Isaac looked up at me. With his face tilted up into the moonlight, I could see his eyes, and they were searching, confused. The lightning might have struck, but the thunder still had to roll in. Believing was one thing. Proof was another.

"Isaac," I said, "did you empty the shotgun?"

"What's wrong?"

"Please, just answer me."

"It's empty?"

I swallowed. I thought I'd felt cold before, but it was nothing compared to what I felt now, like plunging into the deepest trench in the Arctic ocean. I tried to swim my way out of it. Why did I think this? I'd just had sex with this man, for God's sake. I couldn't be that wrong, could I? It was a gut feeling, but gut feelings could lead me astray.

And yet, there were pieces—maybe not of proof but an accumulation of coincidences that by themselves could be brushed off but that together made that possibility very real. It was more than Isaac saying Tom was mean. It was the weird sense I'd gotten that Tom could see better than he was letting on. He'd driven here. He'd walked in the woods by himself. Was he really going blind, or had he used a fake diagnosis of macular degeneration as cover? Or was the fact that he was *really* going blind the reason he hadn't exactly been operating in his usual manner these past few weeks? The reason I'd felt like he was playing some new game?

As a moderately successful author of children's books, Tom Shelby certainly had the kind of independence that allowed him to rove the country without raising suspicion. No boss. No coworkers. Would some of his killings coincide with his book tours? My hunch was that they probably would. A fan might recognize him when he was on the hunt, but not if he wore disguises.

Disguises.

That word troubled me for a reason I couldn't explain, not yet, but I sensed there was something key about that too. Mr. Grim had worn a disguise when he'd watched me from the sailboat on Buck Bay. He'd worn a disguise when he tried to strangle Maya on the ferry. That could have been Tom both times—he had the build for it—but it was more than that.

I'd seen his stubborn insistence on remaining at the cabin as an act of bravery, but maybe he'd just wanted to keep us isolated. Why? To eventually frame us for murder? And why would he unload the shotgun? The only reason I could think of was because he was planning on killing us, probably this very night, and he'd wanted to remove the possibility of another loaded weapon in the house. In that sense, Isaac's freakout was a stroke of pure luck for us. Otherwise we might both already be dead.

But why not kill us the day we arrived on Casper Mountain? Why wait? A couple answers came to me. The first was that he'd wanted to make sure Isaac and I were seen as the chief suspects in the various murders. He had his own computer, so he could have been going online all this time. It might also explain his sneaky forays into the woods, where he could make calls or use a smartphone to access the internet, planting evidence against us without worrying that we'd catch him in the act. From what I could tell, the cell signal was pretty weak all over Casper Mountain, but maybe he'd found a spot in the woods where he could get good reception.

The second reason he might have waited was far more chilling to me personally: Because he'd wanted to seduce me.

He might have considered having sex with me as the ultimate act of dominance.

While Isaac stared up at me, waiting for me to explain my strange behavior, I did my best to remain stoic even as the bile rose up in my throat. I was a strong woman. This was not to say that I was responsible for everything bad that had ever happened to me, but I'd always refused to see myself as a victim. Even in that terrible, nauseating moment, I still didn't, but I certainly felt used. Deceived.

Violated.

It was not something I could ever remember feeling before. Had I been raped? It might not have fit the technical definition, but I certainly felt dirty, a sense of revulsion and even self-loathing. He'd taken the most intimate thing I could offer, and I felt like a fool for letting him have it without a fight. Standing there in my underwear in that moonlight clearing on Casper Mountain, his sweat, the smell of him, still clinging to my skin, I felt vile. I felt humiliated. I felt like not even a thousand hot showers would make me feel right again.

The distant howl of a coyote, a lonely, forlorn sound, shook me from my reverie of shame. What was I going to do now? I was naked. I was weaponless. I'd been used and deceived. At each step along this gruesome journey, he'd stripped more of me away—

clothes, confidence, even my sense of self-worth. Was this his plan all along?

I felt weaker and more vulnerable than at any point in my life, but I knew I had to be strong. I had to be strong because I wasn't going to run. Why? First, I had to prove that my gut feeling was true. Second, even if I *knew* it was true, I couldn't run anyway. It wasn't just because I wanted revenge—although I would have been lying if I'd said that wasn't part of it—but because the best way to stop him was also the riskiest.

I stepped away from Isaac and squatted down so we were eye to eye.

"Listen," I said, "I'm going to tell you something, but I need you to be calm, okay?"

He nodded. I was pretty sure he was staring at my breasts, not my face, but it wasn't the time to make a "hey, buddy, eyes up here" sort of comment. I looked over my shoulder, back toward a faint yellow smudge between the trunks that must have been the cabin. So far, I hadn't heard a car start, a door slam, anything. No footsteps in the darkness. If he'd left, he'd been sneaky about it.

"I think Tom's Mr. Grim," I said, turning back to Isaac. "I don't think he's quite as blind as he's been letting on either."

Isaac blinked. Other than that, he didn't react.

"Did you hear me?" I asked.

"Yeah."

"Do you want to know why I think that?"

"No."

"No?"

"No, I believe you. If you think he is, he is. That's enough for me."

"And doesn't it bother you? That one of your favorite authors turns out to be, well, you know?"

He shrugged. I would have felt better if he'd been looking me in the eyes. I was worried that my boobs were making him say whatever I wanted him to say without him weighing his answer on its own terms, but there was something almost comforting in the fact that even in a crisis, male sexuality was never entirely absent.

"Well, I'd say I'm only 80/20 that he is," I said, "and I'd like to tell you why, but right now I appreciate you just trusting me. Now listen. This is important. I want you to head to the road through the trees there, then make your way to the first lighted house you find—or to the campground if you don't come across anyone. Have them call the police and come to this house. You remember the address?"

He nodded and told me what it was. "You're not coming with me?"

"I'm going back. To the cabin."

"Why?"

"Because if I don't, he'll know the game is up and probably take off. I don't want him to get away."

"But he has the handgun."

"I know. That's why I don't want him to have the slightest idea I'm onto him."

"I want to go with you."

"No, you can't."

"I won't let you do it alone."

"Isaac, no. I appreciate your offer, but I really need you to get the police." I put my hand on his shoulder, surprised to find that he was trembling. "Listen to me. This isn't just to get rid of you, okay? This is important. My job is to keep him at the cabin. Your job is to bring in the cavalry. It's actually a huge thing you're doing because right now the police are looking for you."

He swallowed. "What if they arrest me without coming to the house? They might not care what I say."

"Don't give them your real name. Make something up, okay? Just say you heard gunshots and a woman screaming at this house. That's enough. You can take off at that point. Hide in the trees. Wait until everything shakes out."

He didn't object, but he still looked dubious. "Are you going to take the shotgun?"

I shook my head. "It's unloaded, so it's not any good to me anyway. And if I take it with me, he'll figure I *know* it's unloaded, right? My only chance is to pretend I couldn't find you."

"I don't like it."

"I know. And I think you should leave the shotgun too, okay? Just leave it here. I don't want a neighbor freaking out and shooting you before you get a chance to call the police."

"Okay."

"I'm counting on you. I can't let him get away. *We* can't let him get away. And this is your part. Can you do this for me?"

It took him a moment, but Isaac finally nodded. He reached for his sweatshirt and tried to hand it to me. I shook my head.

"Why?" he said.

"I want him to think I couldn't find you, remember?"

"Oh, right. But what if he heard us out here? I was kind of loud."

"Then I'll make something up about how you got away anyway. Listen, we have to get going. He's probably getting suspicious already."

I climbed to my feet and extended my hand. The way Isaac looked up at me, his gaze sweeping up and down my body, it wasn't so much a leer as an appraisal of my chances. I didn't blame him for his doubts. I was about to go up against what might have been the worst serial killer the world had ever known, one who'd duped both of us and shamed us in different but equally powerful ways, and I was topless, barefoot, and weaponless. It was insanity.

And yet I had to do it.

"Take my hand, Isaac," I said.

It took him a moment, but he did. I pulled him to his feet. He put on the sweatshirt. We regarded each other in the darkness, the night still and cool, until he did something unexpected. He kissed me.

On the cheek.

"Good luck," he said and jogged toward the road.

———

AFTER ISAAC LEFT, I stood in that moonlight clearing for a lot longer than was wise given that Tom could have conceivably left the cabin at any moment. Yet except for the softest whisper of the breeze and a barely detectable rattle of aspen leaves, it was so quiet that I definitely would have heard the crunch of tires on gravel. I would have heard the thump of his shoes on the dirt. I might have even been able to hear him breathing.

I heard none of that. I *did* hear my own breathing, quick and shallow, as I contemplated what was to come. My toes felt numb. Goose flesh exploded across my arms. I felt the cold in my bones. I'd never felt so cold, so utterly exposed.

I refused to give into fear.

The key was to keep things simple: Return to the cabin. Act concerned that I hadn't found Isaac. Find a way to get the handgun.

As I left the clearing and the empty shotgun behind, the forest swept over me like a shroud. The glow of the cabin was such a tiny, insubstantial thing. A jagged rock scraped the bottom of my right foot. A stick scratched my left ankle. There must have been rocks and sticks before, but I hadn't noticed them in my panic to find Isaac. Now it was as if I was creeping blind across broken glass. Maybe it was because the wind was still, but the smell of mold and decaying wood was so much stronger too.

When I reached the clearing that surrounded the cabin, I stopped behind a ponderosa. The clouds smothered most of the moonlight, but the porch light and the light rimming the curtained windows lit up the area well enough that I thought I'd spot him if he was lurking in the open, but there were so many shadowy pockets that he could have been standing just about anywhere else unnoticed.

For just a second, I thought I heard a police siren in the distance, maybe all the way down in Casper. I might have imagined it, but even so it was a reminder how easily the cops might blow this. If they came in with sirens wailing, Tom would surely flee. I couldn't let that happen. I had to get the handgun before they got here.

Feeling like I had a bull's-eye in the middle of my bare chest, I jogged to the front door. If he was going to take a shot at me, this was his best chance. I kept low, glancing left and right, doing my best to look like I was still worried that Mr. Grim might be skulking about.

On the deck, a plank creaked and I tensed. Deep breath. I was about to knock when Tom spoke from inside.

"Karen?" he said. "Isaac, is that you?"

There was something about his voice, how nervous he sounded, that gave me pause. Maybe I was wrong. I had to at least allow for that possibility.

"I'm armed!" he called out. "And I just called the police!"

"Hey, hey, it's me!" I said. "Karen Pantelli."

"You didn't knock."

I winced. Silently scolding myself for my stupidity, I knocked three times, paused, then knocked three more. "Sorry—just not thinking straight. I—I couldn't find Isaac. Let me in."

At least I didn't have to sell the part about not thinking straight. There was a pause, only a second or two, but I imagined him standing there with the handgun pointed at where he'd heard my voice.

Did he know? Had something in my voice given me away?

Then the door opened, and there he was.

He took a step back, blinking at me through his thick lenses, the Smith & Wesson held at his side. I could have lunged for it right then, but that would have been risky. Better to play it cool. If there was even a tiny chance I was wrong, I didn't want him to get hurt.

His hair, blocky chunks sticking in random directions, looked as if a child had drawn it with a crayon. It was a reminder of our roll in the hay, and I had to concentrate to keep my disgust from showing. In my absence, he'd tossed on gray denim jeans, a partially zipped black cotton sweatshirt, and black Sketchers without socks. He wore no shirt underneath the sweatshirt, his chest hair exposed all the way to his naval.

I walked into the well-lit living room. Tom closed the door and locked the deadbolt. I noticed that his finger was still on the trigger even if he was pointing the gun to the right. He leaned closer, squinting.

"Jesus," he said, "you look like you were in a backstreet brawl. Are you okay?"

"I'm fine. I just … I fell, chasing him."

"You didn't find him? I thought I heard him yell."

"Yeah. I heard that too. I think he—he ran into a tree or something. By the time I got there, he was gone."

"Oh. God, I'm sorry. I kept waiting for the sound of the shotgun. I'm at least glad you're okay."

He reached for me with his left arm, hugging me close while he kept the handgun extended away from us. The feel of his hand on my bare back, my breasts pressing against his cotton sweatshirt —it was all I could do not to cringe. Even then, I may have flinched a little, an involuntary response. Again, I thought about going for the handgun, but not yet. I'd wait for him to put it down. I just had to make him comfortable enough to do that.

If he really was Mr. Grim, I wanted him to think I was just as ignorant as before, along for the ride with whatever sick game he was playing. When he pulled away from me, I even did my best to smile. A worried smile. A smile that felt like drying concrete even as it formed, but a smile. His face was so close that I got a whiff of the peanut butter he'd eaten earlier.

"What do you want to do?" he asked.

"Well," I said, "*first* I want to get cleaned up and get some damn clothes on. Then … I don't know. Wait and see if he comes back, I guess. Maybe he'll come to his senses."

"You're not worried, you know, about that shotgun? That he might—"

"Yeah, but what should I do? He could be anywhere now. And if he really wants to take his own life, can I really stop him? I just hope he comes to his senses."

Tom cocked his head to the side, studying me. This time, I barely believed myself.

"Hey," I said, "while I'm getting cleaned up, could you make me some of that lemon tea? I need to settle down a bit, calm my nerves, think about what to do."

"Oh," he said, "sure, sure, I can do that. We have a couple tea bags left. Take a minute to get the hot water going."

"That's fine. I appreciate it."

I smiled. He smiled. There we were, just like any happy couple —except, of course, he was holding a handgun, and I was standing there only in my underwear, scratched, bruised, and coated in dirt. With a nod, I started toward the bathroom. When I heard the thick rubber soles of his Sketchers squeak the hardwood, I glanced behind me.

Just as I'd hoped, he set the handgun on the breakfast counter on his way to the teapot.

Jackpot.

His back was turned. He was so nonchalant that I was seized with more doubt, but I couldn't let that stop me. Once I had the handgun, we could sort out the details. Waiting until he'd picked up the teapot and turned on the kitchen faucet, hoping the noises would provide cover, I grabbed the bathroom doorframe.

Then I pushed off, using the doorframe to springboard me toward the gun.

Two lunging steps and I had it in my hand. Not only did Tom not lunge for it, he didn't even notice. He tested the water by running it over his index finger, holding the stainless steel teapot with his other hand. Pointing the handgun at his back, I backed into the center of the room, free of obstructions and with a clear shot.

Other than that stainless steel teapot in his hand, an empty ceramic fruit bowl on the breakfast bar, and a couple of oven mitts hanging on the wall, I didn't see anything that could even remotely be used as a weapon.

"Tom," I said.

He didn't hear me. Or if he did, he didn't acknowledge me. I almost hoped he *hadn't* heard me. There was a hitch in my voice, a choking off of his name that betrayed my nervousness.

"Tom," I said, "turn around."

This time I'd been louder. Still running the water, he glanced over his shoulder. He smiled the way people often do when their name is called and they have no expectation of conflict.

When he saw the handgun, that smile petrified. The skin around his eyes tightened. His skin, usually possessing a rich, honey-oak sheen, paled to a sallow yellow. His reaction kindled even more of my doubts. Was I crazy?

"Karen?" he said.

"Turn off the water, and put down the teapot."

"What—what's going on?"

"Just do it. Then turn around, real slow, hands up."

"But—but I don't understand—"

"Do it!"

He didn't so much as flinch as jerk back, as if I'd already fired a bullet into his chest. The running water sounded menacing, like a hissing snake. He swallowed, then, never looking away from me, fumbled with his free hand for the faucet handle until he got it off. When he set the teapot on the countertop, his hand shook so badly that the metal clattered.

"Hands up," I said. "No sudden movements."

He raised his hands, the confusion reigning in his eyes giving way to fear—or at least that was how it seemed. "It's you, isn't it?" he said.

"What?"

"You. You're Mr. Grim."

I snorted. "Don't be ridiculous. "

"You planned to kill me all along. You—you probably killed Isaac already. That's why you were gone so long. I didn't hear the shotgun. What did you do, bludgeon him to death? You probably—"

"Will you shut the fuck up? Isaac is fine. He's gone for the police."

He stared. His eyes, behind all that thick glass, were as big as blue coasters. I caught a glimpse of something there, genuine surprise, a dropping of a mask, just a little flicker, but it was enough to fortify my resolve. He *was* hiding something.

"But—but why?" he said.

"Because of you."

"I don't—"

"You know what I mean."

"Wait, you … you think *I'm* Mr. Grim? Are you insane?"

"Stop the bullshit, Tom. The shotgun wasn't loaded."

"Huh?"

"You unloaded it! You were planning on doing something to us tonight, weren't you?"

"Karen—"

"But Isaac's freakout threw off your plans."

"That's insane!"

I tightened my grip on the gun. "Here's what we're going to do. We're going into your room, together, real slow. We'll search your things. I'm willing to bet we'll find some stuff that will raise all kinds of questions. Another phone. Another computer. Another weapon. Something."

"I can't believe you're doing this. I thought we had a real connection."

He was so smooth that it made me doubt myself again. "Let's just go search your room, okay? Then we'll take it from there."

He gazed at me for a long time. His shoulders dropped, a shift in posture that could have signaled defeat, but I sensed that it was more akin to a panther crouching to spring on its prey.

"No," he said. "I won't be doing that."

His voice had changed. It was neither the easy Wyoming drawl or the clipped Massachusetts twang, but something else altogether, raspy and low, a voice that still seemed somehow familiar. Why? I didn't know, but there was something there, some mystery that, even more than his change in tone, knotted up my stomach.

"Maybe you haven't noticed," I said, "but I'm the one holding the gun."

"I wish you hadn't sent Isaac to the police," he said.

"Stay where you are."

"But it doesn't change my plans. It just accelerates them."

"Don't move. I'm warning you, Tom."

"I do like the way you say my name. I knew we'd have a special connection. I knew it all along."

I swallowed. "I was right then. I was right about you. About who you are."

"Listen to me very carefully, Karen. I have no plan to hurt you tonight. So if you pull that trigger, you're making a choice that has nothing to do with my intention."

I didn't see him move, but he must have. He'd reached the breakfast bar, his gaze flicking briefly toward the top drawer on his side before returning to meet my eyes, not even a hint of blindness now. He saw it all. He saw it all with vivid clarity.

"Stop," I said. "Whatever you're doing, stop."

Without looking away from me, he opened the drawer.

"Tom," I said.

"I'm going to take a gun out of this drawer."

"Don't."

"It's a little backup, just in case things went south. I won't pull the trigger unless you shoot first. I'm going to walk out of here, Karen. It's your choice whether you shoot me or not."

"You don't have to do this."

"I think we had a real connection, Karen. I think you have real feelings for me."

"Don't flatter yourself."

"I don't think you'll shoot me."

"I absolutely will if you pull a gun out of that drawer."

His right hand moved lower, dropping out of view.

"Stop," I warned.

He didn't. I saw his hand coming up. I saw the walnut handle of a small Remington revolver, black chrome and stainless steel, a little six-shooter. It didn't happen in slow motion. At least that wasn't my perception of it. It didn't happen fast either. It happened the way he might have lifted a TV remote out of the drawer, with purpose but no real urgency. If it had happened in slow motion, maybe I wouldn't have done what I did, given more time to weigh the risks and consider the options, and if it had happened fast, I might have been able to absolve myself of any responsibility because I wouldn't have had time to do anything but react.

But I had time. I had enough. I saw the gun rising out of the drawer, the end of the barrel so much blacker than everything else, like a hole straight to hell.

I pulled the trigger.

30

Looking back at that fateful moment, I should have known what was coming. It was as obvious as the smirk on Tom's face. After all, he'd telegraphed this outcome with Isaac and the shotgun. Why would he unload one gun and not the other?

When I pulled the trigger, nothing happened. There was no explosive *pop*, no jerk of the handgun, and no ammonia-like whiff of modern gunpowder. No bloody bullet hole blossomed in the middle of his black sweatshirt. He didn't stagger into the kitchen sink. There *was* a sound: a click, dull but loud, like the first nail being driven into a coffin. My coffin.

"A little test," Tom said. "Two tests, really. First, having you think you had me at gunpoint was the only way I could know for sure you'd sent Isaac to the police. That was information I needed. Plus I just wanted to know if you had it in you. It pleases me to no end that you do."

I stared at the gun dumbly. "You wanted to know if I could pull the trigger?"

"I wanted to know if you're still a stone cold killer. And let me tell you, it's *very* sexy."

"You're a sick fucker, Tom."

"Aww, see that's not a very nice way to take a compliment." He nodded toward the breakfast counter. "Go ahead and put the gun down ... please."

There was something about the way he said the word "please," so pedestrian, so ordinary, that alarmed me even more than if he'd shouted. It came out like an actor who'd just realized he'd forgotten a line. He was annoyed, yes, but it was like he was annoyed more with himself than with the situation at hand.

"And if I don't?" I asked.

"Then our story will come to an end. That would make me very sad, Karen, because I still don't want to shoot you tonight."

He didn't sound sad. He sounded like someone who might have to reschedule a hair appointment. But even ascribing that much emotion to him may have been too much. He definitely *acted* human, but it was more like an android pretending. It was a very good act indeed, but there was something missing even if I couldn't say what it was. I sensed it, though. I sensed the void in him.

I didn't know how I was going to play this, but if Isaac did his job, the police would be here soon enough. I placed the handgun on the counter.

"Thank you," Tom said, then nodded toward the door. "Now we need to go for a little walk."

"Outside?"

"Yes. It's not far."

"I thought you were just going to leave?"

"Oh, our business together is not yet finished. Besides, how could I leave a woman who had the balls—if you'll pardon my expression—to pull the trigger on a man she'd just had sex with when he hadn't shot at her yet? A man she'd started to develop feelings for."

"I have no feelings for you. None at all."

He shook his head. "You're an amazing woman, but you're an extraordinarily bad liar. Even now, you're trying to reconcile the man who was so tender with you in bed, so vulnerable, with the monster you built up in your mind who killed all those people."

"Bullshit. The only thing I feel for you now is hate."

"You really should leave lying to those who have a talent for it."

"Oh, you mean like you?"

He shook his head. "It's not lying when you can *make* the lies true. I'm a god, Karen. That's what I am. I may walk among the living, but I'm a god. I decide who lives and dies. I do it in my stories all the time. I'm a god in a sense there too, but that was just pretend. I'm a god in the realest sense there is."

"Jesus. Can you even hear yourself? You're delusional."

He smiled. It was the same Tom smile, a little impish, a little cocky, a smile I'd found attractive but now found repulsive because I knew what the smile was hiding underneath.

"I'd be happy to talk more about my sanity later," he said, "but right now we need to leave. Let's go."

I hesitated. I didn't hear any approaching cars, no sirens, nothing to indicate help was on its way. It felt like it had been hours since Isaac and I had parted, but it had probably only been ten minutes. The cabin felt colder than before, but it might have just been the coldness of his gaze on my body. I started to cross my arms over my chest, then stopped. It gave me an idea.

"Can I at least get dressed first?" I asked.

"You're just delaying. Go. *Now.*"

"Just let me put on a shirt and some shoes, okay? It'll only take a second. You know I don't have a gun in my room. You can watch me the whole time."

"I said no."

"Come on, it's cold."

"It's not that cold. Besides, a little cold never hurt anybody. Look at your breasts, after all. They're quite beautiful. A little chilly outside air has only made them look more magnificent. Not too big, not too small, right in the Goldilocks zone of perfect breasts. No, I like you naked. Maybe you should take off your underwear too and go completely au naturel?"

As he spoke, it felt like ants were crawling all over my breasts, but I didn't want him to know he was getting to me. "If you're really not planning on killing me tonight, then why can't I put on some clothes?"

"I'm losing patience. Let's go. Right now, and I mean it."

I nodded toward the black vinyl Columbia jacket hanging on the hook by the front door. "How about your jacket? Can I at least put on that on the way out?"

"No."

"Well, I'm going to. Shoot me if you have to."

"Don't do it, Karen. "

I walked toward the door, slow and purposeful in my bare feet but no rushing, not giving him a reason to shoot me unless it was just out of pure spite. I heard his Sketchers on the hardwood as he fell in behind me, but I didn't look at him. I didn't know why it was so important for me to put on some clothes, but it was, and it had nothing to do with being cold or exposed. It was mostly because I needed a victory, even a small one, some way to prove that he wasn't in total control.

He may have thought of himself as a god, but he didn't determine *my* fate.

When I got to the door, I reached for the jacket. My fingers were closing around the slick material when I felt the cold, hard barrel pressing into the base of my skull.

"Are you sure you want to do this?" he asked. "If you're dead, you'll never learn the truth about your mother."

He was so close that his warm breath blew across the nape of my neck. Way too close if he wanted to keep himself out of danger. There were a dozen moves I could have pulled in that moment, all of them risky, most with a high probability of me ending up dead, but as soon as he made the comment about my mother, I wouldn't have tried any of them. He knew it too. He was playing me again. I knew he was playing me, but that didn't make it easier.

My mouth had gone as dry as a Wyoming hardpan during a drought. "What about my mother?"

"I know where she is." His voice was closer, his lips brushing against my skin. "I'll tell you too if you just cooperate."

"She's dead. You killed her."

"No, we never crossed paths. Colin Welk may have been right about many things, but he was wrong about that."

"You're lying."

"Don't you want to find out for sure? I want to tell you, but you have to do it my way. Open the door and go. Or die here. The choice is yours."

I heard the beating of my own heart, a steady, violent thumping. I heard air whirring through the vent to my right. I heard water dripping from the bathroom faucet. I heard all this inside the cabin, but the outside world was so still that it could have been outer space. The gun still pressed against my skull. I didn't care. I wasn't going to pull a move to try to disarm him, but I wasn't just going to do what he wanted either.

With the left hand, I turned the knob and started to open the door, enough to let in a jet of cool, pine-smelling air, but with my right I snatched the Columbia jacket off the hook.

Tom laughed. "You're really something, aren't you?"

I looked over my shoulder at him. "Maybe it's *you* who can't shoot *me.*"

"Oh, I can shoot you, trust me. It would be a disappointment since I've come to enjoy your company, but I can't let you interfere with my plan."

"What plan?"

He jabbed me in the back with the Remington. "Never mind that. Listen now. You can wear your jacket, but there's one other thing you should know if you're thinking of crying for help, running, or any such stupid thing. Not only will that get you killed, it will get your sister killed too."

A ball of ice slid into the pit of my stomach. "How? You're here with me."

"Let's just say there's all kinds of amazing things you can do with a cheap drone. One doesn't even need to be present to have it carry out a preprogrammed flight plan."

"Liar."

"After everything I've done, don't you think I'm capable of it?

If I don't cancel its program, your sister is dead in ..." He glanced at the microwave clock. "Forty-two minutes. At midnight our time, 2:00 a.m. their time. Your sister's family should all be snug in their beds."

"It's bullshit. You're just trying to get me to cooperate."

"I've cut the landline and hidden both your phone and mine where you'll never find them, so don't think you could call from this house without my help. Now let's go. The clock is ticking. Head past the shed there—to the north and into the trees."

"I need shoes."

"Go."

This time, his tone left no room for debate, or at least I wasn't willing to push it. I peered into the clearing. The moonlight, gauzy and yellow through the cloud cover, spread yellow strips in the clearing like a whittler's wood shavings. I heard no cars. If the cavalry was on its way, they were a long way off. I still thought Tom was lying about the drone, but I had to operate as if it were true, which meant I had to wait for my very best opportunity to subdue him. He'd make a mistake. I just had to be ready.

Slipping on the jacket, I stepped off the porch and headed toward the trees. The man behind me had broken me down bit by bit, stripping away my self-confidence, my pride, and even my clothes. Getting the jacket on may have been the smallest of victories, but it was a start.

31

———

Forty minutes. As I walked barefoot past the shed, past the fading reach of the porch light toward the aspens and pines to the north, that was how much time I figured I had before midnight—or 3:00 a.m. in Atlanta, Georgia. Forty minutes before some explosives duct-taped to a drone smashed into my sister's house.

I was 99 percent sure Tom was bluffing, but it was the remaining 1 percent that kept me from trying to subdue him. I also wanted to know about my mother, even if I was pretty sure he was lying there too, but that need was nothing compared to my desire to keep Hope and her family safe.

"Walk faster," Tom said.

"That's hard to do barefoot."

"You want me to force you to take off that jacket? How about your underwear? I really would like to gaze on your bare derriere in the moonlight. It's only slightly less perfect than your breasts."

I didn't answer. At that moment, I would have rather had shoes than the Columbia jacket even if I had to put up with him staring at my ass. The thin vinyl that barely extended beyond my underwear did little to ward off the chill bite in the air anyway, and it was bulky enough that I worried it would get in the way if I tried to make a move on him. At least it was black, though. If I had to run, it might provide some camouflage in the darkness.

"I usually like a little more junk in the trunk," he continued to muse, "and your bum is more on the athletic side. Still, as I said, quite beautiful, especially because it suits you, the raw power of it."

"Jesus," I said.

"What? You didn't mind me saying this sort of thing an hour ago."

I bit down on my lower lip. If there was a button on my back that read MAKE KAREN MAD, he was doing his best to push it. If he wanted to keep me from attacking him, he was doing a piss-poor job of it. Or maybe he wanted me so wound up that I couldn't think rationally? An irrational person couldn't come up with a plan. His voice, not quite Wyoming, not quite Mass-achusetts, something more clipped and annunciated, again struck me as familiar, but I couldn't grasp why.

I stepped on more than a few sharp rocks, but I bore it all without so much as a groan. The breeze picked up, and I caught a whiff of woodsmoke. Someone was still awake around here, someone close. It made me think of Isaac. Had he called the police yet?

I could tell by Tom's footsteps that he was staying about ten feet behind me. Close enough that he could easily put a bullet in the back of my head but far enough away that I couldn't get the jump on him. We reached the first aspens on the north side of the property, like white pillars fronting an abandoned coliseum, only darkness within.

"Where are we going?" I asked.

"You'll see," he said.

"Gonna put a bullet in my head in the woods?"

He sighed. "Come on, Karen. I may be a vengeful god, but I'm not a lying one. I told you I wouldn't shoot you tonight as long as you ... cooperate."

The pause came at an odd time, his voice pinching on the

word "cooperate." I looked over my shoulder at him. We hadn't yet crossed into the net of tree shadows that would make reading his face difficult, so his wince, even in the moonlight, was clear enough.

"What's wrong with you?"

"I'm fine," he said.

"It's not macular degeneration, is it? You're obviously not blind. But it *is* something."

"I *told* you, I'm fine."

For the first time, I thought I heard genuine emotion. There was real irritation there. That was the tell. That was the doorway to what was true, what was actually true. I turned and faced him, the glow from the cabin a halo around his head.

"You're dying," I said.

He snorted.

"Cancer?" I said. "Brain tumor?"

"Get going," he said. "It's just allergies, all right?"

Then I had it. It wasn't just the voice. It wasn't just the wince either, though that was a big part of it. It was him blaming his wince on allergies. *That* was what finally helped me see a connection that had eluded me earlier.

"Oh Jesus," I said.

"What is it now?"

"That was you. Back at the Orcadia, in the hotel room. It wasn't Colin Welk in that wheelchair. It was *you*."

"Absurd. You're just trying a new delay tactic. Walk!"

It might have been an act, but his shout seemed real enough. An act. That was the key word, wasn't it? It had been an act from the first moment I'd walked into the Orcadia, a play staged for an audience of one. *Me.* The face wasn't quite the same, nor was his build, but I knew I was onto something. He must have been wearing a lot of makeup, a wig of curly red hair, and some sort of fat suit, but I was sure now that the man standing before me, a man pointing a Remington revolver at me at this very moment, was the same man who'd pointed a S&W .38 Special at me while sitting in a wheelchair in room 1109 at the Orcadia. He'd kept the room dim and positioned himself so he was partly in shadow to make it harder to see through his disguise.

"The bathroom," I said. "Oh my God."

"I told you to get going."

Walking backward, I edged out of the moonlight. "Colin Welk —the real Colin Welk—was dead in the bathroom all along, wasn't he? Jesus. He was dead even when I first came in to clean. *You* were sitting in the wheelchair, dressed up as him."

He followed me into the forest, the shadows wrapping about him like a cloak, the gun flashing as moonlight glanced off the barrel. "Do you want me to shoot you right now? I will, you know, if you keep up this nonsense."

The dream I'd had in Butte, the one where Colin Welk had interrupted my make-out session with Ben in the car, came back to me now. *I'll be in the bathroom if you need me.* My subconscious must have been trying to tell me this all along. "That's why you had the bathroom door closed," I said. "That's why you had it smelling like air freshener. It wasn't because you had an upset stomach. It was to cover his smell. You shot him, then disguised yourself as him to talk to me. To set me on this path."

"Karen—"

"That's how you brought me to you. By putting your name second on the list. It's the only way it would have worked, and ... and it made me sympathetic to you. I wanted to protect you. You preyed on that instinct."

We kept walking, me backward, him trailing just out of my reach. The cabin receded in our wake, another source of light trailing off to nothing.

"That's it, isn't it?" I said. "And my sympathy blinded me to the fact that you were a perfect candidate to be Mr. Grim. The right age. An occupation that allowed you to roam the country. You were toying with me all along. Why?"

We'd traveled some distance into the trees, toward what I didn't know. I felt disembodied, half-crazed with everything I was saying, and so I wasn't paying attention to what was in my path. I tripped over an exposed root and fell hard on my backside.

A featureless shadow, Tom loomed over me like the angel of death. He didn't say anything for a long time.

"Smart," he said. "You're very smart, Karen Pantelli. All right, yes, it's true. Like the Norse God Loki, I sometimes disguise myself and have a little fun. Telling you this doesn't change my plan, though. A god's plan cannot be altered by the doings of mere mortals."

"But how did you even know Professor Welk was onto you?"

"I told you, Karen. I know all."

"Bullshit. You're not omniscient."

Tom chuckled. "Welk *was* extremely careful, comically so, but I grant you that he did make one mistake. Have you heard of Websleuths?"

"It's that website for amateur detectives, right?" I was getting him talking. This was good. I didn't know where it would lead, but sitting here listening to him was better than walking straight to my doom. If nothing else, it bought me some time. "We used to make fun of it when I was in the FBI."

"Correct. It's an internet community with thousands of active forums focusing on all manner of crime and missing person cases. It's been around for decades, and I like to keep my eye on it. After Welk's wife died on that hike, he posted about her death in there —anonymously, of course, speculating that it might have been murder, but I knew exactly who he was. He only posted a few times, and he deleted it when he began to theorize that I existed, but it was too late. I started watching him very closely."

"Was Welk even going to talk to me? Or was that all an act?"

"No, that part was definitely true. His research was real too. The technology isn't *quite* there yet, but his particular algorithms, his use of geographic profiling, combined with some of AI's large learning model pattern recognition ... Well, let's just say the technology is advancing too quickly for me to take any chances."

"I didn't see any high-powered servers in his home office. All he seemed to have was that one laptop."

"Oh, he was far too paranoid for that. All of his computational analysis was decentralized, encrypted, and processed in the cloud, but I'm certain he had materials in that safe that might lead another brilliant mind to me, which was why I destroyed it. I almost got you, too, but you managed to pass that test, Karen, as you have managed to pass all the tests I have given you—until now, at least." His smile, what I could see of it in the darkness, was demonic. "Welk really was a genius, you know. And he really did want your help—for most of the reasons I said. I just decided to replace his little scheme to stop me with a plan of my own. To bring you to me."

"But why? Why me, exactly?"

"I was aware of you, of course. Even before Colin Welk zeroed in on you, I was aware of your exploits. You might even say I was … a fan. That's why I couldn't resist testing you."

I thought of the last person who'd called himself a fan, that police officer on the side of the road in Wyoming. Try as I might to keep a low profile, my fame was ironically going to be what got me killed. It figured. "But why go to all that trouble? Just so I could be, what, some sort of sex slave, one that was *worthy* of you?"

"Don't cheapen what we shared."

I glared up at him, pine needles poking into the palms of my hand, my legs prickling as the sweat cooled on them. I knew it was stupid to anger a man pointing a gun at me, but I couldn't help myself. "We didn't share anything but a quick roll in the sheets. And you weren't even that good."

He chuckled. "I suppose the next thing you're going to say is that I have a small penis? Come on now, I counted at least three orgasms, and you, my dear, are not the actor I am."

I felt heat spreading across my face. If he could have seen me well enough, he would have been able to see me blushing, and I hated him for it. I hated him because even after what I knew he was, what he really was, he could still get me to feel this way.

"What do you *want?*" I said.

"I told you, all will be revealed. Our destination is just up ahead. Now get up."

I couldn't see his face either, not well, but I heard the wince in his voice again, the way it skipped like a vinyl record. Everything kept coming back to that wince.

"That's it, isn't it?" I said. "Everything you're doing, it has something to do with you being sick?"

"Get up, Karen."

"Isaac said you were afraid—did you know that? He said he thought that's why you were doing things differently."

"I don't need to explain myself to you. I've told you enough already. Now get going. I won't ask again."

"Are you afraid of dying? What is it you have, anyway? Some kind of disease? Some kind of—"

The gunshot was so close that I felt the boom as well as heard it. It hit me like a hard shove to the chest. For just a second, I thought I'd actually been shot—the sensation of being struck was so real, so visceral—but then my mind caught up with the direction of the muzzle flare. He'd shot to the right, the bullet sailing harmlessly into the darkness. If it struck something, the sound was lost in the steady ringing in my ears.

"I told you I wouldn't ask again," he said. "The next bullet goes somewhere else."

"All right, all right," I said. "I'm going. Jesus."

"That way. Now."

I got up, brushing dirt off my legs, and started walking north again. If he was dying, was this some sort of swan song? The darkness thickened. The forest was as silent as a mausoleum. Finally, I heard a siren in the distance, a mile or two off. Took them long enough.

"I hear it too," Tom said. "Just remember what happens if you run. Even if you somehow manage to elude me, your sister will die."

"I remember."

"If you shout, scream, do anything to draw attention to us, same result."

I still thought he was bluffing, but I wasn't going to make a move, not yet. How much time had passed since we left the cabin?

Ten minutes? That left about half an hour before the drone strike if it really was happening.

We were heading in the direction of the campground. Was that our destination? I kept walking, my head down, using all my mental energy just to keep from tripping. The siren, a distant wail for a long time, grew louder. I glanced to my right to see if I could spot the telltale sweep of red-and-blue lights, but all I saw were different shades of darkness, the tree trunks like slender monks standing vigil over hallowed ground.

"You're not completely wrong, you know," Tom said behind me. "Gods don't die, but sometimes they fall out of favor. People stop believing in them. Or they make them into a joke. When that happens, gods sometimes have to reinvent themselves—even if it's a trial by fire. They must be *reborn.* "

"What's that supposed to mean?"

"Hmm. Like faith, it's difficult to explain. But sometimes, after a trial by fire, something wonderful rises from the ashes—a Phoenix of truth, one might say."

"You're babbling. You're just worried about what's going to happen when the cops get to Riche Rich's cabin. "

"Nothing's going to happen—at least nothing I don't expect. You do realize that there is no Richie Rich, right? At least not one with any connection to me?"

I *hadn't* realized it, but I saw now that I should have. "Your Subaru is there."

"Not mine. It was … borrowed. If anything, they'll think you stole it."

"Your things—"

"—will be assumed to be yours and Isaac's. Nothing connects me to that either."

I swallowed. "Fingerprints. Your fingerprints are—"

"Wrong again. What do you think I was doing while you were outside looking for Isaac?"

"Ben. Ben Wilde, he knows you were here with us."

"Well, he can *claim* that I was, but he'll have no proof. And people know how close you two are. They'll think he's lying to protect you."

We walked into a pocket of fir trees, both of us silent, me stewing in rage and despair. He'd played us, and I'd sent Isaac right into the hands of the police. Even if Isaac was hiding somewhere, the cops would comb the woods until they found him. But they'd keep looking for us too. That was something.

"Ah, Karen," he said, chuckling, "I can guess how depressed you must be, realizing I've made you dance like a marionette. But take heart. When I said sometimes truth rises from the ashes, I wasn't just referring to me."

"What are you *talking* about?"

"Your mother. You see, I told you where she was the first time I met you. You just didn't know it."

"I have no idea what ..." I began, then realized he was talking about the list he gave me, the list that I'd thought was coming from Colin Welk but was actually coming from Tom Shelby in disguise. Phoenix from the ashes. "Jane Doe," I said. "You're saying that's my mother? That she's, what, in Phoenix, Arizona?"

"Is that what I'm saying, Karen?"

"Bullshit. Just more bullshit, all of it."

When he spoke again, I could hear the smile in his voice. "I'm not saying she's there under the same name. But if you know her birthday, you can find her. Think of it like a treasure map. X marks the spot. Perhaps we'll go together in a couple of days? If you cooperate, anything's possible. We'll see. We're almost there."

"Where?"

"I'm surprised you haven't guessed it already. You've been there once."

I realized what he was talking about an instant before it came into view—the two-level green house with the overhanging ponderosas. We passed out of the smaller aspens at the edge of the dirt driveway, and there it was, just as dark and abandoned as it had been when I'd scouted it a few days earlier. There was no porch light, but there was enough dappled moonlight that I could see much better than when we'd been in the thick of the forest. Even more pine needles littered the front deck.

"*That* place?" I said.

"If you come inside like a good girl and do exactly as I say, I'll cancel the drone."

I heard the wail of two sirens now, one close, one distant, but the close one could have been barreling down this very driveway. That was how near it sounded. I knew it wasn't, though.

The gun pressed into my back. "Just walk in the front door," he said. "It's unlocked."

"You planned this," I said. "You planned to come here all along."

"The front door. Now."

"Did you break in or actually rent this place?"

"Go!"

Thoughts a jumble, I crept toward the door. What was his play? What was he trying to do? I remembered his swift negative reaction when I'd suggested foraging this place for food. That had just been yesterday evening. On my way through the forest, I must have cut myself on the bottom of my right foot because hot, stabbing pain flared up my leg each time I put pressure on it.

"You're walking too slow," he said.

"I'm going, I'm going. I cut my foot, you know."

"No excuses."

I took a step, then another, playing up the pain with lots of wobbly steps, lots of little groans and grunts. The first siren had fallen silent, but the second was close by. After he'd quickly shot down the idea of ransacking this house, he'd propositioned me that very night. I'd been a willing partner, but it wouldn't have happened without him sneaking into my room. Had he been getting worried I might figure out what he was up to?

"On the deck now," he said.

It was a low deck, just one step up all the way around, vinyl that looked like wood. I knew this not by how it looked but by how it felt when I stepped on it. What was Tom's plan? The answer was tantalizingly close.

I took another step. Our sexual escapade had been interrupted by Isaac's threat of suicide. If not for that, I might not have figured out that the shotgun was unloaded, and I certainly wouldn't have gone out of the house when I did.

I took two more steps. The door, a bare outline in the shadowy alcove without a porch light to spotlight it, drew closer. He was going to do something tonight. That was why he'd slept with me. He'd wanted to check that off his list, and he knew he was running out of time. Was he going to shoot both Isaac and me, make it look like a murder-suicide, then hide out at this other house until someone found us?

What I actually needed right now was a phone, and whether he was bluffing about the drone thing or not, I had a hunch there was one in the house. I needed to make my move either out here or in there, but I needed to do it soon. By the thud of his hiking shoes on dirt, I could tell he was almost at the deck.

When he stepped up with one foot, that would be my chance. He'd be off-balance, concentrating where to put his foot and how to shift his weight. If I executed the move just right, I could drop and deliver a side kick, sending the handgun flying. It was going to be tricky. I didn't dare look back, but I sensed that he was a little out of range.

Timing was everything. I might not get a better chance. I had no idea what awaited me in the house, and a *dangerous known* was better than *unknown danger* nine times out of ten. I couldn't plan for what I didn't know.

I was going for it.

I heard the *thunk* of his shoe on the deck. I felt the vinyl plank lift beneath me as his weight bore down on the other side. How far away was he? Eight feet? Ten? I could do this. Do or die. This was my moment.

I started to lift my right foot when Isaac shouted behind us.

"Stop or I shoot!"

———

32

By the sound of his voice, Isaac was in the woods behind us but up the dirt driveway. Not far. Twenty feet, maybe. I looked over my shoulder—just as Tom did the same—and saw Isaac stepping from behind a Douglas fir. He emerged from the shadows into the moonlight like an actor steeping from behind a curtain. The only thing missing were the gasps of the audience.

The police sirens had fallen silent. I was so stunned by Isaac's sudden appearance that it took me a second to realize he had Big Shot Bob in his hands and that he was pointing it at Tom.

"Nice try, kid," Tom said, "but that one's empty."

"Not anymore," Isaac said. "If you even twitch, I'm pulling the trigger."

"Isaac," I said. "What are you *doing?*"

"Making sure this fucker doesn't get away," Isaac said. "He's going to the electric chair for what he did."

There was enough authority in Isaac's voice that it must have given Tom pause because he said nothing. Isaac had chosen his spot well. The angle gave him a clear shot of Tom without much chance of me getting hit in the crossfire.

Still pointing the revolver at my back, still with one foot on the deck and one foot off, Tom hadn't moved other than that first head turn. "You never could have found the shells," he said finally. "I hid them well, trust me. Now put it down, or I'll put a bullet in Karen's back."

"This guy at the campground, he had twenty-gauge rounds in his truck. He gave me some."

"Oh really? How convenient." Tom chuckled, but I heard the doubt creeping into his voice. "I think if that gun was loaded, you would have shot me already. You wouldn't have stepped out like this. You were close enough to hear me talking. You could have shot me long before now."

"I *told* you, I want to see you fry in the electric chair. That's why I didn't shoot you. Now drop your gun."

"Okay, go ahead and shoot then. I dare you. I killed your father, Isaac. How does that make you feel?"

"Shut up! Just—just shut up! The cops will be here soon. We can just wait for them."

"See? Someone like you, someone with a damaged brain, someone defective, really—there's no way you could keep yourself from pulling the trigger. Now put down the gun. If you don't, I'll shoot her, then I'll put one right between your eyes."

"Stop."

"But maybe you won't die, right? You lived through the last time I tried to kill you."

Isaac started crying. "Stop talking."

"Maybe you'll live through this one too, but your brain will be even worse. Is that even possible? Could you get any stupider? Come on, Isaac. Pull the damn trigger! Do it!"

Isaac didn't pull the trigger, didn't even lower the barrel, but the sobs got louder. Thinking this might be my chance, I readied myself to kick the gun out of Tom's hand, but then, as if he sensed what I was going to do, Tom took a lunging step backward onto the dirt—too far from me now to reach him.

"Ha!" Tom said. "Still no shot! I knew it. And now I'm going to count to three, Isaac. I won't kill Karen. I'll just shoot her in that pretty leg of hers. It will be painful, but she'll live. You, on the other hand, are going to die a miserable death. I'm going to make sure of it. Now put the shotgun down, or I shoot you."

"No."

"One," Tom said.

Isaac, still racked with sobs, looked at me helplessly. "Karen."

"Two."

"Put down the gun, Isaac," I said. "Tom, don't shoot him. Please. I'll do whatever you want."

"Oh, whatever I want, is it?" Tom said. "How lovely. Did you hear that, Isaac? And hey, if you put down that gun, maybe I'll even let you watch. *Three.*"

"Okay, okay," Isaac said, lowering the barrel. "I'll p-p-put it down. Don't shoot."

Still struggling for breath between each pitiful sob, Isaac eased the shotgun to the ground. I watched Tom closely, waiting for his revolver to swing toward Isaac. Tom was too far away now for me to try something that didn't end up with me getting shot, but I knew one thing for sure: I would not let him shoot at Isaac, no matter what happened to me.

Tom didn't move the revolver. The shotgun was down. In the scattered moonlight, with the barrel disappearing into the shadows, the long metal cylinder looked more like a sword. Isaac's blocky, gray sweatshirt could have been a suit of armor, an ill-fitting one. He made me think of a young squire who'd failed some test of knighthood.

I felt a heart-wrenching stab of sympathy, but at least he was alive. For now.

"All right," Tom said. "Now move over with Karen. We're all going inside."

Isaac hesitated.

"Did you hear me?" Tom said.

"I'm just—I'm trying be like Two Tufts," Isaac said. "From the Isle of Mirrors. He said—he said if you don't stand up against evil when you have the chance, nobody will. Didn't that mean anything when you wrote it?"

Tom laughed. His revolver still hadn't swung toward Isaac, but I kept waiting for it to do so.

"Quoting my own words back to me again, are you, kid? Of course they meant something. But gods play by different rules. To a god, good and evil are the same, don't you see? They are the *same.* Two sides to the same coin. You cannot have one without the other. You must have balance, and gods provide that balance. Now, if you want to live, get over there with Karen. I won't ask again."

Still, Isaac didn't move. The night grew still. The two of them shared a long look, and I sensed a recognition of some sort pass between them. Isaac, anguished, turned to me.

"Karen," he said. "He—"

Tom's revolver fired.

Hearing Isaac say my name, I'd turned my attention toward him, so I wasn't looking at Tom. I hadn't been ready for him to pull the trigger. There was no powerful boom. Compared to most guns, the Remington produced a sound that was almost polite by comparison. Like a loud, sarcastic clap.

For a second, Isaac just stood there. It was too dark to make out a bullet hole in his sweatshirt, but I thought—*hoped*—that shot had missed.

Then blood darkened the cotton, a spot near where his naval would be, then bigger, not red but a shimmering, oily black, spreading in all directions like tentacles. Isaac looked down.

"Oh," he said.

He collapsed onto his knees. I looked at Tom and saw a grin stretch across his face. If he hadn't taken that extra second to appreciate his handiwork, I doubt I would have had time to make a move.

But he had, and I did.

If I'd had to make a conscious decision, I would have thought too much about body positioning, about dealing with the baggy Columbia jacket, about dozens of other things that would have just gummed up the works. Instead, I just acted—a spin, a leaping front kick, and a leap halfway to him before Tom realized what was happening.

He brought the revolver to bear, but too late. My foot made impact with his arm.

I didn't quite land the kick on his gun hand, but it was close, the ball of my right foot connecting with his wrist. It might have been better. Flesh on flesh instead of flesh on metal. He managed to squeeze off another shot, but this one sailed wide as he whirled backward. The revolver spun away from his outstretched fingers.

He went down. With the Columbia jacket fluttering behind me like a parachute failing to unfurl, I landed on all fours, but momentum and the tilt of the driveway carried me forward. I rolled, dirt spraying me in the face, and rolled some more, deliberately now, putting some weight and speed into it, until I'd somersaulted back to an upright position.

Tom was up on hands and knees too, the two of us glaring at each other like prize fighters in a ring, just long enough before we both realized what the next move was.

The revolver. Where was it?

I spotted it first—there, to my right, nose-deep in the soft dirt like a black tongue lolling out of the ground.

I lunged for it. Grabbed it. Spun it around, expecting Tom to be charging at me and was surprised to see him already on the deck, sprinting toward the front door.

Ten feet away. Then twelve. I probably should have shot him right there—I certainly had a clear shot—but thinking about Hope and the girls stayed my hand. What if Tom wasn't lying about the drone? What if I needed his help to stop it? I was also thinking about his many victims, about the loved ones they'd left behind and how they might not ever find solace until we could prove what he'd done.

I was thinking that if he went in that house, he was never getting away again anyway.

It turned out I was thinking like a fool, but right then I watched him throw open the door and slam it behind him. The click of the deadbolt followed. He might have had another weapon inside, but that at least told me he wasn't coming right back out. Keeping the revolver leveled at the door, I turned to Isaac just as he toppled onto his side.

He hit the dirt like a punching bag that had been set on the ground, no effort to get his hands up to brace his fall. Keeping some of my attention on the door, I ran to him. I dropped to my knees. He clutched his chest as if afraid his innards were going to spill out, his mouth pressed into a thin line. Blood darkened his hands. In the poor light, I couldn't get a good look at the wound.

"Roll onto your back," I said.

"You—you didn't shoot him," Isaac said.

"I know."

"You should—should have shot him. He killed Dad."

"We'll get him. You come first."

"Oh God. It hurts."

"Just let me see."

Groaning, he rolled onto his back. With his bloody, shredded sweatshirt in the way, it was difficult to see much, but he was alive, breathing, and could move all his limbs, which were good signs. He wasn't coughing blood either, which was another.

The wound was probably three inches or so to the left of his naval. With my free hand, I reached under him and slipped my fingers under his sweatshirt. His skin was clammy and warm. I felt along his back, looking for an exit wound, and didn't find one. That *wasn't* such a good sign. It was almost always better if the bullet passed through.

"I—I need to tell you something," he said.

"Later," I said. "I've got to run for help. Keep your hands pressed tight against the wound."

"N-n-no. Don't let him get away."

"That doesn't matter right now. You need an ambulance. That's the important thing."

"Phone. Phone … inside."

His eyes closed even as his voice trailed off. I felt for a pulse on his neck. Steady. For now, at least. And he was right. We were far enough from any houses that calling from a phone inside was the fastest way to get help. Smart kid. Even as he lay there dying, he was smart.

But he wasn't going to die. I wasn't going to let that happen.

I stood, crouching low, scanning the house. The curtains were closed. For the first time in years, I was glad I had a gun in my hand. The clock was ticking on Isaac. The clock was ticking on my sister. I didn't want to leave Isaac where he was, so exposed, but it was risky to move him, and I didn't want to waste any time.

No sirens. No approaching vehicles. If the police had heard the gunshots, they weren't on their way yet.

Knowing the door was locked, I briefly debated trying to shoot out the deadbolt, but that would take time and waste precious bullets. Plus Tom might be waiting on the other side of the door. Instead, I ran down the south side of the house.

Bark chips bit into my feet. I pushed past a juniper to get to the retaining wall, the spindly branches within the bush raking my thighs. I hopped onto a paver patio that was as dark as a cave. It was so dark, in fact, that I almost landed on the barbecue, barely missing it by pushing off the retaining wall at the last second and landing farther out, on stone pavers as cold and hard as blocks of ice.

I could just make out a glass slider leading into the basement. No light from within. Tom could have been standing right there. I couldn't chance checking to see if the slider was unlocked because he might take a shot at me. I needed to catch him off guard.

I raised the revolver and, bracing my shot with both hands, took aim just to the right of the handle and squeezed the trigger.

Finally, I was rewarded with a live round—and a cacophony of shattering glass.

I'd been hoping for a hole at least big enough to reach through without cutting myself, but the entire slider burst, bits of glass pelting the pavers outside and the tiles within like a hailstorm.

Leading with the revolver, I approached the slider. With the threat of Tom taking a shot at me, I couldn't afford more than quick, flitting glances at the ground, so I stepped on a shard. Then another. So far, keeping the steps gentle, I avoided cutting my feet.

My eyes began to adjust. I saw a wet bar. A leather couch. The corner of a pool table. No Tom.

Faster.

I had to move faster.

I had to get a phone. I had to get it now.

I made it over the threshold without cutting my feet, but the second step inside got me. Pain blazed from the small of my left foot, a hot, searing pain, and I clenched my jaw to keep from crying out. A shard was embedded, I could tell, but I couldn't do anything about it. Not yet.

I saw carpeted stairs to the left, an open bathroom door to the right. I also smelled something odd, something like ammonia or bleach, a powerful bathroom cleaner maybe. There was no place for Tom to hide unless he was crouching behind the couch, so I kept the revolver focused there, side-stepping around the couch and using only the ball of my left foot. I felt blood pulsing from the wound.

Tom wasn't there.

I didn't see a phone. If there was a landline in the house, the best place to look was probably the kitchen. If there was a cell phone here, Tom would have it with his things. Leaning against the wall next to the stairs, which doubled back halfway up, I extracted the shard from my foot. Like removing a plug from a bathtub, this turned the trickle into a gusher and painted the fingers of my left hand black. The blood felt hot and sticky. I felt momentarily faint, but I shook it off.

Up.

I had to go up.

The pale red dot from a smoke detector illuminated the carpeted stairs up to the landing, beyond which I couldn't see. Ignoring the throbbing pain in my foot, I took a step. The strange, pungent cleaner-like smell was even stronger. It wasn't cleaner, though, was it? Aiming the revolver high and center, I took another step. The stair felt wet, just a few drops here and there, but it was definitely moisture.

When I stepped again with my bad foot, nearly to the landing, the next stair was even wetter—and a split second after that sensation the pain radiating up from the cut on my foot intensified a thousand fold. Someone could have cut the whole leg off and I doubted it would have hurt more.

It was then, as the scent of fir and pine from the breeze billowing into the house started to recede behind me, that I realized what the strange smell was. It wasn't ammonia. It wasn't bleach.

It was gasoline.

That was why the stairs were wet. The bastard had sprinkled gasoline on them.

Trial by fire.

What Tom had said earlier came back to me now. Was he going to burn the house down? Was that always his plan, or at least a backup one? Crouching just before the landing, still not able to see the floor above, I tried to think of why. I didn't smell smoke.

"Ohhhhhhhhh, Karrrrrrrrren!" Tom called down to me in a singsong voice, his voice muffled as if behind a door. "I know you're in the house! Come *fiiiiiiiiiiiind meeeeee!"*

It might have been a trap, but the thought of Isaac dying outside gave me few options. I ducked my head around the corner, saw more stairs, an open doorway, and some white vinyl flooring. The stairs were even wetter, but the moisture was inconsistent, dry in some spots, soaked in others. I charged up to the main floor.

My blood-greased left foot slipped on the vinyl, and I crashed into a refrigerator, but I stayed upright. The smell of gasoline was overpowering. My right foot stepped in a puddle. There was gasoline everywhere. The kitchen, with walnut cabinets and a U-shaped white tile countertop, was off to the right. The front door and a sunken living room was to the left. A short hall, with the same brown, eighties-era carpet, led to three doors, only one of which was closed. The one on the end.

"Karrrrrrrrrrrrr-ennnnnn!" Tom sang out again, obviously behind the closed bedroom door. "I'm *waiiiiiiiiting* for you!"

Afraid he might shoot me through the door, I stepped out of

the way. The door on the left was another bedroom, the door on the right a bathroom. I spotted a sink. I scanned the kitchen and saw a corded phone mounted to the wall next to a wall calendar. I snatched up the receiver and held it to my ear.

A dial tone.

Thank God. Watching the hall, I punched 911 with the pinky of my gun hand. The blood on my left hand smeared the receiver. Before the dispatcher had even finished asking me the nature of my emergency, I was talking, telling her there was a man with a gun in my house on Casper Mountain, come quick, he'd already shot somebody. I didn't know the address, but she could trace the landline.

"Ma'am?" the woman said. "Can you give me—?"

"You already have officers at a house to the south! Just tell them to go the next house and … and …" I trailed off because I caught a whiff of smoke. From down the hall. "Jesus. He did it."

"I'm sorry?"

"He's going to burn the whole house down!"

"What's your name, Miss?"

"Karen Pantelli! Does that get your attention? And Isaac Welk is outside—a gut-shot wound. Send an ambulance!"

I left the phone dangling from its cord so they could trace the call. Smoke, acrid and black, billowed out of the hall. I needed to get out, but I still feared this was some kind of trick.

"Tom?" I called out to him. "Tom, get out of there!"

"You shouldn't have done that, Karen!" he called out to me. "You shouldn't have called the police!"

"You don't have to do this! You can turn yourself in!"

"You didn't have to call them! We could have been reborn together. I wanted to wait, there are things we should have done together, but you ruined it."

I tried to speak again, but this time the smoke, a hazy gray cloud filling the hall, made it impossible, and I ended up coughing hard just to breathe. I knew I had only seconds before the whole house lit up, but I still didn't want to leave, not yet, not until I was sure he wasn't going to escape again. What if there was a bedroom window in there?

"Tom, get out!"

Still no response. I heard the crackle of fire—then something thunked and clattered, noises like furniture falling over.

"Tom?"

Nothing. I didn't see flames under the door, so maybe I had a chance to get to him. Holding my breath, staying low and to the right, I rushed to the door. I tapped the door handle. Still cool. Good. I tried to open it, however, and found it locked.

I stepped back, far enough away not to be hit by a blizzard of wood, and squeezed off three rounds into the door jamb. Then I kicked it hard with my good foot. The wood crackled but didn't give. I kicked it again. Finally the door burst open.

Smoke plumed into the hall, thick and black, along with a pulsing wave of heat. Covering my mouth with the jacket's sleeve, I ducked below it and plunged into the room. Fire ringed the room, climbing the walls, roaring across the bedspread with flames so high they licked the ceiling. No one was in the bed. The windows were closed. My eyes teared up, making it hard to see anything—pine dressers, a closet with slatted doors, and a bathroom door behind a veil of thick black smog.

When the smoke in front of the bathroom door cleared, I saw him there. It took me a second to understand *what* I was seeing because at first I thought he'd become a giant, eight feet tall and filling the doorway in the flickering orange light, his head brushing the top of the frame. But that wasn't it. His shoes were extended as if he'd been trying to stand on tip toes, but they didn't quite touch the floor.

He'd hung himself.

There was one of those pull-up bars at the top of the frame, and he'd affixed a noose to it. A folding chair lay on its side near him.

"Jesus."

His eyes bulged grotesquely. Was he alive? He wasn't moving, but it had only been a minute since I'd heard the sound of the chair falling. I started toward him, but the flames rose up like a wall between us. Still worried that this was some sort of trick, I took one last lingering look, but there was no doubt it was him. Same face. Same black hoodie. Some hiking shoes. I saw a suitcase. Water bottles, bags of chips, and granola bar wrappers were strewn everywhere. The fire, fueled by a new breath of air from the hall, rose up and engulfed everything.

The last thing I saw, before running for the front door, was a pair of handcuffs on the dresser. Had he been planning on handcuffing me to the bed? Thinking about insanity was like thinking about fire. The longer you sat there, the more it burned you alive.

I ran. The flames, invited along by the gasoline, roared into the kitchen behind me. They ripped across the carpet, nipping at my heels. I heard sirens outside. The cops, finally. My bloody foot throbbed. I grabbed the front door, but it wouldn't open, and in a moment of panic I kept yanking the knob until some part of my rational brain realized that it was the deadbolt.

I clicked it open. Stumbled onto the deck. Fire spat out of the house like a dragon chasing me out of a cave. Two police cars roared up to the house, sirens blaring, lights flashing, tires skidding across the dirt. Isaac was exactly where I'd left him.

I sprinted for him. One of the cops jumped out of the vehicle and shouted at me to drop the gun, which I did, but I didn't stop running. I yelled that I needed to save my friend and prayed he wouldn't shoot at me.

He didn't. There was lots of yelling, more sirens, a maelstrom of noise—fire consuming wood and plastic and everything else in its path. I had to get Isaac out of there. He was too close. Too close to the fire.

He blinked, so he was alive. Moving him was dangerous, but there was nothing else I could do. I grabbed him under the arms and dragged him up the drive, toward the cops, away from as much of the house as I could. One of the cops, a kid, had a Beretta trained on me. The other, yelling at his younger, thinner partner, helped me pull Isaac to safety.

"Hold on, kid," I said.

He didn't answer. I leaned my ear close, but I couldn't feel breath.

"Isaac, don't you die on me," I said.

He closed his eyes.

"Isaac!"

33

It took me three days of searching in the boiling hot sun, but I finally found what I was looking for on the first Sunday in July. Mesa Cemetery was technically in Mesa, not Phoenix, hence the name, but it was in the East Valley part of the Phoenix metropolitan area. It was all one big sprawling city of stucco siding and saguaro cacti as far as I was concerned.

There were more than thirty thousand graves in Mesa Cemetery alone, but like the five other cemeteries I'd visited since checking into my motel, I'd started with a list of "Karens" with Mom's birthday. That had narrowed it down a lot, but there was no way to find exactly what I was looking for without inspecting each gravesite individually. My left foot hurt like hell. No matter how many bandages I wrapped around it, the nasty cut kept re-opening from all the walking.

It was going on four o'clock. The sky stretched overhead like a taut blue tarp, not a single cloud providing relief from the unrelenting sun just beginning its descent toward the bulk of Phoenix that lay to the west. It smelled like parched grass, clay, and diesel fumes from a garbage truck that had just rumbled past. There were still plenty of Fourth of July decorations everywhere—red, white, and blue flags, banners, balloons, flowers. Olive, ficus, ash, and pine trees lined most of the interior roads, but the flat gravestone I was looking for was in the North View section, in the middle, with no shade to provide refuge.

The printed list in my hand was stained with sweat, dirt, and ketchup, plus it was so wrinkled that I could have used it as a tissue to wipe my brow. Sweat pasted my V-neck shirt to my back and greased every part of my body: my neck, under my arms, even between my toes. I'd worn a baseball cap for most of my Tombstone Tour, but I'd neglected to put on sunscreen until yesterday. The back of my neck ached from the burn.

I found the gravestone I was looking for—a simple granite square with white engraving—and squatted in front of it.

Karen Whiteside.

Late in the day, the dry air had wicked most of the moisture from my eyes, so there was a lot of blinking, but I still spotted what I'd been hoping to find straight off, even before I'd verified that the birthday was right.

An X.

It had been engraved in the middle, but not professionally, a jagged X centered above the name and probably put there with a chisel and a hammer, big enough that it was no accident but small enough that few would notice unless they were looking right at it. Like me.

Feeling my heart pick up its pace, I looked around. There were plenty of people, no surprise for a Sunday, even on a blistering Arizona day, but we were spaced out. To my left, a groundskeeper in a gray uniform edged the grass around a young ficus tree. To my right, farther away, an old man in a tan suit set flowers in front of a gravestone. I saw others, people alone, people in pairs, whole families, but nobody was looking at me.

Nobody cared.

Still, I waited until I was back in the Honda to make my call, partly for privacy and partly out of respect for other visitors. I was parked by the grave of Waylon Jennings, the famous country singer—I picked the spot out of curiosity, but the gravestone was just as plain as any of the others—and the sun was low enough that the nearby ash tree blocked some of the sun. It still felt like an iron forge inside the car. Rolling down the windows barely helped because there was no wind. I'd eaten so much fast food lately in the Honda that it smelled like a McDonald's.

Hope answered so fast that it was like she was waiting with her phone in her hand.

"Hey, it's me," I said.

"Did you find it?"

She sounded breathless, so I figured she *had* been waiting for my call. I didn't blame her. She'd always been the one who wanted this more than I did. I heard something sizzling on the stove. I heard canned laughter in the background, like from a sitcom.

"X marks the spot," I said.

"Wow, really?"

"Really."

"You were right then about what he meant about the birthday thing. I've been praying for this moment. You think it's really her?"

"I think it's what he wanted me to find—if I somehow managed to beat him. I don't think he thought I would, but this was like his … I don't know, his *reward* to me if I did."

"Wow. And to think she was right there, just a couple hours away from Tucson. From *us*. Crazy."

"We don't know that it was really her, Hope. Not yet. I told you I'd call you right away if I found it, and that's what I'm doing."

"Right, right. But it could be her, right? It could. Okay, give me the details. I want to write it all down."

I did—the name, the cemetery, and the date of death. I heard her pen scratching across a piece of paper. Sweat trickled from underneath my hat and into my eyebrow, which already felt heavy like a wet sponge. I wondered how hot it was in Atlanta. Hope had air conditioning. All the modern conveniences. I could imagine her leaning over the green Silestone countertop, using one of her husband's UPS pens to jot down the information, the cool air blowing on her bare legs from a wall vent. Dressed in a cute yellow summer dress. Comfortable.

She lived in a middle class palace, and I lived out of my car. I felt a mix of loneliness, revulsion, and—most troubling—envy, a familiar but rare mix I seldom felt unless I was talking to Hope, for some reason. She didn't bring out the best in me. She didn't bring out the worst either. She just brought out the parts of myself that I most wanted to ignore.

"You mean Mom only died a couple months ago?" she said.

"Well, this lady did."

"Sure. Okay. I'm just … Wow. Still trying to wrap my head around all this. I mean, she really could have been watching over us, right? Why would she do that? Why would she not come talk to us?"

"Hope …"

"Right, right. We need to make sure it's her. I'll do some research. Got to finish making dinner, get the kids to bed, that sort of thing, but—call later? Like really late?"

"Sure. I'll do some research too when I get back to the motel."

"Sounds good. Hey, um, Karen?"

"Yes?"

"I just wanted to say … I'm sorry about that kid, you know. About him dying on the way to the hospital. I read about it in the paper. I should have said something before, but with everything happening, the craziness of it all, I just, well …"

I swallowed. "It's okay."

"Are you, though? Okay?"

"No."

"Oh."

"But I'm working on it, all right? Don't worry about me. That's part of why I'm in Phoenix. It's … a kind of healing, I guess. A way to make things right."

Hope chuckled, but there was a ruefulness to it that made it sound more like a stifled sob. "And here I thought you were just trying to avoid the press."

"That too."

"Well, at least that Tom Shelby guy is dead, right? And all that stuff they found in his house in Casper. The journals. The pictures. Wow. I mean, it's … I can't believe somebody like that really existed. And a children's author too!"

I didn't say anything. I didn't like the undercurrent of glee, the same morbid fascination that I'd been hearing in the news, the pleasure that many people, maybe even most, seemed to take from the exploits of someone so evil. Was it a kind of coping mechanism? I supposed it was, but it wasn't one that worked for me, especially with Mr. Grim. He'd fooled me. He'd fooled lots of people, but he'd fooled me most of all, and I'd always burn from the shame of it.

"Sorry," Hope said, "I know you probably don't want to talk about all this stuff. You actually lived it. I just want you to know, you ever want to talk about…"

She trailed off, and I heard Ronnie, her always controlling, sometimes abusive, and only occasionally charming on-again-off-again husband, asking who it was before she muffled the phone. I heard him yelling. I heard her trying to placate him. I didn't like the yelling or the placating, but I was glad not to talk about Mr. Grim.

The back and forth went on for a while before she finally returned with a sigh.

"Sorry about that," she said.

"Ronnie still pretty mad at me, huh?"

"Well, Karen, you did have a couple cops staking out his house without even telling us."

"I know. Technically, one FBI agent and one San Juan County detective."

"And then you had those cops drag us out of the house in the middle of the night."

"For your own safety."

"Yeah. I get that, even if it turned out to be a false alarm. Ronnie just feels that your friend, that black guy? He was kind of rough, the way he grabbed Ronnie."

"Hmm."

"You know, you can at least act as if you're sorry about that."

"Well, you know, Dad did teach us not to lie. "

"Right. Okay. You're making it into a joke. Ha ha. I know you don't like Ronnie. Would it hurt you so much just to pretend that —you know what? Forget it. I don't want to rehash this today. We'll talk later."

"Hope, hold on."

But she'd already hung up.

———

THE DESERT STAR Motel was just off Highway 87 in Chandler, the cheapest place I could find and still be in the Phoenix metropolitan area. By the time I drove across town, grabbed an early dinner of burger and fries at Wendy's while soaking in the air conditioning, and finally parked the Honda in front of the drab stucco building that looked more like a pioneer fort than a two-star motel, it was nearly six o'clock.

I wouldn't have known it by the sun, which stubbornly perched high above the flat roofline. Arizona didn't observe daylight saving time, but even so, there were hours to go before sunset. In the lobby, the clerk was watching a CNN anchor interview an author of a book on serial killers. Tom Shelby's photo was featured in the corner of the screen. Keeping my head low, I picked up some chocolate chip cookies from a tray on the counter and was out of there before the clerk turned to look at me.

I knew from previous experience that the cookies tasted like sugar-coated cardboard, but they were free. Free may not have made things taste better, but they lowered my expectations, so I wasn't disappointed. Not being disappointed wasn't quite the same thing as being pleased, but when you're dirt poor, it has to do.

"Honey, I'm home," I announced to my squalid room, but my squalid room, with its saggy queen bed, puttering mini fridge, and carpet that both looked and felt like damp moss, didn't answer. That was good. Nobody wanted a chatty squalid room.

The mini fridge would have kept me up at night if it wasn't for the wall-mounted air conditioner, which did the job admirably by itself. It sounded like someone pouring a bucket of tacks on a concrete door. It did keep the room cool, though, if a balmy seventy-eight degrees counted as cool.

To the left, between me and the bed, was one of those double interior doors that allows families to share rooms, but it was hard to imagine families wanting to stay in a place like this. I flung my sweaty ballcap on my suitcase and collapsed on the bed, flat on my back.

The bed smelled like an aquarium, or maybe a bait and tackle shop, which was odd for many reasons but chiefly because the motel was not only in the desert but also because I'd heard on the radio that Phoenix hadn't seen a drop of rain in three weeks. It made me wonder who'd been in the room last. It made me wonder who'd slept in the bed. A mermaid who'd always wanted to see the desert?

I was exhausted, and I desperately wanted to rinse off the sweat caked to my body, but I didn't want to delay the inevitable. I reached under the bed and grabbed my Chromebook, then leaned against the headboard and tucked my knees up. I brushed off the clumps of dust and set the computer on my lap. The motel's Wi-Fi was spotty, but this time it worked fine.

My heartrate kicked up to blind date territory. Crazy. In a way, that's what it was, a blind date with Karen Whiteside. Would she be the one? I brought up a search site and typed her name in the magic box plus the date of birth, death, city, and all the other relevant details.

I expected it might take a while, but it didn't.

I sat with the information a minute, listening to the death rattle of the air conditioning and studying a crack along the ceiling that looked like a fissure in the desert. Had Hope already found what I'd just discovered? If she had, she would have called. Or maybe not. Maybe she needed to sit with the information for a while too. Maybe she was putting her kids to bed, trying not to think about it, comforting herself with the family she'd built, the family she'd never really had as a child.

I felt another stab of loneliness. How had my life come to this, a desperate search for a mother's love in all the wrong places, like somebody trying to quench their thirst by digging deep where it seldom rained?

I needed to talk to someone, but not Hope. I grabbed the cell phone off the nightstand and dialed. He answered right away.

"Bad news," I said.

My voice betrayed me, a hitch there that embarrassed me, but to his credit Ben didn't pause before chuckling, "Come on, Karen," he said. "I told you to come up with a better nickname for yourself."

"Ha ha. Yeah, I am bad news, aren't I? No, I found the X. Her name is Karen Whiteside. But it's not her."

This time there was a pause. It was hard to hear over my air conditioner, even pressing the phone against my ear, but I thought I could make out a saxophone, static mixed in with the melody. Something else too. The whisper of traffic?

"Are you sure?" he asked finally.

"Yeah. She's black, for one thing. Her picture came right up on a funeral site. She was a kindergarten teacher. A widow for the past ten years. No kids. Didn't seem like she had a lot of people in her life at the end." I shrugged, forgetting he couldn't see me.

"I'm sorry," Ben said.

"Yeah, just a crazy wild goose chase. I don't know what the hell Tom was trying to do. Maybe he found it funny that a woman named Whiteside was black? Who knows. Joke's on me."

"Do you think he knew your mother at all?"

"I have no idea."

"I'm sorry."

"You should probably stop saying that. I feel like punching something."

"Right. What are you going to do now?

"Take a hot shower and try to forget this whole thing."

"I meant after."

"I have no idea, Ben. I'll figure something out. I always do."

"Back to wandering, huh?"

"Don't start. How are things in DC?"

He blew air between his lips. "Oh, you know. Same old bull-shit that has nothing to do with catching bad people. I'm actually on my way to a stupid black tie event right now. Shake some hands. Repeat the same inane platitudes about how the FBI is more than just a job. It's a calling."

"Don't try to sound so cynical. I know you actually believe that bullshit. Where's this thing being held?"

"Oh ... The White House."

I snorted. "That's nothing special?"

"The president won't even be there. Just the first lady. He's in the Middle East right now."

"Uh huh. What a hardship. Having to settle for an evening with the most popular woman in America."

"Well, it's mostly because of you, Karen. Once again, you made it sound like I was the brilliant mastermind and you were just a minor player in all this. Like I singlehandedly made sure Tom Shelby will never kill again."

"If it was even him," I said.

"No, no, it was definitely Tom Shelby. It's not a twin either, so don't give me that bullshit. Dental records, DNA tests, it's all preliminary, nothing's official, but I can tell you it's a match."

"I see."

"Even after all that, you still don't believe that was him hanging in the house?"

"I just figured he had another trick up his sleeve. If his original plan to frame me for all the murders failed, I thought he'd have some sort of backup."

"I think we have to face the fact it's really him, Karen. There was not a lot left of the body, but the science says it's him, and you saw him face-to-face yourself. Maybe, when his plan was falling apart, he just decided to go out on his own terms?"

"I guess you're right."

"I *know* I'm right, so you can stop beating yourself up. You may have managed to fool most people that you didn't do the world a huge favor here, but you haven't fooled everyone."

"What are you talking about?"

"Only this. The FBI wants you back."

"You're shitting me," I said.

"No, this comes all the way from Director Steele. I think he wants to let the smoke clear for a bit, but he wants you in the Bureau again, Karen. I think you can name your price too. A raise. Lead a special task force. Whatever you want."

I studied the crack in the ceiling again, which seemed to be growing, cleaving the room in two. I didn't want anyone to fix the crack. I was fine with it exactly how it was. What would I look at if not for that crack?

"No," I said.

"You don't even want to think about it?"

"I did think about it. For three point five seconds."

"Jesus."

"I gotta go, Ben."

"Really? Where?"

I sighed. "Let's not end like this."

"All right, all right. I'm pulling into the gate now anyway. Hey, come see me soon, okay? "

"Sure," I said. "And thanks, Ben. For what you did for Hope. For me. For everything."

"Always. And I meant what I said about you visiting me. I miss you, Karen. Really."

"Talk soon," I said and clicked off before he could say anything else mushy.

I put the phone on the nightstand. I put the Chromebook under the bed. I lay there for a long time in that squalid room, alone with the dying air conditioner and the mini fridge on life support, comforting myself with a ceiling crack that would probably be there long after I was gone. Gone from the room. Gone from this world. It would probably still be there when the desert turned green and the dinosaurs came to reclaim what was rightfully theirs.

I heard people outside talking, lots of coming and going. The walls were so thin that the windows rattled every time a door closed. Only when the sunlight rimming the closed curtains began to fade did I finally muster the energy to slide off the bed and slink my way to the bathroom. It was no bigger than the bathroom on an airplane, and somehow they'd fit a shower in there too. The water was hot, though, scalding hot, and I stayed under it as long as I could bear. Then I stayed under it even longer, until my chest turned pink and my toes began to prune, until the air grew so thick with steam that I could no longer tell up from down.

I might have stayed even longer if it wasn't for the phone. I heard it ringing in the other room. It stopped, then started again. Hope. She wanted to talk to me. She needed me. That was enough reason to get on with things. For now, anyway.

She called a third time when I was drying myself off. When I came out to answer it, wrapped in a towel, water dribbling down my neck and steam rising off my bare shoulders, somebody was sitting on the chair by the wall-mounted desk. Armed with a Beretta 92FS fitted with a suppressor. Pointed unmistakably at me.

It was Tom Shelby.

34

———————

"**S**urprise," he said.

It was Tom Shelby all right. The same lean build even if he'd tried to make himself look bulkier by wearing a baggy green tracksuit. The same brown hair streaked with silver, though I could only see a little of it sticking out from under the black Arizona Diamondbacks baseball cap. The same broad but tight-lipped smile, like he was sitting on the perfect joke and he was just bursting with the need to tell it to someone.

During all this, my phone kept ringing. It finally stopped. Water ran down into my eyes. I blinked it away, but Tom was still there. He wore black surgical gloves. A pair of mirrored aviator sunglasses sat on the desk next to him along with a North Face backpack roughly the same green as the carpet. I also saw what I thought was a furry brown caterpillar next to the backpack until I realized it must have been a fake mustache. He'd taken it off just for my benefit. He'd wanted to make sure I recognized him.

"It can't be," I said.

He smiled. "Amazing, isn't it? Just like Jesus, I've risen from the dead."

"Impossible."

"No. A miracle? Maybe. I told you I was going to be reborn. Well, here I am."

The voice, the facial expressions, the mannerisms, they were all the same. I shivered. Either the grumbling air conditioner had found new life, or my body temperature had dropped dramatically. I became keenly aware of how naked I was, with only one of those scratchy, never quite big enough motel towels tucked tight around my body. I also became keenly aware of just how long that suppressor was.

A Rugged Obsidian 9. One of the best. Even without my angry chorus of failing equipment to cover the noise, it would have been hard to hear a gunshot. We were separated by at least fifteen feet, far too much distance for me to try anything.

"So you're going to shoot me, is that it?" I said.

"Yes."

"Wow. Just like that, huh? You're not even going to pretend otherwise?"

He shrugged, the movement mostly disappearing in all the loose folds of the tracksuit. "There's no need to pretend at this point. But whether I kill other people important to you after leaving this room is entirely up to you, Karen. If you shout, scream for help, or make some stupid attempt to stop me … Well, other people will suffer."

I shook my head. "Another drone threat? You expect me to fall for that crap again?"

"Hardly. I admit that was a ruse. No, I'll hunt down the people you care about one by one in person. Hope. Her daughters. Ben. I'll do it over a few years. Most will look like accidents. Some won't. They'll all die, but some will die more painfully than others."

He recited this with the emotion of a tax auditor explaining why your deductions didn't quite add up. It was all the more chilling because of it. I glanced at the door. Not only had he turned the deadbolt, he'd hung the chain.

"There's nobody coming to your rescue," he said.

"People know I'm here, you know," I said. "I just called Ben. He knows."

"It makes no difference. I'm just going to make it look like a robbery gone bad. Place like this, nobody will be surprised."

"I don't have any money. Nothing valuable worth stealing."

He nodded toward the backpack. "Oh, I'll leave a few things. In your depression, it will look like you were turning to drugs for comfort."

"Who are you? Who are you really?"

He smiled. "Tom Shelby, of course. I told you, I rose from the dead."

"Bullshit."

"Why, Karen, you need to have a little more faith. All right, if I'm not Tom Shelby, then who could I possibly be?"

"I saw you die in the cabin," I insisted. "I saw it with my own eyes!"

"No, you saw Tom Shelby die. Or actually, you saw Tom Shelby's body hanging in the bedroom. Come on, Karen. Think! Do you remember seeing the handcuffs? In my haste, I forgot them. Did it ever occur to you that maybe Tom Shelby, the real Tom Shelby, had been my prisoner in that house? That I'd kept him there just so he could die at the right time?"

"To frame him," I said. "To frame him for all the murders."

"Now you're finally getting a clue."

"But ... but he looks just like you."

He chuckled. "Karen, Karen, I *so* thought you were smarter. I actually told you everything from the first moment we met. You remember how I said you looked just like your mother?"

"What?"

"At the Orcadia. When you thought I was Colin Welk. I told you the world was full of doppelgängers, remember? With almost eight billion of us, there's more people that look just like us than most people realize. I admit, I got a little lucky. Years ago, I stumbled across one of his books and saw his author photo. The resemblance was uncanny."

"You mean he was just another innocent person?"

He sniffed. "Innocent. Who among us is really innocent? He was a shitty husband and a conceited asshole."

"And he wasn't really going blind?"

"Oh, no, that part was definitely true. That was why I had to speed up my plan, you see. Back when I saw how much Tom and I looked alike, I filed that information away, thought I might use that to my advantage someday, but the fool started going blind. I was originally just going to kill Welk, you know, and leave it at that. I don't like being forced to do things I don't want to do, but I was getting around to it. But then Welk set in motion his pitiful little plan to bring you to the Orcadia, and it occurred to me that if *he* might find me someday, somebody else might too. The time had come for me to be reborn. Plus I thought I could have a little fun with you while I was at it."

"That was all true? Welk bringing me to Orcadia? You didn't just make that stuff up when you told me that back in Wyoming?"

"Oh, he was a smart fellow, I will give him that. If I hadn't been watching him closely by that point, he might have even gotten away with it. As I told you before, I just co-opted his plan. Killed him, stuffed him in the bathroom, and made it look like a suicide. You figured out that I was pretending to be Colin Welk, but you didn't figure out that I was pretending to be Tom Shelby too."

"And you're not dying? All that wincing you did, that was just … part of the act?"

"Exactly. I needed to give you clues, put out the bread crumbs just so. I didn't want anyone else involved, but you made that easy, Karen, you're such a loner, so insistent on doing everything your-self. I played my part—from the first time you saw me in the wheelchair all the way to the end."

"But why tell me this at all then? What do you want from me? One last roll in the hay?"

He dismissed this with a wave of his hand. "Please. Nothing so tawdry."

"Then *what?* You obviously lured me here with that X marks the spot business. You must have been watching the cemetery, waiting to see if I would show up, and then you followed me back to the motel. You *wanted* me to come to Phoenix. Why? At least tell me the truth. I deserve that much."

"Deserve? That's a funny word, isn't it? Did I deserve to have someone like Colin Welk obsessed with finding me? Did I deserve to live in a world where the technology was emerging that would stop me from doing my work? Did I deserve to have Welk's annoying son tagging along with you, almost ruining everything? I'm just glad the little shit is dead."

His tone had turned self-pitying. If he was a god, he was one of the old Greek gods, impulsive and quick to take offense, full of all the usual imperfections. I would have told him so too if he wasn't currently pointing a Beretta at me. Outside, a woman yelled at her kids to bring back two Cokes and a Sprite. They couldn't have been more than a couple rooms away. I glanced at the door. He saw me do it.

"If you shout," he said, "you're dead right now. And don't take another step. I've seen what you've been doing, creeping closer."

He was right that I'd tried to get closer, inching forward a little at a time, but I hadn't succeeded in shrinking the gap more than a few inches. The gulf that separated us could have been the Grand Canyon for how much good my effort had done me.

"You ask why I brought you here," he said. "The truth is, I would have been fine had you died when I blew up Welk's house in Seattle. I would have been fine if you'd gotten caught by the police in Butte. And I would have been fine if you'd died next to the man the world believes is Mr. Grim, his last victim before he hung himself and burned the house down on Casper Mountain. But this works too, don't you see? You provided an eyewitness account to Tom Shelby's death, which is even better. And now I get to go on doing what I do, no one the wiser."

"What about my mother?" I asked. "What happened to her?"

"I let her go," he said.

"Come on."

"She wanted a ride. I gave her a ride. I have no idea what happened to her after I dropped her off in LA."

"Liar."

He shrugged. "I don't kill *everyone* who wanders into my path, you know. It's the power of deciding that I relish most."

I couldn't tell whether he was telling the truth, but then, I hadn't been able to tell much about him at all. "Who are you then? What's your real name?"

"I'm nobody."

"You don't have a name?"

He shrugged. "I left my name behind the first chance I got. I knew what I was from a very early age, you see. Gods aren't born with names. They are *given* names by their believers. Welk gave me the name Mr. Grim. It helped him believe in me. But on one level, at least on a level you'd understand, I'm a lot like you, Karen. Another dead-eyed drifter. I'm just much better at it than you."

"We're nothing alike."

"Oh? You have no permanent address, no personal attachments, no future. The only difference between us is that you keep clinging to your past. If only you'd let it go forever ... Well, you could have become a god like me."

I couldn't quite keep my anger in check. "A mass-murdering psychopath? No thanks."

He sighed. "I thought you were a worthy opponent, Karen. You almost were too. You passed all my tests—save one. The final one. You didn't see the truth of who I was before it was too late. If you had, you never would have come to Phoenix. You would have known it was a trap. It's a pity, really. It would have been a lot more dangerous to me if you *had* figured it out, since that would mean the world would go on looking for Mr. Grim, but I admit part of me wanted to continue playing our little game despite the risk."

I shook my head. The towel was slipping, and I grabbed it to keep it from falling. I could tell by his eyes that he enjoyed looking at me. I felt ill at the prospect of him touching me again, but there was still a kind of power there, the power of my sexuality. It was something, anyway. Then I realized what his weakness was, one I might be able to exploit. "You want somebody to talk to, don't you? Or at least to hear what you have to say?"

He didn't answer.

"That's why you haven't shot me yet. You could have done it at any time, but you're desperate for some kind of connection."

"Ridiculous."

"You're lonely."

"Nonsense."

"That's what this is really about, right? You may tell yourself you just wanted a worthy opponent, but on a deeper level you needed somebody to know what you've done. To appreciate the *real* you, even if it's only for a moment."

"Just stop. You're embarrassing yourself."

"Isaac was right. You *are* afraid—of not mattering. Of doing everything you've done without anybody caring. Even your pattern, spelling the word God on a map—that was your way of reaching out to the world. You *wanted* somebody to figure it out. Otherwise, it's like you don't even exist. Does a god exist if nobody believes in him?"

He shook his head, but I could see that I'd gotten to him. Rattled him. It was a dangerous game, but I wanted him rattled. Off-kilter. Anything to keep him from thinking too much. There was still way too much distance between us for me to try anything without ending up dead, but I had one more thing I could do to throw him off-balance. To scramble his brains. It was the obvious thing—for a woman, anyway.

I took off my towel.

I let it drape from my right hand, fully exposing myself to him, naked and glistening. I made no attempt to cover myself. I knew he'd see through anything obvious, so I just stood there in the balmy, squalid room, letting his gaze sweep across my body.

"What are you doing?" he said.

"I know loneliness too. I've known it my whole life."

"Whatever you're trying to do, it won't work."

"We made love. There was a real connection there. I know it."

"I was just playing a part."

"For a moment, you felt less lonely. You wanted to feel it again."

It was a very subtle thing, the way his mouth parted, the way his eyes lingered, the way the Beretta dipped just a tiny bit, not even a millimeter, but I noticed it. His lizard brain had taken over, if only for a second. Even in a serial killer, male sexuality was never entirely absent. It wasn't comforting, but it was useful.

There was a loud knock, but it wasn't my room. It came from next door. "Housekeeping!" a woman shouted. Mr. Grim, a.k.a. Colin Welk, a.k.a. Tom Shelby, a.k.a. who knew who else, glanced in that direction. It was hardly even a glance. The pupils shifted a millimeter to the left, nothing more. If I would have tried something right then, he would have shot me for sure. He was too good to be fooled by a naked woman and a housekeeper at the door.

But then the door between the motel rooms crashed open.

The interior door was even farther from Mr. Grim than I was, with a bed between him and the wall-mounted desk where he sat, so it wasn't ideal, but if we'd tried to control too much, he would have been onto us.

A lot happened in a span of a few seconds. Ben Wilde, my steadfast former partner, dressed in a bulletproof vest armed with his Glock, burst into the room. I tossed the towel at Mr. Grim's face. Knowing he'd probably squeeze the Beretta's trigger, the plan was for me to dive to the right, or anywhere not in the line of fire, but I wasn't going to do that. I knew he'd take a shot at Ben first. Ben had taken a huge risk. He'd insisted, but there was no way I was letting him die for it.

Instead I dove forward, low and slightly to the right, but mostly following the towel. Mr. Grim's Beretta did fire, a muffled explosion that burst a hole in the middle of the towel and sent the bullet whizzing past my left ear. The bullet was so close that I felt the burn, but I was alive and unharmed.

And I was on the move.

I turned my dive into a somersault, covering more than half the distance as I rolled naked over the spongy carpet. Puffs of cotton floated in the air. Mr. Grim fired again, but this shot went high and wide—blowing a hole in that ceiling crack, of all places.

By this point, I was springing back to my feet. All my many martial arts moves were well-practiced, honed from hours of diligent work, never stopping even as I became a drifter. With my left arm, I swiped a block, pushing his gun arm away not only from me but from Ben too.

He squeezed off another shot, but with the ungainly length of the suppressor working against him, I was too close for him to bring the Beretta back around. It was what I'd been counting on. I saw his eyes, wide and ferocious like a caged animal, but then my closed right fist was surging toward those eyes with more power than I'd ever hit anything before.

And I'd hit a lot of things in my life.

He took the punch in the nose, a sickening crunch. His head flopped back. I followed the punch, the two of us crashing against the desk.

I'd hit him hard enough that it might have killed him, but I knew by the way he screamed and grabbed his nose that he'd been spared that fate. There was blood everywhere. Blood on him. Blood on me. Blood on the sad, damp carpet, which probably improved it.

By now, Ben had descended upon us, snatching the Beretta away from fake-Tom and cursing me out for not following the plan. Maya was right behind him. The three other FBI agents who'd been staking out the room next door followed him into my room more cautiously. They all wore bulletproof vests and were armed with Glocks, but somehow Maya was the only one who made them look like a fashion choice.

While Ben pinned Mr. Grim to the floor, I used the handcuffs in Ben's vest pocket to shackle fake-Tom's arms behind him. It was hard to think of him as Mr. Grim anymore the way he carried on like a two-year-old having a tantrum, sobbing, bucking, and jerking about to no avail. Oh, how the mighty had fallen.

He didn't sound like a god. He barely sounded human. I didn't know what he was, some abomination of flesh and bone that shouldn't exist and, if it were only up to me, wouldn't. At least not beyond the day. But it wasn't just up to me anymore.

Now that Ben had subdued him, I stepped away and picked up the towel, once again tucking it around my body. The bullet hole exposed part of my thigh, but the towel did the job well enough until I could put on clothes. Ben was nice enough to look away. The other FBI agents in the room, not so much.

At least nobody was taking photos.

Mr. Grim's sobbing had become a rhythmic, high-pitched keening. Maya ducked under the bed. When she reemerged, she held a digital recorder in her left hand, the backup. The main attraction was the tiny wireless microphone in her right hand. Smiling, she held both up so fake-Tom could see them. I didn't see any fear in her eyes at all. Whatever demons she'd wrestled with on that Anacortes ferry were gone.

Only then did Mr. Grim fall silent. He stopped jerking and bucking about—slowly and then all at once, like the death throes of a stray dog that had been hit by a bus. It wasn't so much that the fight went out of him. *Everything* went out of him.

It could have been a still life for how motionless everyone was, five law enforcement people in bulletproof vests, a serial killer in a tracksuit, and one dead-eyed drifter wearing nothing but a towel. It was so quiet that once again the rattle of the air conditioner and the groan of the mini fridge filled the stillness. It was so quiet that when I spoke, I felt like I was standing on a stage.

"You were wrong about one thing, at least," I said, looking down at the bloody face of a serial killer who would never hurt anybody again. "You said I always have to do things by myself. Well, this time I brought a few friends."

35

———

After they hauled Mr. Grim away, after the room was secure, and after I got dressed but before we were all set to meet in the room next door for a general debriefing to ready ourselves for when what had happened at the Desert Star Motel blew up the daily news cycle like a neutron bomb, I went for a quick walk to clear my head.

Sunsets were long in the desert. The sun was fully down, but twilight was still singing its last hurrah as I headed over to Highway 87. A thin purple band held back all the dark sky weighing down on it. I just wore jeans and a thin white T-shirt, but I still felt warm. Was it the warm night air or my racing heart? At least I wasn't sweating.

When I could no longer hear my heart beating in my ears, I returned to the motel, bought an Aquafina from a machine, and grabbed a plastic cup and some ice from the empty motel office. The clerk was in the parking lot with a lot of other looky-loos trying to figure out what had just gone down. I headed into the parking lot, away from the madness, and holding the ice water against my still-throbbing right hand.

I hadn't broken anything when I'd punched Mr. Grim in the

face, thank God, but I knew that my knuckles would hurt for days. It was a small price considering the enormous satisfaction I'd taken from that punch.

My Honda was parked at the back, the white hood caked with a layer of orange grime so thick that I could have grown succulents on it. I was leaning against the driver side door, watching the FBI agents conferring in front of the motel room, when Ben walked up. He no longer wore the bulletproof vest. His tie was loose. The moisture rings on his arms were as wide as tire treads. In the fading light, his forehead gleamed like black chrome.

"Ice water, huh?" he said. "You don't want anything stronger?"

"Ice water will do for now."

He nodded and leaned against the Honda next to me. "That was some crazy ass shit in there, Karen."

"Thank you."

"I didn't mean it as a compliment."

"I know."

"You should have followed the plan. He could have shot you."

"He didn't."

"But he could have."

I shrugged. I didn't want to argue with him, not after what he'd done. What he'd done for *me.*

"Thank you," I said.

"You already thanked me on the phone."

"Yeah, but the team was listening. This is just between you and me."

We stood there in the warm silence, neither of us saying a word. I thought about what he'd seen when he'd burst into the motel room. To my knowledge, it was the first time he'd ever seen me fully naked. I wondered if he'd liked what he saw. I wondered if I should say something about it—a joke, a sarcastic remark. I wondered if it could lead to anything. A doorway to somewhere good. I thought again about the one time we'd kissed, back in Houston.

I was still thinking about that kiss when Maya walked across the parking lot, smiling tentatively, holding a cell phone out in a way that made it obvious that somebody was on the line. She glanced at Ben, and he glanced back, and the look wasn't much, but there was something there, a shared intimacy. Something had happened between them.

I didn't know how far they'd gone with it, but I knew that whatever door I was looking for with Ben was closed.

"You okay?" Maya said.

"I will be," I said.

She handed me the phone. "Somebody wants to talk to you."

"Is that who I think it is?"

Maya just smiled. I took the phone, both Maya and Ben watching me. That was fine. I didn't mind them watching me with this. Soon the two of them would go off together, and I'd be alone. Again.

But no matter what, I at least had one more friend in the world. I might have been able to count my real friends on one hand, but at least I could count them.

"Hey there, guy, " I said. "How are you doing?"

"Hospital food sucks," Isaac said.

I laughed. "I think you just stated a universal truth."

"Thanks for getting him," he said. "I just—I want you to know that. Thank you."

"You're welcome," I said. "And thank *you* for agreeing to lie low for so long. I know it must have been really weird, especially when people on the news were talking about you being dead. But it worked, Isaac. Our little trap worked just like we hoped it would. He'll never hurt anyone again."

He didn't say anything for a long time. I knew what he was thinking. He was thinking that the only way we'd know for sure that Mr. Grim would never hurt anyone was if Mr. Grim was dead. *That* was what he really wanted. It was what I wanted too, if I was honest with myself. I could tell him this was better, letting the hands of justice work their magic, but it was hard to say something I didn't really believe. At least not this time.

"Do they know his real name?" he asked finally.

"Not yet, but they will."

"It doesn't really matter, though, does it? Because he's a nobody."

"That's right. Nobody that matters, anyway."

"Not like the real Tom Shelby. He was somebody. He didn't deserve that. I feel real bad for him."

"Me too. A lot of innocent people died. But we stopped him, Isaac. We stopped him, and you played a huge part in that. So again, thank you."

"And all because I made up a fake quote," he said. "I didn't know for sure he wasn't really Tom Shelby until then, but I kind of started to wonder. He might not remember stuff he'd written word for word, but he wouldn't say he'd written something I completely made up. Because there's no Two Tufts, and there's no Isle of Mirrors. I mean, there might be some fan fiction out there that has stuff like that in it, but not that I've read. And I've read a lot of *Fur and Fang* fan fiction."

It was such an Isaac thing to say that I had to laugh. "It was a good quote, though. 'If you don't stand up against evil when you have the chance, nobody will.' Well, you stood up, Isaac. You stood up, and I'm proud of you."

"Aw, I don't know."

"No, really. You were awesome. You tried to tell me in that moment he wasn't who he said he was, but I didn't—I couldn't … Well, I just didn't see it. And I'm sorry."

"It's okay. He tried to shoot me so I wouldn't tell you, but if he hadn't … Well, then we couldn't have fooled him today, right?"

"Right. I just … Well, anyway, I just want to say again there's no way I could have done this without you, okay? I mean it. Seriously."

We were both getting choked up, I could hear it in our voices, so it was time to end the call.

"Hey, listen," I said, "I've got to get back, but I'll come visit you in a day or two, okay?"

"Sure," he said.

"And then I'll help you with everything else—next steps, that sort of thing. We'll figure it out. You're not going to be alone with all that."

He was silent. I thought I heard a nurse talking to someone in the background. Distant beeping.

"What is it?" I said.

"Well, um, Maya kind of already offered to help me with that stuff. She said I can come live with her until I get my feet set, if I want. I guess she was up for a job in Portland, and she got it."

"Oh," I said.

I looked at Maya, raising my eyebrows at her. She cringed and patted her chest, as if to say *my bad.*

"I hope that's okay?" Isaac said into my ear.

"No, no, it's great."

"I thought it would be good. A fresh start, that sort of thing. I mean, you don't have your own place, you know, and I just thought ..."

"Isaac, it's fine, it's awesome."

"Really?"

"Yes, really. Hey, I do have to go, but I'll call again tomorrow, okay? We'll make plans."

He said that would be great, and we hung up. When I handed the phone back to Maya, I made sure to really glare at her.

"Sorry," she said. "I was going to tell you, but I literally got offered the job two days ago. And we weren't supposed to talk to you, you know? Pretend like we didn't know you. And I thought ... well, maybe it would be good for Isaac. I called him to just float the idea. He hasn't even met me in person, so I didn't think he'd go for it, but, well, he kind of jumped at the chance."

She looked oddly guilty, like I'd caught her reaching for the last Coke in the fridge. It was a cute look for her, and I wanted to enjoy it, so I just kept glaring. But Ben spoiled it by punching me playfully on the shoulder.

"Cut it out," he said.

"She's not mad?" Maya said.

"No, she's not mad."

"I'm so mad," I said.

"Really?" Maya said.

She was so earnest, so out of character for the ice queen of police detectives, that I had to laugh. They joined me. It was good to laugh. It made me forget about how lonely I was, if only for a second. But like many such moments, when the laughter died a sobering silence followed.

A motorcycle roared by on the highway. The twilight faded a little more, the purple ribbon on the horizon reduced to little more than a thread. I pressed the plastic cup against my forehead. Ben smiled at me, a weird smile, the smile of someone who had something to say. Maya looked from me to Ben.

"What is it?" I said. "You two about to tell me you're getting married or something?"

Both of them looked so shocked at my question, regardless of my playful tone, that now I *knew* something had happened between them. A lot more than a kiss too.

"What? No!" Ben said. "What are you talking about? I was just thinking that Maya isn't the only one who has to weigh a job offer."

"What are you talking about?" I said. And when Ben just leaned into his look, I shook my head. "The FBI thing? You were actually serious about that?"

"Absolutely."

"No way."

"Yes way. They really, really want you back."

"Hmm. It's nice to be wanted, I guess."

He sighed. "Your answer is still the same, huh?"

"It is."

"All right. But if you ever change your mind …"

I let this hang in the air, taking a sip of my ice water, not wanting to say anything else because I was afraid that if I did say anything else, no matter what it was, no matter how strong the denial, he'd hear the doubt in my voice. It wasn't doubt about whether to go back to the FBI. It was doubt about everything. About my life. My choices. I didn't want him to hear that doubt.

If he was starting something with Maya, I didn't want my doubts weighing on his mind.

Fortunately, the blonde FBI agent was waving us back to the room, sparing me the need to say anything else. Time for the debriefing. That loneliness weighing down on me was as black as the sky. The three of us started walking across the parking lot. Maybe it was the walking, the act of moving forward, but I thought of a possible cure for my loneliness. A step in the right direction, anyway.

"So," Ben said, "since I utterly failed to convince you to return to the Bureau, what are you going to do now?"

I sighed. "You know, you always ask me some version of that question, and I always give you the same answer."

He shook his head, annoyed but obviously bemused at the same time. "You don't know."

I nodded. "Right. That's what I usually say. But this time I do."

"Really?"

"Yep."

"You're not going to tell me, are you?"

"Nope."

36

There was a lot to do, so it wasn't until the first week of
August that I finally boarded the ferry in Anacortes. Maybe
nerves got to me too. In any case, it was a good time to be on the
water. Even perpetually soggy Seattle was being blistered by a heat
wave ravaging most of the Pacific Northwest, but when I drove
the Honda off the ramp onto Orcas Island late on Sunday,
windows rolled down, Survivor on the radio, I was greeted with a
cool seventy-degrees that smelled of the sea.

Just like the last time I'd been there, the sky was an unblemished blue, and the Douglas firs crowding Olga Road were a
verdant green, which shouldn't have been remarkable but was
because it was so much cooler than over on the mainland and
because I knew from my previous visit how rare a truly cloudless
day was on Orcas Island. Was it a sign? I hoped so.

The whole way to Olga, I rehearsed what I was going to say,
feeling like a girl about to cross the gym at a middle school dance,
but when I actually parked in front of the cozy two-bedroom
cottage that looked like something out of a fairy tale, I forgot all
my lines. Her pink Volkswagen Beetle was parked in the driveway.
So she was home. Good. Fine. That was what I wanted, right?

367

Getting out of the Honda, I wondered if I should have called first. The wildflowers were no longer in bloom, but the white picket fence looked like it had been freshly painted. I wondered if she'd done it herself. There were no guest cars parked in the gravel area. It was late, almost five, so most of them had probably checked out. I rang the doorbell, and nobody answered, though Peanut, her toy poodle, started yipping inside. I passed through the gate with the sign that read COZY CABINS, following the step-stone path.

I figured she was probably cleaning them for the next guests. I was right. I found her coming out of the farthest one, the one with the best view of Buck Bay. She wore a tie-dye dress and carried a wicker basket of dirty linens, navigating past all the hand-painted birdhouses.

The view over the top of the blackberry bushes was even more spectacular than usual, the sea so smooth it looked like blue crystal, no haze at all among the various islands and land masses. There was almost no wind, just a gentle, cool breeze, which made it easy to hear the water lapping against the rocks below. Before I said anything, before she saw me, I took a deep breath, filling myself up with the smell of the sea. For once, it felt like coming home.

"Hi, Bev," I said.

She jumped a little, dropping her basket on some daffodils whose blooms were all long gone. For a second I misread her surprise as irritation, at being disturbed, at me, all my thoughts turning dark, but this all vanished when she lit up with a wide smile.

"Karen! Oh God! It's so good to see you!"

We embraced, there in the middle of the yard with Buck Bay behind us. It was a warm hug, long and genuine. There was nothing fake about Beverly Ann Braun. There were a lot of breathless questions—how I was doing, how I was handling it all, questions about what had happened and why. I answered everything as patiently as I could.

Like most people, she wanted to know who Mr. Grim really

was. I told her they *thought* they had a real name now—and not one of his many fake identities—but they were withholding it until they were absolutely sure. He'd been born at home. He'd never been fingerprinted as a child. He'd been a drifter. Held a lot of odd jobs. It really was the perfect cover for a serial killer.

I told her there was a sad story there about being orphaned at a young age, but otherwise there didn't seem to be anything all that special about him, which was kind of what made it so frightening. He could have been anybody. A lot of people had sad stories and didn't become serial killers. Why him?

Bev didn't seem entirely satisfied with this, but then, almost nobody was. After that, there was some chiding about me not calling her, and I apologized profusely, telling her I was afraid she might be mad at me for the way I'd left.

She waved this away as if it were nonsense. "Don't be ridiculous. How could you even think about me with everything you went through? I'm just glad you're okay. Did you find out what happened to your mother?"

"No," I said. "I'm kind of back to square one with that—or at least back to somewhere between here and Los Angeles. I'll keep looking, though. Something happened that made her not go to that appointment with Marv Friedman. I'll figure it out."

She nodded, looking at me with such sympathy that I could have melted right there. She gave my arms a warm squeeze, and I almost cried.

"As interested as I am in all this," she said, "I have a hunch you didn't come all the way to Orcas Island just to tell me this. I'm so glad you're here, of course! But you could have done it by phone."

I swallowed. "That's true."

"So ... have you come back for a job?"

"No," I said.

I didn't like the disappointment on her face, but it actually gave me hope. "Oh," she said. "I thought—since you were here— that you—"

"I got a job over in Eastsound," I said, "washing dishes at the

Buena Comida. A housekeeper I knew at the Orcadia, Elena—her son owns it, and she hooked me up over there. I just ... I didn't want to impose on you."

"Ah. I see. Well, it wouldn't have been—"

"But I did come back mostly because of you," I added quickly. My throat was getting tight. This was a lot harder than facing down Mr. Grim, so I needed to pull the usual Karen Pantelli and barrel forward without thinking too much. "You see, I, uh ... I hated leaving the way I did. I really like you, Bev. I was hoping ... well ..."

I was still making a mess of it, but she smiled, a twinkle in her eyes, and then regarded me the way she might have regarded a half-starved kitten, with both compassion and pity. That was all right. I didn't mind pity. I didn't mind anything so long as she didn't tell me to hit the road.

"How about we go inside and have some tea?" she asked.

"That sounds fantastic, Bev."

"Good, good." She gave my shoulder another squeeze, then turned toward the main house. "One thing, though."

"Yes?"

"Call me Babs. All my best friends do."

ABOUT THE AUTHOR

SCOTT WILLIAM CARTER's first novel was hailed by *Publishers Weekly* as a "touching and impressive debut" and won an Oregon Book Award. Since then, he has published dozens of books, including the popular Garrison Gage mystery series set on the Oregon coast. His book for younger readers, *Wooden Bones*, chronicles the untold story of Pinocchio and was singled out for praise by the Junior Library Guild. In past lives, he has been an academic technologist, a writing instructor, bookstore owner, the manager of a computer training company, and a ski instructor, though the most important job—and best—he's ever had is being the father of his two children. He lives with his family in Oregon.

Visit him online at
www.ScottWilliamCarter.com

ALSO BY SCOTT WILLIAM CARTER

Garrison Gage Mysteries

The Gray and Guilty Sea

A Desperate Place for Dying

The Lovely Wicked Rain

A Shroud of Tattered Sails

A Lighthouse for the Lonely Heart

Bury the Dead in Driftwood

A Deep and Deadly Undertow

A Cold and Shallow Shore

———

Myron Vale Investigations

Ghost Detective

The Ghost Who Said Goodbye

The Ghost, the Girl, and the Gold

———

Karen Pantelli Novels

Throwaway Jane

Lethal Beauty

Dead-Eyed Drifter

———

Other Books for Adults

The Dinosaur Diaries

A Web of Black Widows

The Man Who Made No Mistakes

Ask Hagan

Looking for Little Red

———

Young Adult Novels

The Last Great Getaway of the Water Balloon Boys

President Jock, Vice President Geek

The Care and Feeding of Rubber Chickens

———

Books for All Ages

Drawing a Dark Way

A Tale of Two Giants

Wooden Bones

The Castle on the Hill at the Edge of the World

The Dragon Lottery